END OF THE LINE

Without food and with his feet hurting, he'd lost track of time. He only knew that he was a hunted animal and had to stay hidden.

He wondered just when the hell he would run into American forces. He could tell by the sun that he was heading west, but how far west had the Germans advanced? Had they gone all the way to the French border? He sucked on some snow to kill his thirst. His stomach had been cramping up and his bowels were barely under control. If he didn't get help soon, he would die in a Belgian forest and it would be a long, long time, if ever, before anybody found his remains. That thought almost made him cry. He was a twenty-six-year-old college graduate with a liberal arts degree. He'd majored in German history and was an associate professor of languages at Dayton University. He'd taught German, which he thought was probably why he'd been assigned to a billet as an intelligence officer in the 106th in the first place. Sometimes, the army does get things right, he'd thought.

He heard someone cough. He looked up and saw half a dozen men standing in front of him and with rifles leveled at his chest. He laid his carbine on the ground and stood up slowly. As soon as he was upright he held his hands up and out. The other men had wraps on their helmets and white cloths over their uniforms so he couldn't tell whether they were German or American. It didn't much matter. His run for freedom was over.

BAEN BOOKS
by
ROBERT CONROY

Himmler's War

Rising Sun

1920: America's Great War

Liberty: 1784

1882: Custer in Chains

Germanica

Storm Front

To purchase Baen Book titles in e-book format, please go to www.baen.com.

GERMANICA

ROBERT CONROY

GERMANICA

Copyright © 2015 by Robert Conroy

A Baen Book

Baen Publishing Enterprises
P.O. Box 1403
Riverdale, NY 10471
www.baen.com

ISBN: 978-1-4767-8170-9

Cover art by Kurt Miller

First Baen paperback printing, September 2016

Library of Congress Control Number: 2015025751

Distributed by Simon & Schuster
1230 Avenue of the Americas
New York, NY 10020

Pages by Joy Freeman (www.pagesbyjoy.com)
Printed in the United States of America.

INTRODUCTION

THE NAZI RETREAT TO A FORTRESS IN THE BAVARIAN Alps in 1945 never really happened. It was seriously considered by those in the German high command who wanted to go on fighting, either in Germany or elsewhere, or those who didn't want to die in Berlin. But Hitler forbade it. The Allied command was divided about the seriousness of the threat. Some were concerned that a large German army holed up in the mountains would be almost impossible to root out without incurring large numbers of American casualties, while others thought that the whole idea was a fantasy. This worry impacted on Allied strategy, including having some influence on the decision to not send the U.S. Army to take Berlin ahead of the Russians. Instead, the Allies concentrated on cutting off large numbers of Germans, thus keeping them from reaching their presumed mountain sanctuary. Berlin was left to the Russians. They took it after desperate and bloody fighting and then savaged the town and the city's population in an orgy of rape and murder. Hitler died in the ruins and his remains were taken by the Russians where they kept them hidden for decades.

The United States was war-weary and there was still the planned invasion of Japan to contend with. Battles in the Pacific had convinced the U.S. leaders that invading Japan would be a bloodbath. Thus, the war with Germany had to be concluded as soon as possible so that the full power of the United States military could be concentrated against it. The idea of a Nazi-led German army holding out in the mountains for months, perhaps years, horrified Allied leaders.

The German high command's idea for the redoubt was not to win the war; that was no longer possible. They wanted the cult of Nazism to survive, along with themselves, of course. Hitler wished to die in Berlin and he did, but it was his potential heirs who wanted to go to the mountains. There they wished to exact enough American blood so that the U.S. would negotiate a peace that left at least a small version of Nazi Germany intact.

Hitler did not change his mind about the redoubt until April 18, 1945, when it was far too late to implement.

But what if he had ordered the development of the redoubt just after the failure of his attack in the Ardennes, the Battle of the Bulge? A mad dash to the mountains would have occurred. Hard and bitter fighting would have resulted as the Nazis did their best to convert the Alps into an impregnable citadel. Would the U.S. have negotiated an end to the war in Europe in order to end the killing? FDR was dead and Churchill had been voted out of office by a war-weary British population. Who knows what might have happened? And what if the United States began to fear that the Germans actually *did* possess at least one atomic bomb along with the means to deliver it? Pressure for peace would have been intense. The horrors of the death camps were only just being discovered, and many still doubted the extent of the killings.

As I have done in previous novels regarding Nazi Germany, I have chosen to use the English equivalents instead of the overlapping and often confusing German and Nazi system of ranks. It's just easier.

Many outstanding histories have been written about the closing months of World War II in Europe and some days I think I've read all of them. The most recent is Rick Atkinson's magnificent *The Guns At Last Light*, and I've shamelessly borrowed a number of facts from that work.

To the best of my knowledge, there was no 105th Infantry Division active in World War II. Therefore, all characters from that unit are fictitious, including the commanding generals.

Robert Conroy

GERMANICA

CHAPTER 1

I FEEL PAIN, THEREFORE I AM. AT LEAST I DON'T THINK I'm dead. Maybe I'm in hell, Tanner thought. If this was hell, then why the hell was hell so cold? He thought that was funny and almost giggled. He realized he was lying down, which made a kind of sense if maybe he really was dead.

"Captain Tanner, you okay?"

The voice came from his left. Tanner tried to speak but his mouth was too dry and he could only gag. He tried to generate some saliva. "Is there any water?" he finally croaked.

"Yeah, but you're gonna have to get it yourself. Or have you forgotten what happened?"

His mind was cloudy and his head was pounding. Exactly what had happened? He began to recall German artillery shells exploding near him, his being slammed to the ground, and clumps of earth falling on him. After that, nothing. Clearly he had been stunned. But was he hurt badly? It didn't seem like it. His arms and hands moved, which was a good sign, and he used them to check the rest of his body. All was present and apparently in good order. There was a bandage on his arm and his right knee had been wrapped.

He was on the ground and lying on his back. There was a large hole in the roof of whatever building he was in and he could see the low-hanging clouds that had hampered American air operations and protected the Germans. Someone had laid a blanket over him. He rolled his lanky six-foot frame onto his side and sat up. The world swam for a minute and then stopped. "You better hurry, Captain, or you're gonna miss the surrender."

"What the hell are you talking about?"

"The regiment's surrendering, sir. Maybe the whole division. I don't think there's been anything like it before in this man's army."

That's ridiculous, Captain Scott Tanner thought. But was it? His mind was clearing some more and he recalled visions of German tanks and infantry coming through the snow, the mist and the rain, overrunning and overwhelming the inexperienced and thinly spread out 106th Infantry Division. Now he recalled men running in panic from the onslaught. He saw them being blown to bloody pieces by shells from German artillery and tanks. Many senior officers had been as bad as the enlisted men and the junior officers. Stunned by the ferocity of the totally unexpected German onslaught, too many had been indecisive. They had done nothing while the division was cut to pieces. Yes, some men and units had fought bravely, but so many men had frozen, unable to give orders or make decisions. Or worse, had abandoned their posts and their men to their grim fate.

Tanner dimly recalled firing his carbine at shapes in the mist and swirling snow. He thought he might have hit someone, but wasn't certain. All had been chaos and confusion and terror. Finally, he'd run in panic with the others and the thought shook him. Army captains were supposed to lead, not run screaming for help that wasn't there. It didn't matter that he wasn't a combat officer, he was supposed to lead and he hadn't. He had failed and it made him ashamed and bitter.

The 106th was a new division and had been put in the line on December 11, 1944 to gain a little experience fighting the Germans. The division had been given far too much front line area for one division to cover. Don't worry, the division's commanders were told. The area they'd been assigned was presumed to be calm and as safe as a combat area could be. The men could train and patrol and maybe get a little fighting experience.

Too bad nobody told the Germans. On December 16th, the Germans had attacked in overwhelming strength.

Tanner managed to stand up. He lurched over to where a canteen lay on a table. He looked around and saw that he was in some badly damaged farm house. He took a swallow and began to feel better.

"You know you could share, Captain."

Tanner recognized the man on the floor as a private named Peters. His legs were in splints and, almost sheepishly, Tanner brought him some water. A second man lay by Peters. His name was Tucker. He too was a private. Tucker was unconscious and breathing shallowly. Tanner dribbled some water on Tucker's lips but got no response.

"He's been like that for a while," said Peters. "Corps-man said he didn't think he'd make it. I didn't look, but the medic said there's a big dent in his skull. If you want to roll him over you can see his brains."

"No thank you. Tell me about the surrender?"

"Well sir, you know we got our asses kicked by the Krauts. We were surrounded and outnumbered and outgunned and outfought and, oh yeah, outsmarted."

Tanner interrupted. "I remember that much. Who decided that anyone was going to surrender?"

"Hell, I don't know. The medic said that two of the division's three regiments were surrendering and that the third one had gotten away. He said our position was hopeless and that he was going down the road to tell the Germans that there were wounded in this farmhouse. That was a couple of hours ago so they ought to be back here pretty soon."

Tanner took a deep breath. Did he want to sur-render, to become a prisoner of war? Hell no. But did he have any other realistic choices? The Germans were all around. Could he get through and go west to where the American lines had to be? The Germans couldn't have pushed the Americans too far back, could they? He decided that he had to try it. The weather was cold and miserable. Snow had started falling again. A prison camp might be dry and warm, but it would still be a prison. He could be there for years, maybe decades or even the rest of his life. Everybody had said that the Nazis were on their last legs and would collapse soon. Sure. The ongoing German offensive had just shot that idea all to hell. Now it looked like the war could go on forever with him in a prison compound. No thank you. He would leave this hellhole and go west. If he didn't make it, he could surrender all by himself.

He picked up his M1 carbine and gear. He had two clips of ammunition, but only a handful of packs of rations. Once more the world moved and stopped. Another deep breath and he was back in control.

"Peters, if anybody remembers there were three of us, tell them that I left right after the medic did. I wish I could take you with me, but you know that's not possible."

"Understood," said Peters. "You can't carry us and you sure as hell can't drag us around by the arms. No, sir, you get the hell out of here and when you reach safety, just remember us."

Tanner reached down and shook Peters' hand. "I will. You won't be forgotten." He was surprised by the depth of emotion he felt. It was terrible to abandon the two helpless soldiers, but there was no way he could take them.

He patted Tucker on the head. No response. "Germany may be hard on Jews," he said to Peters, "but I've heard they've been treating prisoners of war pretty decently. You'll be okay. The war can't last all that much longer." Too bad he didn't mean it. This last German offensive proved that the Krauts were a long ways from dead.

He saluted them and stepped to the doorway. I hope they'll be okay, he thought. He looked outside and down the muddy road. A German vehicle was approaching, although very slowly. Tanner ducked out the back way and used the farmhouse to shield him from the approaching Germans. Even though he knew there was nothing he could do, he hid in some

hay and threw snow over himself while he waited to
see what would happen when the Germans arrived.
He had an awful feeling that it would be something
dreadful. He prayed that he was wrong.

The German vehicle was a Kubelwagen, the German version of a Jeep. It stopped by the house. Four
men got out and Tanner saw to his dismay that they
were all SS. One appeared to be a fairly senior officer.
All four went into the house. Tanner pulled out his
binoculars and watched and waited. After a moment,
he heard harsh laughter and then screams followed
by the staccato burst of a German submachine gun.

All four Nazis came outside, laughing. The senior
officer's weapon was smoking. The German took a
number of steps in Tanner's direction and he thought
that the German had seen him. But his luck held. The
bastard unbuttoned his fly, pulled out his penis and
began to urinate into the snow. When another German joined him, the officer laughingly told him that
this pissing spot was reserved for field grade officers
only, which they all thought was hilarious.

Bastards, Tanner thought. How can you butcher two
helpless men and then laugh? He focused the binoculars on the senior man. His SS rank was equivalent
to colonel. He was stocky, in his thirties, and there
was a rose-colored birthmark in the shape of a star
on the Nazi's left cheek. He would remember that.
He would also remember Peters and Tucker.

The surrender of the 106th took place on December 19, 1944. Tanner would never forget that date.
To him it was even more important than December
7, 1941, the date of the Japanese attack on Pearl

Harbor. He quickly found out a basic truth. An army is difficult to hide, but one man is not. He moved slowly but steadily westward. His few rations quickly ran out and he realized he was in danger of starving. He tried eating some grasses and even kept some of them down, but chewing twigs simply made him sick and gave him diarrhea. His boots were soaked and his feet had felt funny for a while, but now were paining him. He didn't think he was frostbitten, but he wondered about trench foot. He wanted to live, but not as an amputee. He sagged to the ground. He needed rest, but allowed himself only a few minutes before pulling himself to his feet. He also needed to keep going.

Without food and with his feet hurting, he'd lost track of time. He only knew that he was a hunted animal and had to stay hidden. He had to reach safety, not just for himself, but for Tucker and Peters. He had gone into the farmhouse after the Germans had left and seen their mangled corpses. He had the horrible feeling that there was more that he could have done for them. Logic told him he was wrong, but he wasn't being particularly logical.

He wondered just when the hell he would run into American forces. He could tell by the sun that he was heading west, but how far west had the Germans advanced? Had they gone all the way to the French border? He sucked on some snow to kill his thirst. He remembered as a kid being told never to eat yellow snow and then wondering what it meant. His stomach had been cramping up and his bowels were barely under control. If he didn't get help soon, he would die in a Belgian forest and it would be a long, long time, if ever, before anybody found his remains. That thought almost made him cry. He was a twenty-six-year-old college graduate with a liberal arts degree. He'd majored in German history and was an associate professor of languages at Dayton University. He'd taught German, which he thought was probably why he'd been assigned to a billet as an intelligence officer in the 106th in the first place. Sometimes, the army does get things right, he'd thought.

Tanner had seen precious few civilians during his wanderings and had stayed hidden. He didn't want them involved with him. Someone might turn him in or, worse, the Nazis would treat them like they had treated Tucker and Peters if they were found out. The SS were everywhere and they were animals. The U.S. Army had begun discovering concentration camps. They'd all been shocked to the core. Tanner wondered if he would have wound up as a skeletal wreck if he had surrendered along with the rest of his men.

He heard someone cough. He looked up and saw half a dozen men standing in front of him and with rifles leveled at his chest. He laid his carbine on the ground and stood up slowly. As soon as he was upright he held his hands up and out. The other men had wraps on their helmets and white cloths over their uniforms so he couldn't tell whether they were German or American. It didn't much matter. His run for freedom was over.

"Give me the password," one of the soldiers said in English and Tanner nearly collapsed with joy.

"I don't know the password. I've been running from the Germans."

"Sure, and maybe you're one of those shits who've been disguising themselves as Americans and blowing up stuff." From the way the others deferred to him, the speaker was likely an officer.

"My name is Scott Tanner and I'm a captain in the 106th Infantry Division. Who are you?"

"Not yet. I ask the questions. Hey, if you're telling the truth, you were one of the yellow bastards who surrendered, weren't you?"

"Not everyone surrendered," Tanner bristled. "I sure as hell didn't. Can I put my arms down?"

"No. Who won the American League batting title last year?"

"Lou Boudreau and he hit .327. Bobby Doerr was second."

"Not bad. Now, who's the coach of the Green Bay Packers?"

"I don't fucking know and I really don't give a shit," Tanner snarled. "I'm cold, tired, wet, hungry, and I ache all over. I think I've got trench foot and I don't want to lose my feet. Unless you plan on standing here talking all day, I'd like to see a medic and get something in my stomach."

"Sounds fair," the American officer said and lowered his rifle. "By the way, you're filthy and you need a shave."

Tanner knew he was filthy but hadn't considered his beard. He checked his chin and realized he'd grown a fairly full head of chin hair. The officer grinned. "You look a lot like Abe Lincoln would've if he'd been a hobo."

Others came forward and took Scott by the arms and gently led him back to where a couple of jeeps were parked. A soldier opened some K-rations and Scott wolfed down some biscuits.

"You know what day this is, Captain?"

Tanner laughed. He had lost track of days. "No idea."

"It's January first, 1945. Happy New Year. Maybe this year will be better than the last."

Couldn't be much worse, Tanner thought.

Life in Berlin revolved around the Allied bombers. The British bombed at night and the Americans during the day. Some days they bombed every day and night and some days they did no bombing at all. Despite the fact that it was a major target, the Chancellery, the hub of the German government, still functioned. Today there had been a pause in the bombing. Everyone understood that it wouldn't last, but people would enjoy the respite while it lasted. It gave them a chance to shop for what limited and severely rationed food was available, and it gave them time to try to repair the damage to their homes.

Josef Goebbels, Martin Bormann, and Albert Speer had commandeered a small conference room and some privacy. They did not want aides and secretaries as possible witnesses. The three men glared at each other. Goebbels and Bormann were rivals and each despised the other, while Albert Speer was the architect of the Nazi's war effort. The men were nervous. Bormann, age forty-five, had insinuated himself into the position of personal secretary to Hitler. It was a position of obvious influence. It also required a very annoyed Goebbels to defer to his rival, a man he thought of as a thug and a snake.

Goebbels was slightly older at forty-eight and much better educated. He had earned a PhD from Heidelberg University in 1921. He was the Gauleiter of Berlin and the Minister of Enlightenment and Propaganda. He had thrived by subordinating his personal ambitions to those of Bormann's. He was also incredibly homely in many people's opinion and walked with a limp because of a club foot. In all, he was an unlikely candidate to be one of the heads of the Master Race. That women found him attractive was generally attributed to the fact that he was powerful.

At forty, Albert Speer was the Minister of Armaments and War Production. An architect by profession and education he had excelled at providing the weapons the Third Reich needed to fight the long war. Despite Speer's efforts, the war appeared to be winding down and defeat was staring at them.

Two other members of Hitler's clique were not present. Heinrich Himmler, head of the SS, was trying to lead Army Group Upper Rhine, while the Hermann Goering was in his mansion at Carinhall and doubtless trying out some new narcotic. Himmler would be kept abreast of the discussions, while Goering's existence would be ignored.

The men were nervous and could not stop shifting in their seats. Enemy bombers were not overhead but they could be at any moment. There had been suggestions that the Party headquarters be moved to the vast underground military complex at nearby Zossen but Hitler had so far vetoed it.

Bormann tapped lightly on the table. "Let's get on with it. Once again, the Fuhrer has changed his mind and not a moment too soon. It is becoming apparent that our offensive in the Ardennes will not be as successful as anticipated."

Goebbels lowered his head at that comment. His analysis of the Ardennes offensive was a gross understatement. The offensive had involved much of the Reich's military reserves and was rapidly becoming a total disaster. The defeat of the German armies west of the Rhine meant that so much less would be available to confront the Red Army as it approached from the east. It also meant that the defenses along the Rhine would be that much weaker against the resurgent Americans. It was a dismal situation.

Bormann continued. "The Fuhrer has decided that the German government must move to the National Redoubt in the Alps, and that includes everyone in this room."

Speer looked up in disbelief. "We have no such redoubt. I was not permitted to go beyond the planning stages."

Bormann eyed him coldly. "Knowing you, Herr Speer, you doubtless exceeded your authority and are farther along than you would like to admit at this time."

Speer flushed. "In a manner of speaking, your words are true. What I did was prepare to move critical production facilities to new areas as we have been doing for some time and yes, that does include the Alps. We have dispersed our factories to protect them from Allied bombers. I also identified and developed storage areas to provide supplies for large numbers of refugees, and we have built living quarters for those who will work and live there."

Bormann actually laughed. "And would the German army be defined as a large number of refugees?"

"It could," Speer admitted, "but that's not for me to decide."

Goebbels was in turmoil. He and his wife had pledged to die in Berlin with his beloved Fuhrer.

They had no wish to live in a world without Nazism. Now he was being given a chance to survive. No, he was being *ordered* to survive. "If it is the Fuhrer's decision we will, of course, honor and obey it. Will he come with us?"

"Most emphatically no," said Bormann. "He is determined to die in Berlin if the army is unable to hold off the Red Army's hordes. Should that need arise, the Fuhrer feels that he should die for the cause of Nazism. He feels that today's Germany does not deserve him or the Nazi Party and should be destroyed. However, he has decided that the seed of Nazism should endure and that it should be nurtured and grown in a national Alpine Redoubt."

"Has he decided who should be the person in charge?" asked Goebbels hopefully. He and his wife had six small children. They had decided that they all should die and would not even think of surrendering. He already had the cyanide pills that would end their lives.

Bormann smiled knowingly. "You and I will go to the redoubt and run Germany together. You, Herr Speer, will also be there, and you will leave immediately to begin developing a new country."

Speer shook his head. "This is a vast undertaking, or it could be. I will need to coordinate with the army."

"Of course," said Bormann. "Logistics and geography will rule the size of the redoubt as well as the population that can be sustained. To assist you, I have requested that General Warlimont be assigned to the group."

Speer and Goebbels were surprised. Warlimont was considered a master at planning operations, but he was not thought to be totally trustworthy by Hitler. Even though he had been wounded in the July 20, 1944, assassination attempt, there were those who thought his support of the war had become lukewarm at best. Perhaps, Goebbels thought, this was a way of getting the general out of Berlin. He also had never served in combat. He was an archetypal staff officer. A brilliant man perhaps, but very limited in his experience.

"Then who will have overall military command of the redoubt?" asked Goebbels. He was clearly annoyed that he didn't have this information in the first place.

"The Fuhrer will be getting recommendations from Field Marshal Keitel. It is obvious that military exigencies will play a large part in making that decision. Generals Schoerner, von Vietinghoff, and Rendulic are strong possibilities. They too have the advantage of being in the south, which means they could be appointed safely."

"Yes," said Goebbels drily. "It wouldn't do for the new leader of the Alpine Redoubt to be killed en route to his new assignment." Quietly, he approved of Schoerner commanding the armies in the Redoubt. Schoerner was a friend and a supporter.

The irony was lost on Bormann. He didn't change expression while Speer turned away. "Schoerner will probably be selected. Hitler likes him and Schoerner is slavishly devoted to him. I believe he will soon be promoted to field marshal. Whoever it is, Herr Speer, it will be up to you to provide for a very large army."

"Not too large," said Speer.

"What do you mean?" asked a surprised Bormann.

"Any army that goes to an Alpine Redoubt will have to confront various realities. That army will need food, shelter, clothing, weapons, and ammunition, and the Alps will have none of those. Right now, that area imports much of its food from Austria, which is about to be overrun by either Devers' Sixth Army Group or the Soviets. If we send too many men to the redoubt, they might just starve to death. Similarly, I have identified a number of areas where large amounts of weapons and ammunition can be stored, but nothing that could sustain a large army in combat for more than a year or two."

"How large an army could be sustained?" asked Goebbels.

Speer shrugged. "Perhaps a quarter of a million, and don't forget that there will be thousands of Party elite sent to the Redoubt along with their families."

Goebbels was shaken while Bormann paled. A quarter of a million soldiers was a drop in the bucket. The Russians and Americans, along with their French and British allies, each had more than ten times that number.

"Then we will make do with what we have," Bormann said softly. "But it must be done and done quickly. And painful though it will be, we must limit the number of civilians and party functionaries no matter how loyal they have been. So too with very high-ranking military officers. We cannot have a rump state that is top-heavy with generals."

Goebbels nodded. The last time he had seen his beloved Fuhrer, the great man had been pale and sickly. His arm had shaken uncontrollably and Goebbels had wondered if Hitler was dying. He was only in his mid-fifties but looked decades older. Clearly, the stress of running the nation and the war had overwhelmed him. Goebbels had urged Hitler to rest for a few days, but had been waved off. He had faith in his personal doctor, Theodor Morrell, a man whom Goebbels considered a quack. Morrell treated Hitler with concoctions containing narcotics. If Hitler died, Goebbels would try to have Morrell prosecuted for murder. Or perhaps he would just have him shot.

But that was for the future. Now he and Magda and the children would have to get out of Berlin and south to the Alpine Redoubt. There they would set up a bastion that would ensure the survival of Nazism. If they were forced out of the mountains, they would cross into neutral Switzerland and wait for the proper time to go elsewhere, probably South America.

"One last thing," said Bormann. "The Fuhrer is adamant that at least a couple of his wonder weapons programs be shipped to the Alps. Of primary importance is the nuclear bomb being designed by Doctor Werner Heisenberg. He and a number of his fellow physicists will travel south as well, along with what equipment can be moved. He has assured me that he is on the brink of a major breakthrough."

Of course he would say that, Goebbels thought. To tell Bormann anything else would guarantee a trip to Dachau. Well, we shall see what comes of his nuclear bomb.

When Lena Bobekova looked in a mirror in her small room in the Schneider house, she did not see the attractive and vivacious young woman who once had dreams of being a ballerina. That Lena Bobekova died several years earlier when German tanks and troops rolled through her native Czechoslovakia and ended her life. The Germans had taken her parents, her brother, her first and so far only lover, and her home.

She was a slave.

Physically there was little difference between the Lena of today and the previous young woman. She was a little thinner perhaps, but food rationing had put everyone in Germany on a diet. Even though she'd been assigned to work in the house of a Nazi functionary, there was still only so much food to go around. Gustav and Gudrun Schneider and their two children, Astrid and Anton, did not care that Lena was always hungry. Why should they? Lena was a slave because her grandmother had been a Jew. Lena's light brown, almost blond, hair was still attractive. She washed and bathed as often as she could. Water was one thing that was not in short supply.

Lena knew she was lucky to have been assigned to the Schneiders. She could be in a factory in the process of being worked to death, or, worse, shipped off to Poland to those places of death that not even the Schneiders were certain existed. They talked of them in hushed voices, forgetting that even slaves have ears. Instead of dying in Poland, she was in a large house in a small village about fifty miles north of Innsbruck in what once had been Austria.

Nor was there any serious sexual burden imposed on her. Herr Schneider had entered her room on the first night at their house. He'd ordered her to strip and lie down on her bed. She'd complied without hesitation. He had fondled her in a perfunctory manner to arouse himself, placed her on her hands and knees and then mounted her. He muttered that he did it that way so he didn't have to look in the face of a Jewess while he was fucking her. He'd hurt her and she'd whimpered. Schroeder had misunderstood and thought that her moans meant she was being pleasured.

After finishing, he'd been emphatic that a good Nazi would never lower himself to fuck a Jew, even one who was only fractionally Jewish and who had never practiced her religion. Before the Nazis arrived, Lena had never even known that her grandmother was Jewish. Herr Schneider said that he'd forced her to have sex with him to prove to her that her life was entirely in his hands. He'd even worn a condom. He said that he didn't want to take the chance of her getting pregnant and bringing another Jew, if only a fractional one, into the world.

Herr Schneider coldly assured her that he had no intentions of requiring her to take him in her mouth.

When he left, the Schneider's housekeeper, a nearly toothless old Pole named Olga came and helped her. "They are pigs," she said. "But you will survive. You don't have a choice."

For several nights after that she'd slept on the floor, unable to sleep in the bed where she'd been humiliated and violated. After those few days, common sense returned and she realized that the only person she was hurting was herself. The senior Schneiders simply didn't give a damn about her or where she slept. She returned to the bed.

This was not the case with the Schneider's two children.

Astrid Schneider was a chubby and unlovely sixteen years old and wondering whether she liked boys or girls. On a couple of occasions, she had climbed into

Lena's bed and insisted that they play what Astrid called "games." Lena went along. A bad word from Astrid might send her to a long slow death in a factory. And besides, it wasn't all that much different than the games she and one of her girlfriends had played during sleepovers during happier times. It was endurable. And it made Astrid happy.

The problem was going to be Anton. He was fourteen and getting bigger and stronger. He was also getting very curious. She'd caught him looking at her smallish breasts and watching how she moved her body. On occasions, he'd contrived to pass her closely in a hallway and brushed up against her. Once, his hand had strayed across her bottom. She'd stopped him with a glare, but she was certain he would try something again. She was reasonably certain that his father had told him that he could not profane his pure Aryan Nazi body by copulating with a Jew, but what else might his father permit? And would an oversexed Anton pay any attention to his father's rules? She tried to dress and behave in a manner that was sexless, but that was not practical. Anton was at the age where everything was sexual.

Lena did not cook for the Schneiders. Perhaps they didn't want to accidentally eat something kosher, she'd thought with amusement. Olga prepared the food. That woman was a servant, not a slave, although she complained that she rarely got paid. Instead, Lena did all the cleaning and any chores assigned to her.

The house in which they lived had belonged to a Jewish merchant who had fled to England before the war. It was very large, opulent, and even had a wing for the servants. Thus, Lena had her own room. Her bondage might have been light, but it was still slavery.

Thanks to her father's insistence on her getting an education, she was fluent in English as well as Czech and German. She recalled someone, possibly Abraham Lincoln, saying that to the extent a man is not free, he is a slave. Well, she was not free and she was always terrified. Not only were the Schneiders capable of turning on her like animals, but the Allied victories in the war represented a threat as well. What would happen to her as the Americans drew closer? Would the Schneiders take her south to the mountains like they were talking about or would they turn her loose to fend for herself? She didn't think the Americans raped and murdered like the Russians did, but she wasn't certain. And the French were known to take vengeance on German women for what the Nazis had done during their occupation. That she was Czech and not German would have no meaning to them.

And if the Schneiders took her with them, then she was condemned to that much more slavery along with the ever-present threat of death.

No, what she wanted to do was run and hide until the tide of war passed over. Then she would emerge and try to begin a new life.

CHAPTER 2

TANNER TOOK HIS FIRST TENTATIVE STEPS WITHOUT crutches. Doctor Lennie Hagerman watched him tolerantly. "Not bad, Captain. You won't make the '48 Olympic track team but you're otherwise going to be all right. Of course, there might not be a '48 Olympics unless this war winds down."

"How long will I need a cane?"

"That's up to you. I would use it for a couple of weeks. Your leg and foot are still weak and sore and, besides, people will feel sorry for you and might give you a break, or even a seat on a bus. Seriously, you don't want to fall down and hurt yourself worse."

"I don't want anyone giving me a break. I want to have another chance to kill the Nazi bastards who murdered my men."

"Understood. However, it is unlikely that you will be assigned to a line unit until your leg is totally up to par, and maybe not even then. Can't have a crippled captain leading troops, now can we?"

Scott had been in worse shape than he'd thought

21

when he got to the hospital just outside of Celles, Belgium. The otherwise lovely but undistinguished village had been the high-water mark of the German's Ardennes invasion. He'd had pneumonia along with a bad case of trench foot that had taken a couple of weeks to clear up. The medics had given serious thought to amputating his right foot after stabilizing his badly twisted left knee. The knee had been easy. It just needed rest. The foot, however, raised concerns that it might turn gangrenous.

Hagerman continued. "You were very fortunate that your foot did heal. The traditional treatment of keeping the foot dry and letting the dead skin slough off and new skin grow back actually worked. We also tried you with some of that new drug, Penicillin. I have no idea if it worked or not or just made me feel better. You are now very unfortunate in that you might be susceptible to it happening again. Ergo, it is highly unlikely that you will be cleared to be in a situation where your feet could become wet and cold for a prolonged period of time."

"What if I promise to bring extra socks?"

"As they say, Tanner, put a sock in it yourself. Keep your socks and your powder dry or you'll wind up being a cripple. That'll get you out of the army but won't do a damn thing about you're urge to kill the Nazis who murdered those two men. Not that they were the only GIs who were executed like that."

Tanner nodded thoughtfully. There had been other massacres of American prisoners. A particularly terrible one had occurred near the Belgian town of Malmedy where almost a hundred American soldiers had been butchered. There would be a lot of Germans facing trials and the firing squad when this war was over.

"Any idea where I'm going to be assigned?"

"Do I look like God? There are ugly rumors that the Krauts are pulling up stakes and heading south to the Alps. That means that this part of the war is going to wind down and the next phase will be up to Devers and the Sixth Army Group. Is that where you'd like to be? I do have some friends in low places who would do me a favor."

"Do that, please."

"Then get into a uniform and we'll go out to dinner. Your treat, of course. After all, you do owe me a foot."

Tanner laughed and agreed. The only place to eat around the hospital was the army's mess hall.

Staff Sergeant Billy Hill sat in the last vehicle in a ten jeep convoy and tried to keep warm as the snow-flecked wind hit him in the face. He would not show the rest of the men that he felt the cold. He would not show the platoon that he was human. After all, he was the platoon sergeant. He would also never let them call him Hillbilly Billy Hill.

If the officer commanding the platoon thought that being last in line was his punishment for being out-spoken, the young and inexperienced second lieutenant was very, very wrong. This was the safest place to be as the officer led his platoon from the front down the paved two-lane highway. It wasn't quite the Autobahn, but it was nicer than anything Hill had seen in or out of his small town home in Opelika, Alabama.

According to the maps, the American army was getting ever closer to the Alps, as were the Germans they were chasing. The land was hilly, not mountain-ous, but there was the idea that the terrain was going to get more difficult. There were many great places for an ambush.

Hill was twenty-eight and had been in the army since a week after the Japanese attack on Pearl Harbor. He'd hitched a ride from Opelika down the road to Fort Benning, Georgia, where he'd enlisted. He hadn't intended to be a lifer, but that's what it looked like was going to happen. He'd seen combat in North Africa and been wounded in the drive towards Tunis. He'd given some thought to going to Officer Candidate School but decided that he'd have to be a gentleman in order to be an officer and that just wasn't in him. He smiled at the thought as he spat tobacco off the side of the jeep, courteously missing the other men with him. They nodded their appreciation.

Of course, if he'd been an officer, he could have told the young shit-eating puppy of a lieutenant that he was doing a truly dumb thing. The captain had said send a small patrol down the road to probe and see where the Krauts might be holed up. The captain hadn't said to take the whole damn platoon and ride down the middle of the highway like a bunch of sightseers. To Hill, the captain really wanted two or three men and a radio to quietly and slowly figure things out. Rumors said that the Nazis were moving south to the mountains, but who could trust the Nazis?

The men wore white smocks which helped hide them in the snow, but the jeeps were painted olive drab and clearly stood out on the snow-covered highway. Hill swore silently and hoped that the Nazis were asleep at the switch while the column moved down the road at twenty miles an hour.

They weren't. Just as he started to grab another

chew, tracers snaked out from either side of the road, smashing into metal and flesh. Bullets swept the column, dropping screaming men from the jeeps. The lead vehicles were quickly driverless and crashed, while the others tried desperately to turn and get away from the deadly rain of bullets. Gas tanks exploded. Men screamed as burning gas enveloped them.

"Turn around!" Hill yelled. The jeeps in front of him were already trying to do just that, but they too were quickly hit with bullets. There was the loud crack of an antitank gun and another jeep simply exploded. He didn't need his radio to tell the others to get the hell out. He was about to radio the company commander when something smashed into the side of his jeep, slowly turning it on its side.

Hill hit the ground and crawled towards the cover of a ditch. The gas tank exploded, sending debris and burning gas over him. His uniform was on fire. He rolled around in the snow and mud and finally put it out after a few seconds that seemed like forever. He hurt like the devil from a number of burns, but he could deal with it. He had to.

More machine-gun bullets sprayed the area and made sure the dead were well and truly dead. Hill and a couple of other survivors lay in the ditch. The whole damn platoon had been pretty near wiped out. If it was any consolation, the idiot boy lieutenant was likely one of the bodies smoldering at the head of the devastated column.

"Damn it," he snarled. He'd only been with the inexperienced unit for a couple of weeks and didn't know any of them well, but they were still his men. Or had been, he thought angrily.

The wind shifted and he could smell burning flesh. He managed not to gag but one of the men with him wasn't so lucky, vomiting violently. After a while, he got up the courage to look over the edge of the ditch. The Germans had come out of their holes and were headed slowly up the road. They checked American bodies and found a couple still living. They called for medics to take care of them. At least, he thought, they weren't SS. One German shot a body that was still burning. A mercy shot, Hill thought. In North Africa he'd killed a badly burned Italian soldier who'd been screaming through charred lips to be put out of his pain.

He signaled to the other two men and they crawled slowly towards the safety of the Austrian forest. Hill waited until after darkness to go by himself to the head of the smashed column. He quickly found the sites where the shooting had come from. The Germans had evacuated, correctly feeling that American artillery or fighter planes would soon bomb and shell the area. Maybe the planes would use that new napalm to cook up a passel of Germans and call them "Fritz Fries." He liked that thought. The Germans also likely assumed that a stronger American column would rescue the one they'd massacred. They didn't know that all the platoon's radios had been destroyed in the attack.

Nobody'd had a chance to pick up the dead and the German positions had been evacuated. He wasn't going to bring back the dead either, but he did want to identify them. He gently removed one set of dog tags from each of twenty-three bodies, including the young lieutenant's.

Hill couldn't even recall the poor kid's name until he saw it on his tags. The boy had arrived only a few days earlier. Now he would be buried in a local cemetery or shipped home in a box. Just because he'd been stupid didn't mean he ought to have died.

The snow began falling again. In a few seconds it was almost impossible to see more than a few feet. Someone had told them that this was one of the worst winters in decades and he believed it. Alabama got bone-chilling cold and damp and of course it snowed every now and then, but this, he thought, was something else. At least the snow would cover their withdrawal. Thank God for small favors, he thought.

They got another small favor. One of the damaged jeeps actually started and ran, although they couldn't get it out of second gear. Beat the hell out of walking, they thought.

General Dwight D. Eisenhower arrived without incident at Lieutenant General Jake Devers' Sixth Army Group headquarters near the old border between Austria and Germany. The U.S. owned the skies so the handful of passengers and crew of the modified B25 bomber had little to worry about except boredom and the weather. Even so, the flight had been accompanied by a dozen P51 fighters. Nobody was leaving anything to chance. The Germans had very few planes left, but it would only take one ME109 or one of the new jet-propelled ME262s and the Allied High Command could have been decapitated. There had also been some disturbing instances where German planes had carried out suicide attacks on U.S. bombers.

Devers Sixth Army Group was the smallest of the three army groups fronting the Nazis in a line that ran from the North Sea south to the Alps. A fourth army group, the Fifteenth under Mark Clark, was clawing its way up Italy. Devers had twelve American divisions in General Alexander Patch's Seventh Army and seven French under General Jean de Lattre de Tassigny in the French First Army.

Coffee and pastries were served by awed privates in a large house that had once been owned by a wealthy German. A large but slashed and mutilated portrait of Hitler decorated a wall. With the bulk of the war raging to the north, there was the feeling that the Sixth Army front was pretty well forgotten. The presence of Ike told them otherwise. Rumors quickly flew saying that big things were in store for the Sixth and that meant bloody fighting.

It wasn't that the Sixth had been sitting on its collective hands. It hadn't. They'd fought long and hard and successfully. They'd just completed eliminating what was called the Colmar Pocket, a German holdout on the west bank of the Rhine. As a result of that effort the city of Strasbourg was once again part of France. Unfortunately, Ike had not been impressed by Devers and the Sixth Army Group's performance in that fighting. If the war in and around the Alps was to become critical, Ike had been thinking that a change in command might become necessary.

Ike gave Devers copies of the latest Ultra intercepts received from the code-breaking center at Bletchley Park in England. Only a handful of Allied leaders were privy to the fact that the U.S. and Britain had been listening to much of the German military's communications for quite some time. He lit up a Camel, his current brand of choice, while Devers scanned the papers.

Devers shook his head and handed the documents back to Ike who stuffed them in a briefcase. They would not be left around for curious eyes to see. "This changes a lot of things," Devers said. "A lot of people thought that the idea of an Alpine Redoubt was a figment of somebody's imagination. The idea of the Nazis turning the Alps into a fortress is a frightening prospect. We've got to get across the Rhine and fast and that isn't going to be easy."

Ike nodded. At least Devers wasn't saying I told you so. He'd been one of the American generals who'd thought that a German move to an Alpine redoubt was a likelihood. He'd even urged Ike to let his Sixth Army Group troops be among the first to cross the Rhine and cut off a German retreat to the Alps, but Ike had emphatically shot down that idea. Without proof that a redoubt was actually going to be built, there was no reason to change Allied strategy. They would press on towards the Rhine and then the Elbe. Thus, the Rhine crossings would be to the north. But now the situation was different.

Ike accepted that Devers was right about the Rhine preventing any move to cut off a German dash to the Alps. Plans were being made for Montgomery to command an enormous crossing force near where the Rhine flowed into the North Sea. Unfortunately, that would place Montgomery's army as far from the Alps as possible. They would be in no position to stop the German exodus. As always, hindsight was a great view.

Ike drew deeply on his cigarette. "Once we're across, Bradley's Twelfth Army Group will give up any and all thoughts of heading to Berlin. As planned, they and Monty's troops will stop at the Elbe. Patton's

Third Army will swing south and east to try and cut off forces trying to make it to the mountains. Patton's angry as hell but he'll deal with it. This seals the fact that we will not send men to Berlin just so they can give it back to the Russians."

The agreement between the Allies made at Yalta specified that the Elbe River would be the boundary between the Soviet sphere of influence and the Anglo-American-French lines. If the American troops crossed the Elbe, they were treaty-bound to withdraw back to it at a later date. Thus, any American casualties sustained in the effort would have been lives wasted. Regardless of how much generals like Patton and Montgomery wanted their armies to make it to Berlin ahead of the Reds, Ike had forbidden it.

Ike continued. "Once Monty's across, we hope there will be other opportunities to cross; perhaps there'll even be a collapse of the German forces on the Rhine. Be prepared to make the jump at the first opportunity. Once on the other side of the Rhine, can your men make an all-out effort to cut off the Germans?"

Devers winced. "You know we'll do our damndest and then some. I've got nineteen divisions, which sounds like a lot, but all of them are understrength, filled with raw and inexperienced rookies, and just plain worn out. The army is scraping the bottom of the barrel."

"So are the Germans," Ike said. "We're conscripting eighteen-year-olds, but they are drafting children who are much younger."

"Understood, but it doesn't change the fact that this isn't the same army that invaded France last summer. The men are counting the days until the war ends and they can go home, and those who don't have enough time in service to get discharged are scared to death at the thought of going to fight the Japs. Until the Bulge, everybody thought the war with Germany was over and nobody wanted to be the last man killed."

"Can't say as I blame them," said Ike. "Everybody's mad and disappointed that the Krauts have shown so much life."

Devers continued. "And don't forget that seven of my divisions are French and they are pretty much fighting their own war. De Gaulle has instituted some troop replacement policies that are just plain nuts and that's left their units badly understrength and undertrained. That and the fact that General Tassigny takes his orders from De Gaulle and not from me is a royal pain. And don't forget that General Leclerc and General Tassigny won't even speak to each other, which is why Leclerc's division is in the Seventh Army and not the French First Army. It's a farce."

"Understood," said Ike grimly. The French had shown a propensity to squabble like children both among themselves and with their erstwhile allies.

Devers had never been Ike's favorite general and he had been considering replacing him. But now he was having second thoughts. Maybe Devers' apparent problems weren't all his fault. Perhaps it was also due to a fractured and fractious command. De Gaulle had been a thorn in the American command's side from the very first. Neither FDR nor Churchill could stand the man and accepted him as the leader of France only reluctantly. Paris had been liberated some months earlier and it was felt that De Gaulle no longer saw any need to expend effort and French lives in a war

that was already won. France had regained control of
Alsace and Lorraine, provinces claimed by France and
lost in 1940, and that further dampened their enthusiasm for future operations or even basic cooperation.

Devers stood and pointed at a map of Europe on
the wall. "Once across, I'm sure I can halt a lot of
German traffic, but that still leaves the road from the
south via Italy wide open. And then there's nothing to
stop the Krauts from coming up through Yugoslavia.
The Reds aren't there yet."

Devers turned a worried look at Ike. "General, am
I allowed to speak ill of our allies?"

Almost from the day he'd taken command, Ike
had issued a fiat that no one could insult the British
or the French. A few officers had made that mistake
and paid for it with their careers.

Ike smiled. "If it's just between us, yes. Of course,
you could always call General Alexander a bad general
who just happens to be British rather than a bad
British general."

British General Harold Alexander had recently been
promoted to Field Marshal and made commander of
all operations in the Mediterranean. Ike and others
felt that Alexander had been kicked upstairs and out
of the way.

Devers laughed. "Ike, I know that Mark Clark is now
in charge of the Fifteenth Army Group and that's got
to be an improvement over Alexander. From what I
can tell, it's been a slow-motion chase for months. And
yes, I know the Fifteenth has been climbing northward
towards the Alps and I also know that we've stripped
it of some of his best units, but Clark won't be able to
stop the Germans in Italy from getting to that redoubt.

The British Eighth Army is run down and they don't want to take any more casualties either. Clark's armies are made up of units from many countries, including Brazil. It'll take time for Clark to sort things out. I mean, does anybody really think the Brazilians can take on even a weakened Wehrmacht? Hell, we all know FDR's big on this new United Nations thing, but Clark's got Canadians, Poles, and South Africans in his army along with those damned Brazilians. I'd like to have the Poles and South Africans but you can keep the others. The Canadians are just as worn out as the British."

Ike nodded and dug out another cigarette. Mamie had written him about his chain smoking. He thought he might do something about it after the war. Now it gave him comfort. Ike was confident that Mark Clark was an improvement over Alexander, but by how much was a question. The man had a tendency to act like a prima donna. He had liberated Rome on June 5, 1944, the day before the invasion of Normandy. Rumor had it that he felt that Ike had upstaged him. There was also the question of his liberating Rome in the first place. Clark's advance had been controversial. By taking Rome instead of cutting across the width of Italy, he had permitted large numbers of Germans to escape to the north where they now confronted the Allies and could be heading for the Redoubt. Jesus, he thought. How many prima donnas could he have? First there was Montgomery, then De Gaulle, add Mark Clark and stir in a dash of George Patton.

Of course, he thought with a small degree of satisfaction, he didn't have to deal with that ultimate prima donna, Douglas MacArthur. That legend in his own eyes was Roosevelt's problem.

"Have you forgotten the soldiers from India and that regiment of Japanese from Hawaii and California?" Devers added with a smile. The Fifteenth Army Group was indeed a polyglot force.

"Intelligence says that the German and Italian units facing Clark are mere remnants," said Ike. He was now regretting the decision to exclude Clark from this meeting. Ike's staff had talked him out of making a dangerous flight over the Alps to Italy or having Clark make one instead.

"Even a beheaded and dying snake might have enough venom to kill a victim if given a chance," answered Devers. "If the Germans in Italy decide to make a run for this redoubt area, I don't see any way of stopping them. Once they get to some kind of sanctuary, they can rest and reorganize and be a real bear to push off of those mountains. Of course the weather continues to be miserable, which doesn't help matters one damn bit. By the way, if Clark can't use the 10th Mountain Division, I'd like to have it. Their skills will come in handy if we have to fight on those peaks."

Ike nodded grimly. While Bradley and Devers would ultimately close the route from northern Germany to the Redoubt area, the door from the south was open and would likely remain that way. Maybe it wouldn't be a huge German army that made it to the mountains, but it wouldn't have to be to be an effective deterrent. Damn it to hell, he thought as he reached for another cigarette. Realistically also, there was no chance of stopping the Germans from moving to the Alps until the Rhine was crossed.

"You can have the Tenth," Ike said. And, he thought,

you have convinced me to give you a chance to either
stop the Germans from making it to the Redoubt in
large numbers, or taking it from those who do make it.

"Do I have the go-ahead to begin planning to cross
the Rhine?"

Ike winced inwardly. It was a reminder that he'd
shot down Devers' earlier plan. "Just don't plan too
long. I want your men across as soon as feasible."

Devers beamed. "Great, Ike. To get started I want
to switch the Seventh Army's location with the French
First Army. I want Americans heading east along the
Swiss border where they can cut off Germans from
the north and east. I just don't think the French are
up to it and you can blame De Gaulle all you want."

Ike laughed. Devers enthusiasm was contagious.
Now all the man had to do was pull it off. "Jake, I
plan on blaming Le Grand Charles for everything."

Tanner tried not to limp too badly as he reported
to Major General Richard Evans of the 105th Infantry
Division. His knee had healed and his foot was getting
better, but was a long ways from healthy. He wondered if he would ever be able to play touch football
or pickup basketball. Hell, or even walk briskly. He
had also picked up an intestinal bug that had cost
him twenty pounds. This morning he'd noticed that
there was a hint of premature grey in his hair. Damn.
The last thing he needed was to look old before he
was thirty. When he got home after the war, how
would he ever find a woman if he looked older than
he was? He had laughed at his reflection when he
realized that first he had to survive the war in order
to get home upright and not in a box.

Evans commanded the 105th Infantry Division. He was at his headquarters in a farmhouse ten miles west of the still uncrossed Rhine and north of the Swiss border.

An officious clerk told Tanner to have a seat. He was informed that the general would be with him in a moment. He took the opportunity to look at the numerous maps tacked to the walls. Evans' division was the closest to the Swiss border. To its left as it faced Germany in the east was the Thirty-Sixth Infantry Division and the other divisions that comprised the U.S. Seventh Army.

The clerk told Tanner to go in. He saluted the general and reported formally. Evans casually returned the salute, shook his hand, and directed Tanner to a chair. Evans was short, pot-bellied and had thinning red hair. Tanner judged him to be in his fifties. He looked nervous and exhausted but greeted Tanner cordially.

"I've read your record, Captain, and it's not my policy to make wounded soldiers stand. It's also not my policy to spend too much time greeting captains, even those who've been wounded and decorated. There are just too many of them. However, your story intrigues me. Just how the hell did the 106th get in such a position that two of their three regiments had to surrender?"

Tanner had told the story so many times that he almost had it memorized. "It's a sad old tale, General. We saw what we wanted to see and believed what we wanted to believe. The Germans were making a lot of noise putting their armor into position but we thought it was them getting ready to pull their vehicles out of the area, not attack us. They also tried to mask the sounds by flying planes low over the area. Some of us thought otherwise, but we were pretty much shouted down by so-called experts. We believed that they knew more than we did, despite what we were hearing and sensing. We were reminded that the Germans were dead, were on their last legs, and, hell, the war would be over by Christmas and we'd all be home by Easter. Sir, I'm not going to insult you by saying I was a genius and disagreed with those assertions. I did to a point, but then I agreed with their collective wisdom. I decided that all those experts had to be right and who was I to argue?"

"How much did the division's inexperience and the fact that you were spread so thin have to do with the disaster?"

"A lot, sir. The higher-ups said our area was a quiet zone and we could gain some valuable experience without getting too many people hurt. And then when the Krauts did attack, we were spread so thin that the German infantry and armor came in hordes and punched through us like shit through a goose. That's when I got wounded and escaped through to our lines."

Evans leaned back in his chair and nodded grimly. "Do you feel that you disobeyed a direct order by not surrendering?"

Tanner answered with barely controlled anger. It was not the first time he had been asked that question. Usually, it had come from men who'd been nowhere near the front. "I never actually got such an order and, besides, sir, I'm not so sure that I'd have to obey an order to surrender when I had an option to escape. I can't imagine getting court-martialed for wanting to continue on fighting."

Evans laughed softly. "I can't either, son. I just don't know what to do with an officer who had trench foot and now can't get his feet wet."

"I'll do whatever you ask, sir."

Evans paused thoughtfully. "A couple of days ago, a young lieutenant misunderstood an order and wound up getting his platoon almost wiped out. The platoon sergeant and three others survived. I hate speaking ill of the dead, but the boy made a dumb mistake. As a result, he and a score of others paid with their lives. Now they're all either dead or wounded prisoners."

Evans lit a cigarette. He did not offer one to Tanner. That was fine. Tanner rarely smoked. "The sergeant's name is Billy Hill and don't laugh or he'll skin you alive. He deserved better. He and a couple of his surviving men are hanging around headquarters. I'm going to assign them to you. You're supposed to be good at intelligence and your report says you'd like to see the Nazi who killed your buddies get justice. You will work for me and you'll be involved in special projects and, no, you will not be handing out socks and underwear. I will try to make sure that you don't get your damn feet wet."

"Magda!" Josef Goebbels yelled happily as he entered their apartment near the Fuhrer Bunker. Until it became too dangerous to travel, she and the children had been estranged and living separately from Josef. "It has been officially decided and I have the orders signed by Hitler himself," he exulted. "We are all to leave Berlin while we can and get to the Redoubt. When we arrive, I will

be in charge until Bormann gets there. He is to leave
Berlin at a later time."

Goebbels' wife smiled grimly. "Perhaps we and the
Reich will have good fortune and he won't make it."

They embraced almost formally, even coldly, and
separated. By conventional standards theirs was a
unique marriage. She had an adult child by a first
marriage and the two had six more children, the oldest
of whom was a girl of twelve. While they might love
each other in their own way, neither had been a particularly loyal spouse. Josef Goebbels was a notorious
womanizer and Magda had taken a number of lovers.
Both were proud that they'd produced six young Nazis
to serve the Reich and Adolf Hitler.

Josef's most recent infidelities had become public
and almost destroyed the remnants of their marriage.
For most of the time, they lived apart with Josef only
visiting his children with permission. Now, however,
the war had forced them to resume living together.

"Now both we and Germany have a chance," the
Propaganda Minister said proudly and Magda nodded
her agreement.

In the distance bombs were falling, but nothing
near the heart of Berlin at this time. They would be
ignored. The work of government went on regardless
of the enemy attacks. After each bombing, thousands
of Berliners would come out of their shelters and holes
and begin the process of clearing the streets, moving
the rubble, and searching for the dead, the wounded
and other survivors. Dust clouds covered portions of
the city and the stench of death was pervasive. The
inhabitants of Berlin looked gaunt and filthy. Food
was rationed and bathing was an unheard-of luxury,

except, of course, for the party and military hierarchy, and that did include the Goebbels' family.

Goebbels had the unenviable job of telling the people of Berlin and the rest of Germany that all was well and that victory was just around the corner. He considered himself the most loyal servant Adolf Hitler had, but even he no longer believed that they could hold out against the Red Army's hordes pressing them from the east. Nor were there any more super weapons to launch at the enemy, unless, of course, Heisenberg's bomb worked. All had been used and the results had been negligible. Defeat was inevitable.

The two had discussed their options and, until recently, had seen death as the only viable option. It was inevitable that the Russians would take Berlin and the fate of the Goebbels family at the hands of the Red Army was almost too terrible to contemplate. Although in her early forties, the blond Joanna Magdalena Maria Goebbels was still an extremely attractive woman and, since Hitler was a bachelor, she was considered the First Lady of the Reich. She had served as a hostess at a number of events and was a celebrity in her own right. She would be a prized prisoner, ripe for humiliation and degradation.

If she were captured by the Reds, it was presumed that many vengeful Red Army soldiers would stand in line and take turns raping her and her children before killing them. Perhaps their ordeal would be filmed and viewed by posterity. Or worse, after being abused by the Slavic subhumans, they would be shipped to the Kremlin and put on display in cages where they would exist as starving naked animals living in their own filth and driven mad by the abuse. Their oldest,

Helga, was only twelve and that fate for her and the others was too terrible to contemplate. No, they already had the cyanide tablets needed to bring all to a quick death. Death by poison would not be painless but they had seen it as their only option. As captors, the Americans might treat them more decently, but the Americans were far away.

But now there was a glimmer of hope. Both were torn. Their adoration of Hitler knew no bounds. But they were human and they wanted the two of them and their children to have a chance at survival. They would obey orders and go to the Redoubt. The cyanide pills were always there, always present. Death was inevitable, but now it could be deferred.

Ernie Janek, late of Chicago, swung his muscular legs out of his bed and thought that war was not always hell. He was twenty-three and a captain in the U.S. Army Air Force, and the mighty Eighth Air Force to boot.

So what the hell was he doing in a cheap hotel in Bern, the capital of Switzerland? Well, he reminded himself, it was because his P51 fighter had a little engine trouble while escorting a flight of B17 bombers. This caused him to drop out of the formation and become easy prey for a pair of German ME109 fighters. He'd fought and danced in the skies and managed to shoot one of them down, but then his engine seized up and the surviving Kraut had poured bullets into Ernie's plane. Almost miraculously, he hadn't been scratched while he cowered and whimpered helplessly and waited for the end. He'd been praying for the first time in years when he realized that the remaining German plane had pulled back and was flying away. Ernie had no firm idea where he was, but he decided that south was best since the German plane was headed to the north.

Ernie had nursed the plane along until the engine started to smoke and flames erupted. He'd then climbed out of his cockpit and launched himself down to the mist-covered ground. He first hoped for a clean landing with no broken bones, and then that the Germans wouldn't kill him. German civilians had begun taking bloody vengeance on the downed airmen who'd rained death on their homes. He'd been told in lectures that the hardest part of surrendering was getting somebody to accept it instead of shooting you first.

He'd landed safely after only a couple of bumps and bruises resulting from being scraped along the ground and was getting out of his parachute harness when a truckload of soldiers arrived. He immediately held up his hands and hoped they would take his surrender. One took his pistol and pushed him into the back of the truck.

"Where am I?" he asked, hoping that someone understood him.

One of them laughed. "You are afraid that you are in Germany, aren't you? Well congratulations, you've had the good luck to land in Switzerland."

And good luck it was, he thought. Switzerland was neutral and felt compelled to treat combatants from both sides as internees and not prisoners. American internees were treated more as unexpected and somewhat unwelcome guests and their confinement was extremely light. Ernie had been put up at an unused ski lodge for a couple of weeks until being moved to his current abode, an inexpensive but clean hotel in Bern. Of course it would be clean. The Swiss were always clean. Here he would be safe until the war ended. He was encouraged to wear civilian clothes, which was fine since his one and only uniform had been shredded by his parachute landing. The American embassy in Bern even made sure he was paid and that he got his mail.

Problem was, he didn't want to spend the war sitting on his ass in Bern. Not only was he supposed to be fighting Nazis, but Bern had to be one of the dullest places in the world. Admittedly, it was a pretty little town of about a hundred and twenty thousand souls, and the medieval city center was a joy to look at. Like his hotel, the place was also immaculately clean, making him think that hordes of cleaning ladies emerged each night and scrubbed down the entire town. It was nice, but it wasn't the U.S. Army Air Force and he wasn't fighting the Nazis. Someday, when the war was over, his grandchildren would ask him what he did in the war. He didn't want to say he spent some or most of it sitting on his ass in a hotel in Switzerland.

He'd had an idea and today he would try it out. On many days, a middle-aged man would come to a nearby park that overlooked the Aare River that snaked through Bern. He would sit and smoke his pipe, apparently pontificating. Ernie sensed that the man was an American, doubtless a diplomat, although he might be from the Red Cross, which had its headquarters in Bern. It didn't matter. Maybe the man could get him out of the boring hole that was Bern and back to the war.

After having watched him for a while, Ernie realized that men and women would occasionally come up to the man, shake hands, and depart. Sometimes they would sit and talk softly. Ernie quickly realized that that some of them were surreptitiously giving him information and documents. Whoever the old guy was, he was likely a spy. Now he *really* had to meet the guy.

Ernie walked across the park and sat by the man at the far end of the bench. He lit a cigarette and tried to look casual. The man had been reading a newspaper. He folded it and laid it down. "Good afternoon, Captain Janek. My name is Allen Dulles. How may I be of service to you?"

CHAPTER 3

WHENEVER THERE WAS THUNDER AND LIGHTNING, Lena would wonder if these were the sights and sounds of battles that would set her free. Always her hopes were dashed when nothing more than wind and rain pelted down. She swore that she would not feel sorry for herself. As her grandmother used to say, each day of life was a blessing. The fact that she was alive and not being brutalized in a factory or work camp was another blessing. The fact that she did not have to spread her legs for Gustav Schneider or take his manhood in her mouth was one more blessing. The fact that Gustav's son Anton and his sister Astrid could still be controlled was another.

Like servants or slaves everywhere, the Schneiders sometimes forgot she was present. Or that she could hear them easily if she simply moved to another room. They had loud raucous voices. Her grandmother would have considered them vulgar and Lena concurred.

She had a lot of freedom. She often went shopping with Frau Schneider and carried her packages like a good and dutiful servant. This gave her an opportunity to see the world around her and gauge what was happening. She was heartened by the growing sense of despair in the faces of those Germans she saw. Wounded German soldiers, many missing limbs or with mutilated faces, sat on benches and stared vacantly at their terribly changed world. She could pity them as individuals, but not the regime they fought for. She felt the same with the growing columns of civilian refugees that were now streaming west. It pleased her to see the men, women, and children of the master race pushing handcarts with all their remaining possessions piled on them. She thought she could tell by the haunted faces of some of the women that they had suffered at the hands of the Soviets before escaping to Germany. Even though she had shared their fate, she felt no sympathy.

The Schneiders had not had the yellow Star of David sewn on her clothing, another blessing. Apparently they and other authorities concurred that there was enough doubt about her Jewishness to permit that exception. Lena didn't think the Schneiders liked being seen in the company of someone who was openly proclaimed to be a Jew.

On occasion they would even send her alone on small errands. They were not concerned that she would run away. After all, where the devil would she go? They did make sure that she carried a permission slip from Herr Schneider in case she was stopped by the police or the Gestapo.

Gustav Schneider was a district administrator and an enthusiastic member of the Nazi Party. He was not part of the Gestapo, but he did run a number

of informants who fed him information about disloyal citizens. This was forwarded on and those who
doubted Germany's ultimate victory would be talked
to. Or they would disappear.

For all intents and purposes, Gustav Schneider's
word was law. He had served in World War I and
had been active in the postwar street fighting that had
brought the Nazi Party to power. Lena suspected that
he had been a peasant before becoming a Nazi. She
sensed that his formal education had been slight, but
he had worked hard and corrected those deficiencies.

But now she had a fair idea of her fate and she was
terrified. She had heard them say that they would not
take her with them to the Alpine Redoubt. No room
for Jews was the reason. Instead, when the time came
for the Schneiders to move south, she would be taken
away to a hidden factory that made small parts for
airplane engines. She'd heard of the place. Rumors said
it was a hell from which no working slaves emerged.
Despite the fact that it was a small factory with only
a couple hundred people confined and working, she
knew she would die if she was sent there.

Thus, she had to escape. But when and how?

Tanner and Sergeant Billy Hill struck up an easy
relationship that was both professional and somewhat
personal. Each had been in the army long enough to
know that sometimes the distinctions of rank had to be
eased, if not ignored altogether, when out in the field.

The American army had advanced beyond where
Hill's column had been ambushed. Still, they went to
the site and saw the scars of battle. The dead had
been removed, although some of the bloodstains on

the road were still visible. The charred and smashed vehicles that could not be salvaged had been pushed to the side where they lay as grim memorials. In the distance, the hills that would grow into mountains seemed to look down on them. A column of trucks drove past them at a prudent thirty miles an hour, evidence that the area was now secure. The German fighting retreat had continued. Almost inevitably, artillery rumbled in the distance.

They turned down a dirt road and drove to where they could see the Rhine. They'd been told that the river was narrower here than up north but it was still a mighty and powerful obstacle. The current was fast and strong and the water was cold. Falling in would result in a quick death if one were not rescued immediately. Tanner looked at the other side through his binoculars and wondered if a German was looking back at him. He fought a ridiculous urge to wave. With his luck, the response would be an artillery round fired right at him.

Sergeant Hill spat some tobacco on the ground, happily desecrating the Third Reich. "Excuse the impertinence, Captain, but what's your take on General Evans?"

Tanner paused. It *was* an impertinent question but one he'd been pondering as well. "I think he's got problems, Sergeant. He's got a brand-new division that's seriously understrength and with a whole new cast of characters and most of them are totally inexperienced. Many of the infantrymen arrived here without ever having fired a rifle and haven't done so yet. Also, the division's filled with inexperienced officers and NCOs. You and I have been in action, although my avoiding surrendering hardly qualifies me as a combat expert. But most of the officers and men haven't really heard a shot fired in anger. And that artillery going off in the distance doesn't count as combat experience either. That's why the ambush of your platoon was such a shock. In the Ardennes it happened all the time, but not to my division and not to yours. The 106th had just arrived up there and most of the men had barely settled in, just like here. A lot of them hoped they could ride out the end of the war in relative comfort and safety. They were hoping to bide their time drinking beer and screwing German women. Then all hell broke loose and the division was effectively destroyed."

"And I'll bet that most of them didn't want to fight too hard either, did they?"

"That's right. They just wanted to serve their time and get home. Nobody wanted to be a hero and that fact is going to plague Evans. It's not that the men are cowards. They just don't want to take a chance on dying when they don't have to. Ironically, some inexperienced soldiers might be talked into taking chances that experienced ones won't. We'll all obey General Evans' orders, but I don't see too many people going out of their way to show initiative, and that probably includes me."

Hill laughed. "Add me to that list, sir."

"When somebody opens fire on them, the men are very likely to go to ground and call for artillery support rather than moving forward under fire. Maybe that's one thing that bothers Evans about what happened to your platoon. Your lieutenant made a foolish mistake and paid for it. But he was showing initiative. He was out looking for bear. Somebody once told me that, after a while, all the heroes in any army are all dead or wounded. What's left are the survivors who do a good job of keeping their heads down."

Tanner realized they shouldn't be sightseeing and shouldn't be talking like this about their general, but what the hell. "I think Evans is afraid of failure and that any failure will result in a lot of deaths. That's why he wants us to provide him with an extra level of security and intelligence. Maybe thinks both of us are survivors and therefore know something about war that other people don't."

Hill laughed softly and bitterly. "I didn't think I was so smart while I was lying in the snow and mud and trying not to get my ass shot off while my men got killed."

"Understood, Sergeant. And I wasn't doing anything special while I was running through the cold and snowy shit that was Belgium."

Major Alfonse Hahn stepped smartly to within a few feet of Field Marshal Ferdinand Schoerner and halted. "Heil Hitler, Field Marshal, and congratulations on your promotion. It is long overdue and well deserved."

Schoerner returned the salute and laughed. "And you're kissing my ass again, Major, but I appreciate it."

Schoerner waved Hahn to a chair. "According to reports, my old friend, you have been a very bad boy. Just how many American soldiers did you have executed?"

Hahn rubbed the star-shaped red birthmark on his cheek. "Just a handful of American prisoners that I deemed useless and, of course, a larger number of German deserters who deserved death for their actions. But why do you ask?"

An aide brought brandies. Before the war, the two men had become close during Schoerner's time spent turning the SS into a real military fighting unit. Hahn had been a very young officer whose ruthless methods had impressed Schoerner. He thought it a shame that Hahn hadn't been promoted to a much higher rank. Perhaps he would be in a position to correct that injustice.

"A very good source has told me that the Americans have put you on a long list of so-called war criminals they plan to prosecute after the war, assuming, of course that they win it and that you are still either alive or haven't fled to someplace like Argentina. Apparently someone witnessed you executing two wounded soldiers in the Ardennes. I'm sure you remember the incident."

"Of course, Field Marshal. One man was unconscious and doubtless dying, while the second had serious leg injuries along with a big mouth. He kept saying that we were going to lose and that Hitler was going to hang. Even if I had wished to, I could not have taken them with me, so I shot them. I was leaving the Ardennes to report our great victory to our mutual friend, Herr Goebbels. It was just a shame that our victory turned so sour so quickly."

Schoerner nodded agreement. Like many senior officers, he'd had doubts about the Ardennes offensive, feeling it was a desperate move. "But now we have an opportunity to turn it all around, which we shall do. Perhaps then we will not be forced to hide in caves."

Both men laughed. Albert Speer and hordes of his

capable assistants along with thousands of laborers, mainly slaves, had performed miracles. Hundreds of large caves now dotted the hills and mountains, including the immense command cave they were now in. It was located a few miles outside the Austrian city of Bregenz, on Lake Constance and close to the Swiss border. Several hundred people worked in the cave and other caves were being constructed. Much of the brute labor came from a small concentration camp in the area, while other workers had been shipped in from the much larger camp at Dachau.

Schoerner continued. "Right now it almost goes without saying that the war has become a disaster. It is going to be up to us to salvage what we can and lead a renaissance of the Nazi Party and, of course, of Germany. The Fuhrer has said that Germany is not worthy of him and he is largely correct. Perhaps the time was not ripe for something as dramatic and wonderful as a world run by Nazis. Someday soon it *will* be and we will be at the forefront along with Herr Goebbels."

Hahn swelled with pride. "I won't let you down."

"I know you won't. How many men did you manage to bring with you?"

"With regrets, only a couple dozen. However, they are loyal men who would be willing to die for the Reich."

Schoerner smiled warmly. "Let's hope they don't have to. I know you're curious as to what your duties will be here in this new capital of Germany. They will be quite simple. You and your men, augmented by other new arrivals of course, will make it your life's purpose to find and stamp out traitors and Jews. You may use any means at your disposal."

Hahn was puzzled. "Isn't that the job of the Gestapo?"

"It would be except for the fact that the Gestapo's presence down here is less than minimal. You are a devoted SS man, which is the next best thing. In fact, it is better since you are also a soldier and this is going to be a totally military operation and will be until some later time. You will report to me until Minister Goebbels arrives. If Bormann makes it here as well, then he will be in charge."

"Between the two of us, Field Marshal, who will rule Germany if the Fuhrer does die in Berlin?"

Schoerner pondered the question. There were a number of claimants for a throne that wasn't yet vacant. Goering was an obese joke, but Himmler was a serious contender as were Bormann and Goebbels. Both Schoerner and Hahn hoped it would be Goebbels. Then too, there was a rumor that Admiral Doenitz was Hitler's designated heir. It was hoped that there would not be a number of pretenders whose infighting could jeopardize the continued existence of the Reich.

Schoerner poured them some more brandy. "To answer your question, Major, the new ruler of Germany will be the survivor."

The dying German plane shrieked across the sky. Flames spewed from its tail and it looked like the pilot was trying to find a place to land. It was also unlike any other plane Lena or the Schneiders had ever seen or heard.

"He isn't going to make it," muttered Gustav Schneider. His wife and children said nothing. As usual Lena hung back. They were outside the house and near a field that abutted the Schneiders' property. They'd been tending the vegetable garden that now provided them with much of their food. The plane slammed into the ground with a loud crack, bounced once in the air and settled on the earth. An instant later, the onboard fuel exploded. Even though it was hundreds of yards away, they felt the warmth from the flames flow over them.

Lena could also smell the contents of the plane burning and wondered if any of the smell was the pilot. Part of her said it was good that the Nazi had died, while another felt it was terrible that another young man's life had to end so violently.

Anton yelled and pointed. "Papa, is that the pilot?"

It was. The pilot had been thrown clear and had landed facedown in the field. He hadn't been burned, but he was still very dead. Behind them they could hear the wail of sirens growing nearer. They walked to the body with Gustav taking the lead and Lena again in the rear. If they noticed her, she was afraid they'd send her back to the house.

Herr Schneider waved his arms angrily. "Look at this. It's another one of Hitler's super-weapons. How super can it be if the damned thing gets shot down?"

Lena was stunned. She had never heard him criticize the Fuhrer. Perhaps he was drunk. Or, like everybody else, perhaps he was frustrated with the war. But from what she'd seen of it in the air and the remains of the wreckage on the ground, the plane was indeed unique. There were no propellers and the shape had been sleek and looked like a predator. She'd heard people talk of jets and presumed that this was one of them. She was not impressed. Herr Schneider was right. How could it be a super-weapon if it could be shot down? The thought pleased her.

Gudrun tried to calm her husband. There were no spies or informers around, but one shouldn't get careless, not even if they were themselves closely allied to the Gestapo. "There will be other weapons and other opportunities to stop the Americans," she said soothingly.

Gustav glowered. "Certainly there are," he said sarcastically. "Just like the V1 rocket was supposed to bring England to its knees, and then the V2 was supposed to finish the job. I've talked to people who know these things and the V1 flies so slowly and predictably that it can actually be shot down. The V2 is much faster but neither of them can be aimed with even the slightest degree of accuracy. They only thing they can guarantee hitting is the ground. Did you know that thousands of both rockets were aimed at the Tower Bridge in London and not one of them hit it? Thousands were fired, but not one hit. Not only that, but their warheads are too small. Even a direct hit on Target 42, which was the Luftwaffe's name for the Tower Bridge, wouldn't have destroyed it."

He angrily and petulantly stamped his foot. Anton had wandered close to the corpse and his mother pulled him back. Astrid averted her eyes. She had no wish to see more death.

"Damn it to hell," Gustav continued to rage. "Germany is being betrayed by the scientists. I'll bet they are all Jews pretending to be real Germans."

The fire was rapidly burning itself out. The local fire and police continents had arrived and contented themselves with containing it. The dead pilot had been pulled from the ground and laid on a stretcher. The impact had flattened the man's body and left a rough outline of his corpse indented in the ground. She shuddered. At least he'd died quickly. Or she hoped he had.

Gustav Schneider decided that the show was over and they all headed back to the house. Lena maneuvered so she was last. They hadn't noticed her and she had not spoken. Only Anton had been aware of her presence. He had turned and looked at her. The glance had turned into a stare and then into a leer. Her dress was an old one and the hem was too short, showing more of her legs than she realized she should have.

He grinned and winked. She turned away and walked just a little faster.

When Ernie Janek presented himself to the Marine guard at the U.S. embassy in Bern, he expected to be told to wait. The summons from the old man in the park had been simple—be at the embassy at ten in the morning. To his surprise there would be no waiting. He was immediately ushered into a small room with a card table and two chairs. Not impressive, was Ernie's first thought.

The old man entered and took a seat. A servant brought coffee and cakes and left. There was silence while they enjoyed the coffee. Switzerland might be neutral, but good, real coffee was still rare and the cakes were excellent. Even better, from Ernie's perspective, they were free.

"My name is Allen Dulles, Captain, and I am in charge of all the OSS activities in the area. I won't be more specific for security reasons and the fact that my job seems to change every day, if not every hour. Just for the record, you do know what the OSS is, don't you?"

"Yes sir. OSS stands for Office of Strategic Services and it involves all kinds of spying and espionage activities. For the record, I wouldn't mind doing something more useful like that than taking up space in a cheap Swiss hotel."

Dulles took out his pipe, stuffed some tobacco, and lit it. He drew deeply and a blue cloud of smoke rose to the ceiling. "You were a fighter pilot. How many Germans did you shoot down?"

"Eight."

"You were a fighter pilot and all fighter pilots are congenital liars. That means you actually shot down four. Is that correct?"

Ernie shrugged and grinned. "Guilty. One more and I would have been an ace, but I guess that's never going to happen, is it?"

"Not in this war. Tell me, do you speak German or any other language and do you have any skills that might be useful in my line of work?"

"No sir." Aw shit, he thought. Was he going to turn me down?

"What about Morse code? Do you know judo or karate?"

"I used to be good with Morse when I was in the Boy Scouts, but I know nothing about Judo and I don't even know what karate is."

Dulles' next comment allayed his fears. "No matter. So many of my agents started out as willing amateurs and you are already way ahead of them. You've been in combat and you've faced down death. But you have always killed at a distance. Could you kill someone who was staring at you and was only a few feet away? If you had to, could you kill with a knife? Could you strangle a man? Could you kill a woman if you had to?"

"I don't know but I think so."

"Good. If you had told me you were certain you could, I would have thought you were a fool as well as a liar."

"I hope I am not a fool, sir."

Dulles ignored the comment. "What you will now do is go back to that hotel and gather up all your belongings and return here. You will be living and training in the embassy until something appropriate comes along. We will issue you diplomatic credentials which give you a great deal of legal immunity and you will not abuse them."

"Understood, but won't the Swiss notice that I've gone from the hotel?"

"Probably not, Captain. I hate to tell you this, but you are simply not that important. And if anyone does notice, a few discreet comments will satisfy them."

Dulles stood and held out his hand. "Captain Janek, welcome to the OSS."

The P51 Mustang was arguably the finest propeller-driven fighter plane in the world. It was powerful, durable and, with drop tanks, had enormous range, which enabled it to fly as an escort to bombers as they attacked far into Germany. With the right pilot at the controls, it could hold its own against Germany's best and that included their vaunted jet, the ME262. The German jet was vulnerable during take-off and landing and required a long runway. Thus, American pilots learned to tail the jets back to their bases and, if they could not actually kill them while landing, damage the runways so they could not be used until repaired. Not only was the P51 a great plane, but there were thousands of them, something that could not be said about the German jets, which maybe numbered in the hundreds. Overall also, American pilots were much better trained then their German counterparts, who were poorly trained because of chronic fuel shortages and a lack of safe places for training.

Lieutenants George Schafer and Bud Sibre were bored. They hadn't seen a German plane in days. This afternoon they flew their birds over southern Germany and were looking for prey on the ground. While George searched the roads below, Bud scanned the skies for Germans. They were not having any luck. The skies were empty and so too were the roads. The only traffic was clearly civilian and they'd been told to not attack civilians, even if they were Germans and doubtless Nazis.

"We know there are Krauts down there, so where are they?" said George over his radio. He was frustrated. They both were. Every briefing said the Germans were moving by night and hiding during the day. On a few occasions they'd shot up some hayfields and barns or some woodlands, especially if they saw tracks that might mean Nazi activity. Aside from destroying some farmer's livelihood or mutilating some trees, it wasn't clear that they'd accomplished anything.

"We need to be able to see in the dark," said Bud. There were rumors that the military was actually working on something that could sense heat, thus enabling a pilot to "see" in the dark. They were not counting on getting it during this war.

"Convoy," said George. The two planes swooped down. Three vehicles were parked by the side of the road. Red Crosses were plainly visible on their sides and tops. "Damn it," he added. They had seen a number of ambulances in the last few days and all were displaying the symbol of the Red Cross.

The military and their own sense of morality told them they could not strafe an ambulance full of wounded even though they were doubtless Nazis. For all they knew, the Germans could be hiding Adolf Hitler in one of the vehicles, but they would not intentionally fire, which was why ambulances often drove in daylight. Less of a chance of an accident, was the reasoning. Nor was there any firing at them from antiaircraft guns.

They flew low and swept over the ambulances. "Somebody's in the road," said George. "I'll check it out."

"Roger." Bud would watch out for any danger to his friend and eliminate that nuisance if it occurred.

"Hey, it's a nurse," George chortled. "And, damnation, she's a blond."

"You wanna land and have her check your blood pressure along with the pressure behind your dick? Or why don't you signal her to show you her tits."

George ignored him. "She's waving and smiling and there's a doctor in front of one of the ambulances. I guess we should play nice."

The two pilots again flew over the ambulances. The waved from their cockpits and wagged their wings. They flew off to their base in France where their planes would be fueled and ammo reloaded. Down below, people were dying in cold and mud and filth. While death in the air could be just as violent and ugly, this night they would eat warm food and sleep in beds.

"Fucking American bastards!" screamed Magda Goebbels as she waved at the American planes. She'd yelled in English even though the two pilots couldn't possibly hear her. The smile was frozen on her face as the planes disappeared.

Despite himself, the "doctor," Josef Goebbels, laughed hugely. "I hope they can't read lips."

They'd decided to heed advice and hide in plain sight. Americans wouldn't shoot up ambulances, they'd been told, and so far the advice had proven right. Despite those assurances, each time American planes looked them over, there was the real fear that a killer pilot would make a small and intentional mistake and strafe them, later saying he couldn't see the Red Crosses. So sorry, he would say. He would apologize, have his wrist slapped, and be forgiven. Each ambulance had a driver and a guard. The Goebbels family occupied two of the ambulances while the third was filled with what remained of their personal possessions. It was galling that they'd been reduced to being able to put all of their possessions into one ambulance.

"Did you learn to swear like that when you visited the United States?" Josef asked. As a young woman Magda had spent a number of months in America and spoke English fluently.

They had stopped by the road so the children could answer calls of nature and had been shocked when the two fighters had suddenly appeared. But now they were gone and the danger was over. She called the children who ran and laughed as they got back into the ambulances.

Josef Goebbels was pleased with their progress. Another day or two would see them at Hitler's mountaintop retreat at Berchtesgaden, the Eagle's Nest, where there had been happy memories of the glory of the Reich. Not enough memories, he thought sadly. The war had interfered with mountaintop festivities. From there they would go deeper into the mountains, and safety in the Redoubt.

During their travels they had seen the stark and brutal evidence of Germany's demise. Roads had been cratered by bombs. Destroyed vehicles and burned out tanks were everywhere. It was impossible to ignore the stench of burned and decaying bodies still inside them. While they traveled during the day, they were able to see camouflaged tanks and troop carriers. They were hiding and waiting until the dark when they could sneak down a road a few more miles to wherever was their destination. Josef Goebbels wondered if many of them were headed south towards the Alps and the Redoubt. He also wondered if many of the other ambulances headed towards the Redoubt would make it.

Even this day, as the American planes had zoomed past, they felt hidden eyes on them. The German soldiers watching them must have wondered who they were to have commandeered the ambulances. Perhaps some of the soldiers had recognized the Goebbels family from the numerous photos taken of them and published throughout the Reich. If so, Josef Goebbels wondered if they thought he was a coward for hiding behind the Red Cross and instead of being in Berlin with the Fuhrer. He decided he didn't care.

"Where the hell is Remagen?" yelled General Evans. He raced across the office and started pawing through maps.

There was a flurry of activity while his staff pored over maps of Germany. "Got it," said Tanner. "It's a small town north of here on the Rhine."

Evans grinned wickedly. "And I'll bet the map shows it's got a bridge, doesn't it? Well, as of a few hours ago, that bridge became ours and Bradley's First Army boys are pouring across it into the heart of Germany. Hot damn! We're in and ahead of that son of a bitch Montgomery."

Cheers exploded in the large tent that was the division's temporary headquarters. If the Rhine had been crossed anywhere, it meant that it would probably be easier for the next force across to exploit. Maybe the German armies on the other side would indeed collapse. Maybe pigs would fly, Tanner thought. On the other side of the Rhine was a defensive line called the West Wall or the Siegfried Line. No one knew how strong those works were and how well they were manned.

Tanner decided to be bold. "General, if you look at the map, Remagen doesn't do anything or go anyplace. It's just a little town with a bridge and one rail line heading east. If we've now got a base in Germany proper, it looks pretty accidental. I just wonder how it can be exploited. And what does that do to Montgomery's planned big jump?"

"That's for Ike and Bradley to decide, just like it's

going to be up to Devers to figure out how to get his army across. When that happens, maybe we can cut off at least some of the German army heading to the Alps. You know damn well that Patton is chomping at the bit to cross and now that we have this Alpine Redoubt to worry us, I've got money that says we'll be crossing just as quickly as possible."

Montgomery's planned massive combined forces jump across the Rhine was code-named Operation Varsity Plunder. Critics of the British general's plans held that Varsity Plunder was overplanned and overlarge. It even included massive airborne assaults that had, in the past, resulted in heavy casualties.

Evans waved grandly to his grinning staff. "The Seventh Army and this division are going to cross that damn river. And when we do, we're going to smash that Alpine Redoubt and then be on our way home."

There were more cheers. Tanner decided he needed some fresh air and stepped outside. As usual, the weather was damp and foggy. He decided that Germany in the winter wasn't the most wonderful place in the world. South of them and closer to the Alps was supposed to be great ski country. Too bad he didn't ski.

Mitch Cullen, a captain and another member of the division's G2, or intelligence section, joined him and shrugged. "Crossing the Rhine sounds like a fine opportunity to get shot at."

"Are you criticizing our beloved general?"

"Horrors, no. It's just that Evans is a lot more enthusiastic about invading Germany than a lot of people, and that includes me. I just want to get this over, get out and go home."

"Pretty much my idea, too."

Sergeant Hill emerged from the tent and joined them. He didn't salute. Nobody did. Even though the area was supposed to be safe, there was always the risk of a sniper. Saluting identified the person being saluted as someone important. Saluting, therefore, was prohibited, particularly by those who were important.

"Captain Tanner," said Cullen, "you missed the best part. General Evans had already gotten a change in orders from Ike. We are to cross that river as soon as possible. In particular, Captain Tanner, he wants you to find and gather as many small boats as you can find."

"Captain Cullen, did someone tell our general that the Germans had either taken or destroyed all the boats along the Rhine?" Tanner asked. He had three weeks' time in grade as a captain. This made him the senior of the two.

"General Evans said he knows that and that he believes you are a very resourceful officer who will solve your part of the problem and do so without getting your feet wet."

"Shit," Tanner muttered while Cullen laughed.

Hill smiled. "It gets better, or worse depending on your perspective. I'm supposed to help you."

CHAPTER 4

TANNER LOOKED THROUGH HIS BINOCULARS AT GER-
many. He was in the upper floor of a two-story
hotel located outside the village of Vogelgrun and
on the west side of the Rhine. He could see the
mist-covered river and Nazi Germany beyond it. The
scene looked peaceful, but it was deceptive. Just past
the Rhine lay the Siegfried Line. It was said that the
wall was obsolete and that the troops manning it were
second and third rate, but no one would know for
certain until the river was crossed and the defensive
line attacked. Tanner had the terrible feeling that the
blood price would be very high, regardless of any
obsolescence or lack of training.

He handed the binoculars to Cullen. "What I would
highly recommend is lining up every artillery tube in
the world and pounding the crap out of everything
within five miles of the river for a week or two and
then sending a thousand bombers over the place to
finish the job."

Cullen nodded. "Sounds like an effective use of

military resources to me. Unfortunately, it ain't gonna happen. Did you happen to notice that there's not much to see on the other side of the Rhine? Like that bridge at Remagen, the Germans don't seem to think this part of the Reich is all that important. There's nothing out there but farmland and that little town of Briesach just to the north."

Tanner disagreed. "Don't you wonder just how many of those farmhouses and haystacks are pillboxes and bunkers in disguise? And how many machine-gun nests could be hidden in a field? Give me a bunch of Boy Scouts with water pistols and I could raise hell with anyone trying to cross. The Krauts didn't help matters by destroying the only bridge in the area. Even if we do get troops across, it's going to take a long time to rebuild it. In the meantime, we'd have to use small boats and pontoons. And did you notice that the river is running high and fast? And oh yes, the water coming down from the mountains is very, very cold. And unless I'm wrong, those are chunks of ice floating in it."

The bridge that had once spanned the Rhine was in ruins. The center span was gone, dumped into the river by German engineers. Germany was so unreachable it might as well be on another planet.

"Answer me a question, oh Professor Tanner," said Cullen. "Are we in Germany or France?"

"Son, this is land that has been shot, fought over, and pissed on for centuries. It was mainly France up until 1870 when the Germans took it. The French got it back in 1918 and then lost it in 1940. I think it's safe to say that right now the fair city of Vogelgrun is predominantly French. Any Germans who lived there are either running for their lives or keeping their heads down and maybe learning French. There may be a number of Swiss in the town since the border and the city of Basel are so close. And we do want to keep the Swiss happy."

Despite all the changes in nationhood, Vogelgrun had been spared much of the devastation of war. Only a few buildings had even been damaged. Some collaborators had been beaten and a few hanged, but there had been no orgy of destruction. Nor did they see more than a couple of cases where women who'd fraternized with the Germans had been punished by having their heads shaved or having "whore" painted on their bare breasts.

If it weren't for the number of armed American soldiers in the streets, Vogelgrun and the neighboring towns could have been quaint tourist destinations. The American army had been greeted enthusiastically and an entire regiment of the 105th had taken up positions fronting the river. Wine and brandy had flowed freely and young French women and even some older ones had been generous with their bodies. Sergeant Hill happily informed them that he'd gotten laid twice. Tanner hadn't yet been so fortunate. Sometimes he wished he'd kept in touch with his ex-girlfriend back in the States. At least he'd have someone to write to and get letters from. But that relationship had just faded away.

"I just want to keep General Evans happy," Cullen said as he squinted through his own binoculars. "He wants to cross here and we're supposed to find boats while he scrounges up a pontoon bridge. Better, he should find a whole lot of pontoons since they have an annoying habit of getting smashed by enemy artillery.

I know I don't see any enemy at all, but you know they are hiding out there and watching us."

They were distracted by a buzzing sound. They looked to the west and saw a small plane, the army's version of a Piper Cub, flying low over the far side of the river.

"I wonder whose mad idea this is?" said Tanner.

"Maybe we'll find out if the Germans are awake," Cullen muttered.

He had just finished saying that when tracers streaked skyward from several hidden German machine guns, probing for the plane. For a moment, it looked like the plane would dart through the fire, but it was like it was trying to dodge raindrops. The plane was struck by a stream of bullets. It shuddered and started to fall but then rose as the pilot regained a semblance of control. More bullets slashed into its thin fuselage. The plane rolled over and dropped straight down into the ground where it disappeared into a fireball.

"The Germans are alive and well and one pilot isn't," Tanner said sadly.

Sergeant Hill had arrived in time to see the plane and pilot die. "Poor bastard."

In response, American artillery began shooting at targets across the Rhine. Shells exploded near where someone thought they'd seen the Germans fire at the doomed plane.

Tanner looked away from the window. "They don't know what they're shooting at. They just want to do something for that damned pilot."

Shells from the American 105mm howitzers continued to dig up the dirt. The Germans decided they'd had enough. Their hidden guns began firing back.

Vogelgrun and the close by city of Muhlbach began
to suffer. A shell struck the hotel where Tanner and
the others were watching. The explosion threw them
to the floor, covering them with dust and debris.
Someone in the distance screamed. They smelled
smoke. Their hotel was burning.

"Let's get out of here," Tanner ordered, and they
clawed their way through fallen roofing and walls.
Civilians and American soldiers poured from the hotel.
Nearby, buildings were burning.

"Why us?" Cullen asked plaintively. "What the hell
did we do?"

Tanner ran to a ditch and jumped in. The others
followed. The German guns found a nearby American
battery of four 105mm cannon and smashed it. Tanner watched in horror as bodies were hurled around
like leaves. In the street by their ditch, more broken
bodies lay and some of them were burning.

Tanner replied. "Maybe because they saw us in the
windows and thought we were artillery observers. Or
maybe they were just bored. Maybe they're just rotten
pricks who like to destroy cities."

More German shells struck buildings in the town
and much of Vogelgrun was on fire. So much for it
being a tourist destination, Tanner thought. Then,
just as suddenly as it began, the Germans stopped
firing. So too did the remaining American guns. A
few moments of bloody, burning hate and it was over.
The surviving American guns from other batteries
were towed away out of range of their tormentors.
The Germans had won this skirmish. Or had they?
If someone was paying attention, they had just given
away the positions of many of their guns.

Tanner gathered his small command and they retreated ignominiously out of range or at least out of sight of the Germans. They passed more men from the 105th Division moving in. The battle for Vogelgrun and a Rhine crossing was not over.

When he thought they were safe, they sat on the ground and rested. Canteens were raised and cigarettes lit. "Okay, Sergeant Hill, what the devil did you find?"

Hill took a long swallow from his canteen and poured a little on his filthy head and face. "Well, sir, you sent me out to scout and snoop and I did just that. And you're right. Just about any boat of any real size was either sunk or dragged over to the other side. However, some very nice people in and around here hate the Germans so much that they'll be willing to sell us some small boats and tell where some others are being hidden."

Tanner laughed sarcastically. "Sell? They couldn't hate the Germans all that much. Still, how many boats are we talking about and what kind of capacity?"

"I think we could get the general a hundred and each could hold a squad. We could get a battalion over with each wave."

Tanner stood and dusted himself off. "Then let's gather up all those boats and see what Evans wants to do. At a battalion per wave, it'd take forever to get the division over, much less the entire Seventh Army. He's trying to scrounge pontoon bridges from Seventh Army and turn this patrol into a major push."

Lena watched stoically as the long line of emaciated ghosts moved down the road, headed south towards the mountains. They moved in daylight. They weren't worried about the American planes strafing refugees. Lena wasn't so certain. Mistakes had a terrible way of happening, and maybe they weren't always mistakes. Some Allied commander might just realize that even slave laborers were part of the German war effort and attack them. I could have been one of them, she thought. Perhaps I should have been and it's still likely I will be.

These were prisoners from the large concentration camp at Dachau and other satellite camps. They all looked gaunt and sickly. Even though it was still winter, they were dressed in rags and many were barefoot. Their eyes were dead and they could barely shuffle. They were being marched south to work on the Alpine Redoubt. She wondered how many of them would make it and how much work they would be able to perform even if they did arrive alive.

They were divided into groups of about a hundred and each group was guarded by members of the Volkssturm, the People's Storm that had been created by the SS a few months earlier. These so-called soldiers were too old or too young or too sick or crippled to fight in a regular force. This did not stop some of them from being sadists. She forced herself to watch as one prisoner fell and was beaten and kicked until he staggered to his feet. How long would he last? she wondered. A few moments later, she heard a gunshot through the window and knew the answer.

She couldn't tell if any provision had been made to feed the prisoners. How could starving men work? she wondered. All of Germany was on short rations because of the war and it made macabre sense that prisoners would only get leftovers. But what was the point of marching them somewhere just so they could die? Of course, the Nazis were anything but logical. She was living proof of that. After all, was she a Jew or wasn't she?

She sensed that Anton was behind her. "You are very fortunate, Lena. You could be one of them."

"I know," she said softly. She wanted to cry but would not let Anton see her weakness.

He put his hand on the small of her back and began caressing her. "Don't do that," she said.

Anton laughed throatily. He leaned into her and she could feel that he was aroused. "My father only said that I couldn't fuck you because you are a Jew. Not only do I think that he'll forget all about that little rule when we have to leave, but I don't believe in it anyhow. Even if he beats me, I think it would be worth it."

He slid his hands around and up, cupping her breasts. "Too small. A real German woman would be bigger."

She reached behind and grabbed his erect manhood. "So would a German man," she said, squeezing hard and twisting. He gasped in pain and let go of her. She released his penis and pushed him away. "I am now going to help your mother with housework. I strongly suggest that you not try that again."

Anton held himself as the pain subsided. To her surprise, he laughed, "At least not until a better time."

He went outside to get a better look at the inmates passing by. He would join other good Germans and abuse them. Spitting on them seemed particularly amusing. Lena watched through a window and realized that she would have to make her decision soon.

She already had an emergency package that contained extra warm weather clothing. She would have to add food and other items essential to surviving in the woods. She had never slept outdoors in her life, but that was likely to change very soon. It would be better, she determined, to die in the woods than to be abused by Anton and then sentenced to a living death helping the Nazis.

Ernie Janek had gone for an evening's walk. He was taking a break from the intense physical training at the embassy and decided that a beer was in order. Previously he'd gone to a tavern a few blocks away, and decided that a visit to a new one was in order. He had taken a seat and ordered. He had only taken a couple of swallows when he noticed two burly men sizing him up. They had short-cropped hair, which marked them as military, and he was willing to bet money that they were Nazis. Like an idiot he had just stumbled into a bar that was frequented by Nazis. He decided to act like he was drunk. With a clatter, he dropped some change on the table. He staggered outside and into an alley where he leaned against a wall and pretended to pee.

Ernie Janek sensed the presence behind him. He willed himself to stay calm. He would be immobile and not even change his breathing, which was shallow and, he hoped, silent. He was not a large man. There wasn't room for anyone with any size in the cockpit of a P51. But he was stocky and powerfully built. He hoped the two German goons thought he would be easy pickings.

The presence was to his left. Good. When it was

only a couple of feet away, he exploded. He kicked the man in the balls and grabbed him by the throat before he could scream. He punched the man in the temple and felt him go slack. Now where the hell was the other one?

Ernie stepped over the first man, who wasn't moving. The second man looked stunned at Janek's sudden transformation. Ernie feinted with his left fist and kicked the man in the meat of his thigh with his right foot. He too went down, howling with pain. Janek silenced him by kicking him in the side of the head. He ran back to the embassy. The Marine guards stiffened as they saw him but relaxed a little when they recognized him. He quickly explained the situation and they grinned at the thought of a little action.

He went to his room and called Dulles at his palatial residence on Herrengasse Street. Ernie had been there a couple of times and it really was a centuries old palace.

"That is most unusual," said Dulles over the phone. "Thuggish behavior like that is frowned up on in neutral countries, especially neutral capitals. Well, I guess it's about time to move you on and out. Tomorrow or the day after, however, I will want you with me when I meet with a Swiss banker. After that, you will be moved to another site. I will tell you more later. You might find what the banker has to say fascinating."

Of course, Ernie thought. He hated it when Dulles was vague, but he understood—The phone might be tapped. Do not divulge future plans. But what about tonight's episode? "Sir, what if those two guys are badly hurt, or maybe even more than badly?"

Dulles chuckled. "Then the master race would

have to admit that they got the crap kicked out of them by one man. Even if you killed them, which I doubt, the Germans are highly unlikely to complain. If they pressed the issue, I suppose the Swiss could have you declared persona non grata and expelled from Switzerland, although I have no idea where you'd go. There is a war on, after all. No, we'll get you out of Bern and somewhere more suitable. Is that a problem?"

"No sir."

"Good and congratulations. I rather felt you had potential. In the meantime, stay where you are and I'll be in touch."

Josef Goebbels had reluctantly come to the conclusion that a pilgrimage to Hitler's Eagle's Nest at Berchtesgaden was a bad idea. His original thought was to gather all his senior military commanders there for a conference where they would be inspired by the spectacular views. Field Marshal Schoerner had sent a brief coded message that quickly talked him out of it. The Eagle's Nest had no real military value, so it had not yet been seriously bombed. But the Americans might find out about the arrival of so many high-ranking Nazis and change their mind. American intelligence was often very good, which led some high-ranking officials to believe that there were spies at work.

Schoerner further convinced him that making Generals Vietinghoff and Rendulic travel over dangerous roads was a chance that should not be taken. Along with being away from their commands during this crucial period of time, their vehicles could be attacked by the swarming

American fighters. Not all of them could be disguised as ambulances, Goebbels thought ruefully.

Magda had enthusiastically agreed. The sooner they got to the relative safety of the Redoubt the better. "There is no point in going to the Eagle's Nest and crying over past glories. We must begin to build new ones. And the children are exhausted. I want them someplace where we don't have to look up at the skies all day and hope that the Amis don't suddenly decide to destroy ambulances."

Her husband sometimes wondered if there was any place in the Reich where the Nazi faithful could be truly safe, but the mountains of the Alps would be much safer than riding down country roads. She looked up into the sky. Contrails marked where enemy planes flew with impunity. How nice it would be, she thought, to wipe away the arrogance of the Americans and their corrupt allies, the French and English.

Josef Goebbels caught her looking at the sky. "A few more days at the most and we'll be safe."

"The Americans will still bomb us."

"Where we are going will be too close to the Swiss border. The Americans won't chance it. Both sides need Switzerland's neutrality."

Assistant Secretary of State Dean Acheson flew to London to visit the U.S. ambassador to Great Britain, John G. Winant. A Republican, Winant had replaced the rich and controversial Joe Kennedy several years earlier, after Kennedy's pro-appeasement stance had offended so many in England.

The meeting with Winant was brief. It was intended to be. Nobody would think it in any way significant that an assistant secretary and an ambassador had met and talked. The media didn't bother to cover it.

Thus, no one noticed when the DC3 chartered to the State Department turned south towards France instead of flying directly back to the U.S. The plane landed at a military field near Reims and Acheson was driven to a private home that had been taken over by the Army just so that he and Eisenhower could meet in private. General Marshall had informed Ike that Acheson was going to arrive and that Acheson had his full support.

After the amenities and a bite to eat, the two men sat across from each other at a table. Acheson opened up his briefcase and took out some photographs. Wordlessly, he slid them over to Ike.

"Dear God," Eisenhower said in shock. "I had no idea he was in such bad shape. These are almost the photos of a dead man."

The pictures were among the latest taken of Franklin Delano Roosevelt. They showed a man who was frail, shrunken, and gaunt. The photos were in color and Roosevelt's skin color was a sickly, deathly gray. Ike shook his head. "He looks like a refugee, or someone who has just been liberated from a concentration camp." He sat back and returned the pictures to Acheson who put them away. "We've all known that he is exhausted, but what these show is well beyond that."

"And that is the point of my showing them to you, General. FDR just began his fourth term. He very strongly felt that, for better or worse, he was the only man who could navigate the U.S. through the end of this war. Now it looks like he won't make it and that his conceit will likely kill him. Certainly, it is extremely unlikely that he will complete the three plus years remaining in his term. It is, therefore, very likely that he will either die or be forced to resign and Vice President Harry Truman will become President of the United States. FDR does not appear to have much faith in the man. Of course, he never had any use for his previous vice presidents."

"Truman? I don't believe I've even met the man. I know he was a senator from Missouri and hadn't been involved in any scandals, or anything else for that matter. But if he is going to be the next president, why in God's name did FDR choose him?"

Acheson shrugged. "Who knows? Franklin has always treated his vice presidents with contempt. But it gets worse. It is strongly believed that there will be elections in England and that Churchill will lose. The Brits are sick and tired of years of austerity and war and they want a chance at a better life. In particular, they want one without bombs, and without telegrams saying that a loved one has perished. And they do want sufficient food for their children. England is a land that is significantly malnourished. Churchill was, is, a fine war leader and a marvelous symbol of British tenacity, but the consensus is that he would be a miserable peacetime leader. If there is an election, Clement Atlee would then become prime minister."

Ike recalled Atlee as a colorless and dour man. Would this be the leader of what remained of the British Empire? Relationships with Churchill were often difficult, but at least the man wanted to fight the Nazis.

"There's nothing we can do about Churchill, is there?"

"Not a thing," said Acheson. "It is very likely that we will have to deal with Attlee. We don't know what his stand on the war will be, although we suspect he will want it ended as soon as possible. We hope that doesn't mean compromises, but who knows?"

"There are other problems," Ike said as he digested that pronouncement. "I presume you're aware of my difficulties with the French? Generals Leclerc and de Lattre won't even speak to each other much less take orders. De Gaulle has threatened several times to pull his army from my command. Only when I threaten to cut off his supplies does he relent and do roughly what we want. Even then his army very liberally interprets our orders to satisfy his needs. I doubt very much that the French will be willing to have their army climb the Alps."

An aide brought coffee. Acheson sipped and smiled. "This is excellent. Yes, General Marshall is well aware of how difficult the French can be and that leaves the Russians, doesn't it? Not so long ago, FDR said that Stalin was a man he could deal with. Now the Soviets are stealing everything that isn't nailed down. They are raping, murdering and plundering their way through Germany and forcibly occupying countries as they go. There will be a big stink about their seizure of Poland, especially from FDR's Republican opposition, but there's nothing anybody can do. The Red Army occupies Poland and we cannot push them out unless we wish to start a new war. However, the consensus is that the Reds will actually stop at the Elbe, the demarcation line agreed on at Yalta, and not move beyond. It is further believed that they are even more exhausted militarily and economically than England and France. Only Germany itself may be in worse shape."

Ike lit a cigarette and drew slowly. It gave him a moment to think. "And now you're wondering just what I can do to speed up the demise of Nazi Germany. In particular, can it be done in time for us to assist in the invasion of Japan?"

"Precisely. General Marshall wanted me to remind you that invading Japan will require much of your army and will also need to divert supplies to the Pacific theater. The invasion of the home island of Kyushu is scheduled for October of this year and is called Operation Olympic. Operation Coronet, the invasion of Honshu and the attack on Tokyo, is planned for about six months later. The army is scraping the bottom of the barrel and drafting men who were rejected just a few months ago. We cannot sustain your army as well as the large force that will be needed to invade Japan."

"Mr. Acheson, are you aware that Herr Goebbels is en route to this Alpine Redoubt?"

The normally poised Acheson showed his surprise. "No. Are you certain?"

Ike's normally cheerful face showed his anger. "Our intelligence intercepted a message saying that he was not going to hold a conference at Berchtesgaden because it would be too dangerous. He was right. We would have bombed the place back to the Dark Ages and the days of Barbarossa. Instead, he said he was going to go directly to the Redoubt. A new Nazi Germany would then arise from the ashes of the Third Reich. I don't want that. I want Nazi Germany destroyed!"

"General, everyone wishes that. The only question is how in God's name do we do it?"

★   ★   ★

Major Alfonse Hahn smiled coldly. The thin and pale boy standing before him and staring at him was perhaps fourteen. He had either lied his way into the Wehrmacht, or the army was so desperate that it was now taking little children. Sadly, he thought the latter. He was so young that his face was covered with pimples. The boy had not been one of the rabble inducted into the Volkssturm. He had been enlisted in the regular army, which meant he had received at least minimal training. That and his eagerness to serve the Reich would suffice.

"Private Gruber, what do you see before you?"

The boy giggled. "A piece of shit, sir."

The man kneeling before them with his back to them winced slightly as he heard the two men talking about him. He was so weak and emaciated that he could barely maintain his balance. His eyes were blank and it was clear that the man would die soon if he wasn't helped, which wasn't likely. They were in a room in a newly dug cave in the heart of the redoubt and it was cold.

Hahn laughed. "An apt description, Private. Now, specifically what kind of shit do you observe?"

Gruber walked around the man, who barely moved except to shiver from the damp and cold and fear. "From his clothing, or the rags he is wearing, it is obvious that he came from a camp. My guess is Dachau, since we are moving so many of those inmates here to work."

"What is this man's crime, Private?"

Gruber glared at the offending prisoner. "He has a pink triangle sewn on what's left of his uniform. This means he is a homosexual. He is a fag, a queer. He is almost as bad as a Jew." Gruber looked puzzled. "Sir, is it possible that he is both a queer and a Jew?"

"No. The camp administration ranks crimes and nothing is more serious than being a Jew. Even if he was a Jew and a queer, he would be wearing the yellow emblem. Now, what do we do with shit like him?"

"Send him to the gas chambers, I would hope, sir."

Does everyone know about the gas chambers and the death camps? wondered Hahn. "Have you ever killed for the Reich?"

"To my sorrow, no."

Well-spoken lad, Hahn thought. There was no braggadocio about having killed hordes of Soviets. "Could you? Could you kill someone who was right in front of you and someone whose face you could see?"

Gruber began to understand the game. "If it was a piece of subhuman shit like this queer, I would do it in a heartbeat."

Hahn gave the boy a Luger. "Then do it."

The boy took the pistol, smiled and walked over to the prisoner. He put it to the back of the man's head and fired. The sound echoed in the cave. The bullet entered the prisoner's skull and blew out his forehead, splattering brains and blood on the earthen floor. For an incredible few seconds, the dead prisoner continued to kneel, but then collapsed soundlessly. Gruber looked shocked at what he had done and Hahn thought the boy would vomit. That would hardly disqualify him, however. Even the best got sick the first time they killed. He had. Instead, the boy fought for control and won.

Gruber calmly handed back the Luger. "Do you want me to clean it for you, sir?"

"No thank you, Private. I prefer to clean my weapons myself. Now, do you still want to join my elite new force?"

The boy smiled. "I want to be a Werewolf, sir. More than anything else, I want to fight for the Reich and kill the enemies of the Fuhrer."

"And what if the Fuhrer is dead, killed in the battle for Berlin?"

Gruber's eyes welled up. His lips quivered as he blinked back the tears. "Then I will fight for whoever follows him. I always knew that Adolf Hitler was mortal. I just didn't think his end would come so soon. It's all the fault of the communists and Jews."

Hahn smiled. Gruber was one of several dozen like him whose fanatical devotion to Hitler and their vision of Germany made them volunteer to be Werewolves. All were young men who were either in their early teens or looked like they were. They'd known nothing more all their lives then to worship their one true god, Adolf Hitler. They all swore that they would be willing martyrs for their god. Hahn stroked the star-shaped red scar on his cheek. He thought that martyrdom was stupid, but if it helped Germany, he would utilize the foolish martyrs.

"Private Gruber, congratulations, you are now a Werewolf. The sergeant outside will send you to your new quarters. Oh, and please tell him to send in some other prisoners to clean up this mess."

in the river, debris or a fish. Tanner had been told that uncharted debris could kill a swimmer and the Rhine was filled with it.

"I think they're across," Hill said softly. "Do they have radios?"

"No. It was decided they'd weigh them down and we couldn't fully waterproof them anyhow. We'll know when they return." If they return, he thought.

After an hour they were getting concerned. Another and they were sick with worry. The thin cable attached to the American side was no help. Sometimes it was slack and sometimes it was tight. Finally, they sensed a disturbance by their side of the riverbank and first one and then the second Ranger crawled ashore. Tanner, Hill, and a couple of other American soldiers crawled to them and helped them into the trench. They removed the men's masks. They were gasping and their faces were blue. One of them did, however, have the cable tied to his belt.

They helped the men out of their bulky and insulated swimming suits and helped warm them by wrapping them in multiple layers of blankets. A little medicinal brandy aided the thawing process as well.

"Great job, guys. You'll get a medal."

One had recovered from his ordeal. "You can keep the medal, sir. I just want to get fucking warm. I don't think my balls will ever thaw out."

Tanner grinned. "Maybe we can get some nice nurse to massage them for you."

"As long as it's a girl, sir, that'd be wonderful. Now, if you're wondering what we saw across the river, the answer is simple—not much. The riverbank hid our view. It would have been too difficult to climb out since we were slowly dying. That and our orders were to concentrate on anchoring the cable, which we did. An elephant couldn't pull that thing out."

Tanner left the two Rangers to get their body heat back to normal. In a few minutes they'd be guided back to where a truck was parked. Their night was done and he would write up the report in such a way that higher brass would have to give them a medal.

"What's next, sir?" asked Hill. "Although I think I know."

"That's right, Sergeant. The light cable is being replaced by a heavier one as we talk, and tomorrow a couple of fools in a small boat will cross and see what is actually out there."

"Any idea who the two fools are, sir?"

"Can you swim, Sergeant?"

Dulles led Janek into the largely empty restaurant where they went directly to a table against the wall. An elderly man with a snow-white goatee awaited them and greeted them with a firm handshake. Janek had been told that the man was Doctor Alain Burkholter and that he was a retired banking official who had also served in the Swiss government. Burkholter was thin and Janek guessed he was at least ten years older than Dulles. He had a stern expression. It was as if he disapproved of everything going on around him. As Burkholter did not have official standing with either the Swiss banks or government, he was free to represent both in an unofficial capacity. The same was true of Dulles. Even though he was head of the Swiss offices of the OSS, it was not something that would appear printed on a business card.

"Thank you for coming," said Burkholter. "I know that your time is important. So much espionage to perform and so little time in which to do it."

"As long as the Nazis are around, I will not run out of things to do," said Dulles.

Burkholter smiled at Janek. "Captain, are you aware that two innocent young choirboys from the German embassy were attacked by a group of thugs last night and are now in the hospital recovering from their beating?"

Ernie laughed. Innocent choirboys? He was, however, strangely pleased that he had not killed the two men. "I wish them a speedy recovery."

"I'm sure you do," said Burkholter drily. Coffee arrived and they sipped with restrained pleasure, even though the brew was not as good as it could have been.

"Let me get to the point," said Dulles. "My government is concerned about the degree of cooperation between the Swiss government and Berlin. It is our understanding that you are shipping food and medical supplies to what both we and the Nazis are referring to as their redoubt. We would like to know why."

"If a wounded tiger climbs on your lap and wants to be petted, what do you do? Why, you pet it, of course. Allen, the Nazis are a wounded and desperate animal. We do not want them trying to take what little we have by force. They might not succeed, but they would devastate Switzerland and kill or wound tens of thousands of our people. We are well aware that our neutrality exists at the whim of the Germans, although now somewhat at the whim of yours. Earlier, we served the Nazis' purposes by being their banker and their conduit to the outside world. Now they want food, weapons, ammunition, and medical supplies. Weapons and ammunition they may

not have. We would have barely enough for ourselves
if the Germans were to strike."

Ernie was puzzled. "Excuse me, sir, but I thought
that Switzerland was militarily quite strong?"

Burkholter laughed. "Good. You actually believed
all the propaganda. Perhaps you would like to enlist
in the Swiss navy? It doesn't exist either. Captain, my
country has a population of just over four million with
perhaps half a million either in the army or in the
reserves. It sounds substantial, but the numbers are
flawed. Our men are not well trained, and we have
no armor and only a little artillery. Our air force is
condemned to fail because it is small and what we
do have consists of German-manufactured planes that
we bought, with many of them being ME109 fighters.
Sadly, a number of them have been shot down by you
Americans who don't bother to read markings, which
brings me to another disturbing point."

"And what might that be?" asked Dulles. He was
not happy at what he was hearing.

"We have compelling reason to believe that the capital
of this Alpine Redoubt will be at the very small city
of Bregenz, which is on the coast of Lake Constance.
Once this is confirmed, I'm certain that your air force
generals will want to bomb it. This must not happen."

Even Dulles looked surprised. "And why not?"

"Because Bregenz is so close to the Swiss border that
it is almost impossible for you to not hit places in Switzerland, which would be a tragedy. This has happened
numerous times already. In fact, the presence of Captain
Janek is a case in point. Were you absolutely certain
where you were when you were shot down, Captain?"

Janek grinned sheepishly. "I had no idea. I knew I

was somewhere over Europe but that was about it. I really thought I was going to wind up in a German Stalag. I am a very lucky man."

Burkholter smiled warmly. "Indeed you are. I am also aware that you have something called a Norden bombsight, which is supposed to be a secret, but clearly isn't. Despite all the claims regarding its alleged accuracy, it is only as good as the pilots using it and they are subject to all kinds of conditions that adversely affect its accuracy. These include weather, winds, visibility, being shot at by antiaircraft and German planes and, of course, the skill of the pilot. Your air force won't want to admit it, but bloody few of the bombs you drop land anywhere near the target. Ergo, we do not want Bregenz or any other place near our border bombed. You may tell Eisenhower, or whoever is in charge of these things, that we will be mobilizing a large portion of our army. It will attempt to protect our borders from any German incursion and we will be setting up every antiaircraft gun we have. We will make a concerted effort to shoot down any plane that even *approaches* our border regardless of nationality."

Janek was surprised at how angry Dulles looked. The man was livid. "Are you telling me, Doctor Burkholter, that we must grant sanctuary to the Germans?"

Burkholter was no longer smiling. "In so many words, yes. Unless you want to antagonize us, your planes should stay a good fifty miles from Bregenz. It this means that the pathetic rump Nazi government is safe from above, then so be it."

The meeting was over. Burkholter picked up the tab and the three men left. "That was very educational," said Janek.

"But not surprising and, no, they are not bluffing. There have been too many incidents where Switzerland has been either bombed or damaged. There was one complete ass of an American pilot who bombed a railroad station in Switzerland when he was supposed to be hitting a different target in Germany. The Swiss rightly complained that the man not only missed the target but got the wrong town in the wrong country. Worse, civilians were killed. It was not one of our finer moments."

Ernie decided to keep his thoughts to himself regarding bombing accuracy. Some of the bombs he'd dropped from his P51 were classified as near misses when they hadn't fallen within a couple hundred yards of the target. "Okay, how does all this affect me?"

"First, I wanted a witness. Second, I wanted you to be educated before you go on to your next location. You will be going to the small town of Arbon on Lake Constance where you will help coordinate OSS activities across the border in Germany. On occasion, you might want to walk to the German border and see the supermen in action. You might even want to go out on a boat. If you do, be discreet. Despite what Doctor Burkholter said about the Swiss navy, they do have patrol boats protecting their border."

"Mr. Dulles, will the Nazis be granted a sanctuary in the Redoubt?"

"Sadly, it is very likely."

Using the cable and a pulley to haul small boats containing American soldiers across the Rhine worked, but with only minimal efficiency. It took too long, was too dangerous, and only a handful could make each trip. And it was only attempted at night. Thus, after a week only five men were more or less permanently stationed on the German side of the Rhine. For a few days, Tanner was one of them. He spent much of his time either hiding in the mud or crawling in it. He recalled Dr. Hagerman's admonition that he should not get his feet wet. How does one do that when there is a war on and you really don't have enough rank to order someone else to get wet?

Tanner noticed few German patrols. He thought it was because they didn't think a crossing at Vogelgrun was likely. During the days he spent on the German side, he did manage to pick up one potentially vital piece of information. That was the location of German minefields. Every morning, farmers would drive their cattle and sheep along proscribed paths that led from the Dragon's Teeth cement barriers to the fields bordering the river. With a sketch pad and a good Swiss camera, he and the other Americans were able to pin down the probable locations of minefields.

"If the farmers don't let their cows get blown up," Tanner said on reporting back to General Evans, "I think it's highly unlikely that GIs will either."

"Could you see any indication that they know we're coming?"

"Sir, I followed the cow paths and crawled on my belly through the Dragon's Teeth and a little ways beyond. I confirmed that farmers had filled in the area between some Dragon's Teeth so their livestock could more easily make it to the fields. Not exactly the thing to do if an attack is expected."

Evans sat back and thought. "With dirt filling the places between the teeth, could we drive jeeps and tanks over them?"

"I couldn't tell how firmly packed that dirt was, but if a cow could make it, so could a jeep. As to a tank, I'm not certain. And I could see the bunkers where the Germans were stationed and everything seemed quiet. There was laughter and talk and, of course, cigarette smoke. They may be concerned about crossings north of here, but I would say that the average Kraut isn't worried about anybody coming from Vogelgrun."

Evans stood up and began to pace. "Since we switched spots with the French, General Devers' plan to have Patch's Seventh Army cross at Mannheim is no longer very viable. Therefore, he is intrigued at the possibility of an American crossing at Vogelgrun. It the attack is a surprise, do you think we can pull it off?"

Why are you asking *me*? thought Tanner. He wants advice, that's why. Evans, Patch and Devers will make the ultimate decision but they want input from people on the ground. "Sir, I think we could make it across fairly easily."

"What about an artillery bombardment?"

"General, the Germans looked so sleepy we might just be able to rush them without a bombardment."

Evans laughed. "And that is why I'm a general and you're not, Tanner. I have been given fifty DUKW landing craft and each can handle at least a squad. We will bombard the crap out of them for no more than two hours then the little DUKWs can race across the narrow river as fast as they can and come back for more. In three crossings we should have at least a battalion on the other side. While our men keep crossing, engineers will be building pontoon bridges. The Germans will try to destroy them, of course, but we're not going to let them, are we?"

Tanner grinned. Evans' enthusiasm was contagious. "Yes, sir. I mean no sir."

"That's right. We're going into the heart of Germany and seal off the routes to their damned Alpine Redoubt. Oh by the way, Captain, I'm commending you for going across and scouting the land for us. You might even get a medal out of it."

Tanner didn't know what to say except thank you. He did not think of himself as someone who had done anything heroic. "Sir, other guys were out there as well."

"Don't worry; we'll take care of them. Look, Captain, this is such a new and virginal division we want our boys to know that there are men who will do what they have to and then some and, oh yeah, survive the experience. You could have huddled in the mud of the riverbank for a couple of days and nobody would have known. But no, you went out and crawled through their lines and picked up valuable information. And how can you be certain you knew where all the minefields were? All you had to do was miss one and we wouldn't be having this cozy little talk, now would we?"

"No sir."

"Good, now we'll be giving you a second chance to prove you're a hero. When the attack comes, you'll be in one of the lead boats so you can make certain nobody strays off the beaten path and into a minefield. And try to keep your feet dry."

Lena was exhausted. Her body ached and she was hungry. She was almost always hungry. Food was becoming more and more scarce. She'd picked up on rumors that what food existed was going south into the redoubt to feed the German armies that were supposed to flock there. She had her doubts. The Schneiders had more than enough but they were not about to share. And especially not with someone who was going to be disposed of in a very short while. Lena was becoming desperate. When should she run? Soon, *very* soon, she kept telling herself.

Lena had been spending most of the past several days helping the Schneider's pack their belongings. If they were going to be refugees, they were going to be extremely well-dressed refugees. She thought that Frau Schneider was in for a rude awakening. Her husband had tried to tell her that she could not bring all her clothing and jewelry. She had even wanted to bring a lot of her furniture. "We'll come back for it," her pig of a husband told her. That seemed to mollify her. But the trunks and suitcases of clothing were mountainous. It would have been funny if it hadn't been an indicator that Lena was going to be sent to a war factory where she would likely die.

She was in her room and had stripped off her dress and slip, and was standing barefoot by her bed, dressed only in her bra and panties. Her dress was soaked with sweat and it would have to be washed. But why? she thought. Perhaps she should take off tonight? After all, the only ones in the house were Anton and Magda. Their parents were off to some Nazi celebration designed to take their minds off the fact that Germany was losing the war.

The door to her room clicked and Anton entered. When he saw that she was partly undressed, he grinned happily. "You are lovely," he said.

"Thank you, but you should leave," she said sternly. "Your father will be home shortly." She cursed the fact that the cook, Olga, had come down with a fever and was in the hospital. She was alone with Anton.

She fought the urge to cross her arms across her breasts and thighs. Such a show of modesty would make Anton think he had intimidated her. Instead, she stood and glared at him. She was wearing almost as much clothing as a young girl at the beach.

He took a step towards her. "I don't think it's time to leave," he said huskily. "I think it's time to finish."

He grabbed her arm and pulled her to him. She was surprised by his strength. He tried to kiss her and then grabbed for her breasts, squeezing them and hurting her. In shock, she squealed with pain.

Anton laughed. "Don't worry about my father. He won't be home for a couple of hours and he's already said I can do whatever I want with you. After tomorrow it won't matter."

Tomorrow? She sagged and he took it as a sign of weakness. His hands roamed over her body, inside her bra and up her legs. He was breathing, panting, heavily.

"I'll do whatever you want, just don't hurt me," she whispered in his ear.

Anton smiled and stepped back. "Then take off your clothes."

Lena stepped out of her bra and panties. "Now it's your turn."

He grinned and in a moment he was naked as well. "Let me touch you," she said. She reached down and stroked his growing manhood. He sighed happily and she cupped his balls in her hand. Suddenly, she squeezed with all her might and twisted them savagely.

His eyes widened. He wanted to scream, but no sound would come from his throat. She jabbed him in the eye with the fingers of her other hand and, when he went to protect it, she kicked him in the testicles. Anton fell to the floor and curled up into a fetal position. She kicked his hands aside from his testicles and kicked him again and again in the groin until he stopped writhing.

"Animal," she said. She took the sheet off her bed and tied him up tightly. A pillowcase made a marvelous gag.

He wasn't moving. She checked for a pulse and there was one. She despised him but had not planned on killing him. Her decision had been made for her. She would leave right now.

Lena dressed quickly, this time in the heavy and practical clothing she'd already squirreled away. These included some of Astrid's ski clothing, including her boots. They were large for her but she solved the problem by stuffing them with rags. She went to the kitchen and filled a cloth sack with food that would both be nourishing and would last. At least that was her hope. She also added some kitchen knives and a cleaver to the sack.

"What is happening? What have you done to Anton?"

Lena had been concentrating so hard that she'd missed the sound of Anton's sister Astrid coming home. "You've murdered him," Astrid yelled again.

Lena screamed, letting go of suppressed rage. She grabbed a lamp and smashed it against Astrid's head. The young woman dropped to the floor like puppet whose strings had been cut.

Lena checked for a pulse. It was there but light

and feathery. A shame, she thought, but she could not, would not, do anything to help either one of her captors.

More bedding was used to secure Astrid. Lena completed her escape plans by breaking into Gustav Schneider's gun rack. His shotguns and rifles would be too obvious and they would be awkward for her to carry. She smiled when she saw the Luger he said he'd brought back from the Great War. He always bragged that he'd used it in combat and had killed Frenchmen with it. She doubted that he'd gotten anywhere near the trenches and had probably won it in a card game.

It didn't matter. She had it now along with several clips of ammunition. The extra ammo went into another sack and the pistol was tucked in the small of her back. There was a shoulder holster and she took that as well. It was too large for her but maybe she could adjust it. Nor did she have to worry about Olga, the cook.

Finally, she found a couple of pieces of Herr Schneider's official Nazi stationery and quickly typed passes for herself, signing Gustav's signature to them. One was in her own name and the other in her mother's maiden name. She was now both Lena Bobekova and Lena Madzyk. Better, the papers authorized her to go anywhere she wished with the blessings of Adolf Hitler.

She went back to where Anton and Astrid were tied up. Astrid's eyelids were fluttering, so maybe she would recover. Good, Lena thought. Anton was more alert and staring at her. She took the cleaver from the sack and held it in front of his nose. His eyes widened in fear and he started to cry. She turned the knife and dragged the flat side down to his swollen testicles and alongside his bruised penis.

"You are an evil little boy. I should cut this off and save everyone a lot of trouble. When your parents come home, you will tell them that I could have killed you but did not. Do you understand?"

Anton nodded. She smiled as she noticed that he had also peed himself. She let herself out the back. With a couple of hours lead, she could be anywhere before the Schneiders started a search. In the growing chaos of the times, she wondered if there would even *be* a search.

Field Marshal Ferdinand Schoerner gave the Nazi salute. He then jubilantly rushed and embraced Propaganda Minister Josef Goebbels. "It is so good to see you, Minister," he said with genuine enthusiastically.

Goebbels laughed. It was good to be off the road and out of an ambulance. Even though he was currently in a cave carved into a mountain, there was a strong feeling of security and safety. And of hope for the future of the Reich.

"I won't ask you if you had a pleasant trip. I think we all know better." Schoerner turned and waved the others out of his office. "I believe it is time for privacy."

When they were alone and behind closed doors, Schoerner poured brandies into expensive crystal and they toasted their good fortune. "Thank you," Goebbels said. "I'm exhausted. I feel like I've been on another planet for the last several weeks. I've lost track of everything. However, I do know that the Americans have crossed the Rhine and that the British have followed suit. Is there any hope of stopping them?"

"None whatsoever," said Schoerner sadly. "Nor is there any hope of stopping the Soviets. Berlin will be destroyed and many of the people trapped inside will die horribly."

"Then I am doubly glad to be here with the children. They and their mother are staying in Bregenz. They are comfortable and their villa is on the outskirts of a town that is almost too small to have outskirts."

Schoerner laughed. He noticed that Goebbels had not mentioned Magda by name. He had already gotten word from one of the ambulance drivers that there had been several flare-ups between Josef and Magda during the last few days. Magda and the children would live in Bregenz while separate quarters were made up for her husband. It was what he had anticipated. He would also arrange for attractive women to be available if the Reich Minister was so inclined—as he generally was.

Goebbels' second brandy appeared to be relaxing him. "And what is the shape of the army, Herr Schoerner?"

"It could be much better and it definitely could be very much worse and I am not trying to be confusing. We have elements of at least fifty divisions in the Redoubt with more arriving daily. Unfortunately, the operative word is *elements*. A full infantry division should have seventeen thousand men. These remnants sometimes only have two or three thousand, sometimes much less. Worse, a disproportionate number of these are from noncombat and rear echelon areas. Our real combat forces have been decimated. General Warlimont has been working tirelessly and brilliantly to reorganize these battered groups into something resembling a coherent force. They will not be the same German army that invented the Blitzkrieg and destroyed France in only a few weeks, but they will do extremely well when well-fortified and fighting on the defensive."

Goebbels was satisfied. "Fighting such a defensive war is why we came to the mountains, Field Marshal. The days of launching huge armies across vast continents and winning great victories are over. At least for the time being," Goebbels added with a smile. "Who knows what might happen in the future. Right now our goal is simply to survive."

"Indeed," said Schoerner. "Our forces have other problems that we are trying to confront. For instance, we have only a few dozen planes and pilots and very little fuel. The Luftwaffe is somewhere between nonexistent and grounded. While we did manage to bring in a goodly number of artillery pieces and antiaircraft weapons, we do not have an excess of ammunition. The factories set up by Herr Speer's minions are just now beginning to produce but they will never be able to supply ammunition in the quantities that we really need."

Goebbels nodded. What he needed and wanted desperately was a good night's sleep. The last few days with Magda had almost driven him mad. The closer they got to safety the more unreasonable and irritable she had become, loudly reminding him of every affair he'd ever had, including some he had totally forgotten. He'd countered by reminding her of her own sexual escapades. Thank God the children traveled in a separate vehicle.

Schoerner was still talking and Goebbels was jarred

back to reality. "I didn't mention armor, but the situation there is reasonably good. Warlimont's ever-changing inventory says we have about five hundred tanks of all kinds. Few are Panthers or Tigers, but most of them are Panzer IVs with upgraded guns. Fuel is again an issue, so they will likely be used as a mobile defense force."

"Excellent," Goebbels said and yawned. "I have some thoughts, although they will not alleviate fuel and ammunition shortages. The Americans were clearly loath to fire on an ambulance. I suggest that additional ambulances be filled with cash, gold and valuable art works that can be used to buy things through the Swiss. A few score more ambulances, perhaps even a few hundred, could provide us with a fortune."

Goebbels shook his head and yawned again.

Schoerner laughed. "I have a feeling I'm keeping you up, Minister. May I suggest we resume again after you've had a chance to rest? By the way, the renowned physicist, Abraham Esau, has made it here as well along with a number of other scientists. We have put them to work developing what he, Heisenberg, and others were developing. Heisenberg is also expected, but obviously has not yet arrived."

Goebbels was suddenly awake. Esau was indeed important. He was perhaps even more important than Heisenberg. Some considered him the founder of the German nuclear program. "Can he make the atomic bomb that Heisenberg promised?"

"He says he can. Of course, if he had said he couldn't we would have had them all shot. He also says that solutions to a number of other difficulties with our weapons were well within reach. All he needed was time and resources. Unfortunately, we have neither, but we will do everything we can for him. I have put him in his own bunker a mile or so out of town and he has a number of scientific toys to play with. He and the other scientists are well guarded."

Goebbels smiled. "Perhaps it is not too late to spring an awful surprise on the Americans."

"Indeed. My only concern is that with a name like Abraham Esau, he might be Jewish."

Goebbels shook his head. "I recall his name and the fact that his family was thoroughly researched. He is not Jewish."

Schoerner was clearly not convinced. "However, he will be watched."

"Will you have any of your men working with him in his bunker or even just watching them?"

"I told Doctor Esau that I would be doing that and he laughed at me. He asked how many of my men were physicists and I had to admit that none were. He then informed me that my men would be in the way, would slow down the scientists work and might just be in danger from radiation. He added that an untrained person might make a catastrophic mistake and cause the bomb to detonate prematurely. For the time being, I have deferred to his wishes."

"What else could you have done?" Goebbels said and resumed yawning. Schoerner got the hint.

"As soon as you've rested, I would like you to meet a representative of the Swiss government and hear his rather interesting opinion of neutrality. I think you will find it very enlightening. If you would like, I will also arrange for a young nurse to come and give you, ah, a thorough massage before you go to sleep."

A female nurse? A massage? Goebbels smiled and thought that would be a marvelous idea. So too would be an atomic bomb. Both thoughts pleased him.

The small Swiss city of Arbon rested comfortably on a peninsula that jutted out into Lake Constance. Ernie's first impression was favorable and a lasting one. The town was lovely and quaint and he decided that if he had to spend the rest of the war in Switzerland, Arbon would be the place to do it. A guidebook told him that the place had been occupied by man since Stone Age times. There were even traces of the Romans along with a late medieval castle. He made a note to see them if the war and the OSS gave him a chance.

He was quartered in a warehouse owned by an export-import company that had done business in both the U.S. and Switzerland before the war. It was now part of the U.S. consulate and was operated by a man in his fifties named Sam Valenti. Valenti was plump, middle-aged and innocuous. He had emigrated to the U.S. as a boy, became a citizen, and then decided to return to Europe as an OSS agent to help defeat the twin fascists, Mussolini and Hitler. Since Italian was one of Switzerland's several languages, he fit in quite nicely.

"What do you think?" Valenti asked genially.

"I've seen better prisons," Ernie replied.

Valenti was unsympathetic. "Be thankful that you're indoors and the roof doesn't leak and, oh yeah, that you're not in a prison camp."

Ernie had a twin bed and what passed for a room. Plywood walls separated him from the rest of the warehouse, now empty, and four other similarly built rooms. A bathroom was down the hall and included a shower large enough for several people. It reminded Ernie of his high school gym.

"You can bring in food, but don't make a mess," Valenti said. "If you want to bring in alcohol, make sure you have enough to share. The same goes with women."

"I'll try to remember."

"And don't bring in any Nazis. I don't want any of them pricks desecrating my property."

Ernie had been instructed to get a newspaper and sit down in the waterfront park. He would then carefully read it. When the right time came, he would be contacted by someone named Winnie. He thought the game was a little silly until he saw German soldiers in uniform walking casually down the streets of Arbon. It was a stark reminder that Switzerland was neutral and that the German border was not only across the lake but only a few miles down the coast. It also said that the border was easily crossed and he wondered what he could do about that. He realized he was thinking like a spy and not a pilot.

After several days of accumulated boredom, he was beginning to wonder if the OSS knew what to do with him. Finally, a young woman about his age walked up to him and smiled. She was short and plump and rather plain. She had poorly cut long and greasy looking brown hair and wore thick horn-rim glasses.

"Cousin Ernest," she said with apparent sincerity. "If you don't remember me from our childhood days, I'm Cousin Winnie from Philadelphia and it is so good to see you. The family will be so glad when I tell them, especially Uncle Allen."

She spoke in a normal tone of voice. Anyone trying

to listen in would hear nothing out of the ordinary. He stood and took her hand in his. Her grip was warm and firm. "It is so good to see you, too, Cousin Winnie. Will you be able to stay long?"

She took his arm and they casually began to walk along the waterfront. They were just two friends, not lovers, enjoying a stroll.

"I'm sorry I was late," she said. "I was terribly busy."

"Doing what, or shouldn't I ask?"

"I was across the border in Germany, in that nest of vipers. I was trying to confirm that Josef Goebbels, one of Hitler's satanic high priests and possible heir to the Reich, had made it to Bregenz."

Janek was impressed. This also confirmed his opinion that the border was very porous. If Germans could walk the streets of Arbon, then plump and drab Winnie could do the same in the new German capital of Bregenz. Or, he thought, maybe he could do the same thing? Going to Berlin was clearly out of the question, but what about Bregenz? It also told him that Winnie was something more than a plump little nothing in a frumpy dress that did nothing for her. He also shuddered when he realized she had bad breath and smelled as if she hadn't bathed recently. Still, he would not judge her skills as an intelligence operative. Getting in and out of Germany proved she had them.

"Well, I did not see the Minister of Propaganda himself, but I did find a villa close to the shore that is well guarded by the SS. I was able to see blond-haired children playing in the back and a skinny yellow-haired frau watching them. I'm almost certain it was Magda Goebbels. If so, could her loving husband be far behind?"

"Are they close enough for someone to cross the border and snatch them?"

She laughed and he decided that at least she had a warm smile and decent teeth. "Mr. Dulles said you would bear watching. Even if we could do that, we wouldn't. At least we wouldn't do it in such a manner as to annoy the Swiss. We are their guests, after all. Word on the street and from Mr. Dulles is that she and her monster of a husband are not on speaking terms. He is probably living at some military headquarters in the mountains. In fact, I would not be surprised if Magda Goebbels and her hatchlings showed up here in Arbon to do a little shopping. The poor dears must be exhausted by their trip from Berlin. Apparently they came by ambulance, which is something else that has to be considered. I believe it violates the Geneva Convention if anybody cares, and apparently they don't."

They'd turned and were back where they'd started. Winnie took his hand and again shook it firmly. "I'll be seeing you again shortly. In the meantime, why don't you use some of the money you've been given and get a car? You can then travel along the border and the neighboring towns to acclimate yourself. When I come back, we'll rent a boat and go fishing or something. Do you like to fish?"

"Not really."

"I don't either," she said. "I suppose we'll have to pretend, though. Maybe we can just throw lines in the lake and pretend."

"Where will you be going?"

"Don't ask."

Lena's thought was that the Schneiders would be looking for her in the south and west. That is, if they looked for her at all. Thus, she initially headed north and east to throw them off her trail. Even though many refugees were using the roads and even though she was armed, she avoided groups. Sometimes she walked with them, but never as part of them. She didn't want to make friends, and she didn't want to draw attention to herself.

The refugees came in all shapes and sizes. Almost all were displaced Germans. They'd been uprooted by fear of the oncoming Russians and they were fleeing Stalin's vengeance-seeking hordes. They were terrified and their goal was to somehow make it to the American or British lines. Murder and rape awaited them if they stayed still.

The displaced Germans all appeared stunned by the terrible turn the war had taken. Not only had their cities been bombed to ashes, but even those who lived in the country had seen their comfortable homesteads devastated. Now they were reduced to carrying their belongings on their backs or pushing them in carts. Few had cars since there was very little gas. The relatively lucky ones had carts pulled by gaunt horses. She even saw carts being pulled by large dogs. She had no sympathy for them. They had brought Hitler to power and cheered when he invaded and plundered country after country, including her beloved Czechoslovakia. Let them suffer. She didn't want them to die, just suffer as she had and learn.

Other groups were spotted and feared like feral dogs. These were displaced persons from other countries and prison camp inmates who'd somehow escaped from the concentration camps or prisons. They wanted revenge, just like the Red Army. They too looted, raped and murdered. Sometimes they burned homes just for the sheer joy of doing it to a German. When they were seen, the refugees either hid or formed protective circles. Each time, Lena clutched her pistol tightly, although she did not let anyone see it. Germany, she concluded, was descending into madness.

There was a group of nuns—Dominicans, she thought—travelling as a cluster. She wondered what the women in their long black habits were thinking. She envied them the fact that they had companions who would support each other. Lena did not miss the Schneiders, not for one minute, but she did wish she had someone in whom she could confide. She was lonely. She had used up most of her food and she had to sleep on the ground with the pistol close by. She had come to realize that no one was looking specifically for her. However, there was always the possibility of an SS or Gestapo sweep. These were generally used to capture deserters and she'd seen several instances where men had been hanged from telephone poles with signs saying "Deserter," or "Enemy of the Reich" attached to their chests. If they checked her identification too closely, it might not hold up. Avoiding the sweeps became a priority, but how?

She used the nuns as a beacon, an anchor. She never approached them or talked to them, but she always kept them in sight. The refugee swarm constantly changed, but the nuns were always there. One heavyset sister appeared to be their leader. She seemed to have noticed Lena although there was no hint of recognition or friendship.

Night came and Lena tried to make herself as comfortable as possible on the ground. One of her folded-up empty supply bags served as a pillow; the pistol was in her belt. She closed her eyes and fell into an exhausted sleep. When she awoke, it was daylight and the encampment was starting to stir. She suddenly felt almost physically ill. The Luger was gone.

She sat up and looked around wildly. The heavyset nun was seated on a piece of wood a few feet away. "Are you missing something?"

CHAPTER 6

THE ARTILLERY BARRAGE BEGAN AN HOUR BEFORE dawn. Targets had been pre-sighted and shells rained down on what intelligence said were German strongpoints. Since he had provided much of the information, Tanner fervently hoped his data was accurate.

As the shelling increased in intensity, columns of DUKWs moved towards the Rhine. He was in the lead vehicle with Sergeant Hill. "Y'know, Captain, for someone who's not supposed to get his feet wet, you do spend a lot of time in little boats."

"Go to hell, Sergeant, and this is a floating truck, not a boat."

Hill chuckled and the two men looked towards the other side of the Rhine. It was obscured by smoke and fire. Overhead, bombers dumped their loads and the shock waves rippled back over them. Could anyone be alive in that horror, he wondered, but everyone knew that they would be. The Germans had proven their resilience. They would have to be rooted out.

At a signal, the amphibious vehicles rumbled forward

112

with each carrying a squad of infantry. The DUKW was a marvel. Built on a GM truck chassis, it could travel by road and then over water simply by throwing a switch. Or at least that was the way it looked to Tanner. He clutched his M1 carbine to his chest. It had been converted to fire full automatic. Hill carried a Thompson submachine gun, his weapon of choice. Captain Cullen would land in a later wave. He did not appear disappointed at crossing later.

The little craft plowed into the water and began the crossing. The shelling and bombing had ceased. "Now we'll find out what we're up against," Hill muttered.

Machine-gun fire began to come from hidden German positions, kicking up splashes around the boats. The Wehrmacht were alive and nasty. Tanner wondered just how much damage the barrage and bombing had actually done. There had been discussions about the pre-landing bombardments. Should they be short or even nonexistent in order to surprise the Nazis? Or should they be lengthy, which would tip off the Germans that an attack was imminent? A compromise was reached. The barrage would be for two hours. Tanner did not like compromises, especially when lives were at stake.

Bullets rattled against their craft's hull and everyone ducked down and tried to make themselves invisible. Men in the craft groaned and someone threw up. That caused others to puke as well. Tanner thought he smelled urine. He checked and was relieved that it wasn't him.

He forced himself to again look over the side. Land was only a few yards away. They'd made it across, he exulted.

No. A German shell exploded by the DUKW, tipping it over and throwing everyone into the water. Tanner gasped. The water was near freezing and the current was strong. He wanted to scream as icy river grabbed at his testicles. He found that he could stand up and began wading towards the riverbank and safety, fighting the current that wanted to sweep him away. Something bumped up against him. It was the soldier who'd been driving the DUKW. A shell fragment had ripped his chest open and water was flowing in. Other bodies bobbed around him.

He stumbled and went underwater. He scrambled frantically to get upright. He could not let the current take control and sweep him away. The water was shallow and he managed to stand up again. Another shell landed nearby and staggered him. Sergeant Hill's strong hands grabbed him and pulled him forward.

"C'mon, Captain. You got to get your ass out of this river before it kills you."

Tanner was about to say that he already knew that when the Rhine water he'd swallowed came up all at once, gagging him.

"I'm all right," he finally managed to say. A wounded soldier lurched by. His left arm was smashed and white bone jutted through the skin. Between him and Hill, they got the man to the riverbank, pushed him up, and followed him to dry ground. A medic crawled over to take charge.

Despite the carnage around them, the overwhelming majority of craft appeared to have landed their human cargoes and were headed back to pick up a second wave.

American soldiers were advancing across the field

towards the Dragon's Teeth. They were following the paths through the minefields that had been carefully mapped out.

Explosions and screams made Tanner turn to his left. A group of soldiers had taken a wrong turn and had blundered into the minefield. Several GIs lay writhing on the ground and the others stood, looking confused and terrified. One man started to run back. An explosion lifted him several feet into the air and ripped his legs off.

"Follow in your own footsteps," yelled Hill, but they were too far away to hear. Finally, somebody got the soldiers calmed down and the survivors slunk out of the field.

More soldiers made it through the minefield's real openings. Enemy fire began to slacken. Tanner looked behind to see that more landing craft filled with troops were already headed towards them and the east bank of the Rhine. Engineers were quickly starting to assemble the first of what were planned to be several pontoon bridges.

"I need a radio. Got to report to the general," Tanner said.

Hill shrugged. "I think it's at the bottom of the Rhine. Don't worry, sir. I think he's got a fair idea we've made it across. By the way, sir, you didn't get your feet wet did you?"

"Hill, go screw yourself."

Lena and the nun sat on the ground and faced each other. "My name is Sister Mary Columba and I am a Dominican. You may call me Columba or sister. Now tell me why you need a pistol?"

"For protection, of course."

"But from whom? I've watched you the last several days. I saw how sick and frightened you looked when you realized there was an SS checkpoint up ahead. The gun is not only for protection, but because you are afraid of being investigated and then arrested. Were you planning to kill yourself with it? So what have you done that a small and frail-looking young woman like yourself would have so outraged the SS or the Gestapo?"

Lena turned away. She did not know if she could trust this woman, even though she said she was a nun. "I would like my property back," she finally said.

"The gun is a military weapon. How did you get it? Did you kill a German soldier?"

"No," Lena said, almost too hurriedly.

"Good," said Columba. "That would have been more than I could handle. Even though I despise Hitler and all he has done, I could not countenance anyone murdering a German soldier, even if he was SS. They SS are misguided fools but they are humans with souls. On the other hand, the men in the Gestapo are not human. Are you Jewish? Did you escape from a concentration camp? What the devil are you doing out here and all alone? Why are you afraid to make contact with others? And, of course, where on earth do you think you are going?"

Too many questions, Lena thought, and they all need answers. She decided she had no choice but to trust the nun. She began to tell her tale.

Half an hour later, Sister Columba quietly handed Lena her pistol. It had been cleaned and wrapped in a cloth. "Now, Lena, we have to get you through the Nazis. How would you like to become a nun?"

An hour later, Lena stood beside the taller Sister Columba, but now she was wearing a nun's habit. Sister Columba said it was left over from an older nun who had died of a heart attack a few days earlier. It almost fit her and it was as dirty as those worn by the others. They had kept it hoping they might find a use for it. Lena also wore the dead woman's sandals. Her other clothing, including slacks and blouse, were in a cloth bag along with the deceased nun's pathetically few belongings.

Columba had chopped Lena's already short hair almost to her skull. A little judiciously applied dirt made it look a shade darker. She spread more dirt on Lena's face and arms, and soon Lena looked as unkempt as the others, most of whom, she noticed were as young as she was.

"We haven't had much chance to bathe," Columba told her. "Now, as we approach the Nazis, all you have to do is look downcast and scared. If these scum are anything like the ones we've run up against before, they'll let us through without checking too deeply. They will probably make filthy remarks about how they would like the chance to make real women out of us withered old virgins, but we will ignore them. One of two of them might even reach out to paw you, which they seem to think is quite funny. Just whimper and pull away. Look terrified if you can. Defiance might make them suspicious. We nuns are supposed to be innocent little creatures who have run away from the world. If things start to get out of hand, I will step in."

"I will have no problem looking downcast and scared. I'm actually terrified."

They moved with the crowed to the checkpoint, which seemed to be moving fairly quickly.

"Aren't they checking anybody?" Columba wondered aloud.

A man on a horse cart stood up and got a better view. "They're not checking anybody because there's nobody there to check. It looks like the SS and Gestapo have all gone. What the hell is going on?"

"Did you pray for this?" Columba asked Lena.

"No, but perhaps I should have."

There was commotion in the crowds of refugees in front of them. "The Yanks have crossed the Rhine just across from Vogelgrun," someone yelled and others picked it up.

"Where's Vogelgrun?" Sister Columba asked.

Lena smiled. "South and, of course, west of here. This means that we don't have to continue to move to reach safety. The Americans will arrive shortly. All we have to do is wait for them."

Sister Columba shook her head. "We will not wait passively. What if the Russians move faster than the Americans? We had always thought about heading west and hoping to find the Yanks. Now perhaps we will."

Ernie did not buy a car. For one thing, Dulles hadn't given him enough money, and for another, gas was in short supply. Instead, he bought an old but sturdy bicycle and used it to pedal the streets and surrounding fields of Arbon. It was a great opportunity to familiarize himself with the layout of the town. The locations of stores and homes that he could use for refuge or escape were duly noted. The lessons given him by Allen Dulles and others were bearing fruit. He was beginning to think

that this life as an OSS was even better than flying a
P51 and being chased around the skies by Germans
who wanted to kill him. Of course, the Germans on
the ground didn't much love him either.

He casually rode up to the border where bored
Swiss and German guards stared at each other. There
was no apparent animosity. Peace reigned. He didn't
go within fifty yards of the border. No sense attracting
unneeded attention to himself, he thought. Instead, he
kept to the road that paralleled the fencing. There was
enough other traffic to keep him from being conspicu-
ous. Of course, dozens of Nazis could be watching him
through binoculars and noting his presence and his
every move. What a happy thought, he told himself.

From what he could see, the German border guards
looked far more nervous and even appeared stressed.
And why not? he thought. Their country was collapsing
into ruins. Their families and other loved ones might
be dead or refugees or, worse, suffering terrible fates
at the hands of the Russians. He wondered if the
border guards could tell him if Goebbels had arrived
safely. He could always say he wanted to send the
Propaganda Minister a congratulatory card.

He wondered if any of the guards or any of the
soldiers he could see might be talked into surrendering
or letting in a commando force in return for a free
pass to the United States for them and their families.
He congratulated himself on an excellent idea that he
would discuss with Dulles as he pedaled back to his
quarters at the warehouse. On arrival he found there
was a message for him saying that Winnie would meet
him at a boat dock at eight o'clock the next morning.
He was to wear casual clothes and bring a swimsuit.

Oh joy, he thought. He had always disliked chubby women in bathing suits. Winnie was attractive enough from her shoulders up, but her body left a lot to be desired, including a bath. Ah well, the things he would do for his country.

Winnie was already on the cabin cruiser when he arrived. As before she was unfashionably dressed in a long baggy dress that did not flatter her in the slightest. "I'm glad to see that you didn't wear leather shoes," she said tersely. "Other than damaging the deck, leather shoes are slippery and you might fall overboard. Even though the lake is a lovely shade of blue, it is very cold and extremely deep. I would hate to lose you so quickly."

"Winnie, I have actually been on a boat before. And whose boat is this anyway?"

"Sorry," she said sounding not the slightest bit sorry. "It belongs to a small corporation owned by Mr. Valenti and thus is the property of the American taxpayer. As taxpayers, I guess this is our boat. Shall we enjoy it?"

They cast off the lines and Winnie skillfully took the boat well out onto the lake. She ran parallel to the German coast, staying at least a mile off shore. Ernie had read that there were disagreements between the Swiss and the Germans as to where borders on the water began. Winnie said they would not do anything to attract attention from either nation. Although they had been warned that boats on the lake could be in danger, they did not think a small outboard cabin cruiser would be construed as a threat by the Germans. Nor were they alone on the lake. A small number of boats were also out on the dark blue water, either fishing or cruising for pleasure. None were very close. They had privacy if they needed it.

Winnie had brought a hamper filled with cheeses, bread, ham, butter, and a couple of bottles of a very popular local Pinot Noir and a fruity white wine called a Chasselas. Ernie generally drank beer, but what the hell? he thought. When in Switzerland, do as the Swiss do—or something like that.

"Do you fish?" she asked.

"I can hook a worm, but that's about it."

"Well, you're ahead of me. We'll cut the engines and pretend." She opened a chest and took out a couple of fishing poles and laid them over the stern of the boat. "If we were serious we could try to catch trout or whitefish. Instead, why don't you go into the cabin and change into your swimsuit. We'll look very natural that way."

Ernie did as told and emerged a few moments later. "Do I pass?" he asked.

Winnie smiled. She really did have a nice smile, he realized. "I was hoping for better, but you'll do."

While she changed, Ernie took binoculars and checked around. He kept in the shade of the cabin to make it difficult for someone to see him. There were no boats that appeared to be official and none were headed their way. He checked the German coastline and again saw nothing in the way of unusual activity. Maybe he was being paranoid, but constructive paranoia was a good way of staying alive.

"Can you see Hitler or Goebbels from here?"

"Not quite," he said and turned. He almost gasped. "What have you done with pudgy little Winnie Tyler?"

The Winnie Tyler now before him was slender and athletic looking. She was wearing a blue one-piece bathing suit that hugged her figure like a glove. "It's an incredible diet, Ernie. It's called how to lose fifty pounds in five minutes. First you wear a lot of padding under an ugly dress that's way too large. Then you have your hair cut very short so you can wear a number of wigs and don't forget thick glasses with clear glass to make you look strange, and then add balls of cotton stuffed in the cheeks. And don't forget to rub garlic and other stuff on your face and hands so you stink to high heaven. We could have met and discussed matters elsewhere but this was a great opportunity to dress and behave like myself and not have to put on an act with the ugly suit. Unless you decide to behave like an animal, today is a holiday for me."

"And for me too?" he said happily. "And I am a gentleman and not an animal. Well, usually."

"You are very nice, but just to keep things straight, I am not going to sleep with you or even kiss you. Today is recreational. I simply need a day off. I don't want to get involved with anyone until this war is over. I owe too much to my brother." Her lips began to twitch as she finished, and a tear ran down her cheek.

"Tell me," Ernie asked softly.

"He's in Honolulu. He's somewhere in the rusting hull of the battleship *Arizona* where he's been since December 7, 1941, and I have a very hard time even thinking about it and him. He was three years older than me and he was my hero. He still is. I joined the OSS in order to strike back at the Japs. Unfortunately, I later found that General Douglas MacArthur has no

use for the OSS and there wasn't much intelligence
work for a woman in other areas of the Pacific, so
I decided to strike at the Japs by hurting the Nazis.
Does that make sense?"

"As much as anything else I've heard lately. I
think it's time to open the wine. May I raise a toast
to your brother?"

She smiled warmly. "I'd like that very much."

Shock and dismay tore through the 105's division
headquarters at the sudden news. Franklin Delano
Roosevelt, thirty-second President of the United States,
was dead in some strange place called Warm Springs,
Georgia. A heart attack or a stroke the news said, not
that it mattered. He was dead and that was all that
counted. The entire army and navy were stunned.
Grown men cried at the thought of a familiar father
figure passing away.

"I didn't even know he was sick," Tanner said to
Cullen, quickly realizing what a banal statement it
was. Who would have told him?

"I guess we should have known in hindsight that he
wasn't well. His most recent pictures made him look
old and isn't it true that he finally admitted that he
couldn't walk? Jesus, we had a crippled sick man in
the White House and never knew it. I wonder how
I would have voted if I'd known."

Tanner shook his head. "That's probably why they
didn't announce it. Besides, what did his being stuck
in a wheelchair have anything to do with his ability to
deal with the Depression and fight this damned war?"

"Nothing I can think of," admitted Cullen.

The news was shocking. FDR had been president

for twelve years. Many had begun to think of him
as immortal. Hell, he was only in his early sixties,
which was quite old, but most of them had at least
one relative who was older. There were people who
had never heard of Herbert Hoover or any other
prior president.

General Evans looked distraught and Tanner could
hear the sounds of sobbing. Soldiers weren't supposed
to cry, he told himself as he fought back his own
tears. It wasn't as if he was in love with Roosevelt.
He had seriously considered voting for Dewey on
the basis that three terms was more than enough.
But then he'd asked himself if it was time to change
captains on the ship of state and reluctantly decided
that it wasn't. Like most Americans, he'd voted for
Roosevelt in 1940. FDR had dragged the country from
the depths of the Depression and had led the fight
against Hitler and Japan. The world had lost a giant
and many people felt that they had lost a member
of their family. His fireside chats broadcast on radio
had calmed and encouraged them, while his eloquent
fury had sent the U.S. off to war after Pearl Harbor.

And now he was dead and who the hell was this
four-eyed stranger with the tinny voice, Harry Truman?

Evans wiped his nose with a none too clean handkerchief and addressed his staff. "Until and if we hear
to the contrary, our orders remain the same. We are
to exterminate the remnants of Nazism. It cost us
five hundred dead and wounded brave men to cross
the Rhine and it is up to us to see that they have
not suffered in vain. I don't know anything about this
Truman fellow, except that he's what we got right now
as President of the United States. The next election

will be in 1948, so, for good or ill, we're stuck with him. I would be shocked if he changed the direction of the war. Hitler's trapped in Berlin and he might just be burning in hell in a short while, and that really ought to change things. Until then, we kill Germans."

There were nods and grunts of approval. After a pause, Evans continued. "There will be a nondenominational service tomorrow. At least I hope there will be as soon as the various chaplains figure out who's going to say what. In the meantime, it wouldn't hurt to honor FDR's memory with a drink or two from the private stores that just about everyone has. Dismissed."

"Well," said Cullen, "Your tent or mine?" It was a joke. They shared the same tent.

"Mine. I've got decent Scotch and you've got that home brew shit some GI cooked up."

Josef Goebbels raised a glass of champagne and saluted the large picture of Adolf Hitler that stared down on them from the wall of the cave. "To the Fuhrer. He is always right. He said that something dramatic was going to occur that would change the course of history and now it's happened. The death of the Jew Roosevelt will bring an end to the unholy alliance that is strangling Germany. Now, perhaps, the people of England and the United States will realize just who the real enemy is."

Field Marshal Schoerner lifted his glass as well, "Death to the Jews and death to the communists. Now if only there is enough time for an Allied collapse before our Fuhrer becomes a casualty in Berlin."

Schoerner put down his glass. An aide quickly filled it. "With profoundest regrets, Minister, I believe it is too late for Adolf Hitler. I cannot see where the death of Roosevelt will mean anything in the short run. The Red Army hordes are in place and will not be deterred. If anything, I believe that Stalin will urge them to fight even more intensely before events and alliances can change."

"Unfortunately, that assessment sounds correct," Goebbels said sadly. "That makes it all the more important that we hang on here in the Alps. And that reminds me. I have been to the lovely city of Bregenz and I cannot see how we can defend it against the Americans if they come."

Schoerner chuckled. "Unfortunately, when people think of Switzerland they think of mountains. Yes, much of the Alps are in Switzerland, but the Alps also extend into Italy to our south and what used to be Austria to our east. Along with those mountain ranges, there are some significant valleys and other areas where the land is hilly but not mountainous. If the land around Bregenz was too rugged, we would not be able to set up a political capital there. We must have roads in order to move our forces and to bring in supplies. So yes, we cannot last forever if the Americans attack with determination and strength."

"And when the Americans come?"

"There are two fundamental ways they can come and both involve their taking the Brenner Pass. American General Mark Clark's Fifteenth Army Group must force its way up the mountains in northern Italy to get the pass. They might win through but it will be incredibly bloody. They can also attack from the north using both Bradley's and Devers' Army Groups, with Devers' forces bearing the brunt of the fighting for

CHAPTER 5

THE RETURN TO VOGELGRUN WAS DONE MUCH MORE carefully and surreptitiously. Even though the land beyond the Rhine had been bombed and shelled several times since they'd been blasted out of their hotel observation post, they were taking no chances.

The hotel that Tanner and the others had used as an observation post had been reduced to a charred pile of rubble. Tanner, Hill, and a squad of infantry dug in the old-fashioned way, with shovels and grunts. The ground was soft and they soon had a decent narrow trench that would protect them from anything but a direct hit. Or so they hoped. They also hoped that the partly cloudy night had protected them from curious eyes.

Hill reached over and tugged on Tanner's sleeve. "Captain, what are those silly boys doing?" Two men with bulky equipment on their backs had moved to the riverbank.

"Sergeant, they are going to swim the Rhine underwater. Or at least they're going to try it. That tanks on their backs contain oxygen that will enable them to breathe underwater. Two French guys thought of it a couple of years ago. They're called aqualungs."

"Jeez, Captain, you mean the French actually once had a good idea?"

"Be nice, Sergeant. Those two men are Army Rangers who've been trained on the equipment. They are going to try and take a thin line across, anchor it, and return. We can then attach heavier cables and use the cable as a pulley to get good sized rafts to the other side."

"Sounds dangerous."

"Yep. If the Krauts don't shoot them, they might freeze to death in the water. I was told they've stuffed their waterproof suits with anything that'll insulate them and even greased their bodies like Gertrude Ederle did when she swam the English Channel twenty years ago. If the Rangers survive their crossing, they're going to do a little bit of scouting, but just a little. Their primary purpose is to bring back that cable so we can send over a raft."

"Why don't they use a snorkel? I've used something like that back home."

"I don't know, Hill, and you ask too many questions. Maybe because they can stay underwater longer and deeper or maybe they just wanted to try out the equipment in truly wretched conditions."

Hill's nod was barely visible in the darkness. "Sounds like the Army."

Lights were forbidden, including smoking. To the enemy, it was hoped that the American side of the Rhine was calm and placid. They tried to watch the swimmers' progress, but gave up. They thought they could see bubbles, but maybe it was just something

the simple reason that they are in place and closest. This is good since I do not believe that Devers'
armies are anywhere near as skilled as Bradley's. We
also believe that Clark's Army Group is as exhausted
as those of ours he is fighting."

Goebbels nodded agreement although he was clearly
unhappy at the thought of American divisions forcing
their way through to Bregenz.

"Bregenz has other advantages, Minister. First, our
sources say that the Americans have assured the Swiss
that they will not bomb the town if we do not make
too big a show of our being there. Second, if it does
appear that the Americans are going to be victorious,
our armies can simply lay down their arms while we
escape to Switzerland and on to South America. The
Swiss might not be too happy, but I have it on good
authority that they will not stop us or fight us. The
vast amounts of money from the Reich and from Jews
that is now in Swiss banks will buy us a sanctuary for
enough time to arrange passage to South America. I've
been told that Argentina is lovely this time of year."

"Or any time of year," said a reassured Goebbels.
"I don't particularly care what happens to my slut of
a wife, but I do want my children to survive. Along
with myself, of course," he laughed. "Of course it will
all be moot when the alliance against us falls apart.
My guess is that it will be the French who collapse
first and then the British. I firmly believe that the
Soviets will see nothing to their advantage in pursuing
us into the mountains, especially if we can confront
them with a nuclear threat. I have been to Professor
Esau's cave and am impressed. He has a pair of V1
rockets and a number of men working on them and

on the bomb itself. He wants more of everything, of course; who doesn't? But he has assured me the bomb and the improved V1s will be ready. He and his assistants are well aware that their lives depend on it. If the bomb is not ready, they will be shot. The Americans are in for a bloody surprise."

"Why did he bring the V1s and not the V2s?"

"He said that the V1 is a more primitive and therefore a more rugged device. He also said they were easier to transport and will be easier to set up and fire when the time comes. I deferred to his knowledge."

"A good idea."

Schoerner continued. "So our war will be against the Americans alone and whoever this Harry Truman person is. Perhaps we should salute Harry Truman with another glass of champagne."

"A splendid idea."

Schoerner laughed. "I still cannot get over the idea that a physicist named Abraham Esau is not Jewish and I don't care how many times his ancestry was checked. I will feel much more confident when Heisenberg shows up."

Goebbels smiled. He was recalling the massages he'd been getting from several lovely and pliant German women since arriving at the army's headquarters. "Then let's drink another toast. Let us lift our glasses to the new Republic of Germanica."

What will the Americans do without Roosevelt? wondered Lena. His death had come as a shock to all of the refugees as they moved towards where they hoped the Americans would come before the Russians. She thought it ironic that a number of

Germans were jubilant that the man they referred to as the "Jew Roosevelt" was gone. In their Nazi minds, it was the Americans who had started the war and who were bombing German cities and slaughtering German civilians. They seemed to have forgotten enslaving Poland and Russia and brutally conquering other innocent nations.

No one had ever heard of Harry Truman. Some even thought his name was Thurman and that he was as Jewish as Roosevelt. She had to remind herself that she was surrounded by Germans and somewhat alone with her feelings of hatred for the Reich. Her consuming fear now was that the death of their president would result in the Americans halting their conquest of Germany and leaving her in limbo. What would she do then?

She still traveled with the nuns and found them a puzzling bunch. With the exception of Sister Columba, none of them spoke to her or even looked at her. She thought they were sometimes laughing at her, but that was almost to be expected. She was dressed as a nun but was absolutely not a Dominican. She was able to confirm that the other sisters were fairly young, which was also puzzling.

"That is because the old ones could not travel," Columba had said. "We left them behind with our prayers. And I told the others not to speak to you," Columba admitted one evening. "The less they know, the less they can tell anyone. Right now I believe we are safe from the Gestapo or the SS, but that could change in a heartbeat. If the Americans show any sign of weakness, the Reich will emerge again."

And where were the Americans? Rumors had them everywhere. The latest said they were a few miles to the north and heading towards Stuttgart. Her column of refugees was moving slowly because they had to bypass the mountains. American planes continued to fly overhead and some of them flew so low that they could see the pilots' faces. What were they thinking? she wondered. Much of an entire nation was on the move, fleeing from the terrors of defeat and the vengeance of those who had been oppressed.

Travelling in large groups meant safety. Too often they had come on the naked, mutilated and desecrated corpses of those who thought they could go it alone or in small groups. Former inmates recently freed from concentration camps were delighted at the opportunities to take vengeance on those who'd persecuted and imprisoned them. Who could blame them? she thought. Some of those former inmates she'd seen were starving and wide-eyed with anger and pain. They wanted food and there hadn't been enough for their German overlords. They'd been kept in vile living conditions for years where they'd been beaten, starved, and many of their friends and loved ones murdered. She found herself wondering what had happened to her father. It was a painful window on her past that she tried to keep closed. But now that the end appeared near, thoughts of her past were coming back. Perhaps the Germans kept good records of those they imprisoned. She thought that he had been sent to Dachau, but she wasn't certain. The Americans had overrun the infamous concentration camp, so someday she might be able to go there and find out his fate. But not now. It was too dangerous.

Later that night there were howls and screams. She pulled out her pistol and tried to see in the darkness. There was commotion to her left, followed by gunshots.

Either the criminals were armed or other civilians had had the foresight to arm themselves.

"Don't even think of trying to help," Sister Columba said as she grabbed Lena's arm. "There's only one of you and God only knows how many of them, whoever they are. Stay here and protect yourself and us."

Lena agreed and spent the rest of the night with her pistol on her lap. The world had gone to hell.

George Schafer and Bud Sibre flew their P51s deep into the Alps. It was a clear day and the sun reflected off the remnants of the past winter's snow. It was not a comfortable feeling. They were supposed to be looking down on mountains, not looking up at them. Granted, their P51 Mustangs could climb to more than forty thousand feet, and granted that most of the mountains in the Alps were well under fifteen thousand feet, they still had to fly low to see potential targets. The tree line above which trees didn't grow was about seven thousand feet.

They didn't want to miss out on any more opportunities. Only a couple of days before, intelligence had let them know that the convoy of ambulances they'd ignored probably contained Josef Goebbels and his wife Magda along with their brood of kids. Just how the intelligence guys figured this out, Schafer and Sibre didn't know. Either they were really good at their work or they had secret sources. The two pilots only understood that they'd blown a good chance to shorten the war. Reports said there were a number of other ambulances headed south towards the Alps. Who or what were they carrying?

They would not make the same mistake again. Any

ambulance, school bus, or hearse would be shot to shreds. They'd taken too much teasing about missing out on Goebbels and not all of it was funny. They'd been accused of lengthening the war because of their squeamishness and there'd been a couple of skirmishes that calmer heads had broken up.

They'd mentioned their intentions to their commanding officer and he'd shaken his head. "Ambulances are off limits. You will not shoot at them unless they shoot at you first. Think about it, guys. Even if you had killed Goebbels, would that have ended the war or would the Krauts simply pick someone else to be their new Fuhrer? And if you did manage to kill an ambulance full of school kids, how would you really feel about that?"

They agreed that the major was correct. They would take the criticism. But they didn't have to like it.

"Jesus, Bud. If someone's hiding an army down there, they are doing a great job of it."

The craggy tops of mountains seemed to dare them to make a mistake. Already, several planes had flown into the mountains, exploding violently and doing nothing to harm the mountains. Just how the pilots had gotten disoriented was a puzzle. But both men knew that only a second's loss of concentration could result in sudden flaming death.

The lower portions of the mountains below seven thousand feet were heavily forested and had lost most of their snow covering. This was too bad. In the snow they might have been able to follow the tracks made by German trucks and tanks. As the mountains got higher and closer together it became obvious that no vehicles of any kind would be travelling near them.

"Are we anywhere near Switzerland?" asked Bud. "I

wouldn't want to piss off those nice neutral assholes by flying over their country."

"I'm not too certain where we are. If you ask me, one mountain looks just like another. Look on the bright side. We absolutely do not have to worry about the Luftwaffe."

The fact that the Luftwaffe had almost totally disappeared was one reason why they were flying as a pair and not as a larger force. Even if the Germans had planes, there were no airbases for them nor gas to fuel them. Now there were numbers of pairs of American warplanes out scouting for German ground forces. The mountains interfered with radio communication, which was another cause for concern. Should something happen to them, it might be a long time, if ever, before someone found them.

"I think we should turn around," said George. "There may be people down there but there sure as hell isn't an army."

A short while later as they left the highest mountains, they were rocked by explosions shockingly close to them. "Where the hell is that coming from?" George yelled. A second shell from a hidden German antiaircraft battery sent shrapnel rattling against their planes.

"Aw Christ, I'm hit and I'm losing oil," said Bud. "I might have to bail out."

"Are you hurt?"

"No. I'm fine but the plane isn't."

There was no thought of trying to locate the German guns. Bud's survival was paramount. George flew underneath his wingmate and examined the wounded P51. Oil was leaking and making ugly streaks on the belly of the plane.

"Okay, Bud. We are going to head north and try to find a place for you to land. It's about a hundred miles to our base, so I don't think you're gonna make it all the way. Unless we can find you a good spot to land, you're gonna have to jump. How many times have you made a parachute jump?"

"This'll be my first and you know it, smartass. And it'll damn well be my last. I mean if I survive it, it'll be my last."

"You better survive, Bud. You owe me money."

CHAPTER 7

THE RIFLE SHOT CAME FROM A CLUMP OF EVERGREENS a hundred yards down the road. Tanner and Hill ducked while their driver swerved the jeep and tried to keep from crashing. Someone was screaming in pain. At least it isn't me, Tanner thought. Hill and Tanner got the men out of their jeeps. The machine guns mounted on them opened fire and began to chew up the trees. Individual American soldiers began firing their M1s in the general direction of the forest.

Tanner clutched his helmet. "If the sniper has a brain, he's far, far away by now."

A second shot and a third followed. "He doesn't have a brain," said Hill. "But the son of a bitch is cunning. He waited for the lead elements to go by his position before shooting. We were a little complacent and now we're paying for it."

Two men had been shot and one looked very seriously wounded with a bullet in the abdomen. The second had a broken arm and medics were caring for both. Tanner shook his head. The one with the broken arm would be fine, but the other had his stomach ripped open. Medics were working on the gut wound, but the looks on their faces said that their efforts would be futile.

"I'm going to take a squad and go after him, or them," Hill said. "We could call in air support but who knows how long that would take. I suggest you stay here, Captain. I don't think you know all that much about infantry tactics."

"No argument."

A few minutes later, Tanner thought he heard gunfire, but the trees muffled sounds so thoroughly that he wasn't certain. He hoped to hell that Hill knew what he was doing. Waiting for the air force to splatter the forest with napalm wasn't all that bad an idea, he thought.

Sergeant Hill's men spread out and, taking turns, moved towards, and then into, the woods. He took a chance and had a couple of his men race ahead to cut off what he felt were only one or two Germans. They quickly found where the sniper had been hiding and there was evidence that he'd had a companion, somebody else to spot for him. Now how fast were they moving?

For a second he was stunned as a bullet splintered the tree next to his head the same time he heard the gun fire. He dropped and swore. "Anybody see anything?"

"I did," one of his men yelled and began firing into a group of trees. Others followed suit, chewing up the forest.

Hill was about to order them to stop wasting ammo

when he heard a scream. Jesus, he thought, they'd actually hit someone.

He called for covering fire and the advance continued, although more carefully. They might have wounded, or even killed, one Nazi, but there was at least one more out there someplace.

The men laid down more covering fire and Hill was only a few yards from the trees. Suddenly, a bloodied German soldier with a hand grenade charged out, screaming "Heil Hitler!" at the top of his lungs. Hill and the others fired and bullets ripped through him. He limply threw the grenade, which went only a few feet before exploding, pulverizing the German's body.

There was a crump sound from inside the trees. "I think the second guy shipped himself off to Valhalla," Hill said. He signaled them forward. Inside the grove, the second German was just as dead as the first. He too had chosen suicide by hand grenade rather than be captured. What the hell kind of enemy is this? he wondered.

He looked at the bodies and felt ill. They were too young. "Private, get the captain."

Tanner had been waiting, frustrated and angry. He should have gone with Hill. So what if he wasn't an infantryman? He was in command wasn't he? He should have pretended to lead and followed all of Hill's suggestions. Damn.

Finally and after what seemed an eternity, a soldier emerged and beckoned. Tanner rose and followed the man into the woods. Hill appeared and led him the last few feet. Two bodies lay side by side on the ground. Both German soldiers had been shredded by their own grenades. They had been dragged there so they could be searched.

"I don't think we need to call for a medic," Hill said sarcastically.

"A mop might be more appropriate." The corpses had been thoroughly riddled. Tanner looked closely at the bodies. "Wait, just how old are these guys?"

"Just out of diapers is my guess. I noticed that too. I got curious and pulled their ID. One is fifteen and the other is fourteen. Just like us, the Nazis have run out of manpower if this is what they're throwing at us. These two Nazis should be in high school, not out here trying to kill us."

Both young men were on their backs and staring at the sky, although one of them had only one eye remaining. "Congress is going crazy because we're using eighteen-year-olds in combat. I think our Congress should come out here and see this. I guess eighteen is ancient to the German army."

"Wait, look at this," said Hill. Each young man had a strange patch on his shoulder. It was a stylized animal face with flaming red eyes. "All right, Captain, can you tell me what the hell this represents? Is this what I think it is, sir?"

"I sincerely hope I'm wrong, but it sure looks like a nightmare version of a werewolf."

The rumble of approaching vehicles awakened the refugees. Lena and the others got only to their hands and knees. Even though it was night, standing up might make one a good target. Crouching made one smaller and it might make running a lot easier.

They looked at each other fearfully. Who was coming?

Was it the Russians? She was thankful it was a cloudy night. The darkness might hide them. They could scatter and maybe live, at least for a while.

But if it was the Russians, they were now between them and any kind of safety the refugees might find with the Americans.

They held their breath as the sounds got closer. Now they could identify individual engines running, each with a chorus of others in the background. "It's an army," said Sister Columba, "But whose?"

They were a good two hundred yards from the road and now Lena could make out dark shapes as they rumbled closer and louder. A long shadowy column of vehicles was going to drive right past them.

The lead vehicles moved by at about fifteen miles an hour. They didn't look like German vehicles she'd seen, but maybe these were a different style or maybe the Germans had captured them.

"Does anybody here speak Russian?" asked Columba. "If they are Reds, maybe we can reason with them."

Lena nearly choked. "One does not reason with the Red Army. They are monsters."

The column had halted. Men were getting out of their vehicles and stretching. The vehicles kept their engines running, so It looked like the pause was momentary. A number of soldiers appeared to be taking the opportunity to urinate, while a couple moved farther away where they dropped their pants and squatted. Under different circumstances it would have been hilarious.

"Watch out for me," Lena said.

Using her dark habit to hide her, she crouched and crawled slowly and cautiously to where she could see the vehicles more clearly. She could hear the men talking but could not quite make out the words. It was maddening.

At first the insignia on the nearest truck was unreadable. Then the moon came out and she could see it. The same with the voices as the soldiers talked and laughed, unafraid of anything. Now she could understand them. These were the conquerors. They were not German.

She crawled back to where Columba and the others waited, their eyes wide with uncertainty and fear. Lena grabbed Columba and pulled herself up. She started to cry. "They're Americans," she sobbed.

This time there would be no meeting in a restaurant. By mutual agreement the discussions would take place in the dining room of a farm house outside of Arbon and disturbingly close to the German border. The Swiss family that owned the farm had taken some money and happily departed for a long afternoon's shopping. A framed portrait of Swiss General Henri Guisan was on the wall. Ernie wondered if the homeowners were sending a message about Swiss strength and the nation's ability to enforce its neutrality. Guisan was the head of the Swiss army.

The man they met was about sixty and looked fatigued. Even though he wore civilian clothes, it was obvious that this man either was or had been a soldier.

"It's good to see you again, Allen. I had begun to despair that anything good was going to come of our discussions."

"I had my doubts as well, Heinrich. One can only hope that it is not too late and that events have not gotten that far past us."

"There is jubilation in Germanica that Roosevelt is dead," the man said. "Goebbels and Schoerner are beside themselves with hope that the Allies will fall apart. Please tell me that will not happen."

"I cannot speak for Harry Truman any more than you represent Josef Goebbels. However, I do not think that the Allies will collapse. France and Britain might reduce their commitments, and Russian advances will surely grind to a halt, but the United States has more than enough resources to deal with your Germanica by itself."

"Of course, but does it have the will? How many more casualties are you willing to take?"

"That remains to be seen," Dulles answered with a candor that surprised Ernie.

Ernie sat still like a statue. This Heinrich had also brought an aide and the two men looked at each other curiously. Apparently both Heinrich and Dulles wanted either a witness or protection. On being introduced to Ernie, Heinrich had stated that the conversations would be in English out of deference to both Dulles and Ernie's lack of German language skills.

"Do your leaders know that you are here?" Dulles asked.

"Yes, but they will deny it if pressed. Even though you and I have met before, this conversation would never have happened, just like the others."

Ernie sucked in his breath. Now he knew who this Heinrich was. He was General Heinrich von Vietinghoff, previously commander of all German forces in Italy. Now he commanded the southern flank of the Alpine Redoubt, or Germanica.

There had been rumors that the Germans had earlier

been trying to negotiate the surrender of all forces in Italy and that a top general was leading the efforts.

Vietinghoff laughed at the surprise in Ernie's face. "I see that Captain Janek has figured out who I am. Congratulations, Captain, but there are no state secrets here. The new Republic of Germanica merely wishes to establish unofficial and deniable contacts with the United States. Herr Goebbels feels that the Alliance against Germany is going to collapse. Therefore, we are here to try to stop the killing."

Dulles saved Ernie from making a blunt comment and offending the German officer. "General, the killing will stop when your forces and your so-called government agree to an unconditional surrender."

"That is what you say today. What will you say tomorrow when the United States is all alone? Already the American people are clamoring for an end to this tragedy if only so you can wreak justifiable vengeance on the Japanese."

"I'll admit that what you say has some merit, but not enough to deter us. Harry Truman is going to surprise a lot of people. He is going to be a very strong president. By the way, General, who the devil thought of the name Germanica?"

Vietinghoff laughed hugely. "That is the brainchild of our propaganda minister, Herr Goebbels himself. He felt that the name of Germany might be distasteful to some, while Germanica might not. Please don't ask me if I think it makes any sense."

The boundaries of the Alpine Redoubt, or Germanica, were firming up. They ran west from the Black Forest and through the Alps past Stuttgart. They continued for more than a hundred miles past the Brenner Pass and then south and across the Danube. From there the borders of Germanica ignored official national boundaries and took in parts of the Italian Alps. Vietinghoff commanded the southern or Italian front, as he had before the decision to activate the Redoubt.

"And what does Herr Goebbels want for his new bastard child, Germanica?"

"For one thing, he will renounce the Nazi Party and everything it stood for."

Dulles almost laughed. "Everything? Will he renounce massacring millions of Jews and other innocent people? Will he renounce the invasions of Poland, Russia, France, and a host of other nations? And more importantly, will he and the others around him admit to their roles in the atrocities?"

"Goebbels will acknowledge that terrible mistakes were made, but claim that a new order has taken over. As to the others, I'm sure they will claim that they were merely following orders, just as I was."

"And what does Goebbels want in what I presume would be recognition of this new state?"

"In return for recognition, the killing would stop and a true recovery could begin. Also, Goebbels and the others who now lead Germanica and who might be considered war criminals want amnesty for their alleged actions. Others on your list of war criminals will not be accepted into Germanica."

Dulles bristled. "That can never happen. The world will want justice."

"As well as being a very subjective term, justice is so elusive," said Vietinghoff. "We will be publicizing our requests to the world. I rather think we will find sympathetic audiences from people in the United States and Great Britain. There are many soldiers who are sick of the war and whose mothers dread the arrival of a telegram that might say that their son or brother or husband has been killed in action. By forgiving a relative few, many lives can be saved. You may hate the thought, even consider it a pact with the devil. But, as the war drags on and the casualties continue to mount, you will find that a great number of people will support it."

"That remains to be seen," said Dulles. Ernie thought Dulles was shaken by the audacity of the proposal.

Vietinghoff continued. "In return for peace in Europe, you will be able to concentrate your considerable resources on those nasty Japs who so treacherously attacked Pearl Harbor."

Jesus, thought Ernie. It sounded all so logical. He looked at his German counterpart and that man's eyes were wide with surprise.

"Nor can you concentrate your forces against our ever strengthening citadel here in Germanica. We are ringed by mountains that only a few expert climbers can cross and are impossible, impassible, for an army. There are only a few ways to get at us and they will all be well fortified. Storming the heart of Germanica would require that you pay a terrible price. Worse, your air forces will find that there is nothing they can effectively bomb and that any of your secret wonder weapons won't be used because they will upset the Swiss."

Vietinghoff continued. "You should let it be known that we too have secret weapons and we will be prepared to use them. I know that some of them have had rather spotty records, but admit it: our jets and our rockets have done well. So let me suggest the existence of a bomb so powerful that it can destroy an entire city, yet is so small that it can be carried in one airplane."

Ernie could not help himself. "That's impossible," he blurted out.

"Is it?" Vietinghoff answered and smiled coldly. "Look at the expression on your leader's face. He has heard rumors of both German and American bombs and knows that both countries are working on them. I assure you that I know nothing about the science involved except that it has something to do with splitting atoms. I am confident that he will immediately communicate what I have just said to his leaders in Washington. Their reactions will be quite enlightening. In the meantime, do consider the sensitivities of the Swiss."

Dulles' face was turning red. "There are many in my government who say the hell with the Swiss. They say there are too many Swiss who are pro-Nazi."

Vietinghoff shrugged. "I cannot argue with that assessment. Many people in many countries, including Switzerland, found a lot to admire in National Socialism. At least they did until we began to lose and the extent of the killing of the Jews became known. The death camps were a terrible mistake. However, soldiers like me were powerless to do anything about it. At least, Allen, I tried. We both tried to end the war in Italy where I had command. We talked to each other and we almost had an agreement whereby the German armies in Italy would surrender.

"In the meantime," the German continued, "we will use the resources we've hoarded in the past several months. When our food supplies run low, we will buy them from the Swiss who will be afraid to deny us. That is if they even *want* to. They, of course, will buy food on the world's markets and have them shipped to Switzerland and then to Germany, I mean Germanica. The Swiss will either extend us credit or they will take appropriate funds from the many accounts we now have in Swiss banks."

"Much of that money was stolen from Jews," Dulles said angrily.

"Yes, and sadly that is another thing over which we have no control. I deplore what was done but cannot change the past. You and I can only impact the future."

Vietinghoff stood and they all shook hands. When the German aide was out of hearing, Vietinghoff turned to Dulles and spoke in a whisper. "Allen, kindly remember that I am the messenger, not the message. Do not forget that I worked for peace once and will continue to do so, despite what Herr Goebbels might want. If this bomb is used, it will unleash horror."

The two Germans departed by car to the border. "Captain Janek, I trust that you found that educational?"

"I found it shocking and stunning."

"Indeed, but I am no longer surprised by what the Nazis might think of in order to save their wretched skins. I do not totally trust Vietinghoff. He is significantly motivated by self-preservation. Nothing wrong with that, of course. In the meantime, Captain, you may do us both a favor."

"Sir?"

"I think we need a drink, a strong one. Perhaps two."

★　★　★

"*Arbeit Macht Frei*," proclaimed the sign over the gate to the Dachau concentration camp. "Work will make you free." It was a hideous play on words as so many of the inmates became free only in death and a terrible end to their lives. The camp in southern Bavaria had been liberated by units of the Seventh Army the day before. General Evans had taken the opportunity to see for himself whether the rumored horrors were true or not. He took Tanner, Cullen, and a squad of infantry for security. A young lieutenant from Patch's Seventh Army staff tried to be their guide. It was apparent that he was emotionally overwhelmed by the scope of the evil they'd discovered.

The stench from the camp was noticeable well before they got to it. Cullen shook his head. "I've been told that the people living around here deny knowing anything about the camp. What the hell, what did they think they were smelling, burned pot roast?"

Their goal was to see and learn, not to help. The Red Cross was working hard to assist the several thousand inmates still in the camp who were alive and the U.S. Army was using former camp guards to bury the dead.

Even so, there had been little time for cleanup. Countless bodies lay about and many inmates looked at the Americans with both hope and fear. Many of the living were little more than skeletons who hadn't yet died. Their guide said that liberated inmates continued to do so despite heroic attempts to help them.

"At least they died as free men and women, although I wonder if many of them knew it," he said.

He went on to add that the largest segments of prisoners in the camp were Poles and Germans arrested as political criminals. There were Jews as well, just not the

vast numbers that had been sent to death camps like
Auschwitz. During the weeks before the camp's liberation, large numbers of prisoners from camps in the east
had been sent to Dachau to prevent the Russians from
liberating them. These had arrived sick, starved, and
riddled with typhus and many of them dying.

"We have no idea how many actually died here," the
lieutenant said, "Although we've got people trying to
work that out. It's got to be in the tens of thousands.
It's almost too many to comprehend."

"I heard that some SS camp guards got shot by our
guys," Cullen said. "Too fucking bad if you ask me."

Their guide grinned. "It's true although nobody
will say how many got shot. Also, the inmates killed a
number of their former captors so we may never have
an exact figure. I have heard that some do-gooders
want some of our boys court-martialed for killing the
guards. Good luck with that if you ask me."

No argument, Tanner thought. They asked a few
questions and found that large numbers of prisoners
had been marched south to work on the Redoubt.
Tanner wondered how many of them made it and
were now working to kill Americans. If they were
anything like the skeletal survivors still in the camp,
they would not be much use.

Civilians from the town were being marched in. They
had stoutly proclaimed their ignorance and now they
would see the proof of the atrocities they'd denied.
The German men and women would also help bury the
dead. The civilians looked shocked and sickened. Maybe
they had deluded themselves into actually believing that
Dachau was merely a work camp. Tough shit, Tanner
thought. Let them see and smell.

Evans shook his head. "We are totally useless here. I had hoped to be able to use what I found here to inspire the troops. But I can't describe the indescribable. I can't tell anyone about the look in prisoners' eyes or describe the stench. Pictures won't even begin to tell the story."

One of the infantrymen they'd brought said he'd been a photographer as a civilian. He'd been given a camera and was trying to record what he was seeing. He said that his efforts would not suffice. The awfulness was too much. No camera had yet been made that could adequately document the horror.

"What's worse," said the lieutenant, "is that this is just the tip of the iceberg. There are satellite camps run by Dachau's administration as well as hundreds of other camps. Most of the others are small, but then you have major ones like Buchenwald and Auschwitz. Of course it doesn't matter a hell of a lot if you've been starved and brutalized to death in a small camp of a large one."

"Can't argue with that," Evans said. He thanked the lieutenant and they drove back to the division.

"I want to take a half a dozen showers with a strong soap and burn my uniform. Maybe that will get the stench off," Tanner said to Cullen.

"But it won't get rid of the memories, will it?"

Being a nun, even a pretend one, had its advantages. The American liberators were courteous to the sisters, even giving them food and rides in the back of trucks. Apparently they were willing to give the sisters the benefit of the doubt as to whether or not they were Nazis. Or perhaps they were afraid. Lena overheard a couple of them talking about the nuns they'd had in school and what fearsome monsters they'd been.

They arrived at the city of Stuttgart in southern Germany. American and French forces had taken it on April 21. What the Allies got were massive piles of ruins. The city had been bombed numerous times and had been shelled by both the Americans and the French before capturing it. The city center area had been especially hard hit. Before the battles, Stuttgart had been one of Germany's largest cities. Now it was a scorched and blackened shell. Lena realized that she had been sheltered while living with the Schneiders. A small blessing, she thought. The destruction around her was almost beyond comprehension. If somebody had attempted to describe it to her they would have failed utterly. Block after city block was totally destroyed. Bare walls jutted up like skeletal remains. People wandered through the ruins like ghosts. Some poked at a particular piece of debris. Perhaps, she thought, they were looking for something tangible that had been a piece of their previous lives.

Worse was the stench. Many bodies still remained rotting under the ruins. Lena and the nuns had seen and smelled death while walking along the roads, but the smell in Stuttgart was overpowering. On a couple of occasions, it had caused them to vomit. Even their American drivers seemed stunned by the devastation.

The people who had survived and who remained in the city appeared to be wandering aimlessly. Their thin pale faces showed shock. Not only had their homes been destroyed, but a foreign power had taken over what remained. Many civilians were dressed in rags. Large numbers were bandaged. They were the walking wounded. Some still wore their military uniforms and they were often in tatters. One of their drivers mentioned that the large hospitals for civilians and German military were totally overwhelmed by the sheer numbers of casualties. Nor was there enough medicine or beds to care for the multitudes.

The driver had shrugged. "It's not like nobody cares. It's just that our soldiers come first and that's just too bad if you're a German. I'm sure that the Red Cross will sort it out in the near future, but, in the meantime, the German hospitals are crap."

Only a few people were working on clearing the massive piles of rubble and they were slowly and methodically moving only one brick at a time. At that rate it would take an eternity to clear debris from the city. But who cared? The only priority was to get the roads cleared for American vehicles. Almost all the workers were old men or women. That was not how she wanted to spend the next couple of years of her life, Lena thought.

American soldiers had set up checkpoints throughout the city. Sometimes they turned people away, and other times they let people through. The nuns were always waved through. Lena was curious. These were the first American soldiers she had seen and their appearance was impressive. Not only were they bigger than most Germans but they positively radiated health in comparison to Germans. Of course, they were getting regular meals while many Germans had been reduced to eating sawdust mixed with flour. Or something the government said was flour.

American uniforms were clean. Even those worn by soldiers who'd been in combat had been mended and patched and showed a degree of pride that German soldiers now lacked. Every so often, they would see German soldiers, prisoners, being paraded off to some camp. Lena was surprised to see how happy many of the Wehrmacht were to be prisoners of the Americans. Since the alternative was to be trucked off to Siberia, who could blame them?

Of course also, the Americans were the winners and winners were always cocky. The Americans exuded confidence. They laughed a lot. Even their current driver joked, though the nuns didn't understand half of what he said. Lena did, and she told Sister Columba that most of what the driver thought was funny revolved around sex with German women.

"Perhaps it hasn't occurred to them that they will have to storm those mountains to our south?" Sister Columba said.

"They are living for the moment, just like I did. For several years, I counted each moment, each hour, each day as a victory. I exulted when I heard of every Allied victory, quietly of course," she added with a laugh. "I nearly cheered out loud when the Allies landed at Normandy. I only began to despair when I thought it was possible that there would be an armistice with all armies staying in place and with me on the wrong side of the Rhine. I saw my fate as being owned by the Russians or the Nazis, what a horrible choice."

"Then you have no regrets about taking matters into your own hands and hurting the Schneider children."

"No. Of course not—and I don't consider them children. Even Anton was physically almost an adult. I hope I didn't hurt either Anton or Astrid too badly, but if I did, they were just two more casualties in a war I didn't start."

"Do you hate them?"

"Not really. They—all of the Schneiders and people like them—were just pathetic little creatures pumped up to think they were important. I no longer hate anybody. I now believe I might have a chance at a life, which seemed impossible just a short while ago."

"What about the people of Stuttgart? What do you think of when you see them?"

Lena smiled. "I see strange little animals running around furtively. They have been in the darkness so long they've forgotten what it was like to be in the light."

Columba laughed. "Are you trying to be profound?"

"Actually, I'm a little hungry. I'd even eat some of those K-rations if you have any left."

Columba did and they munched happily. That was another thing about Americans, Lena thought. They really did not know how well they had things.

The driver slammed on his brakes, throwing them forward, and quickly apologized. As the designated English-speaker, Lena asked what was happening. The driver leaned out his window and pointed at a loud and jubilant crowd of GIs.

"Hitler's dead!" they yelled. "The fucking paper-hanger is dead," one of them added. "He shot himself, the Goddamned coward."

German civilians had picked up on the announcement. "Hitler *kaput*," they said. Some looked jubilant, while others were simply stunned. Hitler was their god, and gods don't die, do they?

"Now I think I would like to be useful," Lena said. "I would like to find an American unit and offer my services. I can be either a clerk or a translator. What do you think, Sister?"

CHAPTER 8

TANNER WOKE SLOWLY. IT WAS LIKE HE WAS BACK IN the hospital in Belgium, only worse. He was in agony. His whole body ached and he was nauseous. He was afraid that his head would roll off his shoulders and bounce onto the floor. Jesus, Jesus, he thought, wouldn't that be a sight. He hadn't had such a hangover since he'd been in college. Or was it his senior year in high school when he woke up in Mary Ann Kutchinski's bed a week before graduation. He'd had to run like hell when he realized that her parents had just come home and were downstairs. He tried to smile at the memory of her naked and nubile young body but it hurt too much.

It didn't matter. In a short while he would be as dead as Adolf Hitler. There was no possible way he could recover from this horror he'd inflicted on himself. He hoped his friends and family could come to his funeral.

He managed to keep his head attached to his shoulders and stood up. He lurched to the latrine where he relieved himself of several days' worth of urine and then threw up. He kept vomiting until he reached the point of almost uncontrollable dry heaves. Other officers had their heads stuck in toilets as well. Well, it had been one hell of a party. After all, it wasn't every day that a bona fide monster kills himself. Hitler was *kaput*. Hitler was dead. But what, he thought, does that have to do with the price of tea in China or the end of the war? As near as anyone could tell, the war would continue.

"Do you believe in mercy killing?" asked Cullen as he knelt back on his haunches. He turned away from his personal toilet lest sight of the contents inspire him to be sick again.

"Captain Tanner, if you still have an iota of Christian charity in you, get a gun and blow my brains out. Wait, I have no brains, otherwise I wouldn't be in this condition."

Tanner stood and found he *could* stand only if he didn't make any sudden moves. Better, his stomach seemed to be settling. Maybe he would live to see another day. "Sorry, but you're going to have to suffer like the rest of us. Besides, like you said we have no brains. They've all been fried away."

"Heartless bastard."

A young and disgustingly sober second lieutenant approached them, stifling a grin. "Sirs, General Evans would like to see the two of you as quickly as possible. He said in an hour or less."

Cullen nodded. "I gather he survived the massacre?"

"Barely, his eyes are flaming red marbles. And I wouldn't dawdle. He's mad as hell although he does understand everybody's situation."

"How did you make it through the slaughter, Lieutenant?" asked Tanner.

"Dumb luck. I had duty. Tonight I'll celebrate but it won't be anything monumental like last night. God only knows what'll happen when this war actually ends. I can only hope I'm there to celebrate."

"Amen," said Tanner. He found a sink and splashed cold water on his face. It seemed marginally refreshing. "You don't happen to have fifty or sixty aspirins, do you? I'd like to take them and end it one way or the other."

The lieutenant laughed. "If I did, I could sell them for a fortune."

Cullen turned on the shower and stepped in wearing his skivvies. He howled as the cold water hit him. "Did the good general say why he wanted us?" he asked.

"Yeah. There was a shooting and two of our guys are dead."

Tanner stripped and stepped into his shower and let the cold water run over his body. By God, it was working. He could feel life returning to his tortured body. "This is still a war, so what is so damned important about two guys getting shot?"

"The general thinks it might have been Werewolves."

"Aw shit," Tanner said. "Lieutenant, do you think you might get us a full pot of black GI coffee along with a knife to cut it with?"

Two hours later and with Sergeant Hill to guide them, they drove to where the two dead soldiers still lay. There had been no attempt to move them or take them to a hospital. They were clearly dead with their heads nearly blown off. Even though sickened by the sight, Tanner acknowledged that it was very good shooting.

"Don't look for the provost marshal's boys to come

and investigate," said Hill. He looked pale but otherwise okay. Tanner and Cullen had each pronounced
the other to be a little greenish.

"Why not?" asked Tanner. "This is a murder. These
guys aren't anywhere near the front lines. Somebody
sneaked up on them and killed them in cold blood.
The cops should be involved."

"Regardless," said Hill, "I was told when I called
that they were busy collecting deserters and black
marketeers. I also think they might have a point.
Whoever did this is military. While waiting for you to
get here, I reconnoitered and found a firing position
that indicated two men waiting and shooting. Just like
that time on the road."

Tanner nodded. "And I'll bet nothing personal was
taken."

"Correct, Captain. These two boys still had their
wallets and ID. They even had some money in their
wallets. All of it was untouched."

"So why were they killed? Just targets of opportunity?" asked Tanner.

"Maybe, even probably. But also they were queer
and you know how the Nazis feel about queers. They
hate them even more than we do. Yeah, I cleaned
up the place and I got the guys who found them to
promise to keep quiet about these two guys getting
caught with their pants down, literally. They probably
got shot with their hands on each other's dick."

"Any chance that the scene was staged?" Cullen
asked. Like all soldiers, he held homosexuals in contempt. If caught they would have been court-martialed
and made to serve long prison sentences. Homosexuality
was one of the worst crimes a soldier could commit.

"No," said Hill. "People heard the shots and the alarm was sounded. The snipers probably ran off first chance they got."

With that new thought, they walked to the firing point. From impressions in the dirt, they could see where two men had crawled up to where they could take a clean shot and killed the GIs. Was it Werewolves or did the two Americans just run into a couple of German soldiers sneaking around? Either way, the Provost Marshal was not going to be involved.

Tanner rubbed his eyes. His headache was returning. "We will report them as killed in action by German snipers, which is close enough to the truth. Ignorance might keep their families from finding out about their relations. Nothing else matters. If there really are Werewolves, then we are going to have to be especially vigilant."

"More patrols?" Hill asked.

Tanner stood and dusted himself off. "Yeah, and maybe this time they'll be sober."

Ernie Janek was worried sick. He had grown fond of Winnie Tyler of Philadelphia and now she was across the German border in Bregenz on some damn fool errand for Dulles. She was supposed to have gotten back the day before, but the news of Hitler's death had changed things. The border was tightly sealed. Clearly the Germans were concerned about some kind of reaction to their beloved Fuhrer's death. Maybe they were concerned that a lot of their loyal followers would desert and flee to Switzerland, taking themselves out of the war. What a happy thought, he concluded.

Ernie had been lying hidden in shrubs for the better part of the day and now it was becoming dark. He was a hundred yards from the fence and a mile from the normal checkpoint. It was where he was supposed to wait if something had gone wrong. Well, it looked like something had damn well gone wrong. It was now an hour past the time when Winnie should have arrived.

He shifted slightly and felt the bulge in his pocket. It was a Walther P38 pistol. Since it was of German make, he hoped it would confuse people if it was found on him. Guns were frowned upon by the Swiss and he generally didn't carry one, but he made an exception for this day. As he always said, what could the Swiss do besides throw him out? Besides, he was reasonably confident that Dulles would intercede for him. Dulles was concerned as well, but he'd told Ernie that delays like this were to be anticipated. The spy game did not run like a railroad. Or a Swiss watch. Still, he didn't like it.

Day became a partly cloudy night and still no Winnie. He wondered if the Germans knew he was lying where he was. If so, he should move, but he couldn't. This was the secondary exit point she was going to use if leaving through the checkpoint like a regular visitor wasn't feasible. He checked his watch. In a few minutes another time frame would have passed. He was to do nothing until he spotted her and then use his discretion about actually helping her.

Out of the corner of his eye, he detected motion and froze. Two German soldiers walked along the fence line, only a few feet inside the border. He'd seen them before and they had a regular route. They did not look terribly concerned about anything. They carried their rifles slung over their shoulders and not in their arms. He could hear their voices and they seemed to be talking casually about something. Probably Hitler, he thought. It would be a good half hour before they got back. If Winnie could see them and was careful, she could get to the fence without being seen.

But then what? He made an easy decision. He would do what he could to make it easier for Winnie to escape.

When he thought it was clear, he crawled to the fence and paused. Nothing. He took out the wire clippers he'd brought and carefully snipped several strands until he thought he'd cleared enough space for a small person like Winnie to slither through. He smiled. The thought of her slithering was intriguing.

"Hurry!" It was Winnie's voice and she was only a few yards away. How the devil had she gotten so close? He snipped the last wire and pulled them aside, thankful that the Germans hadn't yet hung any bells on the wire.

She crawled up to the wire. Her face was filthy and contorted. "Help me. I'm hurt."

Ernie crawled through the opening and grabbed her arms. He crawled backwards and pulled her. She groaned and stifled it. "I'm sorry," he said.

"Just pull me, damn it. Be sorry later."

He braced himself and pulled hard. A piece of wire gouged along her arm and she barely stopped a scream.

Ernie pulled again and she was free. He knew they should crawl back but he doubted that she could do it. She looked like she'd been through the proverbial wringer. Nuts, he thought. Let Dulles fire me.

He stood and scooped her into his arms. She put her arms around his neck and he thought she was crying. He walked back into the shadows just as he heard someone on the other side yell, followed by an angry response. They were safe, at least for the moment. He didn't think the Germans would send any soldiers across the border, or even shoot into Swiss territory.

"Can you walk? The car's a little ways down the road."

"Yes, but you'll have to help me."

"Do you need a doctor?"

Winnie took a deep breath. "I don't think so." The clouds cleared and he could see her more clearly. Her face was a mass of bruises. The dress that made her look overweight was ripped and filthy. "Don't look at me," she commanded angrily.

Ernie put his arm under hers and they hobbled down the road. She groaned with almost every step. He finally got her in the back seat and drove back to the warehouse. She had her own apartment in another building, but didn't argue when she took him to his Spartan quarters.

"Please let me have a towel and a washcloth and a few minutes to clean up. I wouldn't mind a couple of Band-Aids for my arm, and, oh yes, a bathrobe. Needle and thread would be nice if you have it."

"Of course, but what happened?"

"In a few minutes, Ernie. Let me get myself back together."

It was closer to an hour when she emerged, wearing the robe. It went all the way down to her ankles. She carried the dress she'd been wearing. It had been badly torn and she'd tried to make some repairs with his sewing kit to keep it from falling apart. He made some instant coffee and she sipped it gladly. The bruises on her face were bluish-black and one of her eyes was black and swollen. The bruises extended down her neck and below her collar. He couldn't help but wonder just where else she'd been hurt and it angered him.

"Are you sure you shouldn't see a doctor? Dulles has one under contract."

"I'm sure. It's just bruises and, no, I wasn't raped, although it almost happened. An angry and drunk German officer beat the crap out of me. Of course he was one of the SS pigs."

He felt relief that she hadn't been assaulted but fury that she'd been beaten. "Why did he do it?"

"I was supposed to pick up some information from an agent at a drop site in a park. Before I could, this drunken lout appeared out of nowhere. He grabbed me and started crying about how bad it was that Hitler was dead and what a great man he was. When I tried to get away, he was sober enough to realize that my accent wasn't German, or even Swiss. Then he realized that my dress had so much padding. He dragged me into some bushes and started to ask me who I was and what was I doing in Bregenz. He wasn't stupid and realized I was an American, an enemy, and a spy."

"I'm going to kill Dulles for sending you across."

"Wait your turn. Actually, I volunteered. Don't worry, Ernie, it won't happen again."

"How did you get away?"

"He was drunk and he decided he would attack me. He pushed me onto the ground and started tearing at my fat girl clothes and simply lost his grip when more came off than he expected. I got up and pushed him down and ran as fast as my legs could carry me. I think he sounded the alarm because the border was very quickly closed, which is why I took so long to get across. Thank you for being there. By the way, the guy's name is Hahn and he's a major in the SS. He also has a bright red scar or birthmark on his cheek so you'll know him if you see him."

She stood shakily. "I haven't slept in two nights. I would like to borrow your bed for a few hours."

He thought about making a smartass comment about her borrowing his bed at any time, but thought better of it. "It's all yours. I'll drag a cot over by the door and sleep outside, just like a faithful dog. Except this dog will have a pistol."

She kissed him on the cheek and hugged him. "Thank you again, Ernie." He became aware that she had little or nothing on underneath his unworthy robe.

Josef Goebbels stood at attention facing the flag of the Reich and the black-draped portrait of Adolf Hitler. Like most of the men in the large room hollowed out of a mountain, he'd been weeping. Even though it had been expected, the announcement of Hitler's death had hit them hard. Magda had been devastated. The last he'd seen her she'd taken to her room and was sobbing hysterically. Despite their long simmering animosities, they had hugged and sobbed together and tried to comfort each other. They even made love or whatever passed for it now. Both of them had found it strangely comforting.

He would have stayed longer, but duty called. Magda went to comfort the children while he met with the handful of leaders of the new Germanican government.

Goebbels wiped his eyes. "Is it possible the communists are lying?"

Field Marshal Schoerner shook his head. He was pale but appeared to not have been crying. "The communists are always lying. However, in this case they are likely telling the truth. Their armies have had Berlin surrounded and have been steadily squeezing the area around the Chancellery. Our Fuhrer always said that he would die in Berlin at the head of the Nazi cause. I am certain that the Reds will publish pictures of his body and proclaim the triumph of their cause. The question remains, Minister, what do we do now?"

Goebbels thought quickly. Even though the Nazi Party in Germany appeared dead, as dead as the Fuhrer, there were a number who would want to become Hitler's successor. "Where is Goering? Is he still under house arrest?"

SS Major Alfonse Hahn entered the room. He had heard the last question. "He was freed by loyal members of his Luftwaffe and may be trying to make it to the American lines as an alternative to surrendering to the Soviets. He should not be considered a factor in our future, Minister. The orders regarding his possible treason are a matter of record. I do not believe that he will be obeyed by anyone of consequence."

Goering had considered himself Hitler's heir until he tactlessly broached the subject, implying that he should take over before Berlin fell and took Hitler with it. With Bormann's backing, an outraged Hitler had then considered the corpulent Luftwaffe marshal's

actions treasonous. He had publicly discredited the
man and placed him under house arrest. No, Goebbels
thought, Hermann Goering was out of the picture.
Leave him to his alcohol and drugs.

Hahn rubbed the bruise on his chin where that
American bitch had hit him. He was certain she had
been an American spy. He had punched her several
times and was going to attack her sexually when she'd
somehow managed to get away.

In the absence of a formal intelligence-gathering
apparatus, Hahn had effectively taken control of that
aspect of life in Bregenz. Along with chasing down Jews
and other enemies, he had established radio contact
with a number of Nazi loyalists in Germany proper.

"Himmler and Bormann have disappeared," Hahn
said. "It is feared that Bormann was killed trying
to flee from Berlin following Hitler's death when it
became every man for himself."

"What a shame," said Goebbels. He didn't bother
to hide his smile. If the detested Bormann was dead,
it was better for him and for Germany. "I suppose
that leaves Admiral Doenitz as a possible pretender."

Hahn nodded. "The admiral has been in radio contact
with us. As you know, he has located his headquarters at
Flensburg, near the Danish border. He now commands
all German military forces not in Germanica and under
our control. He considers himself the current president
of Germany, but not of Germanica."

"Just as well," said Goebbels. "We could do nothing
to support each other." He laughed bitterly, "Too damn
many Allied armies in the way." It occurred to him
that he should promote Hahn to some higher position. The man obviously had skills and was needed.

"Minister," said Schoerner, "The admiral wishes to know what to do about surrendering his armies to the Allies. He wants desperately to avoid surrendering them to the Soviets."

Goebbels thought for a moment. "Let him work out whatever arrangements he wishes. He can surrender all the damn armies and ships under his command. The armies of Germanica, however, are not under his command and any announcement that he is attempting to surrender them will be rejected. Germanica is an independent country and does not answer to any rump German government in Flensburg."

Goebbels lit a cigarette and puffed angrily. Smoking in the caverns was supposedly prohibited, but who was going to stop him. He was Adolf Hitler's successor. He took a deep breath and continued. "It has occurred to me that we have been too focused on the bare needs for our survival. Now we must go beyond that if we are to become a true nation. We need other nations, preferably a number of them, to recognize Germanica. That way we can send people out armed with diplomatic immunity. Ergo, we need a diplomatic corps, albeit it will have to be a small one. Anyone have suggestions?"

"I assume von Papen and von Ribbentrop are not possible," said Schoerner, referring to the current and previous foreign secretaries.

Goebbels agreed. "Ribbentrop is an ass and von Papen is too old. That assumes, of course, that we could find him and bring him here. Albert Speer might be acceptable, but where is he? The last I heard, he was headed towards someplace near Hamburg."

"I will make some contacts, Minister," said Hahn.

"If he is in the Hamburg area, it should not be too difficult to bring him here, via Switzerland of course."

Schoerner was dubious. "I have serious doubts that anyone will recognize the nation of Germanica, much less negotiate with us. The Americans are in total control and will exert enormous pressure on countries to ignore us. Even some otherwise sympathetic nations like Argentina might wait a long while before recognizing us. I would think that the same would hold true with Spain. It may be quite a while before any major or even second tier nation acknowledges our existence."

"That's ridiculous," said Hahn. "How can anyone ignore us? We are here, aren't we? We aren't spirits or ghosts."

Goebbels smiled tolerantly. "You still have a lot to learn, Major. Nations, especially victorious ones, can do what they wish and not necessarily what is right. And by the way, your work here in Bregenz has been above and beyond the call of duty."

"Thank you, Minister."

"It has occurred to me that you do not have enough rank to do your job properly. Therefore, I am promoting you to the temporary rank of SS-Brigadefuhrer. I understand it is equivalent to being a brigadier general in the American army." He held out his hand, which was taken by a stunned Hahn. "Congratulations, General, now go and continue your good work. And someday you must tell me the truth about how your face got so badly bruised. I'll bet she was a real tiger."

Hahn laughed indulgently. He would never tell his leader and new Fuhrer that he'd been momentarily bested in combat by a woman and that his bruises had nothing to do with a sexual encounter. Well, almost nothing. In private he'd already contemplated the fate in store for the woman if he should ever find her.

"One other thing," said Schoerner. "Has there been anything on the whereabouts of the physicist named Heisenberg? The non-Jew Abraham is very upset that he hasn't turned up. Apparently, he is very important to the success of our nuclear program."

Goebbels shrugged dismissively. "I don't understand. He's already told us he will succeed with the resources he currently has. Perhaps you should tell him that failure will not result in his being shot. Instead it will entail his being hanged by the neck by piano wire while his toes barely scrape the ground. I'm told that dying that way is lengthy and excruciating. Perhaps that bon mot of knowledge will motivate him."

Lena and Sister Columba walked through the crowd of people waiting at the gate at the sprawling American army base. There seemed to be a line of sorts and there was some grumbling when they walked right up to the front of it. The guard, a young sergeant, seemed amused by the disturbance.

"And what can I do for you sisters?" he asked politely and in passable German.

Lena shocked him by responding in fluent English. "I would like to see a Roman Catholic priest and it is a matter of some urgency."

"Perhaps I should call the officer of the guard and let him decide. Does what you want to talk to the priest about have anything to do with the Nazis?"

"In a way, but not what you suspect. It is also very personal, which is why I want to see a priest. I believe that chaplains are also officers, so why not let him decide about the officer of the guard after I have spoken to him."

"Sounds fair," said the sergeant. "Although I can't imagine what kind of sins a nun like you has committed that requires such personal service."

A few minutes later, Captain Richard Shanahan, chaplain and captain in the U.S. Army, arrived at the gate. "Why do you wish to speak with me, Sister, and I am told you understand English. That's good since my miserable high school German hasn't improved at all."

Father Shanahan was short and slight. He wore glasses and was nearly bald. Lena guessed that he gave long sermons. "May we speak privately?"

Shanahan waved her inside the compound. The sergeant looked away. As always, what officers did was their business. "Now what is it, Sister?"

Lena spoke quickly to prevent Father Shanahan from cutting her off. "First, I may have killed two people. Second, I am neither a nun nor a Catholic. I was kept as a slave for several years by a family of Nazis. When I found that they were going to sell me to a munitions factory where people were worked to death, I escaped. Their two adult children tried to stop me and I know I hurt them badly. These nuns have sheltered me. They are saints, or they should be."

"How much of this can you prove?"

Shanahan looked away when she reached under her habit and removed the cloth-wrapped pistol. The priest took it and whistled when he unwrapped it. "This came from the first war. It's quite valuable," he said.

"For a man of God, you understand weapons quite well."

He chuckled. "I took vows of chastity and obedience,

but not poverty of any kind. I like to hunt and, after all, I am in the army. So yes, I do understand weapons, and I do have many other vices. Now, what else do you have for me?"

She also showed him her identity papers, the ones that said she was a Jew. "But I am not a Jew." She then gave him the papers she'd forged on Nazi letterhead and a pass once given her by Frau Schneider.

"You've been quite prudent and clever," the priest said admiringly. "Now, what do you want from me?"

"I need a job, and a job in which I can use my skills to hurt the Nazis. I want to punish the people who killed my fiancé and probably murdered my father. I want to punish the people who kept me enslaved."

"Your enslavement wasn't all that horrible compared with others."

"Agreed, but wasn't it your Abraham Lincoln who said that to the extent a man is not free, he is a slave? And besides, they were about to sell me to a factory where I would have been worked to death."

"Can you type and file?"

"Of course. And I can translate as well. As you see, I speak fluent English, which I can also read and write. The same is true with German and Czech."

Shanahan grinned. "Well, we don't have all that much call for Czech speakers, but one never knows. I do know that we are hurting for locals who weren't members of the Nazi Party. Of course, everybody swears on their mother's grave that they were never Nazis. So many do that it makes you wonder just how Adolf and two or three other guys took over Germany and much of the world. You certainly qualify for the honor of genuinely being a non-Nazi."

Lena took a deep breath. Is this going to be the first step in leading a normal life? She turned and saw Sister Columba edging away. She waved and Columba waved back, still slowly leaving.

"Are you dressed decently under the habit?"

"Yes, and I have other clothes in the bag I brought."

"Good. I'll find you a place where you can change into something civilian and then I'll introduce you to some people."

"Thank you," she said and started crying.

Father Shanahan gave her a handkerchief. It wasn't terribly clean but it did help dry off her tears. "Lena Bobekova, let me be the first to welcome you to the 105th Infantry Division."

The next morning, Winnie was still in terrible pain and could hardly walk. She managed to clean herself but she looked awful. The bruises on her face had darkened and the eye that was nearly swollen shut also had a ruptured blood vessel that made the white of her eye look scarlet. She looked like something from a cheap horror movie. She'd insisted that Ernie go to her apartment and get her a pair of sunglasses.

It also hurt her to breathe. It was difficult for her to stand up straight. This finally convinced her to go to a doctor who informed them that she had at least two cracked ribs. There might have been a third, but the x-ray machine he was using wasn't very good. The doctor also added that nothing could heal broken ribs besides time.

On hearing of Winnie's problems, Dulles had flown into Arbon in a five-seat Cessna AT-17. Two other men flew in with him but they disappeared quickly.

Ernie assumed that they had OSS-related jobs to do and he was not about to inquire about them.

In deference to Winnie's injuries, they met at Ernie's quarters. He had moved out of his room and been assigned another one. The remaining two units were still empty.

Dulles was visibly upset. He'd had agents killed and wounded in the line of duty and hated it. "Winifred, I very much regret getting you involved in that mess. You were fortunate to survive. Had we lost you, I would have been devastated."

"So would I," she said with an attempt at humor, "It's all right, sir. After all, who could have known that Hitler would choose that day to join his friends and relatives in Hell? But was anyone able to finish my task?"

Dulles smiled. "That is being taken care of as we speak." It was an obvious reference to the men who had flown in with him. "On the other hand, Captain Janek, I understand you had a little, ah, fun this morning."

"I was just doing some reconnoitering, sir."

"What in God's name did you do?" asked a shocked Winnie. "You didn't cross the border, did you? You wouldn't have lasted ten seconds if you'd been stopped."

Ernie was quietly delighted that she was concerned. "Nothing of the sort. I just wondered if the hole in the fence I'd made had been fixed, so just before dawn I went and checked it out. At first it didn't look like anything had been done to it, so I crawled closer. Then I noticed a bunch of wires and realized the place had been booby-trapped by the Nazi swine."

He smiled at the memory. "So I went to the garbage

dump and found a really ripe dead cat. I put it in a bag and crawled close to the wire. When I figured I was close enough, I took the stinking animal out of the bag and hurled it into the hole in the fence. Sure enough, it triggered the booby traps and they exploded. Dead cat went flying all over the place. Lights went on and German soldiers went screaming towards the pieces of the poor little dead kitty. When I left them, I think they were trying to figure out if it was the cat who'd set of the explosives or something else. It was nice to see the Germans grubbing through debris and dead cat."

Dulles shook his head. "Do me a favor and don't do it again."

"But I did it for Winnie."

Winnie leaned over and clutched herself. "I told you not to make me laugh."

Ernie decided it was time to change the subject. "Sir, what plans do you have for us?"

"For the time being you are to sit tight and observe. Check the border and note any changes. Take the boat out and observe, but only after Winnie is cleared to swim in case something should happen."

"What was the information I was supposed to pick up?" Winnie asked.

Dulles smiled tolerantly. "Are you wondering just what was worth risking your life? Well, I can't tell you that right now, but someday I will. Trust me, though, it might have been worth many lives. And if we can still get it, the info will indeed be worth it."

Eisenhower and Devers looked over the several pages of information they'd just received courtesy of someone. "Amazing," said Devers. He had flown into Reims at Ike's request. "It certainly looks like we have people high up in the Redoubt."

Ike was not so confident. "You're assuming that the information is correct. If it is, it is a godsend. How many generals would have loved to have all this much detail about an enemy army before a battle?"

"I can think of a few who did and still blew it," Devers said and Ike chuckled.

What they had before them was a detailed listing of all German units in or near the redoubt. It gave their size, location, and a succinct analysis of their fighting ability. It said that the Germans had reconstituted twenty-five divisions out of the retreating remnants. These totaled one hundred and eighty thousand men. An additional twenty thousand Russians who had turned against Stalin were included along with a division of ten thousand Croats. The Germans also had four hundred tanks. All of the German units were said to be above average in fighting ability. The two generals had their doubts.

Devers gave his own analysis. "First of all, I believe this analysis tells Goebbels and Schoerner what they want to hear and not what is necessarily the truth. I sense some lower-ranking staff officers trying to save their own skins. I just can't believe that all the German units are such rabid and diehard Nazis. After all they have been surrendering by the thousands, the hundreds of thousands north of the Redoubt. Why should these guys be any different? They weren't chosen for any particular skill or dedication. These are just the poor schmucks who happened to be in the area when the Redoubt was formed. If they'd been more fortunate, they'd be in prison camps awaiting repatriation instead of the opportunity to get blown to pieces."

"Are you saying they might surrender if given a chance?"

"Couldn't hurt to find out."

Ike agreed. "Any other thoughts?"

"Yes. The Russians and the Croats will fight like cornered tigers because they know they are all dead if they are captured. Any captured Croats will be murdered by Tito and the Serbs, and the Russians will be turned over to Stalin who will either shoot them outright or send them to Siberia to be worked to death. If there was some way we could promise either group sanctuary somewhere, perhaps they would not fight so desperately."

Ike conceded that Devers had a good point. The current agreement with Moscow required the U.S., Great Britain, and France to turn over to the Russians any captured Red Army deserters. Already there had been incidents of suicides and suicidal resistance from those preferring death with a rifle in hand. Killing one's self was preferable to either being executed or spending a horrible brutish existence in the snows of Siberia. He did not know of anything regarding the Croats. He made a mental note to check it out.

"It may be a lost cause, but I will contact General Marshall regarding your thoughts. Any soldier we can get to surrender will be one less that we will have to root out and kill while he's killing our boys."

"Ike, I could not help but notice that those non-German troops are all stationed on the west side of the Brenner Pass. I wonder if that's a coincidence. Or maybe they don't trust them all that much."

Ike had noticed it as well. "Very interesting," was all he said.

Wolfgang Hummel and Martin Schubert had known each other since the day they'd been inducted into the German Army some six years ago. Now they had each risen to the rank of corporal and were still close friends. The men were a team. They operated the MG42 machine gun. Hummel did the actual firing while Schubert supplied ammunition and generally assisted whenever he could. Sometimes they'd switch, but not for long. Hummel was by far the better shot.

They'd lugged the twenty-five pound weapon along with many pounds of ammunition across several European countries and now found themselves in Germany with the Alps to their back. They considered the gun to be a marvel. It could easily fire twelve hundred rounds a minute, had a range of more than a thousand yards and this one even had a telescopic sight. It also gave off a horrible screeching noise that could easily terrify an enemy soldier. They treated their new gun like a queen, keeping her clean and oiled. And why not? She had helped keep them alive.

Hummel looked around to see if anyone could hear them speak. He had to do it casually since any furtive movements attracted suspicion. "Martin, do you think we've come far enough to stop retreating?"

"I think we went far enough a month ago. When the Americans landed at Normandy I knew it was all over. We couldn't stop either the Russians or the Americans. Germany had to sue for peace, but our leaders didn't and now it may be too late."

"Agreed." Hummel pulled out a pack of cigarettes

and handed it to Martin. They lit up and enjoyed the smoke. The cigarettes were Americans, taken off a dead GI. He would no longer need them, they'd thought. Besides, they had laughed, cigarettes were bad for your health.

"So what are we going to do?" Schubert asked, almost plaintively.

Artillery was rumbling in their rear. American spotter planes had found something and their guns were trying to kill it. At night when they were trying to sleep, the rumbling would be accompanied by distant flashes of light. The Americans were not going to leave them alone. "If the Yanks push us, we're going to have to climb those damn mountains. I can't climb mountains. Christ, I sometimes can't even climb a ladder."

"I can't either. Are you suggesting that we should surrender?"

Hummel finished his smoke and field stripped the butt. He thought about saving the shreds of tobacco in case he had to try and roll his own, but figured the hell with it. He let them go with the wind.

They were in a foxhole that they had turned into a small bunker. With skills learned from years of experience, they had made it strong and practically invisible. They had solid fields of fire and were confident that they could decimate any attacking force, just as they had so many times before. They didn't particularly enjoy seeing enemy soldiers being riddled with bullets and turned to bloody pulp, but this was war and nobody wanted to finish in second place.

Their small fort also had places to relieve themselves, although they joked that it didn't much matter. It had been so long since they'd been able to wash or put on a clean uniform that their personal stench would overwhelm that of body waste. All the German soldiers were in the same condition. They joked that the Yanks would find them from their smell.

Hummel just wanted the war to finish. "I would like to surrender, Martin, but I don't know how to go about doing it. We can't just tell the others to have a good war and then go walking up to the Americans with our hands in the air. First, the Yanks might shoot us as revenge for some of the atrocities the SS and others have committed, and second, Lieutenant Pfister would have the others kill us before we got twenty feet."

Schubert again looked around. Lieutenant Pfister was walking towards them. "What the hell does the idiot want now?" Pfister was a devout Nazi, to put it mildly. They'd heard that the lieutenant had howled like a dog when he'd heard that his beloved Hitler was dead. He had vowed that he and the platoon would die to the last man before surrendering. Sadly, Hummel and Schubert and the others believed him.

They did not stand and salute when he arrived. The Americans were too close and they had their own snipers.

"What are you two plotting?" Pfister asked.

Hummel almost froze before answering. Then he realized that their usually uptight lieutenant was just making a small joke. "We were just talking about some marvelous carnal adventures that we will have when we win this war and get to go home."

Pfister laughed. Some days he actually had a sense of humor, proving that he used to be human. "Don't get your priorities mixed up. Gather all your gear.

We're going to be maneuvering again. As usual we will move when it's dark so the Yank planes can't see us."

The two gunners nodded their understanding. "Maneuvering" was another word for retreating. "Any idea where we're going, sir?" asked Schubert.

"I've heard that we're going to the northern head of the Brenner Pass."

Hummel looked intently at the lieutenant. "Sir, when are we going to stop and fight the Americans? I'm sick and tired of retreating. I want to stop and kill the bastards who are violating our nation."

Pfister looked impressed. So too was Schubert who knew that Hummel meant not a word of the bullshit he was spouting. He wanted to know when they might make contact with the Americans so they could give up.

Pfister smiled broadly. "Corporal, our opportunity will come soon enough. When we get to the pass there will be no more retreating. There we will stand and fight. Then we will destroy the swine who have invaded our land and who are violating our women."

"That was most impressive," said Schubert after the lieutenant had left. "It almost brought tears to my eyes."

"Not to mine," said Hummel. "Once upon a time I thought Hitler was God. I thought that Germany would conquer the world and then there would be a true peace, one that would be based on Nazi values. For the longest time I even enjoyed fighting in Poland and Russia. The fire bombings of our cities opened my eyes and cleared my mind. Germany doesn't stand a chance, if indeed she ever did. I know longer wish to fight for a cause that is lost. I don't care if Jews take over the world. I want to go home and find my family."

Schubert shook his head. He felt infinite sadness. "I just hope we have families to find." They both came from cities that had been leveled by American bombers. They'd heard nothing from their families and expected the worst.

Harry Truman was still growing into his job as President of the United States. He was mad as hell at Franklin Delano Roosevelt for shutting him out of the decisions that had been made and now had to be enforced by a very inexperienced Truman.

He had been considered such a nonentity that he'd lived in an unguarded apartment until Roosevelt's death. Now, however, he had Secret Service crawling all over the place trying to protect him. He'd joked that they even wanted to go to the john with him. He liked to take brisk walks and now he did so surrounded by guards. It was a little unsettling.

He still hadn't moved into the White House because Eleanor Roosevelt hadn't yet left. In a moment of generosity, he'd told her to take as long as she needed and now he wondered if she would ever move out.

Truman wanted to be furious at the military and diplomatic leaders who'd quietly humiliated him by shunning him, but he knew it wasn't their fault. It had been Roosevelt's and they'd had to follow his orders. But why, he wondered, and realized it no longer mattered. FDR had made a pattern of ignoring his vice presidents, so why should his experiences or lack thereof, have been any different?

He was seated behind Roosevelt's massive desk in

the Oval Office that he'd already decided to retain for his use. Many of the former president's personal items had been removed, either taken by Eleanor or packed up to be moved. A few pictures of his own wife Bess and his daughter Margaret graced the desk. Thank God he had them as his anchors, he thought.

A glum group of men looked at him. He wondered if they thought they were having a bad dream and would wake up and find that Roosevelt was still president. Someday he would tell them that he'd had that same dream.

Shortly after becoming president, he'd been informed that the U.S. was making a super-bomb, an atomic bomb. He'd been staggered to realize just how much money and effort had gone into the project. Almost as astonishing was the fact that it remained a secret. Even from FDR's vice president, he thought angrily.

Truman forced himself to smile. "Gentlemen, I trust that the first test of an atomic bomb is still scheduled for mid-July?"

"That is correct, sir," responded General George C. Marshall, the Army's Chief of Staff. He was accompanied by Major General Leslie Groves.

Groves was very overweight and pear-shaped, which somewhat bothered Truman. He felt that soldiers should look the part. Still, Groves had been the man who'd ramrodded construction of the Pentagon and now the physical parts of the development of the atomic bomb. The unmilitary looking Groves was reputed to be one tough son of a bitch and Truman did like that. Groves was not a physicist, but he understood enough of the bomb to explain the military aspects of it.

No one was present from the State Department.

Edward Stettinius was the current Secretary of State and he was high on the list of people Truman wanted removed. They disagreed on too many things. Nor was anyone present from the navy. The discussion points related to the army only and, of course, the air force, which was part of the army.

As president, Truman was the first to speak. "General Marshall, General Groves, I think I understand that using the atomic bomb in Japan would be a catastrophe for the Japanese and might bring them to the surrender table. A bomb dropped on a wooden Japanese city would cause massive fires and devastation along with God knows how many thousands of civilian casualties. It would be even worse than the fire-bombing we are now inflicting on them. I can and will accept responsibility for those casualties if the bomb ends the war in the Pacific without the need to invade the home islands of Japan. But what about using it in Europe? How can it be used to end the fighting that is otherwise going to happen in the Alps?"

Groves was blunt. "I don't see a use for it in Europe."

Truman was aghast. "After all the money we spent on it? And wasn't it intended to be used against Germany and Hitler in the first place?"

"Yes, sir, it was," Groves responded. "And it still would be if there were any proper targets remaining. We planned on dropping it on Berlin or Hamburg, or some other major city. We'd even configured the bombs to be carried by a B29. They are just too big for a B17. There aren't any B29s in Europe that I know of, although that can be changed quickly enough. The simple fact is, there are no major targets left in

Germany and we won't have enough bombs to throw around."

"This Germanica is a legitimate target, isn't it?"

"Of course, but let me explain. In mid-July, we're going to test one of the three we will have and we will do it in New Mexico. We're overwhelmingly certain it'll work, but not totally so. I agree with Oppenheimer and the others who insist on a test. We have to know that it'll work before we drop it. If it fails, we'd look like idiots. That and we'd have given away a lot of our secrets."

"That much doesn't concern me," said Truman. "If it doesn't work, our precious secrets won't be worth much, especially if the bomb was dropped from thirty thousand feet. I imagine the bomb would exist only as fragments. But I guess you're right. Test the damn thing."

"That leaves two bombs left and they are designated for Japanese cities."

"But not Tokyo," Truman said.

"Not Tokyo," said Marshall.

It had been agreed that the capital of Japan would not be hit with anything other than conventional bombs. It was a small honor. The fire-bombings of Tokyo had burned vast sections of the city and killed tens of thousands of civilians.

"There are other issues," said Marshall. "An atomic bomb set off in an alpine mountain valley would be somewhat contained by the mountains and its effectiveness would be reduced dramatically. The three bombs that I've mentioned are all that we'll have for the foreseeable future. We will produce more, but not until we determine which type works best. Then there is the issue of Switzerland and her neutrality."

"Damn the Swiss," snapped Truman.

Marshall was unfazed. In a way he was pleased by Truman's directness. FDR had the maddening habit of talking in circles and leaving listeners to try and figure out what it was he wanted.

"Mr. President, any bomb set off anywhere near the German city of Bregenz could cause thousands of casualties among innocent Swiss civilians."

"I would rather have Swiss casualties than American," Truman snapped. "The Swiss have been coddling and protecting the Nazis for too damn long if you ask me. This asinine Republic of Germanica would not even exist if it wasn't for the protection provided by the Swiss. And now you're telling me that we can't use the bomb because of the Swiss? Bullshit."

"There are good reasons," said Marshall, ignoring the outburst. "We all know that high-level bombing is inaccurate. We are planning to drop the bomb from thirty thousand feet but it will not detonate until it drops to fifteen hundred. This means that any mistake by the bombardier or even strong gust of wind could send the bomb off its course by many miles. It is conceivable, but admittedly not likely, that we could wind up dropping an atomic bomb on Switzerland and not Germanica. Or worse, it could detonate in some desolate mountain valley and no one will notice."

"Shit."

It was Groves' turn. "Sir, I think we should talk about radiation."

"Go ahead."

"Since no bomb has yet been exploded, no one knows what is really going to happen with radiation. There are those who feel that we could unleash unknown forces that could destroy life on earth. Most scientists, however, feel that the explosive forces of an atomic bomb will be absorbed by the planet without any significant problem. The real concern is the possible lingering effects of radiation. We know that radiation burns and can kill. What we don't know are the long-term effects. We've had some accidents in which men and women have been exposed and burned. Some people have died. Although a large number of scientists believe that radiation burns are like any other burns and just need to be treated, there are those who think that deadly radiation will remain in the ground, or buildings, or human flesh for many years. There are also those who feel that lethal doses of radiation will be spread by the exploding bomb's shock wave and debris cloud. We simply don't know what could happen. Some scientists visualize a black cloud of death crossing Lake Constance with a large part of Germany and Switzerland being uninhabitable for generations."

Marshall looked even more glum than usual. "I had hoped to use the bomb to clear a path through the valleys and the Brenner Pass. The Germans have built strong defenses in depth. I'd hoped the bomb would simply obliterate them and that our boys would literally walk over the rubble and into the heart of their Germanica. Radiation may dissipate over a period of time, but I don't think I can take a chance with our boy's lives like that."

Truman swore under his breath. He had seen combat in World War I as an artillery officer and thought he understood bloody death. But not death on the magnitude being described, and certainly not caused by something as sinister as radiation. Workers in watch factories had died from radiation when they licked small paintbrush tips dipped in some radioactive material to make the dial glow in the dark. Many of them suffered from horrific cancers to the mouth that further indicated that there would be long-term consequences.

American soldiers would not die from radiation poisoning if he could help it. But there was still the terrible equation confronting him. If the atomic bomb, or any bomb, could stop the killing of American boys, it had to be used.

"All right," he said unhappily. "We will continue to plan to use the atomic bomb on Japan only. However, we will hedge our bets. I want a squadron of B29s available to fly over this damned Germanica. After we kill some Japanese cities, perhaps the Germans will realize what we can do and how little they can do to stop it. Maybe the Nazis will recognize what a threat the atomic bomb is. Maybe it'll put pressure on them to surrender."

Maybe, Truman thought glumly, the moon is made of green cheese. "And what about Germany's nuclear threat?"

Groves answered. "We believe it no longer exists, if indeed it did. We have teams of scientists scouring the areas of Germany we now occupy for their nuclear scientists as well as any facilities for the making of atomic weapons. It is called the Alsos Project and the Alsos teams have seen nothing that would indicate that the Germans have an atomic bomb."

Truman nodded. At first he'd thought that Alsos was another secret that had been kept from him. In a way it was, but it wasn't that major. He had been amused to find that the name, Alsos, was Greek for "grove" and that it had been decided on by General Groves. He hadn't known the man had a sense of humor. He could only hope that the Alsos information was correct. If what he had found about the bomb was even halfway correct, having it in the possession of an enemy was a terrible thing to contemplate.

Truman stood and paced. "Then can you guarantee me that this report from Switzerland about the Nazis having an A-bomb in Germanica is nonsense?"

Groves winced. "I've spoken to Oppenheimer and others, and they do not believe the Germans are capable of building an atomic bomb. First, we don't believe they have the resources and the scientists to build the bomb and, second, they have no means of delivering it even if they were to build it."

"Does that mean you are a hundred percent certain there is no possibility of the Germans building one of the infernal devices?"

Groves turned red. "Nothing is a hundred percent, sir. It is, however, considered highly unlikely and that the Germans are bluffing."

Truman shook his head angrily. "I want one hundred percent. The risk of the slaughter of American soldiers or the destruction of a major city like Paris or London is too awful to contemplate."

As Truman was making this pronouncement, another thought was forming in his mind—a thought that he didn't like one damned bit.

Gustav Schneider was bitterly disappointed by the reception he and his family received on making it through to the Alpine Redoubt now called Germanica.

It was unenthusiastic to the point that he thought the bureaucrats in charge had been *disappointed* by his safe arrival. He had spluttered and complained to no avail. One Nazi Party functionary had even told him that he'd been fortunate to be allowed access. Only important members of the Nazi hierarchy were eligible for rescue, and not the minor ones. Fortunately, Schneider did have at least one friend.

Gerhard Unger was a civilian administrator in the Redoubt. He reported directly to the still absent Albert Speer and was responsible for the ongoing construction in the area. He was fifty and had once been a physically powerful man. He had somewhat gone to fat but still looked like he could kill with his massive arms. Schneider recalled that he had done so on a couple of occasions when the Brownshirts were engaged in street fights with communists and other riff-raff opposed to Hitler.

"Gustav, I know you're unhappy, but you are truly fortunate to be here at all. The criteria for entry into Germanica are very specific. You must bring something significant to the table. Let's be honest, all you were was a low-level Party functionary and let's be even more honest. You weren't very good at it. The only thing you did of any consequence was to administer a group of informers. If it wasn't for the fact that you and I were so close in the old days, we would have sent you away. Germanica cannot hold everyone in Germany. Our resources are extremely limited."

"So, you're saying I should quit complaining and be thankful."

"Precisely. Now, I've gotten you a job as a clerk in my office. I would appreciate it if you did not fuck it up, at least not too badly," he added, softening the comment with a smile.

Schneider had visions of himself and his filthy and starving family trudging down roads and looking for refugee camps. He shuddered. He would rather die. "I will do my best."

Unger smiled. "Excellent. Now how is your family?"

"Gudrun is well. As a result of the food shortages, she's even managed to lose a little weight. As to the children, they are a different matter. You are aware that they were ambushed and brutally beaten by that Jewess we took under our wing."

Unger nodded solemnly. "I am. That was a terrible betrayal and so typical of a Jew. You saved the child from the ovens and for that she assaults Astrid and Anton. It's almost unspeakable. How are they recovering?"

Gustav had no trouble speaking frankly to Unger. "It is coming slowly. For Anton, the physical pain is gone, but the psychological terror is there. He is now afraid of women. I even tried to have him serviced by a prostitute. She said he had a terrible time getting it up and couldn't function at all unless it was dark. It was as if he was afraid of seeing a woman. I will bring this whore around whenever he feels like he can handle it."

"Terrible," said Unger.

"Astrid has had no problems like that. She sometimes gets severe headaches from being struck in the head, but even they seem to be less and less frequent. I am confident that she will recover fully in time. It's Anton that I'm worried about. He has got to get over this irrational fear of women. If I could find a good psychiatrist here, I would like to use him."

"I am not aware of any in Germanica, but I will check around." It was not lost on either man that many of the better psychiatrists had been Jewish.

"It would be greatly appreciated. In the meantime, I take great joy in planning terrible revenge on the Jewish slut who almost killed my children. If I find her, she will die a long, agonizing death."

CHAPTER 9

THE MAN THEY BROUGHT IN TO BE INTERROGATED was so malnourished and skeletal that Tanner wondered just how he was able to stand and walk. Yet somehow he had summoned up the strength and had traveled a ways to get to them. He was still wearing his tattered striped prison suit and there was a group of numbers crudely tattooed on his left forearm. His head had been shaved bald by American medics to get rid of lice and he had gratefully taken a bowl of broth. A medic had told them to feed him very, very slowly. Too fast and he could easily cramp up and die.

Not only did they not want him to die as a matter of humanity, but they thought he was trying to tell them something, something he considered important. It was frustrating for all of them that no one could understand him.

The former prisoner looked around at the bustle in the schoolhouse that had been taken over by the 105's command. "American?" he asked with a terrible smile. Most of his teeth were jagged and broken.

"Yes," said Tanner. "Do you speak English?" he asked and got a puzzled response. "Deutsch?" he asked. The man's expression turned to fear and then anger. He spat on the floor.

Tanner grabbed the man's skinny arm. "No, no." The man seemed to understand that spitting on the floor was bad.

Tanner had an idea. "Somebody get me a map of Europe, please."

"But only because you said please," Cullen said, handing him an atlas. It was turned to Europe.

Tanner pointed to the man and then to the map. He had to do it a couple of times before the man understood. He pointed at a place on the map. "Ah," he said and smiled again.

"Czechoslovakia," said Tanner helpfully.

"Czech," the man insisted. "Czech, Czech, Czech."

Tanner patted the man on the arm. "I understand," he said. "Yes, ja." And the man has something important to say? What the hell. He stood. "Does anybody here speak Czech or whatever they speak in that country?"

"I do," said Lena.

Lena could not contain her shock on seeing the nearly dead refugee. He was the right age to have been her father. Two American officers were beside the man. She knew who both of them were although she had never been introduced or even spoken to them.

She spoke in Czech to the man in a gentle, soothing tone. He responded quickly and began chattering away. Finally, he took a deep breath and began to sob. Lena put her arms around his shoulders and comforted him. When she finally turned to Tanner, her eyes were

glistening. "He says he was assigned to a small factory
about five miles from here. Their job was to repair
rifles and machine guns. He said that at one point
there were a couple hundred prisoners, slaves. Now
there are about fifty. The rest either died of starvation
or were worked to death."

Cullen was confused. "What the hell are they still
doing hanging around. Didn't anyone notice that the
American army had arrived?"

Lena asked the refugee a few more questions.
"He said that the manager is a fool. He felt that the
Americans would be driven back so he made no effort
to move the factory or the prisoners. Thus, they are
still there, but not too much longer. The manager
recently got orders to pack up and move. What could
not be moved was to be destroyed."

"And we all know what that means," Cullen said
bitterly.

"Yes, the prisoners are to be murdered," said Lena
and this time tears did run down her cheeks. "You
have got to stop them."

Shit, thought Tanner. They had to do something.
"How many guards at the site?" he asked the man.

No more than six came the answer. And all of
them were Volkssturm who were poorly trained and
equipped. "We can handle that with a platoon," said
Tanner. "Cullen, why don't you wake up Sergeant Hill
and tell him we have a job for him."

"I will go with you," said Lena.

Tanner blinked in surprise. "Out of the question.
Women do not go on combat missions."

"Then it's time to make an exception. I have to go
with you or you'll never find the place. This man's

instructions were vague. You need me to translate and guide you. Otherwise the prisoners might be dead before you stumble on it."

They might already be dead, thought Tanner. But the girl was right. He hadn't really noticed her in the few days she had been assigned to help with clerical duties. She was really intense and could be pretty if she could get some food in her and some meat on her bones. She was wearing old olive drab fatigues that someone had cut down to fit her smaller frame. Her shoes looked like old worn tennis shoes.

"We could be going into an ambush," he said.

"I have other reasons for going with you and they are important and personal."

"Should we explain this to the brass?" Cullen asked.

"Of course not," said Tanner. "They'd just turn it down. Let's just go and ask forgiveness later."

It was late afternoon and shadows were getting long when they got to within a mile of the suspected prison site. It was off a dirt road and in a heavily forested area. Lena had been right. It might have taken them a week to find the place, and it was no wonder that the American army hadn't discovered it.

Tanner and Lena were in the second jeep along with the Czech whose name was Vaclov. He was only forty years old but looked eighty. He said he'd been a watchmaker before the Nazis had imprisoned him and made him a slave laborer. His crime was being a communist. He had a wife and two children and hadn't heard from them since being arrested. When he began talking about them, he started to cry. Lena tried to comfort him but wasn't successful.

Sergeant Hill was in the first jeep. Behind them in a short column of trucks and jeeps was a full platoon of infantry. It should be more than enough to overwhelm a handful of Volkssturm. If their calculations were off and there were too many more Germans, they were screwed.

The closer they got to the factory site, the more agitated the former inmate became. Lena kept talking to him and calming him.

She tugged on Tanner's arm. "He says it's just over this hill."

The column halted and all but a squad left behind to guard the vehicles began to move up the hill. "Now you can stay behind," Tanner told Lena.

"No," she said and continued on. Damn it, he thought.

From over the hill they could see the factory. It was really little more than a very large wooden barn. What gave it away was the barbed wire enclosing it and the guard towers and machine guns looking down and inwards. They were clearly intended to keep people in, rather than keeping intruders out. Tanner was puzzled. The towers were empty and the main gate looked like it was ajar. Jesus, he thought, had they gotten there too late?

A side door on the building opened and a couple of men came out. They looked up into the sky as if it was something unfamiliar. They were wearing prison garb and looked as bad as Vaclov. A few more followed and Tanner was surprised to see that a couple of them were carrying rifles.

"Miss Bobekova, Lena, any idea what has just happened?"

She started laughing and crying. "I think the inmates have taken over the prison."

She called out to them in Czech and then in French. A prisoner responded in French. "He wants us to show ourselves."

"Nuts," said Tanner. "It could be an ambush."

The former inmate, Vaclov, stood and walked slowly towards the compound. He kept his hands in the air while he yelled at them.

Once more, Lena interpreted. "He's telling him who he is and that he's with a bunch of Americans. They want to see an American to believe him."

Tanner took a deep breath. "I think this is where I earn my pay."

He slung his rifle over his shoulder and walked with Vaclov to the gate. He became aware that Lena was a few paces behind him. More inmates had emerged and they had no weapons. They looked at him in disbelief as if he were something from another planet. Vaclov was recognized and they peppered him with questions.

An older man came out. He was leaning on a cane and appeared to be their leader. "So, you do not speak Czech," he said in German. "What the hell, who does in this bitch of a world?" he said sarcastically. He told his people to lay down their weapons, which they did. With that, several dozen American soldiers came out of hiding and took charge of the inmates who were now elated by their deliverance. They had begun hugging each other and sobbing. Surprised American soldiers were hugged and kissed as well. They asked so many questions in Czech that Lena was overwhelmed. Those who spoke French and German got quicker answers. To their astonishment, a couple of inmates spoke English.

Tanner saw Lena moving around and talking to the inmates.

"Where are the guards?" he asked.

The man on the cane laughed harshly. "In the back and in a ditch, which is more than they deserve. When they heard that Hitler was dead, they got drunk. They were very easy to confuse and overwhelm. And now they are all dead. And I don't care if they were elderly Volkssturm. They were going to follow orders and butcher us as soon as they worked up the courage the liquor was giving them. I only regret that the piece of shit Nazi who ran this place managed to escape."

Tanner didn't care if the warden had escaped. He had a bunch of liberated prisoners to get back to the camp. Sergeant Hill was doing a superb job of getting people ready to go back to the base. Hill also reported that he'd been shown the guards' bodies. They had been pounded and stomped to pulp. They would not take the time to bury them.

American soldiers and liberated slaves gathered about the vehicles. It would be crowded with all the inmates, but they'd manage. It had been a good day, Tanner thought. But where was Lena?

He found her sitting on a fallen tree. He wanted to tell her that she should be helping to get the inmates moving, but quickly changed his mind. She had her head in her hands and was sobbing bitterly. He sat down beside her. "Tell me," he said gently.

"My father," she said. "They came one night and took my father and it wasn't the Nazis. They were Czechs who sympathized and collaborated with them. They never gave a reason why and I never heard from him again. I've always hoped he survived and was in a place like this where I could come and rescue him. When I heard there were Czechs here I just hoped and prayed, and it's been a long time since I prayed. I always hoped but I'd forgotten how to pray." Her body convulsed. "Damn the Nazis. Damn them."

Tanner took a deep breath and sighed. There were no words. He put his hand over hers and let her continue to cry. Finally, she shook her head. "Enough. We should get these people to a hospital."

Ernie Janek decided that getting Winnie Tyler out on the boat again would be good therapy. They were now working close together and he could tell that she was withdrawn and haunted. The beating she'd taken from the Nazi, Hahn, had deeply affected her and it was more than physical. She looked frightened, and sudden noises startled her more than they should.

She hadn't changed into her swimsuit. Instead she wore slacks and a long-sleeved blouse. She said the bruises were too ugly. She didn't want him to see them, and she didn't want to look on them and be reminded of her ordeal. He disagreed but kept quiet. From what he could see, the marks were going away but it would be a long while before they faded entirely. He was afraid it would take even longer before they faded from her mind.

"I'm stupid," she said after lying on the deck and soaking up the sun for a while. "I guess I knew that danger was always present, but it was always in the background and something that happened to somebody else. Now I know better and I'm not too sure I like it and I don't know what to do about it."

Ernie sat down beside her. "Everybody goes into

battle thinking they're invincible. I know I sure did. Even after a couple of my buddies got killed, shot down by the Germans, I still felt it wouldn't happen to me. Getting my butt shot down was my big epiphany. First, the canopy stuck for a few seconds, so I was afraid that I wouldn't be able to get out of the plane. Then I prayed that my chute would open and when it did I whimpered like a baby when I landed and saw men with guns staring at me. I really thought I was going to die. Now I know it can happen to me. It can happen to anyone."

"And to me," she said softly. She rolled onto her elbow and looked over his shoulder. "Am I seeing things or is that a Swiss patrol boat headed towards us?"

It was and it came directly alongside. A grim-faced young ensign hopped on board. He was armed with a pistol holstered at his waist and two other crewmen had German-made submachine guns. He wasn't certain, but they looked like MP34s. Since they weren't pointed at him, it wasn't important. True to the rules of neutrality, neither he nor Winnie was armed.

"Papers," the ensign said in English and in a firm voice.

"Say please," snapped Ernie.

"What?"

"I said say please. We are diplomats and you are supposed to treat us with courtesy and respect. Therefore, you should have said please," Ernie said as he handed over his and Winnie's passports. The man glared at him and muttered please while the two crewmen looked puzzled. Apparently they did not understand English.

The ensign looked over their papers and handed them back. "You do not look like diplomats."

"And some of those Nazi thugs you permit to walk around Arbon do? Please do not insult me."

"The Germans across the water, the ones you are pretending to not look at, have informed my country that they are annoyed by your continued presence. For some reason they think they are being spied on."

"Then tell them to go away," Ernie said. "We have as much right to be on this lake as they do. Let them come out in an unarmed little boat and maybe we'll drink some schnapps together. We could even toast the fact that Hitler is rotting in hell."

The ensign smiled tightly. "I would drink to that, although some of my countrymen would not. However, I do have my orders and they were to check you out. Having done that to my satisfaction, I will leave you to your sunbathing or fishing or whatever you're pretending to be doing. I would warn you, however, that Germanica is now an armed camp filled with thousands of very nervous German soldiers. If someone should get in his mind to stop you from watching them, they have cannon that can easily reach this little boat."

"Point taken, Ensign. When we're through we'll head back and stick much closer to the Swiss shore."

"Then let me also remind you that the Germans are even more nervous than usual since some American units have made it to the northern shore of Lake Constance. While you might have diplomatic immunity, the Germans can't see that and might think you are scouting them for an invasion."

With that, the ensign stepped back on his own boat and went his way.

"That was interesting," Winnie said after the patrol boat had departed. She ducked into the cabin and emerged in her swimsuit. "If the Germans are watching through their good Zeiss telescopes, they can see what they did to me."

"You look great, Winnie, and I mean that." He had not seen all of the bruises on her body, but even he could tell that they were healing. Still, she had taken one hell of a pounding. This Hahn son of a bitch hadn't missed too much while he was kicking and punching her. It was a wonder that she had been able to walk, much less wait a night in German territory for him to show up and save her. Jesus.

She dived into the water and swam for a few strokes before climbing out. The water glistening on her body made her look like a goddess. "You know what they say, Ernie? That which doesn't kill you makes you stronger. I can't recall who said it, but I think it might have been a German. Let's go back and you can buy me dinner while I quit feeling sorry for myself."

This time George Schafer and Bud Sibre were part of a much larger force of American fighters and bombers flying over what the United States insisted was Germany, not what the State Department referred to as the pirate state of Germanica. Several dozen fighters were escorting an equal number of American bombers. There was little concern regarding the Luftwaffe. The German air forces had been almost totally destroyed. The real danger to the planes would come from the countless antiaircraft guns that covered the Brenner Pass and other parts of Germany's Alpine Redoubt.

"Hey, Bud, try not to lose another plane."

"Go to hell, Georgie."

Bud had managed to nurse his wounded P51 until he

was less than ten miles from their airfield. He'd bailed out and landed in a farmer's field. The farmer and his wife had confronted him with a pitchfork and an ax. He had returned the favor by covering them with his .45 caliber pistol. The standoff had continued for about two hours until a truck with American soldiers in it showed up. The farmer and his wife had then become cordial and pro-American, professing that they had only tolerated Hitler because it was necessary to survive.

Bullshit, Bud thought.

At any rate, he'd been driven back to his base where he'd been subjected to some serious questioning. The fact that so many well-hidden guns were in the area was a problem. The German 88mm antiaircraft could hit high-flying bombers while the high-flying bombers could not hit small targets with precision unless they flew much lower. Flying lower, however, could prove fatal.

He'd been given a new plane with instructions that he was to take better care of this one. He'd endured too much ribbing from his so-called friends, although he understood that they were glad he'd made it.

This bombing run would involve no bombs. To the disgust of most of the pilots, they were to escort the bombers who would drop tons of *leaflets* on suspected German positions. The Allied command had even informed the Germans that this would be a paper run and not a bombing run. It was hoped that this would keep their superb 88s from killing them. The fighters were along to keep the Germans honest. Germans honest? They'd all laughed at that.

As they approached the scenic resort town of Innsbruck, bomb bay doors opened and a flood of papers fell out, falling downward like millions of white feathers, or snowflakes.

"Wow," said George. "That'll show the Krauts we're serious about ending this war."

"I am just stupendously impressed," Bud said sarcastically. "It just kind of makes me want to surrender myself. With all that paper, they must know how desperate we are to go home."

In the background, other pilots were making similar comments. They did not like endangering themselves in a propaganda run of dubious merit. Normally, their squadron leaders would be carping at them to shut up the idle chatter, but even they were silent. Let the troops bitch all they want. The next time it might not be so easy.

Leaflets covered the ground several sheets thick in some places. Wolfgang Hummel and Martin Schubert clambered out of their two man foxhole and ran towards a pile of papers. They scooped them up with both hands and ran back to their dugout and then returned for more.

"What the devil are you doing?" screamed Lieutenant Pfister. "If the Gestapo sees you reading that American propaganda, you'll get a bullet in the back of the head."

"They're probably picking up their own," laughed Schubert. "Just feel how soft this is."

The lieutenant grabbed a couple of sheets and squeezed. "By God, you're right."

"Not even the Gestapo can complain if we wipe our asses with American reading material," added Hummel. "Let's face it, Lieutenant, Germany has been short of so many things and toilet paper has been one of them. My ass is raw from using whatever sandpaper they send us or whatever we can find."

"Good point," said Pfister as he reached for some himself. "If anybody asks, tell them that I gave you orders to keep the area clean and to keep this sick propaganda from contaminating younger soldiers."

The men returned to their little fort where they divided the paper into two scrupulously equal piles. How much each man used each time would be up to him. They jokingly reminded each other to wipe with the inked side out so it wouldn't run. When they were done, they sat down and read the sheets of paper.

Hummel spoke first. "This one says we'll get plenty of good food, clothing, and shelter, and we'll be sent back to our families within a few weeks. Do you believe it?"

"The Americans always have enough food, more than enough if you ask me. So yes, I believe we'll get better food than we're getting now. Of course," he laughed harshly, "I'm not too sure how it could get any worse."

"But what about getting us back to our families?" asked Hummel. He could not keep a sense of longing from his voice. "That's the problem, isn't it? We have no idea where our families are or even if they're still alive. We may never see our families again. The cities have been destroyed and the roads are no longer there. How would we even make the trip?"

Schubert agreed. "True, but how much chance of finding out do we have while we're sitting on our asses in a dirty hole in what used to be Austria?"

"Then we will continue to try to surrender without

getting shot by either the Americans or some Nazi fanatic like Pfister."

Schubert shook his head. "I'm beginning to wonder about Pfister. He has to make a lot of Nazi noises because he's an officer, but I wonder just how sincere and devout he is."

"Are you confident enough to let him help us try to surrender?"

"Hell no," exclaimed Schubert. "I think it's more likely that we'll have to kill him than it is that he will help us."

"A shame," said Hummel, "but we're much more important than he is."

There was more than one version of the leaflets. A second one was titled "Are These Your Leaders?" and showed photos of various high-ranking Nazis either dead or in captivity. They laughed at the picture of Goering in a chair with an American MP beside him. "I wonder if he knew where he was?" laughed Hummel. Goering's problems with drugs and alcohol were common knowledge. Additional photos showed Admirals Doenitz and Raeder and Field Marshals Jodl and Keitel. The most shocking photo was of a very dead Heinrich Himmler.

"But no pictures of the Fuhrer's body," said Schubert. He spoke softly. Even in a foxhole he did not want to be overheard. "Does that mean he might not be truly dead or is it that no one would recognize his body?"

Hummel shook his head. "Once upon a time I worshipped the ground he walked on. Now I don't know. And I don't think it matters if he is alive or not. Germany has been well and truly defeated, and I just want to get out of here and go home."

"Wolfgang, don't you wonder how many others feel like we do?"

"Are you thinking of planning a mutiny, then go someplace else. I trust you and you trust me, but we can't possibly talk to anyone else about our feelings. The SS or the Gestapo would be on to us in an instant."

SS Colonel Hahn had been unable to discover any Jews in Germanica. Indeed, as he told Goebbels, he would have been astounded to find any. "Any Jew fortunate to remain alive in Germany and with even a fraction of a brain would have headed across the Swiss border and sanctuary."

"But the Swiss did not always admit Jews," said Goebbels. "Although I think they would have in this instance. Once again the Swiss are caught between two powers. If they toady to us and turn back or return Jews, then the Americans will be outraged. Open up their borders and we will be angry. Frankly, I would let them take any Jew who wants to leave. After all we've done to chase them and capture them, there just can't be that many Hebrews still remaining within a hundred miles of Germanica."

"I totally agree, sir, which is why I am focusing on this kind of danger to the new Reich," he said as he handed over several sheets of paper. "Our soldiers are being bombarded, literally, with this kind of filth. American planes fly overhead with impunity and drop these pieces of propaganda on our soldiers."

Goebbels examined them carefully. "As propaganda minister, I must admit that they could be fairly effective. Has there been any indication that the men are reading these?"

Hahn laughed and told him that many soldiers were using them as toilet paper, which Goebbels thought was hilarious. "Perhaps, Colonel, we should issue toilet paper with the pictures of Truman, Stalin, and Churchill on them. But first, of course, we have to start production of toilet paper. It is just one item in the very long list of things that are either in short supply or not available at all. More important is whether or not any of our soldiers are taking these inducements to surrender seriously."

"Indeed, Minister, which is why I wish authorization to suspend any searches for Jews in the Redoubt area. If there are any left, and I doubt that there are more than a handful remaining, I believe they should be ignored and our efforts focused on searching out malcontents in the army."

Goebbels stood and paced his office. Once again he was annoyed that it was so small. He made a mental note to get Speer's people to create something more suitable for the head of the state of Germanica.

"Hahn, you are absolutely correct. Instead of searching for phantom Jews, we must totally and ruthlessly suppress any signs of discontent. Our situation here is very fragile and I am well aware that most of our army does not consist of people who would die for us. Therefore, you must show *no* mercy. Don't let anything distract you from that goal, not even your wish to punish the spy who escaped from you in Bregenz."

Hahn winced. "I didn't know that you were aware of that little incident."

Goebbels could not help but smile. "I believe just about everyone in Germanica has heard about it, Colonel."

Hahn smiled tightly. This would be all the more reason to make the little bitch suffer.

"Minister, I do anticipate soldiers either trying to surrender to the Americans or trying to cross the border into Switzerland. I request permission to greatly strengthen the border fence and send some small boats of our own out on the lake to stop soldiers from either trying to get to Switzerland or to the Americans who are also on the lake."

"Do it. And make sure our ships are armed and that the crews have permission to shoot to kill."

Since shooting that sick old Jew, Werewolf Hans Gruber hadn't had the opportunity to kill anyone. He didn't even like to think of that Jew with his brains splattered all over the floor of the cave. What he had done sickened him. He understood what the SS officer who was now a brigadier general was trying to do. He'd been trying to toughen young Hans Gruber and mold him into the kind of fighting man who would bring pride to the Werewolves. The more he thought about it, the more Gruber still didn't like killing the man even though he had been a Jew. He was proud to be a German soldier and even prouder to be a Werewolf, but he wanted to kill real enemies, not sickly scrawny kikes. His parents were proud that he was a Nazi but he wondered if they would have approved of the murder—and that's exactly what it was, a murder. He wanted to go after the Reich's real enemies, the Americans.

One of his problems was that he just wasn't a very good shot. He'd had several chances but none had panned out. He'd twice fired at Yanks and missed. For his troubles he'd had to run for his life. Now he was in a clump of small trees near a road the Americans frequently used. He wanted to find a solitary vehicle, and preferably one with only a driver and no passengers. He wanted to fight for the Reich but he was not suicidal. He would die if he had to, he thought nobly, but he didn't want to rush things.

Gruber heard vehicles moving down the road. He would not attempt a kill. There were doubtless too many Americans to do so safely. Still, he wanted to take a peek. He had made a wise decision. At least a dozen trucks were headed towards him and they were filled with soldiers.

He had to pee. One of the less glamorous sides of being a Werewolf was finding a place to relieve one's self. He stepped a few paces deeper into the woods and laid his Mauser against a tree. He opened his fly and, with a contented sigh, solved his problem.

Suddenly it was dark and he was on the ground. There was a bag or something on his head. He couldn't see and he could only breathe dust. He felt helpless and had wet himself. Strong arms pinned his hands behind his back and he was tied up. The bag on his head was quickly replaced by a blindfold. He felt himself being thrown into the back of what he assumed was an American jeep and felt the jeep driven down a road. He had been captured. He was a prisoner of war and no longer a Werewolf. Hans Gruber was ashamed. He had been an utter failure as a warrior for the Reich. His only kill had been that old Jew and he now deeply regretted that.

Worse, he heard people laughing, laughing at him.

★   ★   ★

Neither Bud nor George liked hospitals and couldn't think of anyone who did. Part of it was the medicinal smell and part was the sight of people in distress. They hated the apparent impersonality of hospitals but knew it had to be.

This evening, however, they had to go. Angelo Morelli was in there and he was one of them. He was a young lieutenant who'd only been in their unit for a couple of weeks before getting badly wounded. They'd had a couple of beers to strengthen their resolve, but it hadn't worked very well and the medicinal smell almost made them nauseous.

Morelli had landed his plane early that morning, if you could call what happened a landing. He'd radioed that he was in trouble. His landing gear wasn't functioning and there was a fire in the cockpit. He'd been hit by some flak. When he was told to get out he said that he couldn't get the canopy to move. Bud and George had listened in horror as he got closer and closer to the ground. The fire spread and his last few seconds were spent screaming that he was burning, burning and howling for help and for his mother.

In what was either superb piloting or dumb luck, he'd landed the plane and it had skidded down the runway, finally coming to a stop only a short way from the emergency vehicles that were trying desperately to catch him. By the time they got to him, the screaming had stopped but precious seconds were lost trying to pry open the canopy. When they finally succeeded, they used extinguishers, and got Morelli out. Bud and George were close enough to see that his flight suit was smoldering.

Later they got word that he was alive and in a

hospital only a few miles from where they were based. They borrowed a jeep and drove to the collection of tents that housed the facility.

Bud glared at the middle-aged nurse who was assigned to guide them. "How come our boys are in tents while the krauts are in real hospitals?"

The nurse was not fazed. "Because there are so damn many injured, both civilian and military, that no amount of so-called real hospitals exist that can hold everyone. Actually, we are under capacity right now since there is not that much real fighting going on. Don't worry, we're taking good care of your friend, at least as good as we can possibly do under the circumstances."

"What are you saying?" asked Bud.

"I'm saying that he was terribly, horribly burned. So badly so that it's a miracle of sorts that he's still alive."

"Is he going to make it?" George asked.

She gazed at them firmly but with compassion. "It is highly unlikely that he will survive the night. And even if he should survive and begin to recover, he may not wish to live."

The comment stunned them. If you were hurt and got to a hospital, you got well, didn't you? Now they knew better. She led them down rows of cots to a separate section. Many were empty but enough held casualties who were swathed in bandages. It was unnerving the way that they followed the two pilots with their eyes. Even more unnerving was the fact that some of the wounded had their eyes covered. They couldn't help but wonder if the men were blind.

"This is where we put the burn patients. Lieutenant Morelli is the first one who is a pilot. Most pilots don't survive what he's gone through. He gets his own area, not only for privacy but so that his screams don't terrify the others."

Bud thought that he would again be ill. "Tell us what to expect."

"Have you seen anybody who'd been burned to death?" They nodded. They had seen violent death. She continued, "In many cases the body looks like a very large overcooked steak or roast. Well, that's what he looks like. The only difference is that he is still alive. His feet are gone and he might have a couple of fingers left. When the nerve endings in his body try to repair themselves his pain will be even more intolerable than it is right now. He is heavily sedated, but the pain still gets through after a while. If we give him too much, it might kill him, although that might not be a bad thing. His eyes are intact, but much of his face simply doesn't exist. Now, do you still want to see him?"

"Can he hear us?" Bud asked.

"We doubt it, but don't take a chance and talk about his condition. And don't even think of touching him."

They didn't. They approached the thing on the bed. They had never seen a mummy before and now wished they hadn't. The rise and fall of Morelli's chest was the only indication that he was alive.

They leaned over him and told them who they were and that they were so glad he'd made it. They said that others would be visiting him as well and that he should stay tough. They added that the government was going to bill him for ruining the plane, but not even that got a rise out of him.

They left, but not before thanking the nurse who

had turned away and was sobbing. "What would happen if he got far too much morphine?" George asked.

She smiled knowingly. "He would go to sleep peacefully and never wake up. He would never have to go through the unendurable agonies that would be his future."

The two pilots shook her hand and went back to the officers club where they ordered more beers for themselves. Nobody joined them. It was obvious that they wanted to be alone.

"I guess there's no good way to die," said Bud. "The life of a pilot is glamorous until you get shot out of the sky or burned like Morelli. Of course we could have joined the bloody infantry and run the risk of being shot, bayonetted, or blown to atoms by artillery or by pilots just like us."

George agreed. "Of course, we could have gotten into the navy but their pilots run the same risks as we do. And our base here is not likely to sink. Did you ever wonder how many sailors lived for how long in the bowels of the *Arizona* or the *Oklahoma* until their oxygen ran out? How many ships do you think went down with living crewmen screaming for help they were never going to get?"

Bud lit up a cigarette. "They say these'll kill you too. I guess there's no real good way to die, just some that are worse than others. What's the old joke? Oh yeah, I want to die of a heart attack while getting laid at a hundred and ten. Only problem is, nobody wants to die. So what do we do?"

George smiled grimly. "I suggest we have another drink."

CHAPTER 10

STAFF SERGEANT BILLY HILL HALF LIFTED AND HALF dragged the trembling and writhing young Nazi into a windowless room and seated him on an uncomfortable chair. He was tied to the arms of the chair but Hill did remove the blindfold.

"How long do you want me to keep him like that, Captain?" Hill asked after leaving the room and closing the door behind him.

Tanner thought for a moment. "Maybe until after I get done with a few things. Maybe I'll go to lunch. That ought to be enough to get him thinking. According to his papers, he's fourteen and lived in Stuttgart. He may think he's tough, but I'll bet he's scared shitless. My bet is that he'll tell us everything we want to know about the Werewolves without much prompting."

Hill grinned. "Sir, you telling me I can't pull out his toenails?"

"Not without first getting his mother's permission."

An hour later, Tanner and Cullen entered the room and sat across the table from Gruber. Hill stood behind him. At a signal, Hill yanked Gruber's blindfold off. Gruber gasped and blinked in the sudden light. He was wide-eyed and looked around in growing desperation. The two American officers were seated in higher chairs and looking down on him, which was intimidating.

Tanner spoke first. "Hans Gruber, you are a Nazi war criminal and you will either be shot or sent to a Russian prison camp."

"I'm a soldier," Gruber blurted. "I'm not a war criminal. And you can't give me to the Russians."

Cullen moved beside the boy. "First of all, Gruber, you were not in anything resembling a uniform, which means you are a terrorist, a *franc-tireur*. German soldiers shoot people like that without even a trial. You are nothing more than a bandit or an assassin and you will be treated as such."

Hans Gruber looked frightened. "I *did* have a uniform. I wore an armband. They said it would be sufficient if I was caught."

Cullen waved a piece of cloth in his face. "You mean this shitty little rag? This is not a uniform and besides, I never saw it." With that he threw it into a wastebasket and Gruber moaned.

Tanner laughed harshly. "Do you like Jews, Gruber? Of course you don't. Jews are the scum of the earth. They are pigs who don't eat pork. Your dead Hitler said that Jews weren't even human and you believed him. You were told that Jews cheat real Germans and that they murdered Christ, weren't you? How many Jews did you beat up? How many did you kill?"

Gruber gasped at the last question. Tanner and the others caught it. "So you have killed Jews. How wonderful. Did they fight you or did you just shoot them in the back?"

Gruber had begun to sob. "It was just one and I had to do it. General Hahn made me. He said I had to do it to prove I was a real Nazi. Besides, the Jew was dying."

Tanner suppressed a shudder. "I'm sure you did, but before we send you to the Reds, the U.S. Army has a special job for you."

He slid a number of eight-by-ten photos across the table. Gruber's hands were untied so he could pick them up. The photos showed men in German uniforms handling mangled and half-decayed corpses. Some of the men handling the bodies wore uniforms with SS insignia.

When Gruber tried to look away, Tanner pushed the pictures into his face. "Do you remember the Nazi joke that the only good Jew is a dead Jew? Well, these were taken at Dachau and most of them are good dead Jews. The German prisoners you see are going to spend the next few months digging up dead Jews, some very long-dead Jews whose rotting flesh stinks to high heaven. They will be identifying them and then burying them with respect. When we leave here and before you go to the Reds, that is what you will be doing. And you will be working for other Jews who will beat you if you slack off. Does the thought of handling dead Jews make you happy?"

"No," Gruber gasped.

"Rachel, come in," Tanner ordered.

A young woman in a nondescript uniform with a white star of David on an armband entered and stared coldly at Gruber. "Is this the little shit who's going to be helping us? Herr Gruber, I'm with the Palmach, the Jewish Army, and we're going to make you work with dead Jews, eat with dead Jews and sleep with dead Jews. You will forever stink of dead Jews. And do you know why?" She rolled up her sleeve and showed him the numbers tattooed on her arm. "I spent a year in a death camp watching Germans kill my people, and now it's my turn. I managed to survive but you will not. You are going to suffer for being a Nazi, you stinking little shit."

The woman glared at him. "Have you ever had a woman, ever had sex with something other than your left hand?" When Gruber whimpered and shook his head, she laughed. "And I'll bet you're not circumcised either. Well, you will be when we get our hands on you and you can bet that your virginity will last forever. You can't get up what you no longer have."

Now Gruber was sobbing openly. "Please don't. What can I do? Please don't let that happen to me? I'll tell you anything. I just want to go home."

"How many Werewolves are there?" Tanner asked.

"There were supposed to be fifty, but a lot of them have deserted. Now there can't be more than twenty and General Red Star is angry."

Tanner was puzzled. "Who or what is General Red Star?"

Gruber sensed an opening. "If I tell you, will you protect me?"

"Talk and keep talking."

"His name is SS General Alfonse Hahn and we call him General Red Star because he has a birthmark like a red star on his cheek."

Tanner drew in his breath. Could this possibly be

the man who had murdered Tucker and Peters so many eternities ago? It had to be. "Where is this General Hahn?"

Gruber was looking hopeful, like a kid who thought he had just passed a surprise test. "He's deep inside the Redoubt, probably in Bregenz. They say he's an important aide to Minister Goebbels himself," he added proudly.

"I need fresh air," Tanner said and walked outside into the still-cold air. Cullen nodded. He would complete the interrogation. There wasn't that much more that a fourteen-year-old boy could tell them about the inner workings of the German Army.

Tanner saw Lena using a cloth she'd dipped into a bucket to wash her arm. "Will it come off?"

Lena smiled softly. "These numbers came from a pen and I wrote them lightly and they've almost completely disappeared. I've seen too many whose numbers were real tattoos and that represented horror. I've been very fortunate." She angrily threw the cloth into the. bucket. "I've never spoken like that to anyone, anytime, much less to a stupid child. And I never thought I would feel so good doing it. I don't know whether to hate myself or be proud."

"Be proud. You were very helpful in there. I thought you would want to help bring down the Nazis if you could."

"You're right. And please call on me again, and *again*, and *again* if I can help." She took up the cloth again and looked at her arm. The numbers were gone. "What are you going to do with that boy?"

Tanner noted that she had referred to him as a boy, not a Nazi murderer. "We're going to find him a

German uniform and send him off to be a prisoner of war. With a little luck, he'll be allowed to go home, if he has a home, in a year or so. As to the Jew he shot, he's going to have to live with that. Hopefully, the handful of other Werewolves out there will somehow get the same message."

"It sounds just. Incomplete and imperfect, but as good as it's going to be."

"Now let's change the subject to something a little more pleasant, Lena. Have you ever had the pleasure of eating in an army mess hall?" Ordinarily, she and the other foreign nationals working for the division either ate field rations where they worked or food was brought to them. It was highly unusual for a foreign worker to eat with the soldiers.

She laughed and he realized that she had a very nice laugh. "How's the food?"

"Generally pretty bad, but I'll bet it's better than what you and the other clerks have been getting."

"Sounds good. If that's an invitation, I accept."

Small world, thought Ernie. The two thugs who'd jumped him in Bern and whom he was afraid he'd killed were sitting in a café along the waterfront of Arbon. They were sipping beers and had a fine view of the lake and couldn't see him approaching from behind. Despite the apparent prohibition against private boats on the lake, a handful of white sailboats were enjoying the day. He wondered if Winnie would have liked going on one. It wasn't going to happen. Word had come from Allen Dulles that they were not to go out on the water again. Nor were they to venture too close to the now reinforced and sealed German border.

With three heavily armed countries now having access to Lake Constance and two of them at war with each other, the lake had just become very dangerous. Ernie sometimes wondered if he should again talk to Dulles about getting back to the air force and becoming a pilot again. The last time he'd brought up the subject, Dulles had calmly reminded him that he was doing an important job in Arbon by keeping tabs on the Nazis just across the border. He'd closed his comments by telling Ernie that the Luftwaffe was almost nonexistent; therefore, who would he fly against? He might not even get a plane. He might be stuck at some base on Iceland doing clerical work instead of intelligence and spying for the USA. Ernie had agreed.

Dulles had then suggested that if Ernie was serious about getting back into the war he could arrange for him to be sent to the Pacific. "I still couldn't guarantee you'd get a plane or, if you did, that there would be any Japs left to shoot at except those fools who want to kill themselves and others. I could, however, assure you of jungle rot, stifling heat, and boredom. Of course you would likely never see Winnie again."

A contrite Ernie said he would love to remain in Switzerland and with the OSS.

But nothing had been said about what to do if he saw Nazis in Arbon. Should he assume that they too had diplomatic immunity? If so, then Germany's diplomatic corps was going to hell. Still, he wondered what the two thugs were up to.

The Nazis got up and paid their bill. He could see that they didn't leave much of a tip. The new Reich must not pay very well. Ernie waited until they were well clear of the café and began to follow them. There weren't many people on the streets so he was careful not to be seen. When the two men turned down a side street, he picked up the pace. They might lead him to where they were staying and perhaps using as their own espionage headquarters.

He'd barely turned the corner when he went flying. He slid forward on his hands and knees. He tried to get up, but he got a kick in the ribs that knocked the wind out of him. He managed to see the two Germans standing above him, smiling. He couldn't get up. He was helpless as more kicks struck his chest, back, and head. I'm going to die here, he thought and his world spun. He could hear the Germans laughing.

Finally, one of them grabbed him by his now bloody shirt and yanked him to his knees. "You thought we were stupid, didn't you? You got us one time, but not a second."

With that, they began hitting him again. He could hear screams and shouts in the distance. One of the Germans swore and they let him drop to the pavement. One more time he tried to get up and failed. His world was spinning and he decided to let it.

Ernie awoke to find himself in his bed at the warehouse. He tried to get up but fell back. The pain in his chest was too much. He wondered if his ribs had been broken. He checked the rest of his body and everything was pretty much there, just a lot of it was swollen and painful. So how the hell had he gotten to his bed?

After several tries he did manage to sit up and swing his legs onto the floor. He realized that he was fully clothed and bloody. He heard footsteps and his OSS landlord, Sam Valenti, approached.

"Welcome back to the land of the living," he said. "How long?"

"Just a few hours. Some passersby heard the fight and the police came right away. It's been recorded as an attempted mugging, but nobody believes that. Dulles has been notified and he's not too happy."

"Is he mad at me or the Germans? The Germans, I hope."

"Both of you, I presume. Winnie's not too thrilled either. She was in earlier and left crying. Anyhow, this is for you," Valenti said as he handed over a package.

Ernie opened it gingerly. It hurt too much to stretch. Inside the package was a German Luger and two clips of ammunition. "Dulles said there's one clip already in the gun, so you should be set."

"I thought guns were illegal in Switzerland?" Ernie said.

"They are, so don't get caught with it."

"Ah, did Winnie say where she was going or when she would be back?"

"She'll be gone for a couple of days, pal. Dulles has her off to Bern as a courier. He said she'll have a gun too."

The last time Tanner had seen so many tanks was that terrible day in December when scores of German Panzers had erupted from their hiding places and overwhelmed the men of the outnumbered and outgunned 106th Infantry Division.

This time it was different. The tanks were American Shermans and he counted forty of them leading an infantry attack on German positions near the entry to the Brenner Pass. Accompanying them was about the same number of M3 halftracks carrying infantry. That was just what he could *see*. Plans called for three full divisions to attack the German lines with two more in reserve. They were positioned to exploit the expected breakthrough.

Bombers and fighters had worked over the area where the German defenses were supposed to be the strongest. A long and thunderous artillery bombardment had followed the planes and preceded the tanks. The ground had shaken and the locations where the Germans were presumed to be had been enveloped by smoke and fire. The force of the explosions could be felt where he was with the division's command.

"Pity the poor bastards," muttered Cullen.

"Ours or theirs?" asked Tanner.

"Anybody who had a mother," he answered.

No one was saying that the attack would be a cakewalk. The Germans were well dug in and well camouflaged. The 105th wasn't the most experienced division in the Seventh Army, far from it, but even the most inexperienced soldier knew that the Germans would be difficult to pry from their fortresses.

Hell erupted. Seemingly out of nowhere there were flashes of light and blasts of thunder as German guns opened fire on the tanks. The main German antitank weapon was the almost legendary 88mm antitank gun, which was capable of easily destroying an American Sherman, as it now began to prove. As they watched, two American tanks were struck and began to burn. One lone crewman emerged from a tank. A few seconds later a third tank was killed and then three more.

Occasionally, an American would manage to escape from the hell that was erupting inside a burning Sherman's hull, but not too often. Even then, a number of the soldiers were wounded or on fire. One poor GI had lost his foot and hopped frantically towards the rear. Tanner urged him on, but to no avail. He collapsed and lay still. A medic finally got to him, checked him over, and left him. Tanner felt sickened.

The halftracks were within range of the German guns and it was their turn to begin to die. Adding to the horror were well hidden machine guns that raked the lightly armored vehicles. Men tumbled from them and tried to advance. When the bullets struck them, they went to ground and stayed there.

"Son of a bitch!" yelled General Evans. "Where the hell are our planes?"

On cue, P47 and P51 fighters began to strafe where spotters on the ground told them the Germans were hiding. The German guns kept firing, with some of them shooting at the planes, forcing them to jink and juke. One was hit. It cartwheeled into the ground and exploded. More planes dive-bombed, this time with napalm. Fires billowed, killing any life beneath or nearby.

"Why the hell didn't we do that sooner?" asked Cullen.

"Probably against regulations," Tanner answered. "Let the infantry suffer before doing anything that makes sense." General Evans glared at him but did not disagree.

The attack was stalling. Even with the Germans pounded by planes and with searing flames from napalm leaping high, the American casualties were too many.

The armor was the first to give up. The tanks moved in reverse to keep their more heavily armored front facing enemy fire. It was a vain hope, as three more tanks exploded. The remaining Shermans then simply turned and raced for safety. More 88mm shells followed and the Germans increased their range. Shells began to fall in and around the area where Tanner and the others now lay on the ground and tried to make themselves very small.

The earth shook and they cowered before they realized their best chance to survive was to get out of sight and far enough away to be out of range of the German guns. "Damn it, I thought we were safe," said Cullen.

"The eighty-eights got a maximum range of nearly forty thousand feet and that's damn near eight miles," said Tanner. "If it can see us, it can kill us."

"Now you tell me," said Cullen as another shell shrieked overhead and smashed into the ground behind them.

General Evans had been quiet. All of the planning for the attack was down the drain. The area before the German lines was littered with smashed and burning vehicles and dead American soldiers. It was beginning to dawn on the American commanders that cracking through the Brenner Pass and connecting with Fifteenth Army Group soldiers fighting up from Italy was going to be a very tough and bloody proposition.

Schubert and Hummel had spent much of their day hiding and trying not to scream as American artillery shells pounded everything near them. Sometimes the concussions lifted them off the ground and sometimes they were deafened, if only temporarily. Debris rained down on the roof of their bunker like hail during a storm. They had heard that the Yanks had an overwhelming superiority in artillery and now they believed it. The German 88 might be a magnificent weapon but there were not enough of them. Worse, the Americans had artillery that was far larger than an 88-millimeter gun.

Earlier, American fighter-bombers had done their part, also proving that the Yanks ruled the skies. Luftwaffe? What Luftwaffe, they thought bitterly. Where the hell were the planes that fat Herman Goering had promised? Had he sold them all for drugs? And where was the Wehrmacht's vaunted armor? Where were the Panthers and Tigers that had savaged the armored formations of Russia and the United States? Why, they were gone, they answered themselves bitterly, destroyed by the Allies' overwhelming superiority in numbers. Now they didn't even care if Lieutenant Pfister heard their complaints.

It was almost a relief when the assaults from the skies ended and the American tanks began to rumble forward. They shifted so they could see the approaching Shermans. "Remember," said Hummel, "we don't shoot at the tanks."

"I'm not that stupid," Schubert said, annoyed, "or as dumb as you look. Or did you get hit on the head?"

Halftracks filled with soldiers were moving behind the tanks, but the two Germans dared not open fire, at least not yet. Expose their positions to the Shermans and their stubby 75mm guns would be fired right down their throats. They would wait their turn.

Finally, scores of carefully hidden 88mm guns opened fire, devastating the coming tanks. Some stopped dead in their tracks while others exploded in billows of flame. Americans in the following halftracks tumbled out and began to move towards the German lines.

"Our turn," said Hummel, almost laughing. It was a relief to be able to do something, to strike back at their tormentors. He began to fire short and well-aimed bursts at the Americans. Their MG42 made a sound like metal tearing when it was fired. Everyone hated the hideous noise the MG42 made, but Hummel and Schubert loved it. The magnificent weapon was keeping them alive.

Most German bullets missed their quickly moving targets, but many did not. American soldiers fell. Some lay still while others writhed on the ground. They were close enough to occasionally hear the cries and screams of the wounded.

Schubert kept feeding belts of ammunition. He too was grinning hugely as they hurt the Americans. The tanks were pulling back, leaving American infantry alone and exposed among the dead and burning tanks and their own dead and wounded. It was no time to show mercy. The man you allowed to live today might kill you tomorrow.

They had to pause as Schubert changed the almost red hot barrel. Regulations said they were to control the rate of fire and stick to short bursts so as to not get the barrel overheated, but people who wrote foolish regulations like that never had scores of American soldiers breathing down their necks.

"The hell with regulations," Hummel said as he helped his partner.

The gun was soon ready and it again spouted bullets. This time they did keep the bursts to short ones. There was no longer a large number of Americans moving towards them. Now they came in small groups of two or three, sometimes only one soldier got up and raced a few feet towards them. Hummel's aim was good as he picked off soldier after soldier and blew them away. Sometimes the Americans just fell like puppets whose strings had been cut, but sometimes they tried to crawl or run back to their own lines. Neither man was cruel. The wounded they let go back, but anyone who didn't look wounded they killed.

Suddenly, Hummel's eyes widened in horror. "Down," he screamed. Seconds later, a napalm bomb exploded uncomfortably close to their bunker. They were lucky. None of the searing flames washed over them, although they could feel the heat that nearly sucked the air out of their lungs. For a few seconds it was uncomfortably hot and they both wondered what was happening to anyone closer to the explosion than they were. They were being fried to a crisp, was what they both thought.

The bombing was over. American infantry had taken advantage of it to withdraw. The two machine-gunners saw no reason to advertise the fact that they had survived and thus draw attention from the American planes, so they settled down and waited.

Shortly after sunset, their wait ended. A runner from Lieutenant Pfister told them to close up and pull back as soon as it was dark enough to be safe. When they asked why, the young private shrugged and said that the officers were afraid that the battle, although clearly won by the Germans, had enabled the Americans to pinpoint the locations of too many of the German defenses. American artillery could commence again at any time, but most likely at first light.

...t Josef Goebbels and his cohorts are ...ape punishment. Goebbels in particular ...hang."

...now that the Russians are willing to help ...Marshall.

...urse they will help us. I may have just become ...nt, but I know that Stalin is a grasping, lying son ...ch. We will likely need him to invade Manchuria ...ewhere in the Pacific to help finish off the Japs, ...o not want him to attack this Germanica and take ...ore of Europe then he now has. I'm catching hell ...the Republicans in Congress because he's now ...ing in Poland and other countries and isn't very ...to leave anytime this century."

"Well sir, what do you suggest?"

Truman sagged. "Unless you or one of General Groves' scientists comes up with a miracle, we can drop an atomic bomb or two on Japan, but not in Germany. There we'll still have to slug it out with the Nazis."

Or, the president thought, we might have to *deal* with the Nazis.

"You look as bad as I did," Winnie said softly. She ...s smiling, but there was deep sadness in her eyes. ...e started to rise, but she pushed him back and ...ked his hair. "I leave you alone for just a little ...and you manage to get into such trouble. When ...ou going to grow up?"

...had to admit that she looked lovely, radiant. ...uises were almost all gone, or at least covered ...eup. She had been shocked and saddened by ...arance after Sam Valenti had let her into his

"Makes sense," said Schubert as the two men prepared to move out. "It's a shame since we definitely did win today. We shouldn't have to retreat after a victory."

"But what did we win," asked Hummel, "besides the right to withdraw farther into the mountains? Someday we'll wind up starving to death on some barren granite slope. As long as the Americans want to keep coming, we can never win."

Schubert couldn't help himself. He had to look around to see if anyone from the SS or Gestapo was listening in on them. No one was, of course. The only thing he could see in the fading light was the large numbers of craters left by countless bombs and shells. It was a stark and ugly moonscape, just like the pictures he'd seen on science fiction novels, only worse. Novels don't smell of burned and exploded flesh along with gasoline and anything else that would burn. They were thankful that the darkness did not allow them to clearly see the debris around them.

"We'll have to wait for an opportunity to give ourselves up." Schubert said.

"If we wait too long," Hummel said sadly, "we'll all be dead."

President Harry Truman looked at the report, shook his head glumly, and put it down on the table. "I thought we had won this war," he said. "Yet this rump part of Nazi Germany continues to hold out and sends thousands of our boys to either the hospital or the graveyard. And I don't care what some generals like to think, it was a defeat. General Marshall, about how much ground did we take?"

As usual, the Army's chief of staff was expressionless. "On average we gained about half a mile."

"Three divisions of infantry, reinforced by an armored division and an infantry division, tried to bull their way through the pass and made only half a mile. That might have been a major gain in the First War, but not this one. At this rate, Devers' armies will meet up with Clark's somewhere around summer of 1948. This first attack on the Brenner was not a victory, was not even a draw. We got our asses kicked."

Marshall did not disagree. The two men were in a small office adjacent to the Oval Office in the West Wing. Truman had recently decided that he liked to use it for small groups. A movie screen had been set up on one wall and a very nervous Army captain had just shown them the latest unedited films from Germany.

"What we have just watched should not be made public for at least fifty years." Truman said.

The debacle at the head of the Brenner had been filmed in glorious Technicolor. The flames were brilliant and bright, and the scenes showing the Shermans being blown up were dramatic and awful. Brave cameramen had gone in with the infantry and the graphic death scenes of American soldiers had shaken Truman to his core.

Marshall was not done. "I have other films for you to see, Mister President. They are from the last war and show the Austrians and the Italians in battle in the Alpine snows. It will give you some idea what we will face if the situation is not resolved before the next snows roll in."

"I will see them, General, just not today. I have

other problems. In just a[...] to meet Stalin and who[...] Great Britain in Pot[sdam...] the future of Europ[e...] that while this Alpine [...] this asinine creation call[ed...] nose at us?"

"Are you having second thoug[hts...] atomic bomb in Germany, sir?"

"I can't begin to think about using som[e...] hasn't even worked yet, and God help us if the[...] possibility that the Nazis have their *own* is true. Ev[en...] if it does work and we use the damn thing t[o blast...] a path through the Brenner, it's now very likely that residual radiation won't let us use that path. Damn it to hell. Now it looks even more than likely that Churchill will be replaced by that dullard, Attlee. God help us, but the situation in Europe looks bleak[...]

"And we still have Japan to defeat," added Marsh[all...] He was glad that the perpetually angry and vol[atile] Admiral Ernest King was not present. He woul[d have] taken the last comment as an insult to his n[avy and] exploded.

"But just like the Germans," Truman [said, "the] Japanese have been defeated but just wo[n't quit.] The Nazi hierarchy knows that they wil[l be...] put in front of a firing squad if there isn['t some...] solution that will allow them to esca[pe...] The same holds true with the Japane[se...] ruling council is a bunch of sadisti[c...] Hirohito is the worst. I know th[ey...] give in and let the four-eyed [...] damn throne, but I don't have to [...]

"Makes sense," said Schubert as the two men prepared to move out. "It's a shame since we definitely
did win today. We shouldn't have to retreat after a
victory."

"But what did we win," asked Hummel, "besides
the right to withdraw farther into the mountains?
Someday we'll wind up starving to death on some
barren granite slope. As long as the Americans want
to keep coming, we can never win."

Schubert couldn't help himself. He had to look
around to see if anyone from the SS or Gestapo was
listening in on them. No one was, of course. The
only thing he could see in the fading light was the
large numbers of craters left by countless bombs and
shells. It was a stark and ugly moonscape, just like
the pictures he'd seen on science fiction novels, only
worse. Novels don't smell of burned and exploded
flesh along with gasoline and anything else that would
burn. They were thankful that the darkness did not
allow them to clearly see the debris around them.

"We'll have to wait for an opportunity to give ourselves up." Schubert said.

"If we wait too long," Hummel said sadly, "we'll
all be dead."

President Harry Truman looked at the report,
shook his head glumly, and put it down on the table.
"I thought we had won this war," he said. "Yet this
rump part of Nazi Germany continues to hold out and
sends thousands of our boys to either the hospital or
the graveyard. And I don't care what some generals
like to think, it was a defeat. General Marshall, about
how much ground did we take?"

As usual, the Army's chief of staff was expressionless. "On average we gained about half a mile."

"Three divisions of infantry, reinforced by an armored division and an infantry division, tried to bull their way through the pass and made only half a mile. That might have been a major gain in the First War, but not this one. At this rate, Devers' armies will meet up with Clark's somewhere around summer of 1948. This first attack on the Brenner was not a victory, was not even a draw. We got our asses kicked."

Marshall did not disagree. The two men were in a small office adjacent to the Oval Office in the West Wing. Truman had recently decided that he liked to use it for small groups. A movie screen had been set up on one wall and a very nervous Army captain had just shown them the latest unedited films from Germany.

"What we have just watched should not be made public for at least fifty years." Truman said.

The debacle at the head of the Brenner had been filmed in glorious Technicolor. The flames were brilliant and bright, and the scenes showing the Shermans being blown up were dramatic and awful. Brave cameramen had gone in with the infantry and the graphic death scenes of American soldiers had shaken Truman to his core.

Marshall was not done. "I have other films for you to see, Mister President. They are from the last war and show the Austrians and the Italians in battle in the Alpine snows. It will give you some idea what we will face if the situation is not resolved before the next snows roll in."

"I will see them, General, just not today. I have

other problems. In just a few weeks I am supposed
to meet Stalin and whoever will be prime minister of
Great Britain in Potsdam, Germany. We will discuss
the future of Europe. How the hell can we discuss
that while this Alpine Redoubt still exists and while
this asinine creation called Germanica thumbs its
nose at us?"

"Are you having second thoughts about using the
atomic bomb in Germany, sir?"

"I can't begin to think about using something that
hasn't even worked yet, and God help us if the remote
possibility that the Nazis have their *own* is true. Even
if it does work and we use the damn thing to blast
a path through the Brenner, it's now very likely that
residual radiation won't let us use that path. Damn
it to hell. Now it looks even more than likely that
Churchill will be replaced by that dullard, Attlee.
God help us, but the situation in Europe looks bleak."

"And we still have Japan to defeat," added Marshall.
He was glad that the perpetually angry and volatile
Admiral Ernest King was not present. He would have
taken the last comment as an insult to his navy and
exploded.

"But just like the Germans," Truman said, "the
Japanese have been defeated but just won't admit it.
The Nazi hierarchy knows that they will hang or be
put in front of a firing squad if there isn't a diplomatic
solution that will allow them to escape punishment.
The same holds true with the Japanese. The Japanese
ruling council is a bunch of sadistic war criminals and
Hirohito is the worst. I know that we might have to
give in and let the four-eyed bastard remain on his
damn throne, but I don't have to like it. But there

is no way that Josef Goebbels and his cohorts are going to escape punishment. Goebbels in particular is going to hang."

"You know that the Russians are willing to help us," said Marshall.

"Of course they will help us. I may have just become president, but I know that Stalin is a grasping, lying son of a bitch. We will likely need him to invade Manchuria and elsewhere in the Pacific to help finish off the Japs, but I do not want him to attack this Germanica and take any more of Europe then he now has. I'm catching hell from the Republicans in Congress because he's now squatting in Poland and other countries and isn't very likely to leave anytime this century."

"Well sir, what do you suggest?"

Truman sagged. "Unless you or one of General Groves' scientists comes up with a miracle, we can drop an atomic bomb or two on Japan, but not in Germany. There we'll still have to slug it out with the Nazis."

Or, the president thought, we might have to *deal* with the Nazis.

"You look as bad as I did," Winnie said softly. She was smiling, but there was deep sadness in her eyes.

He started to rise, but she pushed him back and stroked his hair. "I leave you alone for just a little while and you manage to get into such trouble. When are you going to grow up?"

He had to admit that she looked lovely, radiant. The bruises were almost all gone, or at least covered by makeup. She had been shocked and saddened by his appearance after Sam Valenti had let her into his

he would have to jump. They teased him about having to jump like Sibre did and got an obscenity in return.

They had destroyed a number of Nazi tanks and word was that the tanks were irreplaceable. If they lost one plane it would still be a good day. If the pilot and plane got back safely, it would be a great day.

"I wonder how the intelligence guys found out about those tanks," Sibre mused.

"Maybe a little bird told them."

"A bird?"

Schafer couldn't help himself. He started giggling. "Yeah, a stool pigeon."

SS General Hahn was in a good mood. A sweep by some of his elite SS soldiers had resulted in the capture of four men who were not only planning to desert, but inciting others to desert as well. He watched as the men were interrogated. They were stubborn but they would soon break. Everyone did. Sometimes just the threat of torture would cause a man to collapse, while others had to endure some pain in order to prove to themselves and others that they'd done what they could. Hahn did not like to wait. Experience had taught him that sending currents of electricity from a car battery through prisoner's bodies via clamps attached to very sensitive parts of their bodies generally resulted in a quick reaction. His favorite places were the nipples and the genitals of both men and women. The anus was another excellent alternative.

Two of the four men were naked and strapped to chairs. They had already lost control of their bowels and bladders and were screaming and babbling inco-herently. In a very short while they would confess and implicate others. Those too would be interrogated and still others would be named. He knew that some of the prisoners would lie through their teeth to put a halt to the agony. Therefore, he had to be very judicious. As Field Marshal Schoerner had said, if soldiers keep ratting on other soldiers, soon there won't be an army left. Hahn had thought that the field marshal was kidding, but there was a distinct message. Don't arrest everyone.

As Hahn watched, the third man began to howl and then the fourth. It was a very nice serenade.

The would-be deserters were asked if they were ready to talk. Three of them said yes while the fourth shook his head. "More power," Hahn ordered and the juice was turned up. The man screamed like he was on fire, which, in a way, he was. His body spasmed and then stopped. His head hung low on his chest.

"Shit," said Hahn and signaled that the power should be cut off. A quick check proved what he'd suspected. The man had died. His heart had likely given out. Well, it had happened before and it would doubtless happen again. He had no way of knowing who could stand what level of agony before falling apart. It was a nuisance when it happened after all his good work.

He enjoyed torturing men, but he truly enjoyed making women howl in agony. Sadly, there were very few women in Germanica and none were part of the military. He hoped there would be other times.

When the remaining three men were finished spilling their guts, they would be hanged or garroted. By order of the field marshal, no bullets were to be used in executions. It was a grim reminder that their existence in the Alps was fragile.

On the positive side, the deaths of the four men meant that their food rations would not be squandered keeping traitors alive. The thought made his stomach grumble. He tried to remember the last time he had a full meal.

His aide, Captain Eppler, approached and saluted crisply. Hahn returned it and wondered if he could get the man a promotion. A general should have at least a major for an aide.

"What is it, Captain?"

"Sir, I believe a prodigal has returned."

"And what the devil do you mean by that?"

"Sir, the young Werewolf, Private Gruber, has returned from the Americans' clutches. He was wearing an American soldier's uniform and carrying an American rifle. He says he's fine but quite hungry."

Hahn paused and then laughed hugely. "I wonder just how the hell he managed to pull off that feat. Get him fed and into a decent German uniform. I will talk with him then."

CHAPTER 12

WHEN IT WAS DECIDED THAT OSS TEAMS WOULD try to sabotage the food shipments to Germanica, Winnie was the first to volunteer. She was also the first to be rejected.

"Your German and French are very good," Dulles said, "even excellent, but you could never pass for a local. Your American accent would give you away immediately. You would then fall into the clutches of the Gestapo who would wrench from you everything you know about us. Then they would kill you. I have had enough agents fall into enemy hands and be executed. They were brave and you are brave for asking, but accepting your offer would be the same as signing your death sentence. I will not permit useless deaths. I have another team coming here and they will arrive shortly."

Winnie moped for a while. She was disappointed that she couldn't go in harm's way, but she understood Dulles' rationale. Another part of her was relieved that she had been rejected. The idea of capture and torture followed by death was frightening. The incident in Bregenz where she'd been brutally beaten for no reason at all by an SS officer was still fresh in her mind. The physical scars were gone, but not the mental ones. Thank God, she thought, that she had Ernie to depend on.

Her spirits were buoyed when the new team arrived. It consisted of two very tall and athletic young men and a short and boyish-looking woman. "Marie!" Winnie screamed on seeing her, and the two women embraced.

"Obviously, you know each other," Ernie said with a grin.

"Absolutely. Marie was a junior and I was a senior in high school. She was an exchange student and we were good friends."

Marie was warm and friendly but did size Ernie up. "He'll do," she said. The two men were introduced as Sven and Hans and it was understood that those weren't their real names. Even Marie would have been using a different name if Winnie hadn't recognized her and blurted out her real one.

"How long will you be here in Arbon before you have to go and do whatever you're going to do?" Winnie asked.

"As long as is necessary. Mr. Dulles did not give us a precise schedule. As to what we are going to do, I understand it involves observing the movement of German supplies from Arbon to Bregenz and out to the troops in the field."

Ernie was puzzled. "No sabotage?"

"Not at this time, although the three of us could certainly accomplish it. I'm sure that we could be supplied with dynamite or nitroglycerine."

"How did they get you here?" Ernie asked.

Marie answered for the group. Apparently she was the spokesperson. Either that or the other two's English wasn't all that good. "We came in the back of a truck. We'd arrived by plane in Zurich two days ago."

"Are you going to be confined to this building or will you be allowed to go out?" Winnie asked.

Marie laughed. "Are you suggesting that we act like the schoolgirls we once were and go shopping in marvelous Arbon? I can't imagine that we'll find anything to match Wanamaker's in Philadelphia. Sorry, but I think we'll stay right here and out of sight until Dulles decides when he wants us to move out."

Winnie was a little chagrined. Of course they could not allow themselves to be seen by any of the Germans wandering Arbon. They could not risk being identified and followed. But it did feel good to have someone she'd actually known from her life as an ordinary person. She wondered if she could ever go back to an ordinary life. She knew that Ernie was thinking much along the same line. How did the old song go? Oh yes, how you gonna keep them down on the farm after they'd seen Paree? Well, Switzerland wasn't Gay Paree, but being part of the OSS was more thrilling and fulfilling than anything she'd done in her life.

Joseph Goebbels did not particularly like General Walter Warlimont. Goebbels acknowledged that Warlimont had worked marvels in creating everything that remained of the Third Reich at Bregenz and outlying areas. There was still the nagging feeling that Warlimont simply hadn't been caught in the July 20, 1944 plot to assassinate Adolf Hitler.

Goebbels slammed the papers down on his desk and spoke harshly. "What do you mean that German soldiers have contracted scurvy? Isn't that the illness that affects sailors?"

Warlimont was unfazed. Contrary to the rumors, he had been a devout supporter of Hitler and felt that Goebbels was a pale and second-rate imitation of his Fuhrer. "Scurvy will affect anyone who doesn't get enough Vitamin C. If unchecked, a patient will die. If Vitamin C can be located and given to a patient in sufficient quantities, the patient will recover, possibly fully. Right now we have several thousand soldiers suffering from the extremely painful and debilitating problem. If we cannot get enough Vitamin C to the men, the German Army will cease to exist."

The blunt answer subdued Goebbels. "Then what do you propose, General?"

Warlimont shrugged. "The answer is obvious, Minister. We must get some Vitamin C. There are vitamin tablets that can be manufactured and perhaps acquired from the Swiss. I very much doubt that we can get much in the way of fruits or vegetables, but apparently eating some meats will help. I suggest that the next shipment of foodstuffs from Switzerland include vitamin tablets and the right meats. We simply cannot have our soldiers existing on field rations for extensive periods of time."

Goebbels sat down and sagged. He had just received other news from Field Marshal Schoerner, who'd forwarded additionally unwelcome information from Generals Rendulic and von Vietinghoff. The gist of their problems was that ammunition and fuel were being expended at a rate faster than anticipated.

Soon, Goebbels thought glumly, what remained of the German Army would be both sick and impotent.

"Marshal Schoerner, what do you propose as a solution?"

"We have enough ammunition for one last major battle. Perhaps we should launch an all-out attack in an attempt to shock the Americans. Perhaps they will think we are stronger than we actually are and begin negotiations."

Goebbels was not convinced. "That sounds very much what the late Fuhrer hoped would be the results of the attack in the Ardennes. It was a failure and led to the collapse of the Western front. If your attack becomes a suicide attack, everything we have here will be destroyed."

"Minister, only the stupid and racially inferior Japanese commit suicide attacks. I do not propose anything resembling a kamikaze attack. I would like to hit the Americans hard and drive them back in a limited assault. Our goal would be to show that we cannot be taken easily. There is no possibility of driving them more than a few miles, but even that might shake them. Thanks to the Swiss, we can monitor civilian radio broadcasts and there are apparently growing numbers of civilian protests in the United States, even riots, over the continuation of the war with us. The American people want peace with Germany so they can concentrate on destroying Japan."

Goebbels leaned back in his chair. What Warlimont proposed made sense. He would have to ask if using the atomic bomb would be an appropriate weapon to support the attack or if it would be better to wait for an American offensive before considering its use.

★   ★   ★

Mildred Ruffino was hot and sweaty. Her several layers of clothing, including a heavy girdle, were clinging to her. The fifty-five-year-old grandmother, however, would not be deterred no matter how humid and sticky Washington D.C. was. She had a goal and that was to help bring home the boys home from Europe. She was not totally consumed by the need for peace. She understood fully that the nasty little Japs had attacked Pearl Harbor and needed to be punished severely. She further understood that it would cost additional lives. For Mildred and her family, some of the price had already been paid. One of her nephews was in a hospital in Honolulu getting over the fact that he'd lost much of his left foot on some awful place called Peleliu. Another neighbor had lost a son fighting in France and that was where she thought it should end. Hitler and Mussolini were dead and what was left of Nazi Germany was nothing more than a little corner of that nation. Some people were making noises saying that the country couldn't trust Joe Stalin, but that was nonsense. For years every American had been told by FDR that we could trust good old Uncle Joe, so who was this little piss-ant imitation of a president, Harry Truman, to tell her otherwise?

Why not just dig a ditch around the place called Germanica and let the Nazi inhabitants all starve to death if they didn't want to surrender? It would serve them right. It would also bring home her oldest son, who was in the 82nd Airborne Division and God only knew what plans the army had for him. Why the devil he had ever volunteered to be a paratrooper was beyond her. Mildred thanked the lord that one of her other sons was a sophomore in high school and too young to be drafted, while the oldest, Joey, had a bad foot that made him 4F. Of course, rules could be changed and they could start drafting infants if the army needed the manpower.

So here she was, marching around the White House along with a couple thousand other Americans, mainly women. They all carried signs urging Harry Truman to get them out of what they felt was the unnecessary German war. They'd enjoyed being interviewed and photographed by reporters but now the heat of the day was getting to them. Mildred congratulated herself on having had the common sense to bring a canteen filled with water and put it in her oversize purse. Still, she gave herself another hour before she would have to surrender to the oppressive weather. Already she'd had to share some of the water with one of her companions who looked red-faced and terrible. She didn't want to be told what she looked like.

"There he is," someone shrieked. Sure enough, there was Harry Truman and he was beginning one of his frequent walks. She had to give the little man credit. He knew that he was going to have to run the gauntlet of angry protesters but he wasn't going to let a little thing like that deter him. The protesters would follow him and dog him and shout at him to stop the war. Truman would wave and smile and continue walking at his usual brisk pace. As always a handful of younger reporters started to walk with him but soon gave up.

Mildred Ruffino snorted. She would not give up. She was made of sterner stuff. Still she wished she'd lost the twenty or thirty pounds she'd been planning to but never managed to. It would have made keeping up with Truman so much easier. She also wished she hadn't worn so much clothing, but standards dictated that she wear not only the damned girdle, but cotton stockings, a slip, and, of course, a bra.

After another mile, Mildred was gasping. Most of the other protesters had fallen back. She gave Truman credit for one more thing. He was in excellent shape.

She looked around and saw that she was alone save for a handful of Secret Service agents and one young reporter who was sweating like a hog. Truman was only a few feet away. He looked at her with some concern.

"Ma'am, you don't look well. Don't you think you should stop?"

Mildred was stunned. The President of the United States was actually talking to her. "I'll stop when you bring our boys home."

"And I promise you that I'll bring them home as soon as I can."

Mildred was feeling lightheaded. "Not good enough. Please bring them home now. Let the Nazis have that little corner of their world, and bring them home now."

Mildred was about to add something to this wonderful conversation that she was having with one of the most powerful men in the world when her vision turned red and the sidewalk rose up and hit her in the face. She felt hands turning her over and heard the sound of a siren in the distance and coming closer. She looked up and saw a very concerned Harry Truman looking down on her.

"Lie still and you'll be all right," the president said gently.

Mildred's world was spinning and she had the feeling that she was about to take flight like a bird. "No, I won't," were her last words.

★   ★   ★

"Do you recall Operation Cobra?" asked General Devers.

"Of course," said Ike. "It was an attempt to break out of Normandy and take the city of Caen." They were in Devers' Sixth Army Group headquarters in Strasbourg, France.

"And Cobra succeeded. Now I want to recreate it and start with a massive carpet bombing of German positions. Bradley used three thousand bombers to blast the Germans and I propose the same thing. And then I want to hit them with all the tanks and infantry I have, at least," he paused, "as much as can fit through the relatively narrow opening of the Brenner Pass."

Ike was solemn. "I recall that the massive and concentrated bombing, while effective, led to tragedy. So many planes dropped their bombs short and a large number of American troops, including General Leslie McNair, were killed and many others wounded. We can't have that again."

"Agreed. We can and must be more cautious and the planning must be more detailed and precise. There was a huge misunderstanding about the direction the planes would come from and that led to the disaster."

Both men knew it hadn't been a misunderstanding. The air force had disregarded orders to bomb north to south and had attacked east to west, thus putting their planes over the American lines for an extraordinary amount of time. During that time, the pattern of bomb dropping had crept back towards American lines while horrified GIs waited, unable to run or dig in. The air force did it that way because they were concerned about German planes and the possibility of dense antiaircraft fire shredding the bomber formations. German planes were no longer a threat, but antiaircraft fire still was. But AA could be heavy and come from any direction.

"Ike, I am very confident that we can break through the German defenses and split this Germanica animal in half. With Clark hitting them from the south and my men from the north, we can deal the Germans a decisively catastrophic blow that might just end the war."

Ike nodded. He would approve Devers' plans, but he would keep close tabs on them. There would be no surprises and the air force would be fully on board. He looked at Devers, who turned away. Ike had the feeling that the other general's presentation had smacked of desperation. Devers had lost weight and looked stressed. He'd been defeated in his first attempt to push through the Brenner, and neither he nor his career could stand a second loss. Damn it. Patch was going to relinquish the Seventh Army because of his health. Would he have to replace Devers as well?

Doctor Lennie Hagerman was still wearing scrubs when Tanner showed up after being requested. "I want to show you something," Hagerman said. "That last group of prisoners had some unusual problems and you might want to report it upward."

"Sure," said Tanner. He'd helped interview several of them and, aside from looking hungry and miserable, he hadn't noticed anything unusual. They were prisoners who'd been beaten down both physically and mentally.

Hagerman pulled out a folder with a number of photographs in it. "I know you're not a doctor, but try to figure out what's wrong with these people."

Tanner agreed that he was not a doctor but agreed to look anyhow. The photos were in color, which made the Germans look terrible. They were all staring at the camera with their mouths open and their teeth and gums exposed. "Okay," he said after a moment, "what am I looking for?"

"See how their gums are discolored? Take my word for it but there were sores all over their bodies."

"Jesus, please don't tell me it's something contagious like the plague. Something like that could wipe out the entire German army."

"Along with a few million other people," Hagerman added. "No, this is nothing that bad. These poor dumb Nazis are suffering from scurvy. Being a kind and gentle soul, I've prescribed vitamin C, which should solve their problems. When they go to a prison camp they'll be somebody else's problem. However, if too many Germans facing us get it, there will be large numbers of men too sick, too lethargic and in too much pain to do much of anything in the way of fighting."

Tanner thought of how Lena had been weakened when he'd first met her. He'd put it down to lack of food and not necessarily to incomplete diet. Perhaps she had been in the beginning stages of scurvy herself. Hagerman was right, however, this was something that had to be bumped upstairs and quickly. Out of curiosity, he would ask Lena if she'd ever suffered any of the symptoms.

After that he would try to find out when the army would make its inevitable next attack through the Brenner.

★　　★　　★

"Private Gruber, it is wonderful to see that you escaped from the clutches of the Americans."

Gruber grinned widely at the compliment from General Hahn, a man he worshipped almost as much as he had his late Fuhrer. "It wasn't all that difficult, General. They had a fool guarding me. I tricked him, hurt him, and then took his uniform and rifle."

Hahn rubbed his hands with glee. What a resourceful and violent boy young Gruber had turned out to be.

"And when you were in their clutches, what information did you give them?"

"I admit I told them everything I knew, which wasn't much at all. They already knew about the Werewolves, so I embellished everything I said. I told them there were hundreds of us and that we were well armed and trained. I begged to be saved and promised them everything if they wouldn't send me off to Russia."

Hahn nodded amiably. He had read the young man's detailed report and didn't doubt that Gruber had told the Americans everything that he knew. While there might have been some embellishment in telling of his escape, Hahn was confident that Gruber had been basically truthful. He also doubted that the Americans had believed everything Gruber had told them. The Americans were not fools, after all. They would know that a skinny fourteen-year-old wouldn't have access to anything important.

"What would you like to do now, Private Gruber?"

Gruber smiled. "I wish nothing more than to serve Germany."

"Excellent answer and you shall. It is an added bonus that you brought an American uniform. We can never have too many of those and, to be frank, they are in short supply. The rifle was a bonus as well. The uniform you brought will be given to an older and more senior soldier to use when infiltrating American positions."

Gruber was crestfallen. He had hoped to wear it.

Hahn reached out and fondly patted Gruber's shoulder. "I know what you are thinking, but, even though the American you took it from was a small man, he was still larger than you. The Americans would not hand out a uniform that was too large and ill-fitting. You were quite fortunate to make it through to us without getting caught and then hanged for hurting that guard. I do admit, Private Gruber, that carving a swastika in his forehead was a marvelous idea. And don't worry about being left out of any future Werewolf operations. There will be a special place for you. Who knows, we might even let you use the rifle you stole."

"Hey Tanner, who the hell is, or was, a Mildred Ruffino?" asked Cullen.

He had been reading the latest issue of *Stars and Stripes*, the newspaper printed for the men and women of the American army. The paper was editorially independent of the Army's hierarchy and frequently printed items that the higher-ups did not always want published. The paper's editors had gotten into trouble with a number of senior commanders including General George Patton who'd tried to have the newspaper shut down—only to be overruled by higher powers.

"Isn't she that lady who passed out and died in Harry Truman's arms?"

Cullen laughed. "If I found myself in Harry Truman's arms I'd pass out too. Yeah, I recall her now.

They're talking about peace marchers using her name as if she was some kind of damn martyr or saint. Hey, I guess she was sort of a martyr, wasn't she?"

The soldiers of the 105th had mixed emotions about the peace efforts. Yes, they wanted the war to end and they didn't much care if it was through a negotiated peace or the abject surrender of either or both Japan and Germany. But they knew they couldn't go home until the Germans gave up. And then it would likely be a brief stop while on their way to invade Japan. There was an uncomfortable feeling that well-meaning people like Mildred Ruffino were inadvertently encouraging the Germans to hang on, that the United States would grow genuinely war weary and give up. That could not be allowed to happen.

All of which meant that the Army was going to have to attack again. There had been a significant lull that was about to end. Ammunition and other supplies had been stockpiled. Destroyed tanks had been replaced and large numbers of replacements had arrived.

"Tanner, do you realize that the division is two thousand men understrength?"

"Yep. We've lost three thousand and only gotten one thousand to fill in. Worse, those replacements are very miserable specimens, both physically and mentally."

"And don't forget morally," Cullen added and Tanner agreed. There had been more and more incidents of soldiers finding ways to avoid combat without getting court-martialed for cowardice or for disobeying a direct order. Large numbers of soldiers had managed to wound or injure themselves. Some of the more creative ones had discovered that you could live quite nicely without a big toe, so they "accidentally" shot it

off. Now such wounds were automatically considere
criminal and court-martials were convened. Sadly, son
soldiers considered jail time and a dishonorable di
charge a better alternative to being killed or horrib
maimed. Nobody either Tanner or Cullen knew fe
that way, but another disaster could change matter

"So when do you think we'll attack?" Cullen aske
"We can't sit here all summer with our thumbs u
our asses. We wait too long and we'll be climbing th
Alps in the dead of winter. Did you hear about th
latest plan to bomb the Germans?"

Tanner laughed. Someone in Ike's staff had a relativ
in Congress who suggested that the air force con
mence low-level night bombing since it had becom
obvious that the Germans were moving men an
supplies at night.

Whoever it was had given no thought to the di
ficulty involved in flying through mountains at nigh
the problems with sudden winds, and, of course, th
inability to hit anything when pilots and crew wei
focused on not smearing their planes all over the Alp
No, that idea had been laughed away with the resu
that the Germans were still safe in the mountains ar
the land adjacent to Switzerland.

Cullen laughed harshly. "So the ghost of Mildre
Ruffino lives on."

"And on," said Tanner.

"What's your best guess as to when we'll hit the
again?"

"Sometime between a couple of days and a coup
of weeks," Tanner answered.

"Jesus, Tanner, you're no help whatsoever."

Lena had no difficulty locating Father Shanahan. She'd been wanting to for a while, but had been too busy. She owed him a debt of gratitude and wanted him to know it.

"You're looking well," he said. "There's color in your cheeks and you've gotten some decent food in you."

"Not too much, Father, I don't want to become some plump German dumpling."

"I don't think there's a chance of that, at least not a *German* dumpling. So how can I help you?"

"Does everyone who comes to see you want your help?"

"Generally, yes. I don't lead that exciting a life, so how can I help you?"

Lena took a deep breath. Some things still hurt. "I understand that the Red Cross is establishing a registry of refugees, or displaced persons as they're now being called. I was wondering if you would be able to help me find my father."

Shanahan pursed his lips. "I don't see why I can't at least try. Now, do you still have that lovely Luger?"

She laughed. "Yes and it's still not for sale. There's a war yet to end, and who knows, I might have to use it to protect myself." And protect Captain Scott Tanner, she realized with a jolt.

The M4 Sherman tank was not the best tank in the world, but it was being mass-produced by the tens of thousands. While it could hold its own against German Panzer III and Panzer IV tanks, it was totally outclassed by the Panther and Tiger tanks. Fortunately, these German monsters did not exist in great numbers. Germany's lack of production capacity was the cause of that shortage, and most of those that had rolled off production lines had been destroyed. It was widely understood that the Sherman was vastly inferior to the Red Army's T34, which was also being produced in enormous quantities. The Sherman tank had been upgraded with a 76mm high-velocity gun, which was superior to the original 75mm gun the tanks had been built with. Still, no one would want to fight a Panther or a Tiger or even a T34. Originally, the upgraded Sherman had been sent to the British, but with them now effectively out of the war, the tanks were going to American units.

The Sherman had a crew of five and weighed in at about thirty tons. Along with the main gun, it had a .50 caliber machine gun and two .30 caliber guns. The tank had a gasoline engine that allowed for a range of one hundred and twenty miles and could go upwards of thirty miles an hour. Mileage and speed were dependent on a number of factors, including terrain and the skill of the driver. Her shortcomings were the fact that she was underarmored and, standing at nine feet, far too tall. Thus, she could be spotted fairly easily by enemies lying low in the grass.

But to Sergeant Archie Dixon, the Chrysler-built tank named "Mimi" was lovely. Even lovelier was the anatomically correct painting of a half-naked blond with huge boobs on her hull. A couple of prudish officers had complained, but Dixon had not received any direct order to cover it up. If he had, he would have used some cardboard that had been painted olive drab to temporarily cover the offending boobs and hope that nobody important noticed when he removed it. Getting Mimi painted had cost the crew ten bucks and some liberated cognac.

Dixon, the tank, and the 14th Armored Division had been in Europe for only a few months and had missed much of the heavy fighting after Normandy, something that didn't bother Dixon one little bit. They had played a minor part in the first assault on the German positions in the Brenner Pass and had taken some casualties. That attack had cost the division dearly when the Nazis fought tooth and nail. They were preparing to launch a second attack and Archie wondered if their luck would still hold. He and his crew considered themselves a band of brothers and he wouldn't want anything to happen to his brothers.

But now the Nazis did not appear to have any armored capabilities. Those splendid Panther and Tiger tanks had almost all been destroyed or captured. What remained were a relatively few enemy tanks in the Alpine Redoubt. As a result, the battalion Dixon belonged to had been broken off from the division and attached to the 105th Infantry as support when they attacked through the Brenner Pass.

"Piss break," said Dixon as he jumped off the tank and stretched. The Sherman was consistently uncomfortable. In the winter it was too cold and in the summer it was too hot. The rest of the four tank column had pulled off to the side of the two lane paved road the treads of the tanks were chewing to pieces. Their crews were also savoring the moment.

As he relieved himself, Dixon had to admit that the land around him was beautiful, heavily forested, and hilly. A city boy from the Bronx, he'd never had the chance to be in the woods, and this part of southern

Germany had some incredible scenery. On the other hand, the hills were getting higher and more foreboding as they drew closer to the Alps.

"At least we won't have to fight in the mountains," Archie said as he buttoned up his fly. He hoped he was right. He'd been a buck sergeant for only two weeks and then only because his predecessor as commander of Mimi had gotten himself shot in the face by a sniper. It was a hideous wound and the man had still been alive when an ambulance carted him off. He had been trying to scream but the blood gurgling up from his mouth kept cutting off any real sound he'd been attempting to make. They'd been in an area they thought was safe and was proof that the Nazis, while defeated, were still able to kill.

It further pointed out that the 14th Division, known as the "Liberators," was through liberating. Now they were conquering and sometimes having a good time of it. It gave them some pleasure to see German civilians weeping and groveling and begging. Fuck them, was the consensus. They had started the war and now they could suffer the consequences. And so what if some buildings got destroyed or some silverware went missing. If anybody resisted, they might get shot. They drew the line at raping frauleins. The brass was hell on that and anyone who did rape a German woman could count on decades at hard labor.

Not that the tankers cared, but being attached to the 105th wasn't all that bad. The infantry had managed to make themselves fairly comfortable while waiting for the big attack to take place.

A jeep pulled up next to Mimi and a captain got out. Dixon successfully fought the urge to salute and simply nodded in recognition. "How can I help you, Captain Tanner?"

"First, you can give me the name of the woman who modeled for Mimi."

Dixon grinned. "You'd have to kill me first, sir."

"Well then, maybe you can tell me where the rest of your tanks are. The division was expecting twenty and it looks like we're short sixteen."

"Sir, I understand that the rest will be along shortly. There were some issues that the colonel wanted to iron out with the men before we came up here."

Aw, crap, Tanner thought. "Let me guess, Sergeant. A number of the men were less than enthusiastic about coming up here to fight in the Pass."

"That's about the size of it, sir," Dixon said. The rest of the men in the small column had left their tanks but were staying out of hearing range. "We got to go because I was the most junior sergeant and the least likely to piss and bitch about the situation."

"Did anybody actually refuse orders?"

"No, sir. The colonel's just letting them sound off about how they felt. We were in the first attack and the division got chewed up badly, which is how I got this last stripe. My guess is that they'll be along in about an hour or so."

Tanner forced a smile. "I guess the war can wait that long."

He had to wonder, though, if the army was getting close to actually refusing to go back into the battle. It had happened before, but not with any large force of Americans. In the First World War, however, a number of French divisions had refused to go on the attack after suffering appalling losses in a number of battles ordered by incompetent French generals. A number of historians felt that the French infantry had been pushed beyond endurance by making a number of futile and bloody attacks on strong German defenses. As a result, the French refused to attack. They would stand on the defensive but not waste men in further slaughters. A number of the mutineers had been hanged, but the French hierarchy became more aware of the anger of their men. They didn't want a revolution like the Russians had. Was this what was going to happen to the American army? Good lord.

"Sergeant, are the men aware that the attacks will be preceded by very heavy bombing?"

Dixon started to laugh but caught himself. Captain Tanner seemed like a decent guy, but he knew he shouldn't push it by being a smartass. "Sorry sir, but most of the guys think that's just so much bullshit, if you'll forgive my language. There are a lot of guys who don't think the bombers can hit the ground, much less a target."

There was a faint rumble and they instinctively looked skyward. "Speak of the devil," Tanner said. A long line of bombers was high overhead and headed down the pass. Another rumble told them that the remaining sixteen tanks were heading into the area.

"Sir, I sure as hell hope you're right about the bombers, sir. It would give me a great thrill to put Mimi in gear and simply cruise through Germany without any incident and not put the brakes on until we hit Switzerland."

CHAPTER 13

THE AIR RAID SYSTEM HAD FAILED. AGAIN. THERE were supposed to be radar stations letting the German infantry know that the American planes were en route. So what had happened? It didn't matter. Hummel and Schuster just wanted to survive the horror that was exploding all around them and threatening to blow out their lives.

The two men were in their strong little bunker but far from safe. Bombs exploding nearby were sending shock waves that threatened to collapse their fort and even suck the life from their lungs. Hummel had lost his hearing again, but that seemed to be it. Schuster, on the other hand, was clutching his knees to his chest and screaming silently. At least Hummel *thought* Schubert was silent. He wouldn't know for certain until his hearing came back. Or if it came back. If he was deaf, would the army discharge him? Fat chance.

Schuster started to rock back and forth and Hummel could see that he'd wet himself. There was a pause in the bombing and, even though his hearing still wasn't working right, Hummel could detect Schuster making loud, keening, screeching noises, lunatic noises.

Hummel reached out and grabbed his friend's arm. "Calm down. It'll be all over in a minute."

It wasn't. Schuster shook off Hummel's hand. More bombers came and dropped still more bombs. The world was turning to dust and it felt like the earth was disintegrating. Hummel looked into Schuster's eyes and saw nothing but madness. Schuster pushed Hummel away and tried to climb out of the bunker.

"Stop. You'll get killed. Stay down here and be safe," Hummel said.

Schuster clawed at the earth and continued to howl. The tips of his fingers were bloody and raw. Hummel tackled his friend and dragged him back to the relative safety of the bunker. Outside, it was raining murderous hot and sharp metal.

An explosion hit close by and caused the roof of their bunker to collapse. Now I know I'm going to die, Hummel thought. Schuster had stopped digging. He simply lay there, half covered with debris, his chest heaving. At least he's alive, Schuster thought.

And then it was over. The bombers were gone until the next time. Hummel started to dig his way out, but it was difficult with Schuster inert and in the way. He called for help. A few minutes later, he heard voices and rescuers started digging. Another few minutes and Lieutenant Pfister and several other soldiers pulled the two men out and laid them on the ground. Someone poured water over Hummel's head and then let him drink.

Pfister looked at Schuster who didn't respond. "What happened to him?"

"It was the bombing, sir. He couldn't handle it anymore."

The lieutenant examined Schuster who lay there until someone sat him up. His eyes were blank. His mouth was open and his tongue lolled around.

"He isn't faking it," Pfister said. "I just hope he recovers soon."

"Sir, should I take him to the hospital?" Hummel asked.

"And what will they do for him?" Pfister asked angrily. "He doesn't have any apparent physical wounds, so the SS will decide that he's a coward and not sick and hang him. No, he's better off with us. Maybe this shock will wear off enough so that he can function, at least a little, but until then he stays with us. We'll all take turns watching out for him until something happens."

Hummel stared at his lieutenant and their eyes locked. They both nodded. Pfister was not going to fight to the death either, at least not if he could help it. It was good to know. Too bad it took turning his good friend into a vegetable in order to find it out.

Fifty-year-old Lieutenant General Lucian Truscott was the new commander of the U.S. Seventh Army. General Alexander Patch's health had deteriorated to the point where he could no longer function in such a stressful position. They said he had pneumonia but Ike wondered if it wasn't something more serious. Regardless, the Seventh Army needed a more vigorous commander and the strong Truscott was such a man. He was also a realist. He looked at Ike and Devers and asked a very simple question.

"I just flew up from Italy and crossed the Alps. We probably flew over German-held territory, but don't worry. I don't want any medals for that. The scenery was magnificent from a tourist's point of view but appalling and horrible from a military one. Just how many men are you willing to lose while pushing south to Innsbruck, and what the hell do we do when we take the place? There are no real roads leading from Innsbruck to Bregenz or any other place that the Nazis feel is important."

Ike winced. The backlash against continuing the war against Germany was gaining momentum. Back in the States, protests had become larger and louder, with many extoling the martyrdom of Mildred Ruffino. There had been no real violence yet, or any large refusals on the part of military personnel to do their duty, but there was tension. A handful of soldiers were being brought up on charges while others had declared that they had suddenly decided they were conscientious objectors. Ike had ordered that any court-martials be held in abeyance until the situation clarified itself. Some historians had likened the period to that just before the Russian Revolution broke out. Most thought that comparison was utter nonsense. It was inconceivable that soldiers would refuse to fight an enemy and form soviets to make collective decisions. Nor was there any inkling whatsoever that the nation's hatred of Japan had receded. Just the opposite. The ever louder cries called for an American exit from Europe so that Japan could be squashed.

"We will do our duty," Ike said tightly.

"Never suggested that we wouldn't," Truscott responded softly. His vocal cords had been damaged years earlier, which made some think he was soft spoken and not dynamic. Those who thought that way quickly found out that they were dreadfully wrong. "But has anybody thought of what might happen if the Japanese were to surrender first?"

"I don't even want to think about that," Ike answered, forcing a smile. "Although I'll admit that I've wondered that as well. While we can be fairly certain that it won't happen, we cannot totally rule out the possibility. The Japs are suicidal stubborn bastards who won't quit until the last one is dead. If they do go first, maybe it will motivate the Nazis to give up. Who the devil knows? Unless something dramatic happens to change the game, we'll be fighting the Japs for a very long time."

"I suppose that's good to know," said Devers. "However, it does mean that our boys will be getting killed by Japs and Germans instead of just Germans."

Truscott was not finished. "It also means that I am not going to send our boys into a man-killing meat grinder. Have either of you seen a lion eat an elephant?"

"Not lately," Ike said while Devers looked puzzled.

"Well, I haven't either. But I understand that the lion eats the elephant one bite at a time. Now the German force is not an elephant. We are larger, you could say that we are the elephant, but they have the stronger ground. Therefore, there will be no more three-division frontal assaults and their subsequent appalling losses. We will isolate an area, pound and shell the crap out of it, and then chew it up and spit it out. It'll take time and be slow but steady, but there won't be anything much that the Germans can do. We eat a chunk and their positions to either side are in danger of being flanked while we expand the chunk. When that happens, they'll either have to come out of their holes and attack or retreat. If they attack, we hit them with bombs and artillery and destroy them. If they retreat, which is the more likely scenario, they will soon wind up with their asses up a mountaintop and nowhere else to go."

Ike nodded and checked his watch. He'd spent enough time in Strasbourg welcoming Truscott to his new position and he'd liked what he'd heard. Truscott would put immense pressure on the Germans and they would, sooner or later, fold. Some thoughts were nagging at him. In his position he heard rumors, or sometimes just rumors of rumors. They all said that the United States was developing some kind of super-weapon. If this was true, wonderful. If not, then life and death would go on and the Seventh Army would push its way south through the confines of the Brenner Pass towards Innsbruck while Mark Clark's armies would claw their way north. After that, anything could happen.

Is there really a war on? thought Tanner. This day was just too idyllic for words. He and Lena were sitting on a blanket spread on the grass in a field and having an old-fashioned summer picnic. They were a few miles away from their workplaces and living quarters. Better, the weather was cooperating. It was pleasantly warm and the sun was shining.

It was the first time he'd been with Lena on a totally social basis and he'd been as nervous as a high school sophomore about asking her. Then, he'd been as pleased as a little kid when she agreed.

Tanner had gotten some good food from the cooks—fried chicken, potato salad, and apple pie with ice cream. A bottle of decent Rhine wine completed the picture.

Lena looked up at the blue sky and smiled. "You have no idea how many times I wished for the simple freedom to be able to do exactly this."

"And with me?" he asked with an impish grin.

"Of course I didn't know you then, but definitely with somebody like you. And that reminds me. You call me Lena and that's correct, but how do I call you? Should I say Tanner or Captain Tanner or Scott, or, God help us, Scotty."

Tanner laughed. "It's always been as if I never had a first name. Everybody who knew me always called me Tanner. I would be very happy if that's what you did."

"Then Tanner it is, Tanner. Except when we are on duty and then I will remember your rank." She looked around again. The not so distant mountains were sharply visible. "And I did not come with you just for the chance at some really good food, although that did help. I think you wanted to know me better and I felt the same way. Or am I being too forward and European."

"I think you're being just great."

He also thought she looked great. Instead of the semi-military uniform she normally wore, she'd somehow scrounged up a white blouse and a full blue skirt that still showed enough of her shapely legs. She'd mentioned that she'd liked dancing and it showed in her lean muscles. Now that she no longer was a refugee, she no longer looked like one. She had a lovely trim and proportioned figure. He was also pleased that, unlike many European women, she did shave her legs. With her dark hair, it might have looked very strange to an American. She had no stockings. Few women did. She had attracted a lot of attention when he'd picked her up at the tent she shared with seven other women and drove her in a jeep to the picnic site.

"Someday I would like to go back to Prague," she said wistfully.

"I don't know if I can help, but I'll try. You may have to wait a while. The Red Army is still setting up shop and things could be nasty until they really get the place under control."

She leaned over and patted his arm. "I understand. I really do rather doubt that my father is even alive, much less waiting for me in Prague. Still, I would like to find out what I can."

"Understood." She had told him that Father Shanahan was going to use the Red Cross to help, but there was no Red Cross setup that she knew of in Prague. He wished that she hadn't let go of his arm. God, he was again acting like a kid and he had the feeling she knew it and was laughing at him.

The day became evening and they talked about life, their pasts, and whatever futures they thought they might have or wanted. He already thought he knew the details of her life before the war and as a slave with the Schneiders, but she elaborated. She held his hand tightly while she told him, purging herself and crying a little. He wanted to kill the Schneiders, but she said no. The Schneiders were not worth it.

He drove her back to the tent where a couple of her other tent mates were lounging and trying not to stare.

"Come with me," she said taking his arm and leading him to the tent. She stopped and looked in. "Both of you, out of here," she said laughing.

A few seconds later, a pair of women came out, stared and smiled at Tanner. Lena took his hand and led him into the tent. The heat was stifling. "Have you ever seen anything quite so grand?"

Eight cots were set up in no apparent order. Clothes were strewn about and duffle bags hung from hooks. A bra lay on one cot. He asked if it was hers and she laughingly said no. "I am not a slob. All my things are put away."

"You are right, though, Lena, this is truly magnificent."

She didn't bother to smile. She simply slipped into his arms and they kissed. The first one was most pleasant, even tender. The next few were much more passionate. She pulled away but kept smiling broadly.

"While it's tempting, dear Tanner, I am not going to make love to you on an army cot with seven other women hanging around."

He kissed her on the forehead and hoped that his erection would go down so that he could get to the jeep without drawing too much attention. "I will work on it. Maybe I will find you a palace for rent in Innsbruck."

Ernst Schneider entered the small apartment he shared with his wife and their two grown children. At least he lived in the sunshine of Bregenz and not in a cave like so many others were forced to. He couldn't decide if he felt foolish or terrified. His wife did not share his indecision.

"Good lord, Ernst," she gasped, "what is that you have and what have you gone and done?"

"This is a Panzerfaust," he announced proudly, holding out the several foot long tube-shaped device. "It is a tank killer and I am now a captain in the Volkssturm and this is one of the two weapons I've been issued. The other is an old Mauser rifle and they gave me a few dozen rounds of ammunition."

"But why?" Gudrun asked. "Have things gotten so bad that the Reich has to enlist older civilians and men who are veterans of the first war?"

"I am not old," he sniffed. "I am barely forty. And if I can help defend our country, I will do exactly that. The army is considering drafting men as young as our Anton."

Gudrun rose quickly from her chair. Ernst could not help but notice how much spryer she was since she and all the others were now on an enforced diet. She had lost thirty pounds and he twenty. Both Anton and Astrid had also slimmed down. It was almost impossible to find a fat person in Germanica. This had led to numerous jokes about how Herman Goering would look if he had made it to the Third Reich's last hope.

Gudrun took a deep breath and composed herself. "I did not mean to impugn your manhood, dear. I am just shocked that events have come to this. Wasn't it just a few months ago that German armies were on the verge of conquering Russia and North Africa and then on to the rest of the world? What has happened?"

Ernst scowled. "The filthy stinking Jews happened, that's what. The Jews and the communists have taken over this war and that is why it is so important that we win so that we can ultimately destroy them. We started sending them to the camps far too late. Can you imagine what it would be like to live in Germany under the vengeful rule of those people? I will fight, and if necessary, I will die."

"I hope it won't come to that," Gudrun said softly. "I still can't believe that you would be able to use a Panzerfaust. You'd have to get so close to an American tank for it to be suicide. At least with a rifle you can kill from fairly far away."

Ernst smiled. He'd already decided that he would not get close to an American tank. He would either fire the thing from a distance or give it to someone else to use, someone young and foolish. "Spoken like a true German woman. By the way, I am considered an officer with the rank equivalent to a captain. Right now I only have a couple dozen men under my command and, yes, some of them are boys, but that will change. I will have more."

"Just so long as one of them is not Anton. He is still getting over being assaulted by that Jewish bitch. If I ever see her, I will claw her eyes out."

"If you ever see her, it may well be because the Americans have conquered us. More likely she has gone back to wherever she came from. She was Czech and has doubtless attempted to return home. I believe she once mentioned she was from Prague. The Russians are in Prague and I can only hope they have taken her and are fucking her day and night."

Gudrun laughed. "You are still quite crude and you always will be, but I am in total agreement with you. Since Anton and Astrid are out working, we are quite alone in this tiny palace. Why don't you lock the door and we can celebrate your promotion."

Ernst grinned and they both began to undress. "I hoped you might feel that way so I brought a bottle of schnapps."

"Only one?" Gudrun asked.

There was muted uproar in the ready room. To say that the pilots were dismayed was putting it mildly. As usual, George Schafer was one of the more outspoken.

"Nothing personal, Colonel, but what asshole thought of this idea?"

Colonel Trent shook his head tolerantly. Tight discipline did not exist in the air force and each pilot felt he was entitled to speak his piece. "I believe the asshole was from the Pentagon and was routed here by the Eighth Air Force."

Schafer was not impressed. "That's a great pedigree, sir, but it doesn't change the fact that radar bombing in the mountains at night is going to kill a lot of American pilots and one of them might just be me."

The United States Army Air Force, to use its full name, had recently developed a small radar set that could be attached to a fighter like the P51s the pilots in this group all flew. It had been derived from and was an acknowledged improvement over similar radars that had been used by the RAF in detecting German U-boats. The German subs had to surface to charge their batteries and, since they were quite vulnerable during the day, they did so at night. With the radar attached to a low-flying bomber, the bomber could strafe and bomb a sub as soon as radar found it. Powerful searchlights were also attached to the bomber to improve aiming and possibly scare the hell out of the sub's crew.

"So elaborate for me just what you think is wrong with this idea?" the colonel asked.

"Sir, it's really quite simple. It's one thing to locate and bomb a ship on a nice flat ocean, but it's totally another to find and hit a tank in a valley surrounded by mountains. And don't forget that the wind might just be blowing like hell. And we are supposed to fly a plane under those conditions? And actually hit something and survive the experience? My wingman and best friend got shot down in the Brenner and was fortunate to live to tell the tale. Will he be fortunate a second time? Will I be lucky? I don't like to plan on luck."

"We have our orders, Lieutenant." The colonel's tolerance was getting thinner with each statement and question. What made it worse was the fact that he agreed with his pilots. The idea was lunacy. But orders were orders.

"And we will obey them to the letter, sir. But don't expect reckless enthusiasm. I would imagine that any pilot who senses anything whatsoever wrong with his plane is going to abort the mission and fly straight home."

Trent's face was turning red. The other pilots in the room began applauding, which didn't help his disposition one bit. It was one thing to be tolerant, but quite another to permit insolence. Still, Schafer and the others had a point. They could not be expected to fly planes that were malfunctioning and, at high altitude, only the pilot would be the judge as to whether something was wrong or not. And what the hell kind of raid could he launch if twenty percent or more of the pilots opted out because of real or imagined malfunctions?

He remembered a military doctrine—never give orders that the men won't carry out.

Trent stood and the pilots did as well, although slowly. "I will discuss your concerns and mine with the powers that be," he said and walked away with as much dignity as he could muster.

The prisoner was shackled to a bed. He was naked and his body was covered with only a sheet and there were cuts and bruises all over his very hairy body. To the doctors and nurses he looked like a pink ape. Completing the scene, he stank to high heaven. He had been found in a trench surrounded by other Russians, all dead. They had fought like tigers and refused many offers to surrender. This one hadn't surrendered either. He had been knocked unconscious and taken prisoner while helpless.

Doctor Hagerman gave up trying to hold his breath to avoid the stench. He made a note to get the man bathed while he was chained. "I've always wanted to see a Russian. I just never realized it would be under these circumstances. Don't let appearances fool you," he said to the others. "He's not badly hurt at all, he's strong as an ox, and, yes, he's listening to every word we're saying even though it's highly unlikely that he understands a word of English."

Tanner leaned over. "Comrade," he said and got no response. "Spasibo. Vodka."

That last word got a flicker of a response. The man opened his eyes and glared at the two men with feral hatred.

"I hope you speak Russian," Hagerman said.

"You just heard my entire Russian vocabulary. I've asked around and still haven't found anybody who really speaks Russian."

"Are you telling me there's a language the lovely Lena doesn't speak? I'm stunned."

The Russian snarled and began to speak, this time in German. His German was poor and he had to speak slowly so that Tanner and the others could understand him. He said that he wanted to die and would they shoot him before the Red Army did. He said that the Reds might just shoot him right off, but not likely. He said that Stalin's monsters would torture and starve him, maybe for years, before finally killing him. He added that Stalin's thugs had likely already murdered his family. He had nothing to go home to.

Hagerman was puzzled. "Why on earth would the Russians do that to their fellow Russians?"

"Vlasov," said Tanner and the Russian nodded vigorously.

Tanner continued. "Andrei Vlasov was a Red Army general who thought he was betrayed by Stalin so he went over to the Nazi side, taking thousands of Russian soldiers with him. He felt that he was actually fighting against Stalin rather than for Hitler. His forces were called the Russian Liberation Army and were about the size of a corps, and the prisoner is right about Stalin wanting them all dead. Worse, there's a treaty between the U.S. and the Reds saying that all of them would be forcibly returned to the Soviets. That Stalin would murder them is a given."

"Is this Vlasov still alive?"

"No idea, but unlikely."

Hagerman was shocked. "Jesus, no wonder they fought like animals. But doesn't it make sense that we should induce them to surrender to us and tell Stalin to go to hell?"

"Good idea, Hagerman, and the next time you see Truman why don't you tell him. All this stuff is way above our pay grade. Besides, there's another issue."

"And what is that?" Hagerman asked.

"Vlasov's troops, what remain of them, are supposed to be to the east. What are they doing in the Brenner Pass?"

"I don't know but you're going to tell me, right?"

"Absolutely. There have been rumors that the Germans were withdrawing from the Eastern portion of the abortion called Germanica. This is the first concrete indication that the rumors are correct. I think they're afraid that we'll cut Germanica in half and leave about a third of their army to be starved into surrender."

"I hope that's a good thing," said Hagerman.

"If they are consolidating their positions, then it's bad. If the Germans are using Vlasov's men to hold us up, that's also bad. In fact, I can't think of anything good about this. We will be kicking the information this man's given us up the chain. I hope they know what to do about it."

"So what do we do with him?" Hagerman said pointing at the Russian whose head had been swiveling as each man spoke.

"He's a prisoner and we'll treat him like one. Once you decide he can be released we'll put him in with the other prisoners and hope for the best. Maybe he'll get lost in the crowd or fall through the cracks or something like that."

"Sure," said Hagerman. "Did you at least find out his name?"

Tanner grinned. "It's Ivan, what else?"

★   ★   ★

The second OSS team led by Marie Leroux had left in the night, a week earlier. Neither Winnie nor Ernie knew how they did it, but they had made it across the border, set up camp, and immediately began reporting on German troop movements. The trio also informed Dulles about the distribution of supplies to the German front lines.

Winnie and Ernie had found out that Marie and Sven were lovers, which made them wonder what Hans felt about being odd man out. "Maybe they take turns or something like that," Ernie said. Winnie said that he was disgusting.

The second team had been in Germanica for only a week when their messages ceased abruptly.

"There could be a number of reasons for that," said Dulles when he arrived in Arbon after hearing of the problem. "First, there could be a simple malfunction with their radio. In which case, there are ways of extracting them or getting them a new radio."

"Do you really think it's that simple?" asked Ernie.

Dulles shook his head glumly. "No. There are other signals they could have sent if they were having a technical problem and these have not been done. I'm afraid that they either have been captured or killed. For their sake, I pray for the latter. It is my understanding that this General Hahn, the man in charge of the SS and Gestapo, is a monster."

Winnie was close to crying. "Are you saying they will break them?"

"Of course they will," Dulles replied bluntly. "Everyone will break under torture, and the Germans are masters at it. It's just a question of how long and how much they can tell their interrogators. I would suggest that, in very short while, the Germans will know of every one of us, where we're quartered and anything else the missing group might have known. We will make arrangements to move immediately. I'm sorry, but this lovely little dormitory will have to cease to exist."

Winnie bristled. "I'm far more concerned about Marie, Hans, and Sven than I am about this miserable place."

"As am I," Dulles snapped, "but I must be realistic. Should a miracle occur and they suddenly show up either in person on the radio, I will rejoice."

"I would trust seeing them in person, but not on the radio," Ernie said. "It would be possible that they had been turned and are providing us with false information."

"Precisely. However, they have all been given different signals to indicate that they are or are not under duress. But I agree with you, Captain, anything and everything can be extorted from them under extreme torture. One of their more sadistic tools is to torture one in front of one of the others, especially if two of them are lovers as I understand Marie and Sven were."

"What can we do?" asked Winnie, her voice breaking. Finding her friend from her teenage years had been such a wonderful surprise and now it was all ashes.

"I will be speaking with my German friend. I will see what I can find out and, more important, what he can do for me. That is, if he wants to. He could still be compromised if the wrong persons find out about our talks. In the meantime, we wait and listen."

Ernie was sickened by what he was thinking, but he had to ask the question. "Did either of them have a poison pill to take?"

Winnie started crying. "Hans and Sven did, but Marie didn't. She told me the afternoon before they left."

Dulles cursed himself for his failure to realize that human nature and passions would intrude. Had he known that they were lovers, he would have broken up the team. He didn't think that Winnie and Ernie had crossed that threshold, but, if he was any judge of character, it wouldn't be long. Of course, he had no plans to send them across into German-held territory.

Dulles sighed. "And why didn't Marie have a cyanide pill?"

Winnie continued to sob. "Because she's still a Catholic and suicide is a mortal sin."

Joey Ruffino was twenty-five and perversely proud of the old foot injury that had resulted in his being categorized as 4F and, therefore, unacceptable to the military. He walked with a noticeable limp that he sometimes exaggerated if he thought that people were wondering why an otherwise healthy young man wasn't in the service. Well, he *was*, sort of. He worked in a factory that produced parts for jeeps and was making a lot of money that he couldn't spend because of rationing.

Joey wasn't a bad kid, far from it. If called, he would have served to the best of his abilities. But he was a realist. While he now had a high-paying job and his choice of chicks, he knew that little bit of heaven would cease as soon as the war ended and the real heroes came marching home. Therefore, he would enjoy today and let tomorrow care for itself. Thanks to rationing there was little for him to spend his wealth on. Therefore, he had decided to take college classes and was getting good grades.

All had been well until his mother died in the arms of Harry S. Truman, President of the United States. Like his late mother, he thought that Truman was an accidental president and not much of one. And, while he hadn't given his mother's antiwar activities much thought, her sudden death had changed his outlook. He had made himself a leader of Ruffino's Marchers, a group dedicated to bringing the troops home. He had inherited all of his mother's followers and added a number of his own. Mildred had gone from being a gadfly protester to a martyr. It was his fervent hope that her death would not have been in vain.

There would be another protest, but not a random one like the event that had seen his mother die. No, this one would be organized. Marchers would be grouped into companies and they would all have plenty of water and there would be doctors and nurses scattered through the crowd.

To his surprise and delight, Joey found that he could organize large numbers of people and, better, get them to follow him. When he talked, he spoke from the heart. He would not be able to bring his mother back, but it was his goal to make that Harry Truman person regret the day he'd become president.

SS General Alfonse Hahn looked up from the papers he was signing. Armies are supposed to fight, he thought, not drown in paperwork. "What is it, Diehl?"

"The prisoners have been broken, General."

"I never doubted your abilities," Hahn said with a smile, thinking of all the bodies, minds, and souls that Captain Rufus Diehl had destroyed.

The young people in the OSS team hadn't been

very good or very smart. They'd kept their radios too long in the same spot and it had been fairly easy to triangulate their rough location in the hills overlooking Bregenz. The fact that they were broadcasting had been noticed almost immediately by German radio experts who'd been on the lookout for just such an event. Locating them more precisely in the rough terrain had taken only a little bit longer.

Nor had they done a very good job of hiding their position. They were OSS, which meant that they were amateurs. He'd allotted one company of infantry to find them. They'd been caught in their sleeping bags. They hadn't even set up a guard. It amused him when he was told that one of the men and a woman were sharing a sleeping bag and had been pulled naked from it. Now he knew just where and how Diehl's interrogations would begin and he'd been right.

Hahn followed Diehl to the interrogation area. Torture chamber would have been a more accurate term, but interrogation had a more benign sound to it.

"Are all three of them alive, Captain?"

"No. The man named Hans managed to swallow a cyanide pill. The others, however, are still among the living."

They entered a room where two people were laid out on cots. They were spread-eagled and their arms and legs were chained to the four corners of the cots. Their bodies were covered with only a sheet. Hahn pulled back the cover on the man. His body was a mass of burns caused by the electrical currents roaring through the clips and then into his body. He was unconscious and breathing shallowly.

"Will he recover?"

"If you wish him to, General."

It was an easy decision. "I do wish it. Alive he can still be a tool. Dead he is only so much rotting meat."

Two steps took him to the other cot. He pulled back the sheet. Despite the fact that the woman named Marie was badly bruised about the face, she was quite lovely. He was mildly annoyed that she had been beaten. Fists only cause pain, which can be tolerated. He preferred the subjects to be in agony and a state of terror. Besides, when he decided to take her, he wanted her looking as attractive as possible. He would have to wait until the swelling went down. He ran his hand down her breasts and between her legs. Her eyes opened wide with fear and horror. She closed them tightly as if doing so would make him go away.

Diehl was proud. "They told us everything they knew. We now know the names of their confederates and their locations in Arbon. We could go in and wipe them all out if that's your wish. You said you wanted the girl totally broken so we did. Once she told us everything she knew, we told her she was a liar and that she was holding back."

Hahn laughed. Giving a prisoner false hope and then snatching it away was a marvelous technique for extracting additional information.

Diehl continued. "We brought out the bathtub and filled it with water. We stuck her head underwater and waited to bring her up until she had half drowned. We did this a half dozen times; then we did it to her lover. I am extremely confident that she will cooperate."

Hahn continued to probe her. Her eyes were open again and the look of terror excited him. She tried to twist her body away from him, which was quite impossible. "Sadly, Captain, we will not go after the OSS in Switzerland. An attack by us on Swiss soil would annoy the people who are providing us with so much in the way of food and medical supplies. Catching this pathetic little group in German territory was fair. Going into Switzerland would not be. Tell me, are there any women in the OSS group still in Arbon?"

Diehl quickly checked his notes. "One young woman named Winifred Tyler. She's short and about in her mid-twenties."

And doubtless the slut who'd tripped him and escaped from him. How nice it would be to have her in front of him instead of Marie Leroux. No, he could not fixate on the Tyler woman. The Americans in Arbon were doubtless scattering to the four winds. Even if he were to get permission to launch a raid, the Yanks were doubtless well away from this area of the world. No, Marie Leroux would have to take Winifred Tyler's place.

Marie continued to stare at him through swollen and discolored eyelids. He again allowed his hands to roam her body, feeling her quiver. It delighted him. She had no further information that would be useful.

"Did you sodomize her, Captain?"

Diehl smiled. "Indeed, sir. She screamed when I entered her, and her lover howled just as much. It went as you ordered."

He patted Marie on the cheek. "You are a lovely thing and you will be quite useful. Your lover is still alive and will remain so as long as you cooperate. Do you understand?"

The OSS had been fools to send lovers on the same journey. Along with pain from electrical currents, Diehl had told the boy that German soldiers would rape his girlfriend in front of him, which was one reason for sodomizing her. Another was that Diehl enjoyed it. Marie's lover was told that the interrogators would mutilate her face and body. He had made much the same threat to Marie with the added proviso that she would watch while his manhood was slowly cut from his body. That had been the last straw. Both had collapsed.

Marie nodded and Hahn continued. "Diehl will be responsible for seeing to it that you are given medical care and that your wounds are healed. We will do the same for your boyfriend. As long as you are a good little girl, he will remain alive."

CHAPTER 14

LIEUTENANT PFISTER'S COMMAND NOW CONSISTED of eight men and himself. Nine if you counted Schubert, who was led along by a rope tied around his waist. Pfister thought he looked like a dog that had been trained to walk upright for extended periods of time. It was a cruel comparison but war was cruel, and, if he thought too much about it, he wanted to weep.

Schubert had improved slightly. He now responded to basic orders and was able to feed and clothe himself. He was also able to take care of his personal hygiene, which was good. Not even Hummel looked forward to wiping Schubert's ass. Hummel talked to him constantly; sometimes, Pfister thought, just to keep himself sane as their world crumbled around them. Constant artillery bombardments and their helplessness under bombing raids had sent most of his platoon either to the hospital or the grave. A couple of his men were simply "missing" and the SS had been justifiably suspicious that that they had deserted.

Having been so thoroughly shredded, the entire

regiment had been withdrawn to the rear of Innsbruck and been replaced by thousands of insane anti-Stalin Russians. Neither Hummel nor Pfister had seen any turncoat Reds before, although they had heard of them. Both men thought the Russians were a scruffy, barbaric bunch. They were horrified at the thought of Red Army soldiers like them turned loose on German soil. Neither women nor property would be safe from those vandals, was their opinion. That German soldiers had committed atrocities on Polish and Russian women was unspoken.

All of them carried what they could of their equipment and supplies and left the rest. Hummel was now an infantryman. His machine gun had been bent into improbable angles in the air raid that had damaged Schubert's mind. He had not been able to replace it. He now carried a simple bolt-action rifle and despised it. He loved the firepower and potential for devastating enemies of the Reich that his machine gun had given him. It had made him feel elite. Now he was nothing more than a humble soldier, and one with a very large pet named Schubert.

"We have orders, Sergeant," Pfister said.

Hummel laughed sarcastically. "I'm a sergeant now?"

"Yes, and I'm a field marshal. Our orders are to retreat west along the valleys until we somehow reach an area near the capital of Germanica, some little town called Bregenz. I've never heard of it and it's probably because it's in what used to be Austria and I never gave a shit about Austria."

Pfister pulled out a pack of cigarettes. They were German, which meant they'd be awful, but beggars can't be choosers, they'd decided. He offered one to

Hummel but not to Schuster, who was staring up at the sky.

Pfister breathed out the noxious weed. "Some days I almost envy Schuster. He is safe in his own little world."

Hummel corrected his lieutenant. "Except when the Yanks are bombing and shelling us. Then he howls and screams and bites himself and shits himself."

Pfister shook his head. "I'd tried to forget that part. We will travel at night, of course. It will be slow since there will be no trucks for us. Fortunately, it's not all that far and the weather is fair. We will also hope for clouds and fog so we can move during the day and away from American planes."

"And Bregenz is where we'll make our last stand, isn't it, Lieutenant?"

Pfister looked around nervously to see who else might be listening. No one was near them. "According to Minister Goebbels, it is where we will turn the tide of the war and emerge victorious, which is as unlikely as me fucking Marlene Dietrich."

Hummel laughed. It felt good. Laughter had become a rare commodity. "Perhaps Herr Goebbels will unleash another one of Hitler's super-weapons and save all our asses."

"With our luck, Sergeant Hummel, the Yanks will unleash super-weapons of their own."

On July 16, 1945, the night sky over Alamogordo, New Mexico, lit up with a degree of brightness described as coming from a thousand suns. Had anyone been looking directly at it, they would have been blinded. Instead, thick and heavily coated glasses, much like those used by welders, had been issued. Even with them, everyone was told to avoid direct contact for at least the initial explosion.

The blazing light quickly dissipated and the billowing, churning mushroom cloud could be watched by the naked eye as it boiled and roared thousands of feet into the sky. It grew like a living thing, terrifying some who watched.

Hundreds of scientists and hangers-on had cowered in trenches and bunkers to await the explosion that they all feared and hoped for. They simply did not know what to expect. A minority of the scientists thought that unleashing the power of the atom would result in the destruction of the earth, that the planet would simply fall apart and all mankind and mankind's sometimes dubious achievements would cease to exist.

Others thought that it would merely be an enormous explosion and represent a weapon that would bring Japan to the peace table. *How* this would occur, they weren't quite certain. When discussed, many were appalled at the thought of such a bomb being exploded over a Japanese city, incinerating tens of thousands of civilians. That firebombing of Japanese cities had been ongoing for months and had already caused many thousands of casualties was ignored. Others felt that the Japanese deserved what they would get for starting the war in the first place.

Most, however, were convinced that it would shorten the war and bring the suicidal resistance of the Japanese to a halt. Once Japan was finished, then all of the might of the United States, nuclear or not, could be turned against the Nazis who still clung on to life in what used to be Austria and northern Italy.

The news was sent to President Truman, who was in conference with Stalin and the new British Prime Minister, Clement Attlee, in the German city of Potsdam, outside Berlin. During the conversations with Stalin, Truman hinted about the success of the test bomb, code-named Trinity. He would later recall that Stalin appeared singularly unimpressed by the news. Truman at first thought it was because he hadn't made himself clear to Stalin or that Uncle Joe just didn't understand enough science to comprehend that a new day had dawned in the history and progress of man. It wouldn't be until later that Truman and others would realize that Stalin's spies, most notably Klaus Fuchs, had been keeping him informed on the Manhattan Project's progress and that the Soviet Union was well on its way to developing its *own* bomb.

Staff Sergeant Billy Hill was the first from the division's headquarters to arrive at the site of the slaughter. A message from his friend, Sergeant Jerome Higgins, had sent him to the site. Higgins met him. His face was pale and it looked like there was vomit on his jacket.

"Right this way," Higgins said, "and you can see what the bastards have done this time."

A short trek through the woods took them to a clearing where three long rows of bodies had been laid out with military precision. They were facedown, dressed in rags, and their hands had been tied behind them. From the grayness of their skin, he guessed they'd been lying there for a couple of days. Birds and squirrels had been at them and most were missing their eyes and he wondered what other soft parts as well. They had all been shot in the back of the skull. At least they'd died quickly, he thought, and then wondered what had been going through their minds as the others were executed. Had one person been the executioner, in which case their wait had to have been excruciating, or had there been a number of men blowing their brains out? He decided he didn't really want to know.

Hill started to count and Higgins interrupted him. "I'll save you the trouble, Billy. There are two hundred and seven of them."

"Thanks," Hill said, again trying to hold down the bile rising in his throat. He had seen death in battle, even caused it, but this was different. This was like Dachau, only on a smaller, more intimate scale. The numbers of dead at the concentration camp were too large to comprehend. But this was different. What made it worse was that the end of war might just be around the corner. Jesus, how much longer could the Nazis hang on?

"Hey, Sarge."

Hill wheeled and recognized the private who had argued with him about the merits of continuing the fighting. He was pale and it looked like he had been weeping. "What do you want, Private?" Hill snapped.

"I want to let you know that I changed my mind and want to apologize for what I said earlier. The pricks who did this have to be dug out of the mud and slime where they're hiding and killed before there can be real peace."

Hill nodded. The private held out his hand and Hill took it. "I'm really sorry, Sarge."

"Forget it. I made a mistake once too. I'm just thankful I can't recall it."

They heard another jeep pull up and a few minutes

later a grim-faced Tanner emerged from the woods along with Doctor Hagerman. After appropriate greetings, Tanner and Hagerman walked down the lines of corpses. "This place is out of the way, Higgins, how did you find them?"

"The birds were a giveaway. That and the stench, of course."

"Of course." Tanner had been so transfixed by the site that he had scarcely noticed the smell. Now it was almost overwhelming.

"Look at how emaciated they are," Hill said. "Either the Nazi shits are deliberately starving their slave laborers or they're running out of food."

"Or maybe both," Tanner said.

"We found someone's briefcase, sir," said Higgins. "The Germans are so well organized that they actually listed the names of the people they'd shot."

He held out his hand. "Let me see the list." He had told Lena where he was going and why. Thank God she hadn't insisted on accompanying him. He scanned it and saw no one by the name of Bobek or Bobekova. It was a small blessing.

"What do we do with the bodies?" Higgins asked.

Hill laughed. "Why not bring up a bunch of German prisoners and let them dig a whole lot of graves?"

Higgins nodded and Tanner smiled grimly. "Great, but first let's find a bunch of correspondents who can record this." But he wondered if they would bother, he thought. The reporters might just think that one more atrocity was small potatoes and no big deal. Sadly, they'd be right.

Higgins was puzzled. "Doc, how come they ain't stiff? Shouldn't they be in rigor mortis?"

"Not necessarily. Bodies get stiffened by rigor after a number of hours and then come out of it and are limp and flexible again. Their condition only proves what we already know, that they were killed a couple of days ago."

"Any other observations?" Tanner inquired.

"I'm not a pathologist, but I'll confirm what everyone suspects. These were slave laborers and my bet is that they came from Dachau to work on the German defenses. It's also apparent that they have been mistreated and poorly fed, if at all. I'd make another bet that they were executed because they were too weak to work."

Tanner nodded. "And that also confirms that the Nazis don't have enough food to keep their slaves alive. That's good to know. By the way, Doctor Hagerman, you're really good at this battlefield analysis stuff. I never did ask you, but what was your medical specialty?"

Hagerman shrugged. "Pediatrics."

Two hours later, Tanner and Hagerman arrived back at the division headquarters. Soldiers and civilians were milling around and talking loudly. Cullen ran up to the jeep. "Gentlemen, you seem to know a lot, so please answer a question."

"Cullen, you have my permission to test both my brain and my patience."

"Great, now what the hell is a *Hiroshima*?"

Josef Goebbels was pale and his hands were shaking. The news broadcast by the Americans was staggering in its implications. Could one bomb have utterly destroyed a city of more than three hundred thousand? It was impossible to comprehend. Or was it? The Reich had killed millions in the camps, so what were a few tens of thousands more?

Now he understood what Doctor Abraham and his cohorts were working on. Until now, it was nothing more than theory. Now, Abraham's bomb had to work in order for any trace of the Third Reich to survive.

And was it so terrible that the bomb had fallen on the Japanese? They were an inferior race whose military successes had been against third-rate powers like China or an unprepared United States. No. A world with a few hundred thousand fewer Japanese and their stupid code of Bushido and worship of their emperor would be a better place.

What concerned him was the *next* shoe dropping. Where there was one bomb, there had to be two. Or three. Or possibly many more. The first bomb over Hiroshima had been a message. The Japanese would ultimately surrender even if it took turning the Home Islands into floating cinders. Now it was obvious that the Americans would not have to invade Japan proper, just burn it from a distance. This meant that many of the American troops being sent to Asia could be returned to Germany for a final and massive assault against the Redoubt. It could also mean that future nuclear weapons could be dropped on Bregenz or anywhere else in Germanica. The Americans had promised not to bomb near the Swiss border, but would the Yanks continue to honor that promise if it meant ending the war? He knew precisely what *he* would do and to hell with the Swiss.

And how many bombs could Abraham develop—one, three, or maybe none. Success had been promised and failure would bring an agonizing death, but what if success was impossible? The Americans had vast resources, while Abraham had a few dozen scientists in a cave. Had he been a fool to believe Abraham?

He now had a mission. He and Magda had once agreed to kill their six children and themselves to keep from falling into the clutches of Stalin and the Red Army. The Americans were not savages like the Russians, and he was confident that they would not harm the children. As for himself, he would hang. Magda might just live, but would likely be imprisoned for a period of time, maybe even for the rest of her life.

It was sad, but so be it. He would speak with Magda and make the necessary arrangements.

Lena and her tent-mates had gotten a little drunk after hearing the news about the American atomic bomb. One of them got her hands on a couple of cases of real beer and not the heartily despised low alcohol beer issued by the U.S. Army. They kept their find to themselves rather than risk a stampede by GIs who hated what they felt was government-issue junk. The soldier's rationale was very simple. They were fighting Germans and risking their lives so what the hell if they got a little drunk every now and then? Even though the women weren't directly in combat, they weren't about to share their find.

Lena didn't drink very often or very much and drank beer but rarely. Her preferred drink was wine. The beer was an Austrian brand and must have been in someone's basement for years. Lena had at least three and possibly four bottles. They all had gotten giggly and it was a good feeling of release. When it was gone, they had gone to bed.

About three in the morning Lena awoke with a headache between her eyes and a bladder that was about to explode.

"Damn it," she muttered. Her fellow sinners were all snoring and sleeping soundly. She slipped on her army pants and, over her T-shirt, a pink robe that she'd bought from a refugee for just a few pennies. She didn't feel she'd taken advantage of the woman who was going to throw it away because she no longer had any use for it. Along with covering her when she had to go to the latrine, the pink color made her feel feminine.

She thought for a moment and decided to take the Luger. The robe had baggy pockets and she didn't think the bulge was too obvious. Besides, even though she and the others were allegedly safe on an army base, there had been incidents where some oversexed and horny GI—was there another kind?—had attempted to assault a woman. Don't take chances was their motto. And if they were assaulted, it was highly unlikely that the soldier would face severe punishment. The men would stick together. The soldier might lose a stripe or get his butt kicked by an NCO, but doing serious jail time was highly unlikely. It wasn't fair, but such was life in their corner of the world.

The latrine was primitive but clean since the women took turns caring for it. She relieved herself and splashed some cold water on her face. Engineers had rigged the piping to deliver warm water, but that wasn't what she wanted. The cooler water refreshed her just a little. She took a couple of aspirins and swore never to drink Austrian beer again, unless, of course, someone wanted to have another party. She could not help but exult in the fact that she was actually, truly free.

As she walked the short distance to the tent, she looked up and saw a million stars. She wished Tanner was there to share it with. So many times when she'd been with the Schneiders she'd done the same thing. Only then she'd been wishing for a way to escape.

She caught motion to her right. She waited and saw it again. Someone was skulking out there. She stood still and put her hand in her pocket, grabbing the pistol.

She wished she wasn't wearing pink. She must be standing out like a neon sign.

The man suddenly decided to cross the roadway and she saw that he was carrying what looked like a German submachine gun. Luck was with her. The man hadn't turned in her direction, but then he did and they recognized each other. It was young Hans Gruber.

"Gruber," she hissed and pulled out the pistol.

"American whore," he screamed and fired a burst in her direction. She threw herself on the ground and almost felt the bullets whistle over her. She fired twice at Gruber and also missed. "Help!" she screamed. "Germans!"

Gruber looked at her, fired again and missed again. He swore and disappeared. More gunfire had erupted in the distance and a siren finally started screaming. She heard an explosion. Gruber had thrown a hand grenade, but not at her. Thinking it was a bombing attack, hundreds of men and a handful of women spilled out of their tents and into slit trenches. Lena needed no prompting and found a corner of a trench. Mud quickly covered her pink robe, ruining it.

Gunfire was increasing and it seemed to be close to division headquarters. She groaned as she realized that Tanner's quarters were near the general's.

She recognized a couple of the men in the trench with her. "This ain't no air raid, is it?" one commented. "By the way, Miss Lena, nice outfit."

The sounds of gunfire had sent Hill out of his bunk and onto the earthen floor of the tent he shared with a number of other sergeants. The others were a little slower on the draw but when bullets stitched the canvas they moved with alacrity, joining him in the dirt. The bullets were joined by the sound of grenades exploding.

"What's happening, Sarge?" asked a confused buck sergeant.

"We're under attack, you flaming jackass. What the hell did you think was happening? Where's your weapon? Everyone, get your goddam weapon!"

There was more scrambling as men moved to comply. Even those with a couple more stripes quickly decided he was their leader. When this was over, he would have to ask for a raise.

He sliced the canvas with a very large knife he'd won from a sailor in a poker game and led them single file out of the back of the tent. The loser had called the knife a Ka-Bar but it looked like a Bowie knife. Just about everyone had complained about having to live in tents, but there weren't enough undamaged buildings to house them. Now it might just save their lives. Instead of having to use doorways, they could cut their way out anywhere they wished.

Hill had a dozen men, all NCOs. He had them

form a defensive line and take what shelter they could find. More gunfire and screams could be heard. He began to wonder if the bullets that had struck the tent had simply been fired wildly or were even spent. He decided that it didn't matter a helluva lot.

"People coming," he yelled. "Hold your fire until I tell you. They might just be friendlies."

The issue was decided when one of the approaching men stopped and hurled a grenade that exploded several feet in front of them. "Open fire," Hill screamed. There were only four attackers and they quickly fell in a heap. The Americans continued to fire until Hill ordered them to stop. "Enough. They're dead already."

Hill's little group began to approach the pile of bodies. Hill had a terrible thought. "Don't anybody touch anything. One of them might be playing possum."

"Screw that, Hill," said a more senior sergeant named Baker. "I'm gonna get me a souvenir. And just remember, Hill, you don't give me no orders." He ran off to the bodies and started moving them around. Suddenly an arm thrust up and grabbed the sergeant by the neck, pulling him down. A couple of seconds later, the grenade the German had been holding exploded. The American sergeant was lifted into the air and dropped back down, but without his head and an arm.

"Son of a bitch," Hill screamed and started shooting again. The others joined in and the four Germans, along with the unlucky American, were shredded.

When the killing stopped, they made another attempt to look at the corpses, or at least what was left of them. What they saw were the remains of four very young men. These were the legendary Werewolves, Hill concluded, and they didn't look like much at all. But what kind of damage had they managed to inflict?

Elsewhere, the firing had pretty much ceased. Only sporadic and solitary gunfire was heard and no more grenades. Hill realized that Tanner was beside him. "You shouldn't sneak up on people, Captain. You might get shot."

"You're right. The next time the Krauts attack, I'll announce myself. Other than the foolish and unfortunate Sergeant Baker, did you lose anybody?"

"Nobody that I'm aware of, sir. How about you?"

"There were about twenty of them, including our former guest, Hans Gruber."

"I hope the little shit got killed."

"No such luck. No one's found his body."

The wind shifted and they smelled something burning. "Aw Christ," said Tanner. "That's coming from General Evans' quarters."

As a major general, Evans was entitled to one of the few actual buildings in the division area to use as his office and headquarters and it was burning fiercely. "Did the general get out?" Tanner asked anyone. He saw Cullen and waved him over.

Major General Richard Evans had again been unable to sleep. He appreciated his staff's concern for him and thanked them for the soft bed and the roof that didn't leak, but it didn't change the fact that he couldn't nod off. The war had ground down both his division and himself. He was an exhausted and underweight shell. Since arriving in Germany, the 105th had suffered more than three thousand casualties. Three thousand bright young men killed, wounded, or maimed along with

several dozen missing. He didn't think any of the missing had deserted. More likely, their mortal remains had
been obliterated by a shell or buried by some explosion.

Mercifully, he didn't know very many of them.
Their names on the casualty lists jumped out at him,
however, and he wondered how many relatives, friends,
and lovers were mourning the dead and hoping that
the wounded would recover.

Of the three thousand casualties, only two thousand had been replaced. The United States Army
was suffering a manpower shortage; thus, the division was understrength as well as unmotivated. The
two thousand replacements were poorly trained and
indifferently motivated. Even so, many of them had
become casualties. Their inexperience led too many
of them to believe that they were immortal or that
this was some sort of noisy and thrilling game.

He grieved for them all and once more doubted if
he was cut out to be a general. How could Eisenhower
or Patton or Devers send tens of thousands of men
to fight each day knowing that many of them would
not come back? At least his division was going to
be pulled out of the line. That was the good news.
The bad was that they were going to be headed to
the German city of Bregenz and be part of the final
assault on Germanica.

The chatter of gunfire interrupted his musings. It
was close, too close. He hopped out of bed and quickly
put on his trousers and boots. Now the shooting was
really close and he cursed the fact that all he had to
protect himself was his .45 automatic. And where the
hell were his guards?

A window crashed below him. Swearing softly, he

made it to the head of the stairs. He saw shadows moving. It was just one man. But was it an American or a German? The answer came quickly. The man must have sensed the motion above him. He turned and fired a burst from a submachine gun. Bullets chewed into the wall beside the general. Evans fired back. The German shot again. This time, Evans took the full strength of the bullets in his chest. He gasped and fell forward, slowly sliding down the stairs.

"General!" Evans tried to focus on the sound. It was Cullen. Good boy, he thought as a red haze started to overwhelm him. There was more shooting and he saw the German buckle and fall, his body shredded by bullets from Cullen's Tommy gun.

He tried to say his thanks, but his body wasn't functioning and he smelled smoke. Nothing was functioning.

Cullen's uniform was scorched and his face was soot-blackened and burned red. "No, the general did not get out. He was shot many times by a German while he was trying to get down the stairs.

"I got the German, but then the place began to burn up and I was barely able to drag him out. In case you're wondering, General Evans lived for a few minutes but soon was well and truly dead with a bunch of bullets in his chest. If he had any last words, I couldn't make them out."

The gunfire had stopped. There were, however, the sounds of people yelling for help or screaming in pain. People were giving orders and trying to get control of the situation.

Cullen borrowed a canteen and dumped some of the contents on his face. "I'd like to know just how the Nazis got through our security. My guess is that the guards were either asleep or not paying attention or were killed by the Germans. For their sake, I hope they are all dead. Letting a general get murdered will put you in the stockade for centuries."

With a chance to catch his breath, Tanner wondered if Lena had made it to safety. The German attacking force was small; therefore, the odds were well in her favor. Good odds weren't good enough. He needed facts.

As soon as he could he ran to where the women had their tent. It was still standing, although there were some disconcerting holes in the canvas. He was about to ask about her when she ran up, grabbed him by the arm, spun him around, and hugged him fiercely.

"I was so worried," she said. Her voice was muffled by the fact that her mouth was against his chest.

"So was I," he said, reveling in the fact that he could feel her breasts against him and the beat of her heart as he held her tightly. "Their attack was a bust. If they wanted to kill high-ranking officers, the only one they've gotten is General Evans. His death is terrible, but we will recover."

He realized that it was a tacit admission that the late Evans had not inspired confidence. There would be new commanding general for the 105th, but who would it be and, more important, would it make a bit of difference?

Joey Ruffino had never been to the White House. Most people hadn't. First, it would have involved a lot of money that most people didn't have, thanks to the Great Depression. Second, by the time his good job had given him enough money to spend on the trip, wartime restrictions would not permit it to happen easily.

Thus, arranging for many thousands of his mother's supporters to arrive in Washington at the same time and find lodgings had proven to be a monumental logistical effort. He was pleased that he and his team of volunteers had actually pulled it off. Although much a much smaller crowd then what he'd hoped, several thousand protestors had managed to make it to Washington. A tent city had sprung up across the Potomac and, while watched carefully by the Secret Service, the army, and the District of Columbia police, the protestors were left alone.

Even though it hurt his foot to walk any distance, he insisted on doing it. It was his duty and it thrilled him to honor his mother. He felt that her spirit walked beside him as he circled the White House grounds and carried the placard calling for the troops to be brought home.

He was surprised that the White House, while quite large, wasn't larger. It was beautiful, but not truly a palace. He'd seen enough pictures in books and magazines to understand what a palace should look like. Nobility did not live in the White House, just an elected president, and now it was Harry Truman's turn. The view was marred by the sandbag fortifications and the large numbers of heavily armed soldiers along with machine guns on the roofs of many surrounding buildings. While there was little danger at this time in the war from either German or Japanese aircraft, sabotage could not be ruled out. He'd been told that there were real fears that some crazy fanatic would steal a plane and crash it into the White House or the Capitol. This was once considered preposterous, but no longer, since the Japanese kamikaze pilots began sacrificing themselves by flying into American ships.

At ten AM, two men in dark suits exited the White House and approached Joey. He immediately knew them as FBI agents whom he'd seen on duty near the White House. They'd been formal and stern but not in a threatening manner. "Will you please come with us," one said, "the president wants to talk with you."

The president? "Sure," Joey said and followed them. He expected to be taken to the Oval Office but instead went to a smaller office in the West Wing. He was told to have a seat and wait. The president would be along in just a minute.

It was two minutes before a grim Truman entered and Joey nearly fell off his chair. Truman shook his hand and told him to sit down again. Joey noted that Truman was a dapper dresser and was much shorter than he. He also noted that the new president had a strong command presence and a really firm grip.

"Young man, who was the Great Emancipator?"

"Why, Lincoln of course."

"Yes, and can you imagine Abraham Lincoln arresting people and holding them in prisons without trial or charges?"

"I cannot, sir."

"Can you imagine Woodrow Wilson doing that either?"

"No, sir," answered a puzzled Joey. Where was this conversation going? "Woodrow Wilson was a man of peace."

"Indeed he was and so was Lincoln. Yet both men

arrested those who were perceived of as threats to the country and held without bail, charges or trial. Now, do you know why they did that?"

Joey was starting to realize the direction of the questions. "Because we were at war," he said softly. He wondered if he would be allowed to leave the building.

"Precisely. Because we were fighting the Confederates in Lincoln's time and the Germans when Wilson was president, Civil liberties were often ignored because it was deemed necessary to protect the country. Were you aware that FDR sent tens of thousands of citizens, both native-born and naturalized, to concentration camps where most of them still remain? Almost all of them are Japanese, but none have been charged with any crime, nor will they be. Do you understand where I am going?"

Joey knew a threat when he heard one and he'd begun to sweat. "If you're suggesting that I'm a threat to the United States, that's ridiculous. I just want to save the lives of United States soldiers. I don't want anyone killed in prosecuting a war that's already won. I say let the remaining few Nazis stay where they are and grow old, die, and rot in hell."

"But what about their war crimes?"

"Sir, doesn't the Bible say something about letting the dead bury the dead? If we can catch them we should punish them, but otherwise let God provide for their punishment. As horrible as it is, nobody can resurrect all the dead Jews."

"Would you feel that way if the Nazis were still committing those war crimes?"

Before Joey could respond, Truman opened a desk

drawer and pulled out a manila folder containing a handful of eight-by-ten photos. "Look at these, Joey," Truman said in a voice that was taut with anger.

Joey looked at the photos and felt ill. Long rows of dead men lay facedown on the ground. Their hands had been tied behind their backs and they'd been shot in the back of the head.

"Joey, these are slave laborers, mainly Poles and Russians that the Nazis forced to work on their fortifications in the Alps. When they were no longer necessary or got too weak to work, the Nazis, the people you would have us live and let live, murdered them in cold blood."

"Jesus, I had no idea."

"I didn't think you did. These were taken about a week ago and our intelligence estimates that there are at least twenty thousand prisoners remaining in various states of declining health. If we don't do something, they will all die. I don't think either one of us has any problems with a couple hundred thousand Nazis starving to death, but I do feel different when it comes to innocent people. I would add that there are a few American prisoners being held in Germanica. What would you have me do with them?"

Joey could feel the force of his arguments slipping away. "What do you want me to do?" he asked in a soft voice.

"I'm under pressure to charge you with either sedition or treason. Attorney General Clark is willing to argue that your wanting our troops out of Germany is giving aid and comfort to our enemy, thus making it treason. J. Edgar Hoover wanted you picked up yesterday and locked up forever, and our previous attorney general, Francis Biddle, agreed with him.

You would have spent the rest of the war plus a few decades in prison if they'd had their way."

Joey was appalled and he began to tremble. He had no idea he could get into trouble simply for doing what he thought was right. The thought of going to prison for possibly the rest of his life horrified him.

"I am not a traitor. If I had known that the Germans were still butchering people I would not have organized this march. My mother wouldn't have wanted it either."

"I didn't think you did."

"Mr. President, what do you want me to do?"

Truman handed over the folder with the photos. "These are going to be officially given to the press later this afternoon. Take them now and talk to the others in the group. Let them make their own decisions. However, I think it would be a very good idea for you to literally and figuratively distance yourself from the movement and anyone radical enough to want to continue on."

Joey took the pictures. He would show them around and tell his new comrades that he was going to bail on them. He had a wry thought. He was going to bail and not go to jail. God, had he gotten himself into water that was way too deep for him.

"There are reporters hanging around our camp. I'll make sure they understand my change of heart."

Truman stood. The interview was clearly over. They shook hands. "I knew you'd see reason when you understood what the facts were. I only met your mother for that one tragic moment, but I know she'd be proud of you."

Joey left with his FBI guardians. Truman was relieved to have solved one crisis, if only a minor one. Now all he had to do was solve the growing problem of Stalin's Soviet Union, which was beginning to make demands that could not be tolerated. He had to concede that poor Poland was again lost. The Red Army was on her soil and not likely to leave. The same held true for Latvia, Lithuania, and Estonia. Czechoslovakia and Hungary also had new masters. Austria and Germany would be partitioned.

Japan had surrendered and millions of GIs were clamoring for what they felt was a long overdue discharge.

CHAPTER 15

"**T**HIS IS DISGUSTING," WINNIE SAID AS SHE watched the first bus pull away from the border checkpoint with Germanica. The bus was trailed by two others and by several trucks, all containing luggage and furniture. The bus windows were closed and shaded. Whoever was inside was safe from prying eyes. However, she and Ernie knew who the passengers were. Allen Dulles had gotten the information from his contacts in the Swiss government. At first it had shocked them, but then it *did* make sense.

"The black widow and her hatchlings have arrived," Ernie said and Winnie nodded.

The bus contained Magda Goebbels and her six children. Whether or not Magda would stay at the very hastily constructed compound surrounding a large house outside of Arbon was another matter. Ernie felt it was likely that she would cross the border at her leisure and be at her husband's side until the end. The children, it was felt, would stay in the relative safety of Arbon, or be moved someplace else in Switzerland. Whether or not either parent would die in the fighting was another unanswered question.

A dozen Swiss soldiers on motorcycles led the parade and chased other vehicles off the road. Allen Dulles sat down beside them on a park bench as the parade passed them. He handed each of them a coffee in a cardboard mug.

"Are we going to follow them?" Winnie asked.

"No point to it. We know precisely where they are going and why. When they arrive, they will be secure and secluded. We will observe them and the compound at our leisure."

Ernie grimaced. The coffee had gotten cold. "From what you've told us, they have a hand-picked group of so-called assistants inside the compound. They are, of course, all SS troops and their one and only job is to keep mother viper and her viperlings safe. And, there will be at least a battalion of Swiss army soldiers securing the outside."

Dulles smiled. "And none of them will be personally neutral. I have it on excellent authority that they've been hand-picked because of their pro-Nazi leanings. Therefore, there's not much chance of their being suborned by sweet talk or money from us."

Winnie sighed. "Well, it would be wonderful to talk with the happy family. In particular, I'd like to talk to the children."

Dulles smiled like the cat who'd eaten the canary. "We will."

"And just how will you do that?" asked Ernie. "Just how devious are you going to be this time?"

Dulles pretended to be hurt. "I'm not going to be devious at all. I've gone about it the old-fashioned way.

I simply contacted the Germans via the Swiss and asked for a meeting. Frau Goebbels is as intrigued as we are and will grant an interview just as soon as they are settled in. It shouldn't take more than a couple of days."

"May I ask her about Marie Leroux?"

Dulles winced. "I have it on very good authority that both she and Sven are still alive. Beyond that, I cannot say."

"Is it safe to assume that your contacts come from General Vietinghoff's headquarters?" asked Ernie.

Dulles shook his head. "I will neither confirm nor deny that. Sadly, I can report that both were interrogated and the interrogations were rather brutal along with being very effective."

"Oh God," moaned Winnie.

"What can we do to strike back at them?" asked Ernie. "If Herr Goebbels should decide to make a conjugal visit to fornicate with Frau Goebbels, could we arrange to either kill him or kidnap him while they're screwing their little Nazi hearts out?"

"Absolutely not. First, it would do nothing towards shortening the war. Someone else, probably Field Marshal Schoerner, would take over immediately. Perhaps the successor would even be the head torturer himself, General Hahn. If there was some way of getting Vietinghoff on the throne, I would consider it."

Ernie didn't argue. He'd expected the rebuff.

Dulles continued. "There is also the fact that the Swiss government would be deeply offended and require us to leave their country immediately. Whether or not we approve is irrelevant. The United States likes having an outpost so close to the heart of the cancerous Nazi tumor; that is, if Nazi tumors have hearts.

"Therefore, you will make no plans regarding any assassination or kidnapping of Josef Goebbels. Nor will you contemplate kidnapping or harming either Magda Goebels or her children. We simply will not sink to their level."

"Even if it meant saving lives?" Winnie asked as she wiped the tears from her face.

Dulles nodded tolerantly. "Winifred, when you asked to cross the border as part of an OSS team, I turned you down because I thought you'd be caught immediately. Now you're feeling guilty because you didn't push me hard enough. Instead, your old friend Marie went in and is suffering the torments of hell. I have no regrets as to my choice and you have no choice but to respect it. It was not your decision, it was mine and mine alone. You did not have a vote. There was no way on earth that I was going to let you enter Germany or, if you prefer, Germanica. Not only would it have been a waste of your talents, but the political implications would have been enormous. The one time I did send you, the circumstances were considerably different and there was a sense of urgency."

He shook his head. "Nor did I feel that there was any real danger in that excursion. It was nothing more than the drop off and subsequent pickup of of an envelope that we'd done many times before. I had no idea that Hitler would decide to kill his wretched self on that date and cause such chaos."

Ernie was puzzled. "Winnie, what the hell is this nice man talking about when he says political implications."

She smiled wanly. "My father is, was, a friend of Roosevelt's. He is a big contributor to the Democratic Party. He's also a buddy of Colonel Donovan's."

"I'm surprised that Winnie didn't tell you too much about herself," Dulles said. "Along with being lovely, graceful, and intelligent, she is quite wealthy and part of Philadelphia's Main Line community."

"Winnie, is that true? What does your father do?"

She was able to manage a real smile. "He buys things. The last time we talked he was thinking about buying Philadelphia."

Having gotten out of bombing German targets in the mountains at night, neither Bud nor George, nor the other pilots for that matter, could complain about escorting bombers on another toilet paper run.

As with this and previous other flights, the bombers they were protecting would drop leaflets over what were presumed to be German positions occupied by turncoat Russians. Neither man had heard of a General Vlasov and his anti-communist army. But if they were fighting for the Germans, then they were the enemy. Nor were any of the pilots concerned about the rumored forced repatriation of the Russians to Stalin's embrace. Hell, they'd fought for the Germans and should be punished. The piper wants to be paid, one pilot had said.

But if thousands of Russians could be convinced to surrender, then a lot of Americans might survive the war instead of getting killed in pointless fighting. The surrender of the Japanese after the second atomic bomb had struck Nagasaki had come as a pleasant surprise to everyone. It had been presumed that the Japs would fight to the last Japanese man, woman, and child, and that the war would continue for many long years. The American body count would run into the hundreds of thousands, if not more. "The Golden Gate in Sixty Eight," was a commonly heard cry from the soldiers in the Pacific. Now it looked like it was the Nazis who wouldn't give up. The Germans didn't stand a ghost of a chance against the Americans, so why were they still fighting, was the constantly asked question.

"Toilet paper away, alert the assholes," said a sarcastic Bud as bomb bay doors opened and tens of thousands of sheets of paper billowed down. Puffs of black smoke appeared by the bombers as German antiaircraft guns took up the challenge.

"Where are they coming from?" Bud asked. He looked below for flashes of gunfire. "I see something, guys. Just follow me."

A stream of four planes plummeted down. When they were low enough, Bud fired his rockets and machine guns, the shells' impacts highlighting what he thought was a target. The other planes saturated the area with their rockets and machine guns. There were no secondary explosions and there was no more antiaircraft fire. They made a second pass and dropped bombs. This time there was a small secondary explosion and they were jubilant. They received radioed thanks from the bomber pilots.

"Well," said George, "do you think we hit them or just chased them away."

"Either way works fine for me. I hate to lose bombers I'm supposed to be shepherding. I think the bomber pilots are arrogant pricks, but they are Americans."

"Yep, and they think we're arrogant pricks as well."

Ahead, the bombers were turning and heading

back to base. The fighters followed in their wake. Other formations joined them and a mighty armada that hadn't dropped a single bomb turned for home.

"What are they having for dinner tonight?" asked Bud.

"Shit on a shingle. What else? Rumor has it that when we run out of that crap they'll declare the war over and we'll all go home."

Bud laughed. "Then let's eat hearty. And when we're done we can go into town and see that new cabaret everyone's talking about."

"Which one is that?"

"The one where all the women are dressed up like nuns."

Once upon a time, the road south to Innsbruck had been paved. It had taken drivers on a comfortable and scenic trip between snow-capped mountains. They would arrive at Innsbruck ready for a holiday filled with skiing and other activities. But it had been shelled and bombed so often that the road had reverted to a far more primitive state. It was now worse than if it had never been paved. Craters that could swallow trucks caused the line of Sherman tanks to snake its way slowly down the remains of the highway. White flags nailed to stakes showed where a path had been cleared of German mines. A tank carrying flails that whipped from a bulldozer-like front led the way. It was based on an idea by British officer named Percy Hobart. It and other creations were called "Hobart's Funnies." What was a real laugh for the Germans was that the minesweeping tank actually worked as the flails caused the mines to detonate harmlessly.

As long as the American armor kept to the cleared path, they were reasonably safe. The GIs were not likely to stray. Intelligence said they were now in the middle of an extensive minefield. It would be a long time before all the mines were located and dug up.

Tanner nervously followed the column of tanks in a jeep with Sergeant Hill. Their job was to check and see if any Russian prisoners had been swept up or, better, if any of them had decided to surrender as a result of the blizzard of papers urging them to do so. Cynics doubted it if or no other reason than that the Russians were largely illiterate.

Sergeant Archie Dixon was in the first tank behind the flail. Even though there was a significant difference in rank, the meetings between Dixon and Tanner had been cordial, even friendly. Tanner thought that Dixon was a good kid and a helluva leader and wondered where he'd wind up when the war was over. Assuming he made it through, of course.

"Movement," yelled Hill. A second later, a dozen men jumped up from where they'd been hiding in the grasses along the side of the road. They were carrying Panzerfausts, the antitank rocket that could be fired by one man if necessary. It didn't have much range, but the Germans were already too close for comfort.

Machine guns cut down several of the Germans, but enough of them got close enough to fire at the tanks. The German rockets arched out and struck their targets. Several struck treads, which was only an inconvenience since damaged treads could be repaired.

Tanner watched in horror as Dixon's tank was hit. It staggered to a halt and smoke began to pour out of it. Men followed and one man was limping on one leg. He was missing his left foot and screaming. The wounded American staggered off the path and into the minefield. He had gotten only a few yards, when a spring-loaded German antipersonnel mine known as a "Bouncing Betty" jumped from the ground, exploded, and disemboweled him.

Tanner ran to the damaged tank, hugging other vehicles and trying very hard to stay on the path. Medics had arrived at Dixon's tank by the time he arrived. They had bravely dared to leave the path to get to the casualties.

One of Dixon's crewmen lay facedown in the dirt. A medic had put his helmet over his face and turned away. A second crewman lay half out of a hatch and the lower half of his body was smoldering. Dixon was leaning against another tank, his face contorted with physical and emotional pain.

Dixon saw Tanner. "They killed my men. Why did they have to do that?"

It's because we're at war, he thought but did not say. It would have been too cruel. "Sergeant, are you wounded?"

"I don't think so, but I wish I was. Maybe I wish I was dead. I think I'm the only survivor from my crew. Would you tell me why that happened?"

"I have no idea," he said. He thought that one of Dixon's other men might still be alive, but it wasn't the time to bring it up.

A medic came and pulled on Dixon's arm until he followed him. "Shell-shock," said Hill. "Maybe he'll come out of it and maybe he won't."

Tanner had seen enough mental cases caused by the war to last a lifetime. He looked around at the terrain. The mountains that used to look scenic and romantic seemed to be glowering at him. "Sergeant Hill, is it just me or are the Alps getting bigger and closer?"

It was movie time in the White House again. The audience was small, consisting of the President and General Marshall. There were no refreshments, although Truman had a bourbon and water. The projectionist had been dismissed after confirming that the five star general could actually run the device. What they were going to discuss would be very sensitive and the fewer who heard them, the better.

A number of scenes had been spliced together, all in black and white and all with that annoying herky-jerky motion that made old movies so maddeningly difficult to watch. It even made war look deceptively funny.

However, each man knew that what they were watching contained no humor whatsoever. The scenes were from World War I battles along the border between Italy and Austria and what they showed were mountains covered by snow deep enough to swallow men, horses, and vehicles. Soldiers moved through the snow with great difficulty, while others burrowed into the massive drifts, made caves, and lived like Eskimos. Some of them actually laughed and played around for the camera.

The Austrians held the high ground and the Italians were slaughtered in great numbers. Black splotches on the snow were bodies—many, many bodies.

The film ended. Marshall turned on the lights. He did not rewind the film. That chore would be left to the real projectionist to handle.

"Sir, those battles lasted almost the entire war and nothing much was gained by them. Italy was almost forced out of the war and that led, at least in part, to the collapse of the Austro-Hungarian Empire. If winter comes and the Germans haven't been defeated, that is where and how we'll be fighting them."

"Are you telling me that you don't want us to repeat those battles? If you are, don't worry. I have no intention of letting that happen."

"Even though I've heard it before, Mr. President, I'm glad to hear you say it again. My point in showing the films is to remind you that winter is going to be upon us in just a couple of months. When that happens, fighting in the mountains is going to be extremely difficult at best. Even though much of the area has a moderate climate and there are many areas that aren't at all mountainous, the Germans will withdraw to the worst terrain and dare us to root them out."

"How much use would mountain troops be?"

"They would be excellent, only there aren't enough of them, Devers has only one division, in fact, and it is being worn down pushing towards Innsbruck. It is now obvious that the Germans are shrinking their alpine redoubt and turning it into an alpine citadel. Their engineers have done a marvelous job of tunneling into the mountains and making giant storage facilities. I'm beginning to think that was their plan all along. The original redoubt was just too big to defend with the forces they had at hand."

"I assume you have more bad news, General."

"That depends on you, sir. When the snows come, which will be soon, serious fighting will effectively cease. We will not be able to go for the kill until the spring thaws. In short, we will be at war with the Nazis for a good eight to ten months longer unless something dramatic is done."

The thought of the war continuing until the summer of 1946 caused Truman's stomach to churn. "What do you propose?"

"That, sir, is not my job. I'm here to give you options. It you want this war ended before the snows, then it is highly unlikely to occur without the use of nuclear weapons."

Truman shook his head violently. "Jesus, no. Already I'm being castigated because of the civilian casualties caused by dropping atomic bombs on Hiroshima and Nagasaki. I have no regrets regarding those two bombs since they ended the war and saved millions of lives, but I don't want to introduce them into the European war. The American public was fine with killing Japs, but they would not feel the same way if we began nuking Germans, even if they were Nazis. There are scores of millions of Americans who are of German extraction and they would be outraged. And, like it or not, we cannot ignore the fact that the Germans are white and the Japs yellow."

"That, sir, leaves a massive and bloody attack by us, the use of poison gas to root them out, or, despite your protests, a nuclear drop in some uninhabited Alpine valley to let them know we're serious. Finally, there's cutting off their Swiss supply lines and starving them out."

"Is 'none of the above' on the list of answers?"

Marshall almost smiled. "Sorry sir, but no."

"And what about the risk of a German nuclear bomb? Nobody yet has totally ruled it out."

Truman stood and looked out a window. The anti-war crowds had dwindled since the news of the latest German atrocities had been published. Joey Ruffino had been true to his word. He had apologized in the newspapers and gone home. Truman wished him well. Maybe when this was over, he'd get in touch, maybe invite him to the White House for a real visit.

But first this war had to end. If it lasted another winter, the clamor for a negotiated peace would arise anew and with greater fervor. Memory of the recent atrocities would fade and Americans would want their boys home safely from Germany, just as they were beginning to return from the Pacific.

Truman thought for a moment and smiled. "General, here is what we will do. First, we will prepare at least one atom bomb to be dropped in the Alps. Publicize the fact that we have it and it might just get the Nazis' attention. Second, we will inform the Swiss that their free ride is over, that they must stop supplying the Germans. Either that or we will take action to ensure that they do."

"General Guisan will not like that," Marshall said. "He's repeatedly said that the Swiss Army he commands will fight and even retreat into the mountains if it is threatened, just like the Germans are planning."

"The hell with General Guisan," Truman snapped. "We will let him know that we might have to violate Swiss neutrality and enter her territory, but it will be only so that we can get those damn Nazis. And if he wants to retreat to his mountains, we'll let him. We won't go after him. He and all of Switzerland can sit there in the mountains and freeze their asses while we chase the Germans. And no, we are not going to launch a massive and bloody attack against German defenses, and it doesn't matter if they have the bomb or not."

Marshall looked at Truman. He was puzzled. "You haven't said anything about the use of poison gas."

Truman smiled wanly. "I know."

Winnie sat on a park bench and pretended to read a paperback copy of *Gone With the Wind*. The novel was one of her favorites and she'd read it a number of times. She'd never been to Atlanta, although she'd like to, and she'd never seen a plantation, or a slave for that matter. Margaret Mitchell's prose had brought those images alive for her. This version was a casualty of the war. In order to save paper and wood, it had been printed on sheets so thin that they were almost sheer. She felt that the pages would fall apart in her hands. If she ever got it home, she would preserve it like the antique it was sure to become.

No matter. She wasn't there to read. Her job was to keep an eye on twelve-year-old Helga Suzanne Goebbels. The oldest daughter of Josef and Magda Goebbels and a couple of large and solemn guards, along with a pair of sturdy looking women, had gone shopping in Arbon. The thought amused Winnie. Arbon was a long ways from being a major fashion or retail center. It was nothing more than a very plain little town of no distinction.

It was clear that Helga's two male guards wanted to be where they could actively protect Helga, using force if necessary. They were very concerned about their charge's safety. They kept looking at Winnie as if they knew who she was, which she thought was highly likely. The two women were far more tolerant and it occurred to Winnie that there had been few excursions like this in quite some time. Even though the Goebbels family was safe in Bregenz, there was still the possibility that someone would change the rules of war and bomb the German capital.

She looked up and glanced across the park. Ernie was on another bench. He caught her eye and made a big production out of pretending to pick his nose. She stifled a laugh and pretended to wipe her nose on her sleeve. Later, she would tell him that's what civilized and cultured people did back in Philadelphia. A microphone was under her bench and they were connected by a wireless radio, and it was linked to a nearby building where anything of note was being recorded.

"Why do you hate us?"

Winnie was startled. Young Helga was standing only a few feet in front of her. Damn it, she thought, she hadn't been paying attention. Helga's guards hadn't been either and they moved up quickly. Ernie stood up and moved closer. Neither she nor Ernie were carrying weapons this day. Dulles had been adamant on that. Thou shalt not annoy the Swiss, was his command.

Helga turned to her guards and waved them back. "No one is going to hurt me," she said in a small but strong voice. Reluctantly, they took several steps back. Ernie found another place to sit and did.

"I don't hate you," Winnie said.

"But you're an American, a spy, and all Americans hate us. I even know you're name, it's Winifred. And the man over there is named Ernie. Are you two lovers?"

"No, we're not," she stammered, surprised by the

blunt question. "And let me repeat myself. I do not hate you. Ernie does not hate you and Harry Truman does not hate you either."

Helga smiled briefly at that and Winnie realized that the girl was really quite pretty. "But you support the Jews and the Jews are the cancer that is destroying the world. Hitler and the Reich were put on this earth to stamp out the cancer. Why have you stopped us?"

Winnie took a deep breath. "Helga, do you consider the Jews to be human?"

The question appeared to puzzle her. "No, of course not, at least not entirely. They are less than human. They might look human, but they are not. They rob and steal from true Aryans."

"What about the Poles and the Russians? What about other Slavs and Gypsies?"

She shook her head. "They are near human, almost human, as well. Everyone knows that."

"And the Japanese?"

"Disgusting vermin we Germans had to deal with. I'm glad they've been destroyed. Sometimes back in Berlin I'd see the little yellow men in their ridiculous uniforms strutting around Berlin and I wished I could strike them because of their arrogance. It was almost as if they considered themselves Aryan and our equal. I'm glad they were punished."

Winnie was amazed. How could an open and pretty young girl say such things and do so without any apparent emotion. "Do you feel the same way about the murders of the Jews in the death camps?"

Helga became solemn. "I'm shocked that you believe that propaganda. There are no death camps. There are prisons and of course people have died in prisons.

People always die. And the people in prisons are, of course, people who have committed crimes. Life in a prison is not gentle and it shouldn't be. I've been listening to my parents. They say that the United States has no right to say they are more moral after bombing Hiroshima and Nagasaki and killing hundreds of thousands of civilians, even if they were Japanese."

"Tell me, Helga, did you ever meet Hitler?"

She brightened like a lamp that had been switched on. "I met him on many, many occasions. He had many dinners with us and us with him. He liked us children and sometimes he got down on the floor and played with the little ones. It was like he could live a normal life for just a little while and not worry about the burdens of the world. He would even bring his dog, a German Shepherd named Blondi. She would play with us too. Her great tail would wag and thump and she'd try to lick our faces. She's dead now too." Her eyes began to glisten with tears at the memory. "Someday, the world will recognize Hitler's true greatness."

Along with being shocked and horrified, Winnie was fascinated. She wanted to learn much more about the daily, even banal, life with Adolf Hitler. One of Helga's female handlers had come within a few steps and coughed discreetly. Helga turned and glared at the woman and then turned back to Winnie. She was clearly annoyed.

"I think my guardian angel wants me to go back with her. I enjoyed this talk. Can we do it again some other time? I hope we can."

"Even though I'm a spy and don't hate Jews?"

Helga shrugged and smiled engagingly. "Perhaps that will make it even more interesting."

Ernie waited a few moments before sitting down beside Winnie. Across the park, one of Helga's male guardians glared at them. Ernie smiled and gave him the finger. The guard's eyes widened and then he laughed and returned the favor.

"Ernie, that was incredible. I don't know if I was just in the face of utter evil or listening to the mistaken ranting of a naive little child. Or maybe it's a bit of both."

"Well, she's been listening to that crap for all of her twelve years. That's plenty of time to be thoroughly indoctrinated. Maybe even to the point of no return."

"I hope not. I can't imagine children like that growing up to be future Nazis."

Winnie stood and brushed off her skirt. "I don't know if I feel filthy and need a bath or angry and need a drink."

"Why not both?"

She took his arm and they walked away. "Let me think about it."

The negotiations had been tense. The ranking Russian commander had been only a senior sergeant who covered his nervousness in front of officers by being rude and arrogant. He did speak passable German, which was a plus.

Tanner spoke first. "What should we call you and the men you represent?"

The question seemed to surprise the Russian. "Whatever you do, do not call us communists or part of the Red Army. Also, we are not Nazis. We were always fighting for our homeland. Why don't you simply call us Russians? My name, by the way, is Sergei Radeski."

Apparently the two other men with Radeski spoke German as well since they nodded their concurrence. Good, Tanner thought. "I see that there are no officers among you. Where are they and why would you be authorized to negotiate in behalf of your entire division."

Radeski smiled and it wasn't a pretty sight. Like so many of his countrymen, he was missing several teeth. Dental hygiene in the Soviet Union was a lost art. "Many of our officers had misgivings about dealing with you. We were concerned so we put them all in protective custody. Some of them are hell bent on dying in battle because they've been told that anyone taken prisoner by you Americans would be turned over to Stalin's thugs to be tortured and then murdered."

Tanner had filled his canteen with vodka. He pretended to take a swallow and handed the canteen to Radeski who sniffed, smiled and took a long swallow. "It's almost as good as Russian vodka."

The canteen was passed to the other Russians. When Tanner got it back, it was almost empty.

"Sergeant Radeski, what you feared was indeed likely to happen. But then Stalin went too far. Our president, Harry Truman, is very upset that Stalin is stealing so much of Europe and murdering Russians who are returned to him and that includes those ordinary prisoners who were captured. Apparently, Stalin feels that they have been contaminated. Therefore, President Truman will not force anyone to return to Russia."

"Where will we go?" Radeski asked, suddenly very solemn. The enormity of their predicament weighed heavily on them. Their cause was lost and they were lost.

"Actually, you have several choices. And by the way, that includes the Croats among you. We will take care of them as well."

Radeski shrugged and spat on the ground. "Fuck the Croats. I am only concerned about Russians. Now, where will we go?"

"Argentina will take you," Tanner said. "It's a lovely country with ranches and farms, good wine, and plenty of beef to eat."

"Do their women like to fuck?"

Tanner didn't have to force a smile. "Don't they all? And then there's France, which will take you, but they will want you to join either their army or the Foreign Legion. Either way, you will probably be sent to IndoChina where the French are fighting a communist group called the Viet Minh."

Radeski nodded. "IndoChina has yellow-skinned women, right?"

"Yes."

"Interesting, Captain Tanner. I've never fucked a yellow-skinned woman."

"I'm sure they'd be thrilled."

Radeski laughed. "They'd be thrilled until the money ran out. I am not a fool, Captain. I think Argentina would be the better choice, but I will have to discuss it with my men."

They all rose and shook hands. "Don't take too long, Senior Sergeant. If the Germans realize what we are doing, they could begin shelling."

"You'll have our answer in an hour."

It took just a few minutes longer than an hour. American soldiers spotted a long and winding column of men coming down the road and keeping to the left side of it. Tanner had told them that, if they were truly surrendering, to leave all their weapons behind, and that included their German-style helmets. There was fear that the helmets would draw fire from confused American soldiers.

As the Russians slogged by, Tanner looked at their faces. Some were sad and some looked utterly defeated. Others looked hopeful and even smiled at him. They knew they'd been given a reprieve from a death sentence. They were all filthy and appeared near starving.

Radeski approached Tanner. "It has been decided. We would like to go to Argentina."

"Good choice. I never asked you, but what about your families back home?"

"They are dead. If they are not already cold in the ground, they soon will be. Stalin's secret police would have rounded them up the moment they found out that we'd deserted the worker's paradise that is Mother Russia. It is sad, but that is life under Stalin. We will start over and someday you will find out that Stalin is worse than Hitler."

The Russian column continued. "Sergeant, how many men did you bring with you?"

"Approximately eleven thousand. There could be more, perhaps less. No one was eager to stand around and be counted. They just wanted to leave. I am confident that other units will surrender once they see that we are safe. Until then, they will just stand aside."

Tanner was flabbergasted at the number of Russians and the gaping hole it must be leaving in the German lines. "And the Germans are just *letting* you go? They've done nothing to stop you?"

The question surprised Radeski. "Germans? What Germans? There are no Germans, comrade Captain. They've all fled west."

"Then what's between us and Innsbruck and the American army fighting its way north?"

Radeski roared with laughter, as if it was the funniest question he'd heard in a long time. "There's nothing between here and Innsbruck. What's left of it is yours for the taking."

The discussion between Allen Dulles and Henri Guisan took place in a small room in the town hall of Arbon and were tense. Guisan's rank was simply "general." It implied that he was the only man of that rank in the Swiss Army, which Dulles didn't think was correct. The Swiss Army was several hundred thousand strong. Logic, therefore, said there had to be more than one general. Dulles had concluded that it was an honorific and simply meant that he was the overall commander.

Guisan, a small, prim-looking man with a thin mustache was, in time of crisis, the commander of all Switzerland. Intensely patriotic and a firm believer in doing everything to keep his country neutral, he had threatened to destroy the tunnels and bridges and move his people into the mountains if the Germans had attacked. The Nazis decided that conquering Switzerland was doable, but would not be worth the time and effort.

But times were now different. Major units of the Swiss Army were arrayed within a few miles the border with Germany. Now they were confident that it would be a fairer fight than it would have been a few years earlier. Back when World War II started, the Germans were strong in the air and had superb artillery and armor. Now they had neither and the Swiss army was larger than the rump German army across the border. Guisan had felt comfortable that his beloved nation would survive the carnage around it.

That is, until he heard what Dulles had to say.

"Let there be no doubt about it, General Guisan, my president strongly feels that the war with Germany must be brought to a swift and relatively bloodless conclusion. The Germans must either be destroyed or capitulate before winter closes down military activities. Therefore, we are giving you notice that our bombers will soon have free rein to bomb any and all targets in the Germanica rump state. These will include the crossing points where trains and columns of trucks are bringing into Germanica what are called humanitarian supplies. If necessary, we propose to starve the Germans. I am well aware that high-level bombing is notoriously inaccurate; therefore I urge you to evacuate areas close to the border, such as this lovely town of Arbon."

Guisan's face was turning red. "That is monstrous. We have done nothing to deserve this."

Dulles shrugged. "Who has, General? You might ask the same question of the Poles, the French and the citizens of just about every nation in Europe. As a great American once said, war is hell. We will not commence bombing immediately. When we are prepared, we will give you twenty-four hours' notice before we start."

"We do not have an air force, but we do have guns and we will shoot down your planes."

"If you do that, the planes escorting the bombers will have orders to attack those guns, wherever they might be situated. Your unique position has spared you the agonies of war, but that time has passed."

"We will move to our own mountain forts and fight you from there."

"We don't care what you do, General. We will not be invading, so you can retreat to the mountains and sit there for all eternity and starve."

Dulles thought he could see Guisan's mind churning. "If you will do your best, we will do ours," he finally admitted.

"Excellent. There are a few other factors to consider. While neither of us has a navy in the area, we will be launching armed gunboats onto Lake Constance. They will not come within three miles of Swiss soil while they bombard German targets. There may also be, ah, other activities on the lake."

"One can only imagine," Guisan said drily.

"And when the war is finally over, there will be the issue of Nazi money now on deposit in Swiss banks. These will be turned over to the Allies as part of German reparations. We are particularly interested in retrieving the money and other valuables stolen from Jews and deposited in your vaults."

"Our bankers will never agree to that."

"Yes they will. It might take a little while, but they will realize that they have no real choice. If they don't, Switzerland will be isolated even more than she is now and trivialized. Financial centers will open elsewhere and all you will have left of your economy is skiing, good watches, and excellent chocolates. If your bankers accept our proposal, you will soon recover from any inconveniences you might suffer. If you play it right, you will come out on the side of the angels and the saints and the world will respect you."

Guisan smiled tightly. "I have never thought of myself as either an angel or a saint, but I do see your point. I will discuss matters with my superiors and will get back to you."

"Excellent. Just don't take too long and don't forget that close-in bombing will commence in a *very* short while."

"If some of the higher-ranking Nazis want to leave Germany via Switzerland, what will be your stance?"

Now it was Dulles' turn to smile and shrug. "You can do whatever you want with Goebbels and his ilk. As the saying goes, they can run but they can't hide. They will ultimately be tracked to the ends of the earth if necessary. I would also appreciate it if you did not hamper our diplomatic operations in Switzerland while these matters sort themselves out."

The two men shook hands and General Guisan smiled, this time with humor. "It has occurred to me, Mr. Dulles, that your new president is quite a bastard."

"Sir, I will gladly convey your compliment."

CHAPTER 16

TANNER WAS WITH THE LEAD COLUMN FROM THE 105th as it was driven slowly down the road to Innsbruck. There had been no shooting. The war had taken a holiday. The only thing to disturb the relative tranquility was the steady stream of Russians heading to internment prior to a trip to Argentina.

Sergeant Hill was driving, which gave Tanner a chance to think. Doc Hagerman was up to his ears giving surrendered Russians a cursory physical. Each one of them, he'd said, harbored an enormous colony of fleas and other crawly things. "I don't think some of them have ever bathed in their lives. And as to sending them to Argentina, it would be a cruel thing to do to Argentina. So many of them don't have any idea what or where Argentina is. All they know is that they hate Stalin and want to be many miles away from his clutches."

Translations were being done from Russian to German to English, which had led to a number of misunderstandings. Fortunately, none had been serious and the Russians even had a sense of humor. As long as they weren't going to visit Stalin, they could laugh.

They passed a sign. It said Innsbruck in six kilometers. The sign had been shot to pieces and was barely readable. "Think we'll find anybody in the town, Captain?"

"There's always somebody," he said.

Before the war, Innsbruck had a population of more than sixty thousand. As the end of the Nazi nightmare drew near, the population had swollen to more than a hundred thousand. This had attracted American fighters and bombers who'd plastered what had once been a lovely city and a center of the winter tourist trade. There had even been talk of Innsbruck hosting the winter Olympics, which wasn't likely given the city's Nazi past.

As they drove they could see the totality of the devastation. What had been lovely chalets were charred piles of rubble. To no one's surprise, there were people still living in the ruins. There weren't many, but at least they had survived, and some of them even waved at the Yanks. As with most Germans in the summer of 1945, they were in rags and looked like they hadn't eaten in weeks.

Hill chortled. "I sure do like what Hitler did with Germany, sir. I'd like to ask some of these idiot people if this is what they imagined their lives would be after fighting all those countries."

"You're cruel, Sergeant, but it is appropriate. The Seventh Army says we should treat the Austrians gently since they weren't Germans but were taken over by Germany."

"With profoundest respects to the brass, didn't the Austrians vote to connect with Germany?"

"Ah, but they say the election was rigged and they were without blame."

Hill snorted. "All elections are rigged, especially where I come from. People don't die; they live on forever as voters and it doesn't matter what dates they have on their tombstones." He looked again at the ruins. "We sure did bomb the crap out of this place."

"Did you know there was a concentration camp in Innsbruck?"

"No sir, but I guess I'm not surprised. The Nazis had camps all over the place. It's a wonder they didn't run out of people to put in them. Since that's the case, the flyboys should have bombed it even more."

Tanner looked up at the mountains, some of which were still snow-capped despite the warm weather in the valley and by the River Inn. The mountains were as scenic as a postcard. If it weren't for the death and devastation in the valley, the scenery would be perfect.

"Hey, Captain. What do you hear about General Broome?"

Brigadier General Augustus Broome had been promoted from brigade commander to the top spot in the division, replacing the late General Evans. Evans had been given an impressive funeral. Ike, Devers, and Patton had all shown up to pay their respects. After the ceremony, Evans' casket had been shipped to the States.

"Sergeant, I've been told that Broome is highly disappointed. He's got the division but he won't get a second star, at least not right away. There are concerns in Washington that we already have too many generals and not enough of an army since the war is winding down. A lot of people are going to be discharged. He was told if he played nice he'd be able to keep the star he has instead of being reduced to colonel, his permanent rank."

Hill nodded. "Almost sounds fair, Captain. Are you sure the army thought of it?"

"Anything's possible. Broome did put a stop to any thoughts of prosecuting Cullen for his sloppy way of handling the escaped German prisoner. Intelligence did conclude that it was the little Unger shit who had led the way through our camp because he'd been here before, and that is why Evans got killed. The brass doesn't think too highly of having generals killed or captured. Heroic wounds are one thing, but killing, no. That Cullen will never see another promotion is now considered punishment enough."

"But he wasn't planning on staying in the army, was he?"

"No, but don't tell Devers or Ike."

They'd reached the center of Innsbruck. Ahead of them there were shouting and cheers. "What the hell?" asked Tanner.

Groups of American soldiers were gathered around, laughing, hugging, and drinking from canteens that definitely did not contain water. They got out of the jeep and walked to a master sergeant who was red-faced and grinning hugely.

"Sergeant, mind telling me what the hell the party's all about?" Tanner asked.

The sergeant belched. "I am proud to inform you that we have just rescued your raggedy asses." He saw the captain's bars and paled. "I mean we're here, sir."

"What the hell are you talking about?" snapped Hill.

The sergeant was a little glassy-eyed. The party had apparently been going for a little while.

"Sir, this bunch of misfits and perverts is from the 85th Infantry and the Fifth Army. We came all the way up from Rome to save you. If I can read maps correctly, this means that the German redoubt has just been cut in half."

Tanner and Hill grinned. It truly was a good time for a celebration. Hill took the initiative. "Master sergeant, you got anything of consequence left in that canteen?"

Lena didn't visit Father Shanahan very often. They both had too much to do and, from her perspective, the search for her father had so far been pointless. But it had been a while, so she made an exception.

"Are you here for me to hear your confession?" Shanahan asked with a gentle smile.

"If I was a Catholic, I'd definitely have you as my confessor."

"Thank you for the compliment. Now, I assume you want to know if I've heard anything about your father. Well, the answer is still no. I've gotten responses from a number of sources and there is nothing to tell you. This does not mean that he isn't alive. It might just be that nobody's found him yet or he hasn't decided to come forward. The world is falling apart and has descended into chaos; there are a lot of reasons for lying low. He could also be wandering toward the Allied armies as we speak and having to make a slow go of it."

Lena was saddened but not surprised. "I sometimes

think I should go to Prague and start searching there. After all, it was where we lived."

"That would be very foolish and extremely dangerous. The Red Army in Czechoslovakia is still wreaking havoc and is only marginally under control. Even if you got through the Russian lines, you'd still have to work your way into Prague. Worse, the commies aren't about to leave. The best thing for you to do is sit tight and let him pop up someplace. If he's going to," he quickly amended.

"You're right, of course," she said sadly. "Like you say, it would be foolish, dangerous and likely futile. But it is so frustrating waiting here."

"If I may comment, you seem even more at peace every time I see you."

"Thank you and you're right. I've even learned to trust people."

Shanahan grinned wickedly. "Who is he?"

She returned the grin. "An American, Father, what else?"

"And what are your plans?"

"Our plans are quite simple. We want to survive this war and then think about whether we have a future together."

"But he will go back to the States. What will you do if you haven't found your father and he wants you to go with him?"

"Do you want me to say wither thou goest I will go? I will if you like, and yes, I would go with him and continue searching from wherever we doth goest. Of course, he hasn't asked me yet. I will work on it."

"Your English has improved also. It was always good, but now it is excellent."

"I'm surrounded by Americans. It's hard not to get better. My big worry is some flagrant obscenity working its way into my casual vocabulary."

"Have you forgiven the Schneiders?"

"No, and I never will. Nor will I ever forget. They enslaved me, hurt me and humiliated me. I've survived, and maybe they won't, and that would be a wonderful punishment. Whatever happens, I won't worry about it. They may be punished here in this life or not. I will not lose sleep over them. They are beneath me."

"Lena, would you like a glass of sacramental wine or would you want me to pray for you?"

"Both, Father."

Harry Truman fought the urge to ask Soviet Foreign Minister Vyacheslav Molotov if he would like a cocktail. He did wonder if the personal envoy of dictator Joseph Stalin had a sense of humor. Molotov was a survivor. He had lasted through several purges and was now one of the most important men in the Soviet Union. Rumor had it that Molotov had to tread lightly. He didn't want to be perceived as too important and a rival to Stalin. Stalin's rivals had a way of disappearing into Moscow's dreaded Lubyanka Prison and never emerging again.

They spoke through translators. While Molotov's English was acceptable for casual conversation it was not good enough for diplomatic conversations where nuances were extremely important. Truman's Russian language skills were nonexistent.

Drinks were served. Truman had his bourbon on the rocks while Molotov had some American-made vodka that he clearly did not like. Truman smiled to himself. He had ordered that bad liquor be served to make the communist a little uncomfortable. It was petty, but he enjoyed it. The Soviets had been such pricks lately.

Molotov put down his glass. "My country's position is quite simple. We want the deserters from the Red Army handed over to us as we agreed upon."

"And we would like the Red Army out of Poland so that the Polish people can have their own free nation and a government of their choosing."

"The two are not related," insisted Molotov. "The Russians you have in your custody are traitors and justice demands that they must be punished and, yes, that punishment will likely include their execution."

"And that is barbaric."

"Not to us. We still have anti-Russian partisans fighting our efforts to bring peace to that area. People are already dying and will continue to die. We must see to it that those traitors do not cause further mischief."

Truman sipped his bourbon. Unlike Molotov's vodka, it was the best. "We have it on good authority that many of Vlasov's soldiers are shot the moment they are taken by the Red Army. That does not sound like justice to me."

"It is our justice. You may think it is rough, but you have to remember the massive wars and upheavals that my country has endured in the last few decades. Any hint of rebellion must be crushed."

"Minister, at Yalta your country promised free and fair elections. We even sent members of the exiled Polish government that had been in London to Moscow after you promised that no harm would come to them. We now understand that they are all dead, executed by your secret police. We are willing to negotiate the return of those who wish to go back to Russia, but we will not force anyone to return to Stalin's clutches."

Molotov winced at the insult to Stalin. He looked around, half expecting to be arrested for simply being in the room where such comments were made. The arm of the NKVD, the Soviet secret police, was long.

Molotov switched topics. "Stalin is concerned that your actions regarding the traitors presages the possibility of the United States negotiating a separate peace with the Nazis, in particular, the vermin holed up in the Alps."

"You can tell Premier Stalin that he has nothing to worry about on that score. We will not negotiate a separate peace with those people you so accurately refer to as vermin. We might negotiate where and when they will lay down their arms, but lay them down they will. Josef Goebbels is deluding himself if he thinks we can be deterred by the mountains and winter and anything else that might stand in our way. If he survives, Goebbels will go on trial with all the other Nazi sons of bitches we hold."

Molotov seemed satisfied, even smiled. "Premier Stalin will be pleased. You might inform the government of Argentina that the Soviet Union will be watching them and how they try to assimilate the Russian traitors. As I said, the NKVD has a *very* long arm."

"I'm sure the Argentines can take care of themselves. Now, and along the lines with Poland, when are your troops going to end their illegal occupation of Czechoslovakia, Hungary, Estonia, Lithuania, and Latvia?"

Molotov smiled grimly. "There is nothing illegal about our forces being in those countries just as there is nothing illegal about your soldiers being in Germany. We require buffer nations to protect us from future German aggression and our troops will leave those nations when we are confident that they are stable. There will doubtless be mutual defense treaties between those nations and the Soviet Union that will guarantee that peace."

The Russian took another sip of the vodka and grimaced. "Did I not hear a rumor that the U.S. was contemplating breaking up Germany into little nations much like it was less than a hundred years ago?"

"That was never seriously discussed," said Truman. "Treasury Secretary Henry Morgenthau proposed it, but it will not occur." With that, Molotov and Truman thanked each other for their courtesy and Molotov departed.

Truman made himself another drink. Son of a bitch, he thought. The Russians are going to be a real pain in the ass. And how could Roosevelt have thought he could get along with Uncle Joe Stalin? Roosevelt must have been a lot sicker than he and everyone else had thought.

Winnie sat on a folding chair she'd brought so she could watch the front of the Goebbels compound. With rumors that the war would encompass the area around Arbon, people were moving out and she'd picked up the chair for pennies. Once more, Magda and the children were moving, this time for the greater security of Zurich. After that it was rumored that the group would somehow get to Portugal where they would take a ship to Brazil. Their ultimate destination was presumed to be Argentina. Both she and Ernie had wondered just how many Nazis and former Nazis, their families and their sympathizers Argentina could handle before exploding.

She decided she didn't care. What she wanted now was for all the Nazis in Arbon to disappear, and if the earth swallowed them up she didn't care if that happened either. She saw Helga walking towards her with a very uncomfortable guard behind her.

"We're leaving again," a grim-faced Helga said. "And once again it's all your fault. My father says you are going to bomb everything so we have to leave to be safe. Why do you have to do that?"

"Maybe it'll end the war."

"Why don't you leave us in peace?"

Winnie decided to be blunt. "I would be happy to leave you and your brothers and sisters in peace, but not your parents. They have to answer for the crimes they've committed, especially your father."

Helga's eyes glistened. "But he's done nothing except try to help and protect Germany and the German people from the Jews and other enemies."

Winnie decided it was pointless to argue. "I think we have to let other people decide that. I do hope you find safety and peace," she said, surprising herself by meaning it.

Helga smiled winsomely. "I hope the same for you and the man who's watching us. Too bad you're not lovers yet. You are a very nice lady, even if you are an American. Oh, you're not Jewish are you?"

"Would it matter if I was?"

Helga thought for a moment. "No, I don't suppose it would, at least not under the current circumstances."

She surprised Winnie by leaning over and giving her a hug. "Maybe we'll meet again."

"May I take your picture?" Winnie asked. Helga thought for a moment, smiled and nodded yes. Winnie took her camera, a very expensive Leica she'd bought in Zurich with her father's money when she'd arrived in Switzerland. She even had color film in it. Helga smiled again and posed herself. It dawned on Winnie that the girl must have had many pictures taken of her. She took a couple and the guard sullenly took one of the two of them. Helga laughed and ran off.

Good luck, Winnie thought. What will your life bring? she wondered. Would you be able to live with the knowledge that your parents—your father in particular—was a war criminal. If he was executed for his crimes, could you handle that? Would you have a good life or would you become embittered? She found herself hoping that the child would grow up to be a human being.

A short while later, a column of trucks and busses departed Arbon. They would travel by road to Bern and then by train to Marseilles. From there they would take a ship to South America.

Dulles entered the compound accompanied by a handful of Swiss police and soldiers. After a short while they emerged. The Swiss left and Dulles signaled for her and Ernie to come with him.

As they looked around the compound, both hers and Ernie's conclusions were that the Nazis had lived a Spartan life. The house was two stories high and made of cement blocks. It looked shabby and run down and badly needed painting. At least it was large, they agreed.

Dulles checked his watch. "Some other agents will arrive tonight about ten, which is about six hours from now. I want you to stay here and watch the place. There should be no incidents. The Swiss are entirely on board with our taking over the facility. Who knows, we may make it our permanent base."

Ernie shook his head. "Not if the bombs are going to be falling close by."

"Good point. I'll have to think about another alternative. In the meantime, stay out of trouble and don't break anything. If you need food, call and someone will send in some sandwiches. The phones are working."

After Dulles left, they wandered about the building and grounds. The Goebbels family had left numerous articles of clothing and many items with swastikas on them. Ernie liberated some monogrammed handkerchiefs and Winnie took some towels, agreeing that they would make wonderful souvenirs. Ernie added a couple of ashtrays and a cigarette lighter to the pillowcase he was using as a swag bag.

The phone rang and Winnie answered it, simply saying hello. As she listened to the voice on the other end, her eyes widened. "Yes, Reich Minister, everyone has safely departed." she finally said in German.

Ernie grabbed a pad and paper and wrote "Goebbels?" Winnie nodded. She was talking to the head of what was left of the Third Reich. Winnie continued and smiled broadly. "Yes sir, I am part of a detail assigned to protect your property."

There was more from Goebbels. Ernie tried to get close enough to hear what he was saying, but all he could hear was a nasally voice.

"Will that be all then, Reich Minister Goebbels?

Good. Then perhaps I should inform you that I am not Swiss or German. I am an American and I work for the OSS. Ta-ta, Herr Scheissen."

Winnie hung up and threw herself down on the couch, doubled over in laughter. When she finally got control of herself she took out a cigarette, looked at it and decided against it. She sat back and looked at Ernie. "This will be something to tell our grand-children."

"Ours?"

She walked over and kissed him on the cheek. "Yes, Ernie, ours. Remember what I said about my brother being entombed in the *Arizona*? Well, the Japs have been defeated and Germany is about to fall. Therefore, I have decided to start living again. For a while after he died, I went a little wild and crazy, actually more than a little bit. My brother was everything to me. My father was gone much of the time and my mother was too busy reading the society pages, so he took Dad's place. He was the one who taught me how to shoot and fix cars. I thought about joining the women's army, navy or Marines, but that wouldn't put me anywhere near the Japs. The only way I could strike back at his murderers would have to be indirectly, so I used Dad's influence to meet Colonel Donovan and he got me in. Working with the OSS has helped ground me." She took a deep breath and smiled warmly. "I know you're in love with me, aren't you?"

"Yes," he whispered.

"Well, I'm in love with you too."

She took his hand and led him to the master bed-room. The bed was huge, twice the size of a normal

double bed. There was a huge red and black swastika
on the blanket. "Get undressed," she commanded and
he complied.

Very quickly they were both naked and they soaked
in the sight of their bodies. Her breasts were small but
firm, and her belly was as flat as any he'd ever seen,
and Ernie was happy he'd worked out and stayed in
shape. "You really *do* like me," she said, laughing as
she saw how aroused he was. They fell onto the bed
and made love quickly. The second and third times
were more passionate yet more delicate.

Finally sated, they lay on the bed and shared the
cigarette Winnie had started. "Will we tell our grandchildren that we consummated our love on Goebbels'
bed?" Ernie asked.

"When they're old enough to understand or we're
too old to care. I just wonder if they'll believe it or
if anyone will remember who Josef Goebbels was. By
the way, Ernie, you will have fun with my father. He's
loud and pushy but he already respects you. I wrote
about you and told him that you were a fighter pilot
and now a spy. He never saw action in the first war.
Like this one; he's a civilian expert and stuck behind
a desk and he hates it. Whatever you do, be firm with
him. He despises weak people. By the way, when was
your name changed to Janek?"

"I understand," Ernie said and yawned hugely. Three
times with this woman who was a tiger. She had wiped
him out. "My grandfather did it shortly after his family landed at Ellis Island. It had been Janikowski and
he felt it was too Polish. Sometimes I wish he hadn't
made the change. I think you should be proud of your
heritage and, besides, I like Polish food."

"So do I, or at least a lot of it. And when we're back home and after we're married, I want to go to Hawaii for our honeymoon. The government is going to make the *Arizona* a permanent grave and memorial. There will be no attempts to recover bodies. Too dangerous, I was told. And there's likely not much to recover after all this time. Still, I would like to visit my brother's grave."

"We will do exactly that," he said and yawned again.

He pulled her over and she rested her head on his shoulder. In a moment, his eyes were closed and he was breathing deeply. She slid out of the bed, padded across the room and got her camera from her purse. She smiled as she arranged a corner of the blanket to cover his exhausted manhood. She took his picture sprawled across Josef Goebbels' bed with the swastika in plain view. Then she set the camera and the timer so she could be part of the scene, again discreetly arranging the bedding. She kept taking pictures until she was out of film. She would develop the pictures herself. It was another skill she'd mastered in Allen Dulles' spy school. She almost giggled as she thought about sending copies to Josef and Magda Goebbels.

Winnie felt Ernie shift and his arm fell across her belly. "Just so you know, I really wasn't asleep."

Anton Schneider put his rifle in a closet and slammed the door. "Father, I don't feel like dying for a lost cause. *You* can if you wish, but neither my friends nor I want to commit suicide. Let's face it. Germany has lost the war and National Socialism has gone down the toilet."

Gustav Schneider stood and barely controlled himself while his wife gasped. "How dare you say that? Yes we have suffered reverses, but we will prevail."

Anton laughed harshly. "Reverses, Father. If these are reverses I'd like to know what you consider a real defeat. We've lost everything including all of Germany—or have you forgotten that where we are was Austria until only a few years ago. We have no friends, no money, and we are now living in a fucking cave."

This time an outraged Gustav did swing his beefy arm, but a more agile Anton ducked under it. "Do you see what's left, Father? Old men like you and boys like me. We have no modern weapons and no real training. When the time comes to fight the Americans we will be like lambs to the slaughter. We should be arranging our affairs so that we can either leave this godforsaken place and go to South America or surrender to the Allies and throw ourselves on their mercy."

"He has a point," said Gudrun. "For the last few years it's been nothing but defeat after defeat and promises of wonder weapons that are never fulfilled."

"We pledged to defend the Fuhrer," Gustav said.

"Father, have you noticed that he's dead? That ugly cripple Goebbels is not my idea of someone I would die for."

"If we are captured by the Americans we will be punished severely," Gustav said. "You might get away with a few years in prison because of your youth, while I would be executed as a war criminal."

Anton was intrigued. "For what? You were a clerk, a bureaucrat. You had no real authority. What could you have possibly done to be considered a war criminal?"

To Anton's surprise, his father looked genuinely saddened. "There are many reasons. I ran a ring of informers who told me who was being disloyal. I either accepted bribes from those cowards or sent them to concentration camps where they doubtless died. I stole food from government warehouses so we could eat better than others. And don't forget, I did rape and enslave that Jewess, Lena. If she's still alive, she could testify against me."

Anton laughed. "And who would believe *her*? First, she's probably dead and isn't going to testify against anyone. Even if she still lives, I've been told that most women who have been assaulted don't want to testify against those who attacked them. By the way, Father, how was she?"

Gustav laughed harshly. "Inert and as passionate as a large piece of meat. You didn't miss much."

"But it nearly cost me my manhood to find that out. Thank God things are back in working order. But let's get back to the point. We have to get out of here. Just about everyone I talk to is saying they'll make their way to Central or South America. There are rumors that Goebbels has sent his family across the border to safety."

"Not all of them. His wife is still in Bregenz. Or at least she was as of this morning."

Gudrun spoke up. "He's right. If we stay, we either get killed or are jailed. If we flee, we might find some form of freedom where we can start over."

Gustav sagged. He looked at the Panzerfaust that was resting against a wall. How futile it all now seemed. "I'm too old to start over and I don't want to spend the rest of my life in jail. Or be hanged," he said bitterly. "Anton, Gudrun, I saw the light a long time ago. Why the devil did Hitler have to invade Russia or declare war on the United States? It was madness. Who was advising him? I do not blame Hitler directly. He had to have been told that he would win. Why didn't he simply wait a few years before taking on either nation?"

"Does that mean you will try to figure a way out of this mess? Why don't we all flee to Switzerland?" asked Anton.

"Because," Gustav answered, "the bastard Swiss are playing both ends against the middle. There already have been a number of attempts to cross and they have all been turned back or the people given over to Hahn and the SS. No, now is not the time to try that."

"I understand," said Anton, "but you will plan for it, won't you?"

"Yes, and by the way, what does your sister think about this?"

Anton laughed. "My precious little sister is too busy screwing her brains out with that Hans Gruber boy who thinks he's a Werewolf."

CHAPTER 17

BRIGADIER GENERAL JOHN BROOME RETURNED TANner's salute and waved him to a chair. "Get some coffee and have a seat. Close the door while you're at it."

Tanner was apprehensive. This was the first time he had had anything other than perfunctory greetings. He thought he'd done a good job for the late General Evans, but who knew what Broome might want out of him?

Tanner passed on the coffee and the general got quickly to the point. "Captain, when you first arrived and General Evans set your group up as a quasi-independent unit, I admit that I was less than thrilled. It was his prerogative, of course, but it was unusual and that offended my very orderly military mind. When I took over, I gave thought to bringing you more under the traditional structure. That would not have been a criticism. You've done well."

"Thank you, sir."

"You know what they say—if it ain't broke don't fix it. Well, what we have here ain't broke. I have no intentions of doing anything that would disrupt a well-running headquarters, especially with the end of the war so close, and, God, I do hope it is close. Ergo, there is no reason for a new Broome to sweep clean," he said, laughing at his own joke. Tanner winced.

"We all hope so, sir."

"You planning on staying in?"

"No, sir."

"Which brings up another point. This man's army is being emasculated by this very confusing point system that lets our best men get discharged. Experienced and qualified soldiers are being sent home and replaced by troops who don't know how to wipe their own asses. It's a helluva way to win a war. And the Krauts know all about it, don't they?"

"Yes, sir. Some of the men we've captured were openly hoping that our army would fall apart as a result. I've got to admit that some of the men we've gotten as replacements are pretty bad."

"Like that Oster fellow? That poor puppy shouldn't have been in any man's army. His draft board should all have been drafted and sent to work cleaning latrines with their teeth. I know that the point system is supposed to build morale by showing that there was an end to this long and winding road. Instead, it's helped make the troops we have pull back and not go into combat with the efficiency and aggressiveness they used to have. I'm sure you know how many points you have."

"Of course, sir, but they keep changing the rules. I'll get out when they open the door and tell me to leave and go back to teaching college kids."

"The way things are shaping up, you might have a lot of customers. I understand Truman and Marshall are thinking of having the government pay for veterans' tuition under some kind of plan. It's a good idea if you ask me and it will mean millions of our men and women getting an education rather than going out and looking for jobs that don't exist. That's what happened when the last war ended and it helped cause the Great Depression." Broome shook his head. "Enough of a lecture from me. Get out of here and take your young lady someplace nice, if you can find one."

Tanner was surprised that the general knew about Lena. "I guess there are no secrets in this man's army, sir."

"None whatsoever, Captain. It's worse than a small town full of old ladies."

He was only in his mid-forties but looked and felt decades older. His once decent suit and shoes were dirty and tattered and he was hungry. It was a far cry from the position of power and respect he'd held in Berlin only a few months earlier. Now, he was a fugitive and he wanted to stop running. There was, however, no place to hide. Hitler was dead and Germany was devastated. American soldiers were everywhere and didn't even bother to glance at him with anything more than contempt.

He was in what had once been the proud city of Bonn. Now it was a ruin. It was time to stop running. His only choice was to give up.

He strode up to an American sergeant who was just standing around and taking in the desolation. "Excuse me, but can you direct me to your military intelligence?"

The sergeant laughed. "Ain't no such thing, Mister."

He caught the joke and smiled. "Then how about your military police?"

He was given directions to, no surprise, a former city police station. Inside, a bored MP corporal looked him over. "What can I do for you?"

He drew himself up to attention. "I would like to speak to your commanding officer. I think he will find that it is important."

A couple of moments later, a stocky major appeared. He was not pleased at being interrupted. "So what am I going to find so important?"

"I believe you have lists of important people who have not yet been apprehended. I think it is very likely I am on those lists. I would also like to be put in touch with one of the local Alsos teams."

The major blinked. He had orders to cooperate fully with the Alsos teams. There was one only a couple of miles away, scrounging through the ruins of some scientific facility.

The major was much friendlier now. "Who shall I say wishes to speak with them?"

"My name is Werner Heisenberg and I am a scientist, a physicist."

"I see water."

"Not yet," Hummel said gently to the still confused Schubert. Every day, Schubert seemed to be getting better, if only so slightly. The bombings had not abated, but they no longer appeared to bother the mentally unbalanced man. Nor had any of them struck as closely as the one that had damaged Schubert's mind and nearly killed them both. Hummel wondered if his friend's periods of lucidity were because he was already at the bottom of his mind and could fall no farther.

Their trek from Innsbruck had to be almost over.

Lieutenant Pfister kept telling them that Lake Constance should be visible just over the next hill, or
the next one. Someday he'd be right. Someday the
world would end, too, and someday pigs would fly,
thought Hummel.

Their journey had been agony. They'd traveled by
night and hidden as best they could during the day.
It hadn't taken long for the Americans to figure out
where the troops withdrawing from the Innsbruck area
were headed. The long columns of German soldiers
had been bombed incessantly, leaving bloody and
smoldering clumps of carnage along the trail.

American bombers dropped their loads from on high
with little apparent regard for the existence of actual
targets. The Americans understood that the Germans
were hiding during the day and moving west at night.
Thus, anything that looked like it could hide troops,
like a forest, was bombed with explosives and napalm.

During the day, American fighter-bombers followed
the trail that would lead to the lake or Bregenz. The
attacks were incessant. American planes circled like
hawks looking for mice. "And *we're* the mice," Pfister
commented where only Hummel could hear.

There had been little food for the men and their
clothes were rags. Their shoes and boots were falling
off. Pfister had wondered if this was what it had been
like when Napoleon's men had retreated from Moscow
or when the Germans had retreated from everywhere
in the Soviet Union. At least it wasn't snowing and
icy, they decided, and gave sardonic thanks for small
favors. And thanks to the mountain runoffs, clean,
fresh water was not an issue.

The sound of a car horn blaring jarred them out

of their exhausted reveries. They quickly moved off the road as a large Mercedes sedan bore down on them, going at a high rate of speed over the narrow dirt road.

"The driver's insane," said Pfister as they moved farther off the road and into a stand of trees.

"In more ways than one," said Hummel. "There must be a score of Yank planes looking at the cloud of dust the car is churning up. The fool is just asking to be killed."

"Maybe he doesn't have much choice, Hummel. Maybe the poor driver has been ordered to drive that way by someone who outranks him. In which case, it's the man or men in the back seat who are to blame. I will bet you that the driver is crapping his pants and looking up at the skies."

Hummel agreed. The car was only a couple hundred yards ahead of them when a bird of prey, an American P51, shrieked down from the skies and strafed the car. The driver must have sensed his danger because he began swerving wildly and trying to escape.

The driver evaded the fighter's first pass and stopped the car. He jumped out and ran into the woods. The occupants of the back seat were halfway out when a second American P51's bullets minced the vehicle. It exploded and a ball of flame rose into the sky.

"If the driver has any sense at all he will lie low for a while," said Pfister. The driver did. They waited a number of minutes. The Yanks again flew over, looking to see if anyone had either survived or come out into the open.

When they thought it was safe, Pfister yelled for the driver to come to them if he was able. He was.

A few minutes later, a thoroughly shaken middle-aged corporal made it to them and collapsed. They gave him some of their water and a cigarette. He identified himself as Herman Farbmann, and said that he had been driving for General Lothar Rendulic, commander of all forces east of Innsbruck and titular second in command of all German forces in Germanica.

Pfister looked at Hummel who nodded. "I'll take a look, Lieutenant. Just watch the skies for me."

The car was still smoldering. Two bodies lay half out of it. One was a badly burned man in the remnants of a uniform and the other was naked and charred and might have been a woman. A few rags of bright cloth fluttered near her now sexless body. There was also a scorched leather briefcase, which Hummel took. In the event it contained anything important, it could not be kept by the side of the road.

"Yes, it was General Rendulic," Farbmann said later as he sipped some brandy they'd found on another body earlier that day. "The fool said we had to wait for his mistress to get ready and the lazy self-centered bitch was impossible to get going. Her idea of getting up early was launching her ass out of bed about noon. I would have left her, but the general worshipped her. I urged the general to hurry, that the Americans had planes overhead watching all the time, but he laughed at me and said I was a coward. I guess he wanted to show the woman just how brave a German general was. Are you impressed by his bravery, Lieutenant? I'm certainly not."

Pfister stood. He kept the briefcase. It was locked and he didn't open it. If it contained secrets, he didn't want to see them. "I think we should begin marching west again. At any rate, we should get away from this site. The Yanks are likely to come visiting again. We're not that far from Bregenz or Lake Constance. Are you joining us, Corporal?"

"I'm honored, sir. Just curious, though. How far away is Bregenz?"

Pfister smiled engagingly. "Why, Corporal, it's just over the next hill."

Josef Goebbels shook his head sadly. It had been confirmed. Lothar Rendulic had been killed, murdered by American assassins. They would not keep it a secret. Too many people already knew about it. It was ironic that Rendulic was an Austrian and not a proper German. That point, however, was a small one. What to do with his portion of the army was the real question.

Field Marshal Schoerner sat across the room from Goebbels. Since they were in a cave there were no windows and Goebbels had the feeling that he was in a prison cell. Would this be his life if the Americans got their hands on him? That could not happen. He would rather die. He already had a cyanide pill in his pocket and was not afraid to use it. Now that the children were safe, he could concentrate on his own fate and that of Magda. In his opinion, she could bloody well do whatever she wished with her life. Whatever fondness he'd once felt for her was gone and not likely to return.

Schoerner removed his glasses and rubbed his eyes. "Minister, I do not think it is necessary that we do much of anything about the army's reorganization. So much of Rendulic's forces had been turncoat Russians

and Croats and so much had been whittled down by
the fighting for Innsbruck that there really aren't that
many purely German units left. Once again, they are
mere remnants. I propose getting them as close to
Bregenz as possible and constituting them as a rear
guard with General Warlimont in command."

"All right," Goebbels said softly. "We're slowly being
strangled. What I once said about preserving the
seeds of Nazism is turning out to be terribly wrong.
We've lost a third of our army, which was already
vastly outnumbered in the first place, and much of
the territory that we so confidently called Germanica."

"But what we have left will be easier to defend."

Goebbels stood and began to pace, quickly aware
that the office was so small that he had no room
to maneuver. Just like his army, he thought wryly,
hemmed in by Jewish-dominated Americans who
wanted to destroy him. At least the children were
safe and Magda would soon be leaving for Bregenz,
but not for the compound she and the children had
recently occupied and had now been taken over by
the Americans. He had initially been furious when he
realized he'd been talking to an American spy at the
family quarters in Arbon but later saw the humor in it.

His mind had wandered and he belatedly realized
that Schoerner had been talking about tanks. "Repeat
that, please," Goebbels said.

"I was saying that the compressed Germanica will
be easier to defend. I have already given orders to
those remaining armored units to pull back and form
a mobile defense force in Bregenz. Sadly, there are
only about fifty tanks left. The idea of using them in
fixed fortifications has proven to be a disaster. These

remaining few would have to be thoroughly hidden." Goebbels understood the logic. Perhaps, just perhaps, they could emerge and smash an overconfident American attack, thus buying the Reich some more time.

But time for what? Dr. Esau had insisted that his atom bomb would be ready shortly. Would that change matters? The Americans had proven that they had at least two bombs while Esau insisted that the best he could do was manufacture one. Goebbels believed the man. They would have to use their one bomb wisely.

Goebbels shook his head. Germany stood alone. A devastated and thoroughly cowed Japan lay prostrate and ready to be crushed by an American heel. Nor did Germany have any defenses against America's overwhelming air power. The Americans were destroying antiaircraft batteries in a manner that defied logic. His engineers said they had developed some way of using their radar to figure out the source of an antiaircraft gun and killing it. They tried to explain the science to him, but he couldn't comprehend it. All he understood was that his hopes for the future were being destroyed. The Americans were gathering strength for an all-out push that would end all dreams of survival.

"Tell me, Field Marshal: are people angry or jealous that my wife and children will be safe?"

"They are. While there aren't many families here in the Redoubt, there are some. May I suggest that you arrange with our Swiss friends to let them cross the border?"

"Are you suggesting that women and children should leave the sinking ship first?"

"I am."

Goebbels pondered for only a moment. If nothing

else it would get rid of a number of "useless mouths" who ate food and took up places in shelters. "And what do you suggest we do about our captive workers?"

Schoerner grimaced and shrugged. "It almost doesn't matter. There are only a few thousand of them remaining. Most have died while working and others have been executed by the SS. If we attempt to execute them all, it is unlikely that our soldiers will comply. They do not want to be labeled as war criminals any more than anyone else does. If we leave them to starve, there is the very real chance that they will escape and either fight for the Yanks or at least provide assistance to them. Again, when the Americans come, anyone who imprisoned them could be accused of war crimes."

"Schoerner, give me a suggestion, not a speech."

"Simple, Minister, just turn them loose and point them in the direction of Switzerland or the Americans, whichever is most convenient. Let them complain about the way they were treated to their heart's content. It won't matter. If the Americans win, we'll be dead, and if a miracle occurs and we are victorious, they will be silent. No one could prosecute us as leaders of a sovereign nation if we win."

"I suppose that pushing them into Lake Constance and letting them drown would offend the Swiss."

Schoerner grinned. "It would indeed."

"We have other prisoners as well. We might as well free them too, the lucky bastards."

Schoerner left and closed the door behind him. A handful of secretaries was at work accomplishing little. It was not lost on him that of the three generals who would now command what remained of the

German army, only Schoerner could be depended upon. Warlimont was still suspected of being sympathetic to the cause of those who'd tried to murder Hitler the previous summer, while Vietinghoff had been openly negotiating with the Americans. That the negotiation was with the Reich's approval was irrelevant. He was tainted.

Goebbels had to wonder if Schoerner was as true to the cause as he said. Or would he disappear one night and find sanctuary in another country? It likely wouldn't be Argentina, at least not at first. Too damn many Nazis now in Argentina. And Goebbels wondered just where he would go if the situation called for it. How do you hide an ugly man with a club foot?

Then he recalled Schoerner saying something about having "other prisoners." Of course, Schoerner had other, higher-value, prisoners. This was something that he should have thought of. Perhaps they did have some bargaining chips after all.

Captain Ted Fulton of the provost marshal's office was furious. "Captain Tanner, I had a clear understanding with General Broome that nothing, absolutely nothing, was to be done about reconnoitering that compound without my permission. Did he not make that clear to you?"

Tanner straightened up and stretched. He had been leaning over a large map of the area that was spread over an equally large table and his back was stiff. He'd met Fulton only once and he'd seemed like decent sort, which meant that the outburst was a little surprising. Maybe he was somewhat in love with himself because of the power wielded by the provost marshal's office, but that was nothing anybody took seriously.

"Captain Fulton, I assure you that I had no such understanding with the general because the general said absolutely nothing to me about it other than to tell me that the compound in question would, if necessary, be raided by men from this division. He further said absolutely nothing about prohibiting patrols or sending men out to reconnoiter an unknown area. This, of course, would be the prudent thing to do before sending in troops."

Fulton's face sagged. "But I told him what to tell you about not doing that."

Tanner laughed. "Maybe, just maybe, generals don't like being told what to do by mere captains like us, even though you live with the gods at the provost marshal's. More likely, however, he's just busy like I am and up to his ass in alligators and just forgot. Or maybe he thought I was smart enough to use my discretion. You are aware that we've gotten word to move the whole division back the way we came and go elsewhere in this fairytale land."

"I heard," Fulton said glumly. "Okay, that's over and what's done is done and I've thrown my tantrum. Would you mind telling me what your man found out?"

Tanner sat down on a folding chair. He waved his arm imperiously and a grinning private brought two cups of coffee. "My man reconnoitering the compound is Staff Sergeant Billy Hill and he could snake his way anywhere without being detected. He's a long-time tracker and hunter from the hills of Alabama. His hobby is killing Germans. When you meet him, whatever you do, don't piss him off."

"Don't worry, I won't."

"Hill confirmed that the compound consists of a large but damaged church with a number of outbuildings and tents. Temporary roofs are over some other damaged buildings. He couldn't see inside, of course. He satisfied himself with looking at the arrangement through some excellent binoculars he took off a German he killed in North Africa. He saw a number of men in what looked like American uniforms going in and out of the buildings. There are, or were, a dozen or so military trucks parked there and there are a number of American flags staked out to keep our planes away."

Fulton nodded. "The flags mean nothing. You can buy them at Woolworth's."

"However, there isn't a Woolworth's or a Kresge's, or even a Macy's anywhere near here. He said the flags looked handmade, which also doesn't prove a thing."

"How many guards?"

"Hill saw only five or six, although there could be more out of sight. Now, what do you have for me?"

Fulton took a deep breath. "This is the ugly part. I have very discreetly queried all units in the area and nobody knows anything about this facility. Somehow it just popped up there one day and, since it looked official, nobody cared or asked. It's in a highly secluded area and it was only blind luck that we discovered it. Some guys from your division went hunting or scrounging or stealing stuff and saw it. They got curious and they had unanswered questions so they finally got to us."

Tanner waved for a coffee refill. What he really wanted was a nap. "So what's your best guess?"

Fulton shrugged, "Deserters or black marketeers or

both. There are thousands of deserters from the U.S., French, and British Armies wandering around and stealing everything they can. Some may be trying to blend in with the locals, but the majority are nothing more than crooks. And yes, they can become violent."

"What about German deserters, or actual criminals who've been released from concentration camps?"

"Again, anything's possible. We sometimes forget that there were real criminals in many of the Nazi prisons, people who'd been convicted of murder, theft, arson, rape, and a host of other crimes that had nothing to do with anyone being persecuted for their religion. When we overran the prisons, those guilty people were freed along with the innocent.

"And don't forget that God only knows how many tons of food and equipment have been stolen by criminal bands. We've heard rumors that they are into kidnapping and extortion to keep the locals quiet about their presence."

"Was your source a local?" Tanner asked.

"Don't ask. Now, what do you have planned?"

"What I have is an under strength and chewed up company of a hundred and twenty men led by a first lieutenant who commands because his captain got badly wounded. The company has its quota of machine guns and I managed to get two M5 tanks attached to it."

The M5 was a lighter tank with only a 37mm cannon. It was no match for most of the newer German tanks. Tanner thought they would do quite well against the damaged walls and canvas coverings at the compound.

Tanner continued. "There are three ways in and out of the compound; therefore, I suggest that we don't split the force up. Each part would be too small to defend itself and would be vulnerable if the bad guys decide to fight their way out. I want to hit them up front and hard and if some of them escape down the other roads we've identified, then so be it. You can scoop them up some other time."

"Sounds fair. How soon can your men be ready?"

"They are ready to go right now. Let them take a leak or whatever they want and we can roll in fifteen minutes. It's about an hour to the compound and it's just after 0800. The sooner the better, is my suggestion."

It took closer to two hours to get the column on the road and moving. The tanks did not slow them down. They could do almost forty miles an hour on a decent road and this dirt road had not been bombed. Sergeant Hill had placed himself on heavily wooded high ground overlooking the target and every few minutes radioed in that nothing seemed out of the ordinary. There was a gated entrance several hundred yards down an access road from the main road, but it didn't look like much of a barrier. One man was stationed there to deter anyone from coming in.

As they approached the cutoff, the column slowed and then stopped. They made one last call to Hill. "Nothing's happening," he said. "It's as quiet as a church on a Tuesday afternoon."

"Go," Tanner ordered and the column made a left turn onto the narrow and tree lined access road.

In a couple of moments they could see the gate and an astonished man in an American uniform staring at them. He unslung his rifle and opened fire. Tanner had the sickening feeling that the sentry didn't realize that the trucks and tanks approaching him were

American. White stars and the letters "USA" were on the sides but not the front.

Two more men ran out of the church, paused and looked at the trucks and opened fire. Tanner breathed a sigh of relief. The men shooting at them might be Americans, but they certainly weren't friendly. A few bursts from truck-mounted .30 caliber machine guns sent them running.

The column of trucks stopped and American soldiers poured out of them. They formed up and, along with the tanks, moved on the buildings. Several defenders came out, saw the overwhelming force that was coming at them, and threw up their hands. Others ran towards the road at the rear of the compound, pursued by machine-gun bullets and 37mm shells from the tanks.

The skirmish had taken seconds. There were no casualties among the attackers and only two among the defenders. One man was dead and another slightly wounded.

Tanner ordered a platoon and one tank to go down the rear road and try to capture those trying to escape. As he and Fulton had agreed, their pursuit would not be too vigorous. If someone got away, they could be rounded up later. The big thing was to break up whatever was going on in the compound.

The church came first. It was the largest building and they gasped as they saw the piles of military supplies stacked to the ceiling where pews might have been. Everything was there: rifles, pistols, ammunition, machine guns and even uniforms. They could equip their own army if they so wished.

In another building they found rations, enough to feed a good-sized town for a week or more. In one of the smaller buildings they found a cache of medical supplies including the rare and expensive super-drug, penicillin. This infuriated Fulton, who wondered how many GIs had gone without the precious medicine because it was sitting here waiting to be sold to the highest bidder.

Hill had joined Tanner while Fulton and his cadre of military police tried to make sense of their find.

"So who are these guys, sir?" Hill asked.

"My money is that most of them are American deserters. Some of the ones we caught were so dumb that they were still wearing their dog tags. They'll be breaking rocks at Leavenworth until they're ninety. I will also bet you that some supply officers at bases here in Europe are going to start crapping their pants when they find out about this raid. A lot of it can be traced back to specific units, which means that men got paid off to let this stuff disappear. Some stockades are going to be crowded."

"I wonder if anybody got hurt or killed during the thefts," said Tanner.

"Same here," said Fulton. "If they've committed murder, I hope they hang. What I wonder now is who the buyers were. I can think of a lot of countries that would like to get their hands on all these supplies. French and Italian communists come to mind, and I wouldn't rule out Jewish refugees who want to start their own country in Palestine. And hell, maybe the Arabs who want to stop the Jews. Anybody who wants to start their own war is a likely buyer."

"Over here!" a soldier yelled. He was at a smaller outbuilding the size of a two-car garage.

The soldier looked shocked and stepped aside as

Tanner entered. It took a moment for him to realize what he was seeing. Several dozen pairs of eyes stared back at him. They were all women and they were all naked. They were also tied up with their hands behind them. As his eyes adjusted to the darkness, he could see that their thin bodies were covered with sores and bruises. They moaned with fear when they saw him.

"Anybody here speak English?" he asked. Nothing for a second, then a woman about forty said she did. "Who are you and why are you tied up?" Tanner added. He was going to untie the women but not until he had a good idea what was going on.

"We are their slaves," the woman said and spat on the dirt floor. "We are all good women from this area. We were kidnapped by the men you chased away, and used for their amusement. Some of us had husbands and fathers murdered by those scum."

Fulton's men arrived and, with Tanner's agreement, began freeing them. The women began searching for articles of clothing they could use to cover themselves. "Fulton, would it matter a whole lot if they took some of the uniforms?"

"Sounds good to me. Why don't you tell them?"

Tanner did and the women raced to the church and rifled through the boxes of uniforms. On their way, a dozen or so GIs were treated to a view until one of their officers told them to go away.

Fulton lit a cigarette. "I wonder how high and how far the rot goes. There are rumors of theft and corruption so vast in this army that this is only a drop in the bucket. Of course, the kidnappings and rapes put a different face on it. This is no longer just plain stealing for profit."

"And don't forget the murders these women say these bastards committed," Tanner said. "I originally wanted them to go to jail, now I hope they all hang." And thank God that Lena was safe with the army, he thought. It could easily have been her in that building with those women. Jesus, what a war.

A few moments later, the older woman, their spokesperson, approached Tanner. She was now wearing an ill-fitting uniform. "You will want to see what is parked in the trees. There are at least a dozen ambulances, all with the Red Cross on their sides. They used some of them to transport the women to places where their bodies would be sold. There are, however, a number of them that have not been opened and, until you arrived, their German guards hadn't run away. It was a bargain made in hell. German soldiers pimping German women out to American criminals."

Fulton looked shocked. "Can you take us to these vehicles?"

"Of course, but I won't have to. There's a path through the woods. Just follow it."

It was roughly half a mile from the church area to the parking lot in the woods. By the time Tanner and a full platoon of infantry arrived, almost all the Germans had disappeared. One soldier with a broken ankle had been left behind and he was angry at being left. Water and a cigarette made him think highly of his American captors.

"I have no idea what's in the trucks. We loaded them up at a small town up north and drove down here. We were supposed to get into the Redoubt and safety. Obviously we didn't make it."

"You're saying you don't know what's in the vehicles?" Tanner asked.

"No idea, but it must be valuable. I drove and an SS asshole sat beside me. There was another SS asshole in the back. We were commanded by a lieutenant who didn't know what to do when he realized that the path to the Redoubt was closed. So we sat here until you people arrived. When the shooting started, he and the others simply ran away. Good riddance, and I hope that the bastards who left me here get caught by the Russians."

They asked if the ambulances were booby-trapped and the soldier told them that they weren't. "They were going in and out all the time and then they left in a rush. They only made certain drivers like me didn't look inside. You want me to come with you to prove it, I will."

They did and the prisoner, using crutches found in the medical supplies, led them around the trucks. Fulton picked one at random and they found that it was unlocked.

"Jesus," said an astonished Fulton.

The ambulance was filled with paintings. Tanner pulled one out. "This is a Van Gogh," he said incredulously. He moved some others with extreme caution. He didn't want to be the one who damaged them after all this time. His memory of art history classes wasn't all that great but he recognized a Matisse and a Picasso. A small painting might have been a Rembrandt. His hands shook as he dared to touch it. Most of the other trucks were also loaded with paintings. Two, however, were not. They were filled with blocks of American one hundred dollar bills.

Tanner pulled a pack of bills and riffed through it. "I estimate each truck is carrying several million dollars of American money."

"Then maybe you shouldn't be handling it. Some people might think you're taking some for your retirement fund," said Fulton.

"I don't think so," Tanner said and laughed.

The platoon had gathered around him. "Any of you guys work at a bank or work someplace where you handled a lot of money?"

A corporal and two privates said yes. The corporal had been a head teller at a bank. Tanner handed him the pack. "Look it over, please, and tell me what you see?"

The three checked the money and returned the pack. It had a face value of ten thousand dollars, which would buy a big house back in the States and was much more than the average person earned in a year. Anyone who did make ten thousand a year was considered quite well off.

Tanner put the pack of cash back in the ambulance and closed the door. He would assign guards to protect the vehicles. First, however, he had a question to ask.

"All right, you three, what do you think all this cash is worth?"

The three of them grinned and the corporal spoke. "Not a damn thing."

Ernie and Allen Dulles rode in an older four-door Mercedes. Rank had its privilege so Ernie drove while Dulles took in what sights there were. Their little excursion was a secret. No one else, not even Winnie, knew of it.

Dulles smiled. "Ernie, have you ever been to Germany?"

"No sir, unless you count the time I was halfway under a fence and trying to drag Winnie out. I have not been to Germany and I didn't expect it to happen this way. I thought it would be nice to take a scenic cruise down the Rhine with a fraulein on my lap and a beer in my hand, but I never intended to stop at a crappy town in what used to be Austria."

"But Bregenz is an important place. It's now the capital of Germany, or Germanica if you prefer."

"I prefer that it disappears into the bowels of the earth. When are you going to tell me why we're headed to the border crossing point?"

"Right now would be a good time, I suppose. We are going to cross and meet with two high-ranking Nazis. They wish to discuss matters with us, and, while I believe I know what they wish to talk about, one does not assume."

The border gate was coming up. Ernie stopped and a Swiss soldier passed them through. A sullen German soldier briefly looked over their identification and waved them through as well. Obviously they were expected. Another soldier on a motorcycle signaled for them to follow him and they obeyed. Ernie was in civilian clothes and wondered just what the German reaction would be if he pranced around in the uniform of an air force captain. Getting shot might have been one option.

"Go very slowly, Ernie. I want to take in as much of this as is possible."

"That and it's really pissing off the guy on the motorcycle because it looks like he wants to go a lot faster."

"What do you see, Ernie?"

"Germans, Germans, and still more Germans. This dismal place is crawling with Germans and most of them are officers. Where are the enlisted men? Oh yes, they're probably out getting shot at and killed."

"Don't be cynical, Ernie. Do you really think it's any different at Ike's headquarters or at the Pentagon? By the way, your observation about the preponderance of officers was correct for other reasons. We believe that a lot of high-ranking Nazis made their escape to this location while the enlisted men, sergeants, and lower-ranking officers were left to their own devices. The enlisted men are the ones we are trying to get to surrender through our pamphlets and such, although, with a little bit of luck, maybe we can land some larger fish, like we are going to try to do today."

"I've also noticed that there are antiaircraft guns every few feet. Pilots like I used to be could be hit hard and a lot of them could die."

"And don't forget that those same guns can be used to kill tanks and infantry. I think that a lot of this is for us to see and report back. Taking Bregenz, Ernie, will not be a walk in the park. Many photos have been taken, both from boats and planes, but we are the first Americans to openly visit this city in quite some time."

Their escort waved them to a brick building that had once been a police station. Now it was surrounded by temporary buildings and barbed wire. "Ernie, we are here to see General Alphonse Hahn and his chief acolyte, Captain Rufus Diehl."

Ernie whistled. "Jesus, the lord high executioner and his head torturer. Why do they want to see us?"

"I believe it's because they want to trade something

of value that they have for something of value that we have."

Ernie thought for a moment, then paled. "Oh my God, do you think they want to trade for Marie and Sven? If so, what can we give them in return?"

"We can give them safe passage to wherever in the world they want to go."

"Will you make such a trade?"

Dulles sighed deeply. "I suppose we'll just have to find out, won't we?"

They were ushered to a small room that barely held a table and four chairs. "Will anybody be taking notes?" Ernie asked.

"Don't worry, everything will likely be recorded."

The two Germans entered before the Americans could even take a seat. Ernie was impressed. The timing meant that he and Dulles would not have to rise for the Nazis or insult them by remaining seated. They introduced each other, but no one shook hands.

"I appreciate your coming," said Hahn. "We have a great deal to talk about. As mentioned, I would like to arrange a trade. We will give you two of your agents in return for safe passage for Captain Diehl and me. There are others I would like to save, but I only have your two agents, Leroux and Hansen."

"I assume they are well," Dulles said. Ernie could see that Dulles was keeping a tight rein on his emotions. He had never met Sven Hansen, hadn't even known his last name for that matter, but he *had* met Marie. More important, she was a close friend of Winnie's.

"They are well, but they could be better. They did fight their interrogations and were, well, damaged.

Their fighting did not last long because we were in a great hurry to get what timely information they might have had. As it was, they really didn't know much that was new. For instance, we've known all about Captain Janek, his career as a pilot, and his tendency to beat up German soldiers."

Ernie had been given specific instructions to be seen and not heard. He looked at Dulles who smiled and nodded. "General, I distinctly recall being attacked by your soldiers on at least two occasions."

"Of course," said Hahn who turned to Dulles. "And I'm also aware that the young lady who works with you is the same one who tripped me on one of her spying excursions, thus causing a great deal of hilarity at my expense."

Dulles answered. "If I recall, you were trying to assault her."

Hahn smiled. "Thus proving that there are many sides to each story. But let's get back to the point. Are you interested in a trade? And before you make that decision, were you aware that Marie Leroux held dual citizenship? Yes, she is also an American citizen."

Dulles took a deep breath. "Yes, we are interested. But first I would like to see them."

Hahn shook his head. "That is not possible. However, I do have some photographs that might interest you."

He handed over a manila folder. Two pictures spilled out. They showed Marie and Sven standing against a wall. Both were naked and their bodies were masses of bruises and burns. Their faces were badly bruised and swollen. Ernie had to restrain himself.

Hahn handed over two more pictures. "These photos were taken yesterday. You will see a vast improvement."

Their bruises were largely gone and Marie in particularly looked fairly healthy. "One of the conditions for letting Sven live was that Marie would become my mistress. She services me whenever I wish, although without great enthusiasm. If she does not improve, or if I tire of her, she will be handed over to the troops for their enjoyment. She has also serviced Captain Diehl, again without passion."

Ernie found himself gripping the arms of his chair and wishing he could break off an arm and use it as a club to bash Hahn's brains in.

Hahn ignored their discomfort. "Captain Diehl and I wish to exit Germanica through Switzerland and from there to a place of our choosing. We will depart with some luggage, of course. You are a man of honor, so we will require your word that you won't even think of chasing us for three months."

"What about Magda Goebbels?"

Hahn shrugged. "Who the devil cares, and, besides, she left for Switzerland this afternoon. Like Captain Diehl and me, she will have various identities she can use. Women are so fortunate. They can change their looks simply by dyeing their hair and having it cut."

"Well then, what about Josef Goebbels?"

Hahn smiled. "The Reichminister and new Fuhrer has determined that he will stay in Bregenz to the last, thus emulating his hero, Adolf Hitler. Of course, he could change his mind at any time. But no, you will not have to worry about Josef Goebbels."

"Good," said Dulles. "That would have been too much to promise."

"Then we have a deal?"

"Yes," said Dulles.

"Then I will sweeten it for you. I will give you the names, account numbers, and passwords to several hundred Swiss bank accounts currently in the name of members of the Nazi hierarchy, most of them dead or captured, and others that had once belonged to Jews. I will also suggest that you take notice of the camps that are being built throughout the area. Several thousand criminals will be housed there. Since your country considers them victims of Nazi oppression rather than the lawbreakers that they are, they will be insurance against your planes bombing Bregenz or any other area close to it. We are confident that Truman would not like to add another massacre of civilians to his list of crimes. After all, aren't Hiroshima and Nagasaki enough?"

The meeting ended. Again, they did not shake hands. Nor did they speak until they got back to Switzerland.

"I want to throw up," said Ernie.

"Be my guest, but not while you're driving. Don't be angry and don't envy Hahn and Diehl. We get our people back and those two will be chased for the rest of their lives. Someday, somewhere, I am confident that justice will be served. Now all we have to do is get the rest of the rats to leave their sinking ship. And as to what Truman will do about the camp inmates, I have no idea. I'm just thrilled that I am not in his shoes."

"You're right, sir."

Dulles yawned. He was exhausted, but he couldn't help but smile wickedly. "By the way, do you have any idea why Winnie had me send a slightly stained Nazi bedspread back to her father via diplomatic pouch?"

CHAPTER 18

LENA SAT PRIMLY IN A CHAIR BESIDE TANNER'S DESK. He had to fight the urge to reach out and grab her and, judging from the smile on her face, she was thinking the same thing. They lived in a world with little privacy, which meant few opportunities to carry their relationship farther than a few swift, almost stolen, kisses. Her tent mates had offered to rent their tent for a couple of hours or simply look the other way while they made love, but the offers had been laughingly rejected.

Lena shook her head. "I have interviewed all of the women you rescued. There were sixteen of them and two of them actually were prostitutes. The rest were kidnapped and forced into it. Where they were being kept in the compound actually wasn't a brothel. They were taken to places where there were GIs and were used there. Their captors kept all the money, of course. The girls were poorly fed and several had venereal diseases."

"Which didn't slow down a bunch of horny GIs, did it?"

"Of course not. Nothing would."

Tanner shook his head, then smiled warmly. "So you've absolutely decided to come to the States?"

"Yes. And as I've said before, I will continue my search for my father from there. Who knows, if he's survived, maybe he's headed to America as well. And yes, I will be following you, so make room wherever you plan on being."

Lena winked at him and walked away.

Almost immediately, Cullen came and took her seat. He looked stricken. "What's your problem, Cullen?"

"Maybe a big one, Tanner. Would you kindly tell me why we're being issued brand new gas masks?"

Harry Truman clenched the edge of his desk. He was so shocked and angry that he could scarcely speak. The idea that the Nazis would use innocent people as human shields was beyond repugnant. The report from Allen Dulles had reached him within hours after he had met with Hahn and had been confirmed by camera-carrying airplanes flying over the area.

General Marshall put down a copy of one of the photos. The quality was poor since it had been sent by wire. Better copies were coming, but would take at least a day. These showed the outlines of camps and barracks just as Hahn had said. There was no way that Bregenz could be bombed without the slaughter of great numbers of innocents. Already he was catching hell for using the atomic bomb on Japan despite the fact that destroying those two cities had effectively ended the war and likely saved hundreds of thousands of American lives. That millions of Japanese had been saved from slow, awful deaths from starvation was also forgotten or ignored by many people.

"How many options are left, General?"

"Not that many. We keep nibbling at them, but it's your decision whether or not to continue planning on a massive attack."

"Keep planning. The bleeding hearts who don't seem to recognize that war means killing people will accept civilian battle casualties rather than bombing casualties. Well, that's too bad. If the innocent people in Bregenz are harmed, it will be on Goebbels' head."

"I assume that a negotiated settlement is still out of the question."

"It is, although I will accept, even authorize, the escape of any of the higher-ups in the Nazi command. If we can in get the chief rats to leave the ship, then maybe the little rats and assorted vermin will follow. Dulles is right. We can always catch them later. We can use the OSS or whatever organization succeeds it to help search for them wherever they might find refuge." He smiled tightly, angrily. "In the meantime, we will also prepare for *other* extreme measures."

Winnie clutched Ernie's arm and watched intently as the steady trickle of humanity left Germany. It seemed strange to not refer to the area as Germanica, but even the Nazis had buried the term. Now, if only they could bury the Nazis, she thought.

A sedan pulled up to the German side of the gate. German soldiers wearing SS armbands pushed other people out of the way. Winnie held her breath. "The short guy is Captain Diehl," Ernie said. "He's a real monster. What happened to Marie and Sven was his fault."

She gasped as two people were led out of the car and towards the gate. They leaned on each other for support.

They would have fallen otherwise. Neither Diehl nor any other soldiers offered to help. She wanted to cry.

And then they were through. Winnie started to run but Ernie grabbed her arm. "Hold back. Walk up to them and greet them warmly. Do not let the bastards see how concerned you are."

She nodded and let Ernie guide her. Marie and Sven had stopped and were standing, looking around. They were confused. They didn't know what had happened or where they were. Winnie quickly walked the last few steps and grabbed Marie's arms.

"Marie, it's me, Winnie. You're safe. Sven's safe, too." But badly hurt, she could tell. He was barely conscious.

Recognition dawned. "Winnie, what's happening to us? Where are we?"

"It's over, Marie. You're in Switzerland."

Marie gasped and sagged. She would have fallen if Winnie hadn't grabbed her. Ernie had already taken control of Sven and was heading him towards a parked ambulance. A small hospital served Arbon. They would stay there until they were strong enough to travel to Bern and then out of the country. It would also allow a chance to debrief them. Neither Winnie nor Ernie wanted to hear the grisly details of their imprisonment, but it had to be done. Diehl and Hahn might get away this time, but a strong case would be built up against them. When caught, they would either spend the rest of their lives in prison or be hanged. Sven and Marie's war was over.

"Now what do we do?" asked Hummel. Before them and below them lay the deep blue waters of Lake

Constance. They were dug in on a hill to the north of Bregenz and along the coast. It was heavily wooded and they hoped it made them invisible. They knew better, of course, and made every effort to hide what they had done. Even so, they froze when American planes flew overhead—which they did with regularity. Both men, along with the rest of their unit that now numbered a dozen, longed to smoke a cigarette. They had been warned, however, that smoking in a forest was not a good idea for several reasons. First, it might start a fire and, second, keen eyes might spot wisps of smoke lifting into the sky. The same applied to smoking at night where the glow of a cigarette could be seen or the striking of a match create a sudden flare.

They also quickly realized that this meant that warming or cooking food would be next to impossible. Cold rations would be the menu for the foreseeable future. Nobody was happy, but it beat getting strafed or bombed.

A battery of four 88mm guns was dug in several hundred yards to their right and another to their left. When the shooting finally started, they planned on being as far away as possible from those guns. American retaliation would be savage and overwhelming. They had even gone so far as to dig bunkers two hundred yards behind their main position and in an area where the hills hid them from prying eyes on the lake.

Lieutenant Pfister crawled into the foxhole with Hummel and Schubert, who was staring at the lake and smiling. It was a beautiful scene and they hoped it gave Schubert some peace of mind. Although he seemed to be gradually getting better, he occasionally suffered minor setbacks.

"Too bad we can't arrange for Schubert to be surrendered to the Yanks," said Hummel. "He might get proper treatment from them."

"Or they might just shoot him. We don't know what they do with crazy people. If we could surrender him, perhaps we could arrange for us to surrender as well. You do realize that we're about as far from the American lines as we can get? I wouldn't mind going on holiday here in the mountains, but that is out of the question thanks to dear, dead Adolf Hitler." Pfister didn't even bother to look around to see if anyone was listening in on them. The SS rarely showed up at the front lines anymore.

Pfister now commanded a company consisting of twenty men. He'd earlier informed Hummel that he might get a battlefield commission. Hummel had told him to shove the commission—which resulted in gales of laughter from Pfister.

Hummel nodded and continued to look through his binoculars. An American gunboat patrolled a couple of miles off shore. It was within easy range of German artillery, but they would not fire and give away their positions or waste ammunition. The squat little craft might have been a tugboat at one point in its life. It had since been heavily armored and rode low in the water. It also had a 155mm artillery piece pointing at the German shore. So far it was the only American vessel they'd seen, but they thought there would soon be others. Their future was grim.

Pfister tapped him on the shoulder and pointed to the sky. Contrails were visible. The Americans were watching from on high. No bombs were dropping. Apparently the informal truce was still holding. Both he and Hummel thought the use of human shields was repugnant but was far better than being bombed to oblivion. They also agreed that whatever fools thought you could apply rules to warfare were out of their minds. Survival was a soldier's foremost goal. To hell with bravery and glory and doing the right thing, was the common thought.

"Lieutenant, so what do we do besides wait for them to attack us?"

"Would you rather attack them? At least we're alive for the moment, while doing something foolish would be absolute suicide."

Hummel laughed softly. "Maybe we could build ourselves a very small boat and row out to the Americans, or maybe go along the coast to Switzerland."

"And maybe both sides would blow us out of the water without asking questions. No, I urge you to forget any ideas like that."

"Lieutenant, do you realize that you merely urged me; you didn't order me."

It was Pfister's turn to laugh. "Hummel, we've come too far for that sort of nonsense. I just want to live long enough to see my grandchildren grow up. Of course I first have to survive this war and then find someone foolish enough to marry me before I can have children, much less grandchildren."

It took a long time to get an infantry division on the road and, when it finally did, the caravan of trucks, artillery, cars went on forever. Pilots in spotter planes, the military's version of the Piper Cub, said it looked like an olive drab tapeworm that had no beginning or end. The division was headed towards the German city of Oberlingen, which was on the northern coast of Lake Constance. The U.S. Seventh Army was firmly ensconced in the city. From there, rumor had them moving down the coast to Friedrichshafen or even Lindau, which was only a couple of miles from Bregenz.

Nor were they alone on their trek. The Tenth Mountain Division was heading for the same location, only taking different roads. Tanner had a sneaking idea that the Tenth would be attacking up the hills while the 105th moved along the coast. It seemed like a decent plan and nobody had come up with a better idea.

Maps and photographs told Tanner and the others what they would be facing. There was a narrow strip of what could even be called a beach that ran along the lake and inland for a few yards up to several hundred. In some areas there were narrow roads leading inland. Everywhere, however, were the steep and heavily wooded hills that ultimately led to the Alps. There would be no climbing the more rugged mountains, at least not by the men of the 105th, although they might have to climb some of the hills.

"Are you confident that you could make it to the top?" asked Tanner.

"Yes," said Cullen. He was quiet and thoughtful and not his normal self. "I just don't relish the idea with somebody shooting down at me or lobbing grenades as I try to haul my ass to the top."

"We'll probably have to carry full packs as well," Tanner added.

"What great joy," Cullen muttered. "Whatever happens I just want it to end the war with Mother Cullen's oldest boy in one piece."

Don't we all? thought Tanner. What was a concern to everyone was the fact that brand new gas masks had been issued, replacing the ones the GIs had so cavalierly tossed away months earlier. And, unlike the past, there were strict orders for soldiers to have them in their possession at all times. Clearly, there was a serious suspicion that the Germans would introduce the horrible weapon as a desperation measure.

Tanner had seen photos from the last war of long lines of gassed soldiers who'd been blinded and were being led by the hand away from the trenches. Some soldiers survived, but many had died and others been seriously scarred, both mentally and physically. Back in the States, he'd seen a man in an army hospital coughing away what remained of his life, the victim of a gas attack a generation earlier. Adolf Hitler himself had been gassed and the consensus was that it was too bad he hadn't been killed. Some gasses required the victim to inhale them, while others needed only a brief touch to the skin to kill.

Nor was gas particularly accurate. Once released as clouds of death, it went where it wished and as the wind blew it. It was like a mad dog that had been let loose among tethered sheep.

No wonder it was so dreaded. One of the smaller blessings was that Germany hadn't introduced it, at least not yet and doubtless for fear of retaliation from enemies who controlled the skies. So what had changed? Was Germany so desperate that she would risk annihilation?

Then he had a thought that chilled him. What if it wasn't the Germans who might introduce poison gas?

★   ★   ★

Sergeant Archie Dixon had gotten himself a brand new Sherman tank and he liked it. The tank was a vast improvement over the one the Germans had destroyed and taken so many of his crew with it. This new tank had a higher velocity 76mm gun and could likely handle anything the Germans had, with the exception of the Panther and Tiger series. But then, he thought with as much happiness as he allowed himself, the Nazis didn't have any more of those beasts.

Along with a fresh tank, he had a newly minted crew and they all hated him, and this was fine by Archie. He'd lost one crew and didn't want to lose another if he could possibly help it. Of the five men in the original crew, he was the only one to survive physically unscathed, although he'd spent some intense time talking to chaplains and psychiatrists before they would let him back into the war. The chaplains tried to commiserate with him and he thought that the head doctors were crazier than he had been. One of the things he now understood fully was *don't ever become friends with the crew*. In his first tank, they had all been friends, buddies. They'd gone through basic and tank training and had become close. They'd partied together, chased women and fought as a team. Dixon had known all about their personal lives and what they wanted for a future. He'd known who had kids and whose wife was giving him a hard time and maybe sleeping with some damn 4-F.

Now three of them were dead and the fourth one spent his time so heavily medicated he might as well be. He had brutally severe burns on his legs. A doctor had told Archie that the man might walk again, but always with a limp and always with pain. Since Archie had been their commander, he'd blamed himself. He knew he was being irrational, but didn't care. They had been *his* responsibility. Therefore he would never let anyone get as close again. Losing strangers was bad enough, but losing friends just hurt too much.

Thus, he kept his new crew at arm's length. He never used their names. They were Driver, Gunner, Loader, and Co-driver. He was Sergeant. Not Sarge, Sergeant. Nor did the tank have a name, and that further pissed off the crew. Tough shit, he thought. People have names, not lumps of metal.

He trained them hard, and that too annoyed them. The war was almost over, he'd heard them say, so why doesn't he lighten up? Because the war *isn't* quite over, you assholes, he'd yelled at them. And until that happy day, he was going to train them and train them. One of them actually went to a chaplain to complain about Archie's behavior. Archie wanted to kill the whiny little shit, but the chaplain calmed him down.

As to where they were all going, it was no secret. There was some town on Lake Constance with an unpronounceable name and they would then be the spearpoint that would drive down the coast and to the German capital of Bregenz. It was almost a given that they would again be alongside the 105th Infantry and that was good. They'd worked together before and knew each other. He snorted and one of the crewmen looked at him, puzzled. He'd just realized that he probably knew more about some of the men of the 105th than he did of his own crew, and that pleased him. At this stage of his life he wanted no friends, no entanglements, no sentiment.

★   ★   ★

Hans Gruber's devotion to the cause of Adolf Hitler
and Josef Goebbels was fading rapidly. He had just
found out that both General Hahn and Captain Diehl
had disappeared during the night. "Disappeared" had
become a euphemism for deserting, and this upset him
deeply. He didn't care about Diehl, whom he thought
was a slimy shit and who had tried to caress Gruber's
leg. But Hahn was his hero, a man who had made
him a Werewolf. He was a general and a confidante
of Josef Goebbels.

What was he supposed to do now? Worse, many
other leaders of the new Reich were also fading away,
leaving the junior officers and enlisted men to their
fates. If the Americans caught him, would they treat
him honorably as a prisoner of war or as a terrorist?
He felt that the Americans at that base had been
legitimate targets, and that included their general.
Would the Yanks feel the same way or would they
call him a murderer and hang him?

He rolled over and stared at Astrid Schneider. They
were in her bed at her parent's quarters and she was,
as usual when she was with him, quite naked. She
was the first woman he'd ever made love to and he
wondered if he was in love with her. She had repeatedly told him that she loved him and he'd told her
that he loved her, but he wondered if he meant it.
Or did he just like getting laid? Whenever he said he
loved her, she became a tigress and that was good.

"Everyone is leaving Germany," Hans said.

"My brother and father are still here. They will
not abandon the Reich."

"Nor will I, although I think you should make plans
to go to Switzerland with your mother."

"I don't want to leave you."

"And I don't want you to leave either. But I would feel better knowing that you were safe. Think about it. You serve no real purpose here, except of course," he added with a grin, "satisfying a brave German soldier's lusty needs."

She laughed and punched him on his thin shoulder. "My father is deathly afraid that he will be considered a war criminal. My mother told him that if the Allies arrested everyone who'd done what my father did, there'd be no one left. My father may have done some things that the Allies will doubtless consider wrong and he may have to spend a little time in a prison, but he's done nothing serious. He's not a Himmler."

"What about that girl you said he raped, the one who beat up you and your brother?"

"What of it? Millions of German women were raped by Russians and others. My mother and I were fortunate to make it here safely."

"Astrid, I would still feel better if you were in Switzerland."

"All right. I will get my mother and we will leave, tomorrow if I can do it."

He sighed happily. He had no idea how deep his feelings were for this girl, but he would be much happier if she was out of the war. Then he could concentrate on his task, if only he could now define it. If the cause of the Reich was truly doomed, then he should be looking out for himself as much as he was looking out for Astrid Schneider.

Astrid smiled. "I have one other piece of information for you, my dearest."

Hans yawned. She had worn him out. "And what is that?"

"I think I'm pregnant."

Shit.

Josef Goebbels took the small box from his pants pocket and looked at it. How many times had he done just that in the past few days? The box was innocuous. It could have held a tie tack or a ring but not anything expensive. It didn't say Cartier or some other elegant jeweler. All it had was a swastika.

He opened it and looked at the small pills inside. They were cyanide. One would be more than enough, but he had asked for two in case he dropped one in his haste to end it all. He would not be taken alive. As he had promised an eternity ago, he would join Adolf Hitler in death. The world would honor him for his bravery and devotion. Besides, he did not want to end up on exhibit as was happening to so many of the Reich's leaders. The Allies had announced that a series of trials would commence at Nuremberg, beginning with the highest-ranking Nazis in their custody and working down to the smaller fish. If captured, he would be the ranking Nazi. He would be displayed and mocked like an animal at some perverted zoo. Magda understood that, but the children would not. Therefore, he could not be captured.

So why then did his hands shake when he held the box? Goebbels took a deep breath. His hands shook, he decided, because he was as afraid of death as anyone. The Nazi empire that had once stretched from the Pyrenees almost to the Urals was now reduced to a few hundred square miles of desolate and useless mountains. The larger portion of the army was still fronting the Americans near Innsbruck, while a decent force remained to defend Bregenz. The generals were confident that the Americans would have to come down the narrow valleys that led from Innsbruck to the small town that was the current capital of Germany. He did not share their confidence, but he deferred to their knowledge.

Field Marshal Schoerner knocked and entered. Goebbels tried to hide the pill box but wasn't fast enough. "I will not take cyanide," Schoerner announced. "If and when the time comes, I will do everything in my power to die in battle."

Goebbels gasped. Had Schoerner just insulted him? "Are you implying that I'm less of a man for considering poison?"

"Of course not, Minister. I merely state the obvious, that we come from different backgrounds. If I cannot get killed, I will try to shoot myself. If that doesn't work, one of my aides will finish the task."

"Will your aide get a promotion for the job?"

"Quite likely," Schoerner said. He flushed when he belatedly realized that Goebbels had been sarcastic.

"Do you have any good news at all?"

"None whatsoever. Our time may be counted in days, or at best, weeks. We are almost out of food and ammunition and the Americans now control the lake. This means that they might try to attack from it."

"The Swiss will not permit that."

"Minister, the Swiss will not have a choice. From what intelligence we've been able to gather it looks like the Americans scent blood and wish to come in for the kill. When that happens, the Swiss will stand aside. Further, the number of desertions is increasing. Only about half the men we brought into the Redoubt remain with us. Yesterday, some enterprising soldiers overwhelmed their officers, stole a small boat, and sailed off towards an American patrol craft. They were welcomed with open arms."

Goebbels laughed harshly. "Do you think they would welcome us with open arms?" Yes, he thought. Open arms—and a noose.

"Minister," Schoerner said softly, "I think it is time to complete plans for using the bomb."

Any plans for the bomb were limited by the capacity and range of the two V1 rockets they'd brought to Bregenz. The rockets had a range of two hundred miles and carried a one-ton warhead. They were also horribly inaccurate at long range. They had chosen the V1s over the V2s because they were much easier to move and launch.

Some thought had been given to arming the rockets with poison gas, but it was quickly decided that a ton of gas would not accomplish much except to anger the Americans and perhaps cause them to retaliate. With a two-hundred-mile range, it meant that major targets, such as Paris, London, or Rome were impossible reaches. They could only hit cities in Switzerland or northern Italy or, of course, Germany, which would be pointless.

Therefore, any target would have to be closer, much closer. The scientists had toyed with the idea of enlarging the warhead to house a greater atom bomb by reducing the fuel that would be unnecessary if the target was close. They had quickly come to the conclusion that reengineering the rocket would take more time than they had. Thus, they were stuck with a short-range rocket with a one-ton atomic warhead. Doctor Esau had been of the opinion that the American atomic bombs had weighed at least five tons. Thus again, they had a small nuclear device. It had to work and they had to convince the Yanks that they had more than one. The second rocket was for show only and some other dummy rockets were being constructed out of wood.

Schoerner smiled. "What do the Americans fear more than anything else, Minister?"

Goebbels returned the smile. "Why, casualties, of course. The American soldier is a coward and his leaders are politicians who are afraid to lose soldiers in battle. If our one bomb can decimate a large American force and if we can convince them that we have more of them, they will negotiate."

"But the bomb has to work," said Schoerner. "And Doctor Esau and his people have pledged their lives that it will."

Generals Truscott and Devers watched as elements of the two-division assault force gathered itself. Devers was uncomfortable with his position. Even though he was the ranking officer, he had the uneasy feeling that Truscott was in charge and that Truscott would complain to Ike if he didn't like what was going on. That would be like being taken to the woodshed, a humiliation that he could not tolerate. His pride would force him to resign.

Of course, he had to admit that the gravelly voiced Texan had done a magnificent job and had given Devers little to worry about.

The Rhine was clear, both of debris and enemy forces, all the way down to Lake Constance. That it meandered all over the place as it approached the Alps was irrelevant. It meant that small armed craft could sail its length and emerge in the lake. It also meant that many scores of landing craft could do the same thing and these were congregating along the shore at Oberlingen. When the army moved south to Lindau, the landing craft would follow. The army would board them and launch an attack from the lake. The Swiss would be even more furious than they already were, but nobody gave a damn about the feelings of the Swiss. Getting the landing craft and other support vessels to Oberlingen meant riding the Rhine along its length and in some cases cruising through small chunks of Swiss territory. There had been no incidents, but the American high command was confident that German sympathizers had relayed precise information about the American movements to the Nazis in Bregenz.

"How soon?" Devers asked, resenting that he didn't know all the information.

"A couple of days at the most. A lot depends on the winds."

Yes, Devers thought sorrowfully, the winds. Was the United States really about to commit an atrocity on the scale of what the Nazis had done?

Tanner and Cullen watched the generals have their meeting on a hill. Many others watched as well. It wasn't every day that high-ranking officers displayed themselves as Devers and Truscott were now doing.

"What do you think?" asked Tanner.

"This means war," he said solemnly. "Oh yes, I forgot. We're *already* at war. This means that we're going to go into battle very soon and that's not a surprise either."

"I hope this is the final one."

He and Lena had managed a couple of minutes together that morning. Each was terrified that the next battle would be someone's last one. While Tanner was in the greater danger, the incident in which General Evans had been killed and Lena shot at had showed them that danger was imminent and everywhere. Their embraces had been intense, as each knew that it could be the last for a long time, perhaps forever. Tanner was somewhat comforted by the fact that she was well behind the lines. But would that matter if long-range artillery came into play, or if someone made a tragic mistake, or, God forbid, the rumors about the gas masks were true.

CHAPTER 19

E RNIE HUGGED WINNIE. "I LOVE YOU; NOW GET THE hell out of here."

She smiled and patted him on the cheek. "I love you too, especially when you talk so romantically. But you know I can't go too far. I have a job to do, too. I don't like it that Arbon is so close to the German border either, but I volunteered for this job just like you did."

They were in the rear of the suite of offices that were the United States consulate in Arbon. Normally, a small town like Arbon wouldn't rate a consul, perhaps just a local person authorized to dispense with routine affairs on a part-time basis, but her proximity to the German border and the newly ordained capital at Bregenz made an exception to the rule a necessity.

"Winnie, people are leaving this one-chalet town. They know the war's going to come and they know that mistakes always happen, sometimes even accidentally."

She released him. "What are you implying?"

"Only that we're pawns in this giant thing called

World War II, and that maybe the U.S. would like to smack Switzerland across the head for being so helpful to the Germans. Rumor has it that some priests in the Vatican are now helping Nazis escape. I'm not accusing Pius XII of anything wrong, but some in the Church's hierarchy certainly are. While we can't bomb St. Peter's, maybe we can hit a small town in Switzerland and let it serve as a warning to those who would help the Nazis."

Winnie was shocked. "Are you saying that the President of the United States is that devious?"

"Show me a politician who isn't devious and I'll show you someone who died several years ago. Don't you ever wonder just what Dulles is really up to? Here we are planning to fight a final battle with the Nazis and the Russians are expanding their reign over much of Europe. What do you think Truman and Dulles think about that? What do you think they might *do* to slow down the Reds?"

"Are you saying there might be another war, only this time with the commies?"

"Winnie, I think you can almost count on it."

Winnie was about to reply when air raid sirens began to wail.

"Once more into the breach," said Sibre. He and Schafer headed a flight of almost a hundred P51 and P47 fighters as they escorted a miles long stream of several hundred American bombers. Most were B17s, but there were B24s and B25s as well. They were headed for Bregenz and most of the men were delighted. It meant an end to the German's sanctuary and hopefully an end to a war that seemed to have gone on forever—with America starring in it.

Deep down they knew that was an untrue and unkind statement. Both Great Britain and the Soviet Union had been fighting for far longer and, in the case of the Soviets, had suffered appalling losses.

Their target was the center of the capital of Germany. They would fly, drop their bombs and then leave by flying over Lake Constance. The stream of planes would turn north and head for their home fields. It was understood that this would involve flying over Swiss territory. It was also understood that they could return the fire of anyone who shot at them, regardless of where the firing was coming from. Nor were they to concern themselves about the likely killing of innocent civilians. If those deaths could help save Americans, then their deaths would not be in vain.

Puffs of black smoke appeared around their planes. Flak. "Can you see the guns?" Sibre asked. A moment later Schafer said he could and dived for the ground. Sibre swore and followed, along with several others.

As they got lower, more and more German guns sent shells up to meet them. "Where the hell are they getting the guns?" Schafer yelled. "They must have been saving them for a rainy day."

They dropped their bombs and strafed what they hoped was a gun emplacement. There was no secondary explosion, which made them doubt it. Regaining altitude, they saw that the Germans were targeting the bomber stream and that several had been hit. One B24 blew up, sending debris and bodies all over the sky. Others were either burning or had chunks bitten out of their wings or tails. A surprising number were either cripples or had turned around. They wondered how many casualties were inside the planes and whether or not the

wounded would live. Their buddy Morelli had died of
his injuries a few hours after they'd visited him. They
convinced themselves that it was for the best but that
was a hard sell. Morelli had been a human being, not
a dog that needed to be put down.

"Once more and this time with feeling," said Sibre.
The raid was becoming a disaster. During their briefing, the intelligence officer had minimized the German antiaircraft defenses. Now they'd like to get the
dumb bastard up in a plane so he could see what
was really happening.

They strafed another possible site and pulled up.
They were out of ammunition. Now all they could do
was try to distract the Germans. As if to mock them,
a B17 flew nose-first into the ground and exploded in
an enormous ball of fire. Neither man said a word, but
each wondered if anyone had gotten out before it hit.

The bomber stream had begun to disintegrate.
Cohesion was lost and planes were flying in numerous directions.

"Where the hell are those idiots going?" Schafer
yelled. A dozen bombers were following another one that
was on fire. Their route was taking them over the border
and towards a number of small towns in Switzerland.

"This is going to be bad," said Sibre, and Schafer
concurred. The lead plane's left wing suddenly broke
off and the bomber began a death spiral to the ground.
They didn't want to, but they couldn't help but watch.
Hatches opened and several men jumped out. They
counted four, but there were ten in the crew. Four
chutes opened, but where would they land? Both
agreed that it would be Switzerland, which meant
that the Americans would be safe.

"Oh no," said Sibre. The other planes' bomb bay doors were open and bombs began to fall out and downward. They were bombing Switzerland. Had the commanding officer made a mistake, gotten lost, or was he pissed at the dense German antiaircraft fire? They would never know. The new lead plane took a hit and fell apart. This time there were no chutes.

Winnie and Ernie huddled in a shelter along with several dozen other people. As the explosions drew nearer, an elderly Swiss gentleman with a well-trimmed white beard glared at Ernie. "Can't you bloody people be trusted to tell Germany from Switzerland?"

"It ain't all that easy from maybe twenty thousand feet and with a few score antiaircraft guns blazing away at you. Trust me, I've tried."

The gentleman was about to respond when more bombs hit and caused the shelter to vibrate. Ernie was going to add to his comments when the old man simply disappeared in a rain of flesh and bone.

Ernie managed to cover his and Winnie's heads with his jacket with one hand and cup his balls with the other as the shelter fell apart. "Winnie!" he yelled as consciousness faded and then disappeared.

Werner Heisenberg had been given American fatigues and been flown to New York in a DC3. He was accompanied by two MPs and others on the flight assumed he was a prisoner. If they were puzzled by the fact that he wasn't in irons, nobody said anything. From there it was time to refuel and change pilots. Then it was another hop to Washington. He was tired and frightened. Were they taking him to America to be shot, hanged, or put on display as a war criminal? He was a scientist, not a criminal. How could he convince them of that?

The major in Bonn had quickly found his name on a list and he had been interviewed by an Alsos team, primarily to make sure he was who he claimed to be. From there he had been flown to an American air base in England where he figured he'd be interned for the duration. He'd been there only a couple of days when he was put on a plane and sent across the Atlantic.

After landing in Washington, he'd been put in a staff car and he'd promptly fallen asleep. When he was awakened, he was astonished to find that he was at the White House and would be meeting with President Truman in a few minutes. That and a cup of excellent coffee had perked him up. Perhaps they weren't going to try him as a criminal after all.

He was taken to the Oval Office and given some more coffee. It was fascinating to see a national capital that hadn't been bombed and devastated. Even during his brief stay in England, he had seen where bombs and rockets had struck.

He was ushered into the president's office. Truman was seated behind a large wooden desk. He was introduced to General Marshall and General Groves. He knew who Marshall was but only knew of Groves as the man who had built the Pentagon.

"Tell us about Abraham Esau," Truman said.

Heisenberg blinked. He hadn't expected that question. "Dr. Esau is an excellent physicist, one of Germany's leading scientists."

"Is he as good as you?" asked Groves.

"No. He is a good man, but definitely second tier."

Truman leaned forward. "Could he and a small team located in the Alps build an atomic bomb?"

Heisenberg smiled broadly. So this is what this is all about. "Doctor Esau couldn't build a bomb if he had all the resources in the world and all the time in the world."

Heisenberg was brought up to speed. He was told about the German threat to use a bomb and that Truman was thinking about halting the attack on Bregenz because of the fear of what a bomb might do to massed American forces.

There was more coffee and some sandwiches. "Gentlemen," Heisenberg continued, "there was *never* a threat of a German atomic bomb. I had already seen to that."

Truman was astonished. "What do you mean?"

"Because I could not abide the thought of a monster like Hitler getting his filthy paws on a weapon like the atomic bomb. There were several competing programs, but mine was the major one. I saw to it that we were constantly going off in the wrong direction. Along with not having enough Uranium, all I had to work with were second and third-rate talents. The Nazis considered physics to be Jewish science and chased the good ones away. I assume that they are working for you."

"That's a safe assumption," said Groves as he reached for another sandwich. "But does Goebbels know that?"

Heisenberg shrugged. "He was the Minister of Propaganda. He might be lying or he might be being lied to. Who knows? Now, may I politely ask what will happen to this information and to me?"

Truman smiled coldly and Heisenberg could see how people could underestimate the short man with the wire-rimmed glasses. "As to your motives, I don't give a damn. For all I care you are lying through your teeth about intentionally derailing the bomb research and really wanted it to succeed because you were a good Nazi until the end and decided it was time to save your ass. In the meantime, you will remain in our custody. You will be kept comfortable and secure. And, if by chance, the German bomb does work, I will personally blow your goddamned brains out. If their bomb is either a dud or a fraud, you will be rewarded. In the meantime, the attack on Bregenz will go on as scheduled, and God help us all."

Heisenberg was led away. He would be sent to the Marine Barracks in Washington and held in confinement. He was confident that he would be vindicated. But then he felt a chill. What if, just *if*, Esau and his people had indeed managed to utilize existing research to develop something that could cause great harm to the United States Army? It didn't have to be a full-fledged atomic bomb. Something close would do just as well.

Josef Goebbels was frightened but safe. His shelter was in the bowels of a hill overlooking Bregenz. Even so, the room shook and he looked at the walls and roof to see if they would stand up to the pressure of Allied bombs.

No senior members of his government were with him. They were all in other shelters, fled to Switzerland, or dead. More explosions and the mountain seemed to rise up from the ground.

He fingered the little box in his pants pocket. Was it time? If he wanted to die, he would have to take the cyanide at the earliest possible moment. He hadn't thought of it, but he now thought it possible that he could be injured in a bombing attack and unable to reach the capsules. The rain of bombs was beginning to taper off. He would live through this day. Still, he *had* to be better prepared. He smelled smoke but nothing to indicate a major fire.

The door to the shelter was cracked open. "Minister!" yelled an officer from outside.

"Over here," Goebbels said and managed to stand with great difficulty. He was shaking, but why? He'd endured far worse while in Berlin. It was because he now realized that any feelings of safety he'd had were an illusion, a pipe dream.

The steel door to the cave was open and his officers were tentatively stepping outside. The sky was clear and there were no fresh contrails in the sky. Much of Bregenz was in ruins. Dark smoke was heavy and firefighters were at work. There would be little shortage of water since the city was close to the lake. Dead and wounded were being pulled from the rubble, proof that not everyone had taken the threat of bombing seriously. Goebbels wondered if this would stiffen the spines of those left to fight for Hitler's vision. Sadly, he doubted it. Instead, there would be an exodus to the Swiss border.

Field Marshal Schoerner stood watching the activity. He did nothing and Goebbels didn't either. The people in charge of handling disasters such as this were doing an excellent job. They did not need anyone yelling encouragement at them.

Schoerner smiled. "Minister, did you hear the good news?"

"What good news could there be? The Americans bombed us. There is no longer any sanctuary."

"The Americans made a huge mistake. For some reason, they bombed Arbon as well."

Goebbels perked up, suddenly elated. If the Swiss were angry enough at the assault on their territory, would they be willing to ally themselves with the Reich? The addition of the Swiss Army to Germany's defenses would cause the Americans to think about the blood price that must be paid. Perhaps this day wasn't such a miserable one after all.

And he still had an atomic bomb to fire at the Americans. Was it time to launch? No, he told himself. Not just yet.

Why am I tied up? he thought. He wanted to strain at the bonds that restricted his movement, but his body wouldn't cooperate. His brain wouldn't function. His thoughts were coming out mushy and incoherent.

And he couldn't see. Am I blind? He twisted as much as he could but nothing seemed to be working. He was able to blink and felt something over his eyes. What had happened? The last thing Ernie recalled was being in a shelter and something exploding. He thought he recalled a man scolding him before the man disappeared.

Oh God. Had Winnie been with him? He couldn't recall. Was she okay? He had to find out. He tried to move again and thought there was some feeling in his right leg but nothing in his left. He took a deep breath. Okay, I'm alive. He tried to say something but only a squawk came out and he wasn't certain he'd made any sound anyhow.

Something grazed his right hand. "Ernie? Can you hear me?" It was Winnie's voice, and he exulted. She was alive and clearly in better shape than he was. "If you're conscious, just nod."

It took willpower but he did. "Wonderful," Winnie said. "Now I'm going to put a straw in your mouth so you can get some water in you."

A few moments later he was sucking on a straw and drinking cold, clear water. A few more moments and he tried to talk. It came out as a croak so he drank some more water. Better.

"Where am I?" he whispered.

"In a hospital in Arbon, and don't try to talk too darn much. Since you can hear me, just listen. You were found in the rubble of that bomb shelter. You were very lucky. Several people were killed."

Ernie nodded, recalling the explosion and the death of the old man.

"You were injured pretty badly. While I was thrown clear and am unhurt except for some more bruises, you've got a broken leg and several smashed ribs. Fortunately, it'll all heal but it will take some time, although you will be up on crutches in a short while. I hope you weren't counting on dancing anytime soon."

He smiled and felt her tears fall on his cheek. "A bunch of American bombers got lost and dropped their load on Arbon. The Swiss government is furious. You and I are technically under arrest, although you are obviously not going to escape. They've decided to let me stay with you for the time being. Dulles is a major diplomat so he has more immunity than we do and he's trying to straighten out the mess with the Swiss government. He thinks he will succeed since the Swiss are such pragmatists."

Ernie reached for her hand and squeezed it. "Am I blind?"

"Oh God, no. You've got some serious cuts on your forehead and around your eyes. You caught a lot of debris with your thick skull, which knocked you out. Your head is bandaged up and you've been restrained so you won't pull your bandages off or thrash around and hurt your leg even more than it is already."

"Take off the bandages. I want to see that you're really okay."

"Tomorrow. Right now a nice nurse is going to give you some more morphine so you can sleep in happy land and get some rest. They tell me that when the morphine wears off, you will be in great pain, so be prepared."

"Will you be with me?"

"Yes, dear, of course." Again he felt her tears and then her lips grazing his. Then it was time for a deep sleep.

Ensign Ted Kubiak, USNR, looked on in disbelief as one of his small crew leaned over the side of the boat and donated his lunch to the little fish. The rest of the crew were laughing hysterically.

"Dalton, you cannot be sick. This is a river and the water is barely moving. There are no waves. You've ridden out storms with no problems. What the hell is wrong with you now?

A very green Dalton stood up. To Kubiak's disgust he had slobbered down his chin and onto his shirt. "Don't know, sir. Maybe it's because it isn't rough enough. I'd love to stop barfing but I just can't seem to."

The twenty-four-year-old Kubiak shook his head and joined in the laughter. Despite his stomach problems, Dalton was a good guy, a draftee from West Virginia. Like Kubiak, Dalton had never seen combat. He and all the others had missed the landings at Normandy and in Southern France. They'd been scheduled to attack the Japanese island of Kyushu, but the Japanese surrender had put a welcome halt to their preparations for what promised to be a terrible fight against an insane and fanatic enemy. They'd gotten new orders and these sent them to France—and now up the Rhine. "Up the Rhine" seemed strange. Every time he looked at a map he wanted to say down the Rhine, but he was assured that they were going up the Rhine towards its source, which he thought was in Switzerland.

The long column of landing craft had made it up the Rhine to the Swiss border. There had been multiple stops for the boats to be refueled and the crew allowed time to eat and sleep. Numerous other columns of boats were towed by tugs with the crew simply along as passengers. None of the craft carried any troops, only U.S. Navy crews. Soldiers would come on board at the small German town of Lindau, a few miles away from the Nazi capital of Bregenz. This was assuming that the American forces had taken the city.

They had been further delayed by the need to ensure that the river was clear of obstructions. Channels had been made through the remains of the bridges that had been destroyed by German demolitions. Buoys had been laid to mark the existence of other potential dangers. Mines were not a major factor, although the possibility of their presence had not been ignored. Minesweepers kept a lookout for them and sharpshooters were constantly present and alert. If a mine was spotted, the riflemen would shoot and detonate the mine.

There were no problems. And the trip had taken on the feeling of a Rhine cruise vacation. The days were still bright and sunny. Numbers of sailors had stripped to their skivvies and lolled the sun, enjoying the scenic cliffs and historic castles as they passed them by. Heidelberg was pointed out along with the Rock of the Lorelei and everyone was curious about an ugly, squatty little fortresslike thing in the middle of the river. One of the men said it had been a medieval toll booth, which the guys thought was funny. The idea of boats paying tolls had never occurred to them.

None of them had ever seen the Rhine, and they had been stunned by the steep earthen walls that nature had carved, forming a natural line of fortifications. It was easy to see that the Germans could have held the river line for a very long time and how fortunate the American army was to have taken the bridge at Remagen before it collapsed.

Earlier in the war there had been problems with a shortage of landing craft. Increased production had partly solved that, while the transfer of the small boats from the now dormant Pacific theater had completed it. Thus, there was an abundance of landing craft of all sizes heading up the Rhine. Their destination was Lake Constance.

Kubiak's landing craft was relatively large. It was able to hold one hundred men or a tank and fifty men. Some genius in Cologne had decided that the tank could be shipped with the landing craft and later joined by a crew, so a Sherman tank was tied down in the hull. Scores of other craft had similar cargoes. Nor was the craft totally defenseless. Two fifty-caliber machine guns were mounted in the prow.

He had written his parents and girlfriend that he'd gotten his first independent command and implied that it was a major warship. He'd then intentionally spoiled the illusion by sending a photo of the squat and homely vessel. The crew had voted to name her *Brunhilde*.

Nor were they alone one their journey. On several occasions they'd had to pull off to the west bank of the Rhine and wait while American destroyers surged ahead, like slow traffic on a highway letting faster vehicles go by. Someone joked that the destroyers were going to take on the legendary Swiss navy. Most didn't think it was funny. The presence of the destroyers simply emphasized the seriousness of their situation and reminded them that their respite was likely temporary.

Kubiak bit his lip at the thought of taking his men into combat. There was no doubt that the landing would be a difficult one. The Germans were dying and those who were left were the worst of the worst. And what the hell were the rumors about *gas*?

Still, they all consoled themselves that they weren't fighting the crazy Japs. At least most of the Germans were willing to surrender, excepting of course the SS.

Allen Dulles was stern and unsmiling. "Of course we regret the tragedy, but it was an accident of war, nothing intentional. We have apologized and, when the fighting is over, we will make reparations."

Swiss General Henri Guisan was equally stern. They were in the lightly damaged Arbon City Hall. Dulles' nose was running, caused by the lingering scent of burned buildings and living flesh. He was fighting the nausea caused by the several comingled stenches.

Guisan declined to notice the other man's discomfort. "More than a hundred Swiss civilians were killed and an equal number injured. Several city blocks have been flattened and burned. We want the guilty parties punished."

"I would too, if there was a guilty party to blame. Unfortunately, the pilot and crew of the lead bomber were all killed. I consider it possible that key members of the crew were injured when the plane was hit and went off course as a result. That led other bombers to follow their leader. If you wish to go higher up the chain of command to try to find guilty parties you will get nowhere. Why don't you pin the blame on the late Herr Hitler who, if memory serves me, started this whole mess? If you want guilt, I would suggest that you nominate yourself and others in the Swiss government."

Guisan nearly jumped out of his chair but caught himself in time. "What! That's preposterous."

"Yes, General. If you had cooperated more fully with us and opened your border to German soldiers who wished to surrender instead of turning them back to the SS, it is entirely possible that the Nazi government would have collapsed. In fact, I urge you to do that now. Announce that you will give sanctuary to any German soldier who crosses over and perhaps there won't be any German soldiers left when the real fighting begins. Wouldn't you like to see Herr

Goebbels walking around Bregenz alone and confused and the world at peace again?"

Guisan's expression softened. "I'll admit the vision has some merit. I will further admit that what happened was indeed an accident. I am, however, required to protest vehemently, but I know that *you* know that as well."

"Then let me make another suggestion. At some point in the fighting, when the moment is appropriate, send the Swiss army across the border to attack the rear of the German forces. This could be done unilaterally by Switzerland without signing any formal alliance with the United States. This would preserve your position of neutrality. You could simply state that it was necessary to protect Swiss lives and property. It would also assure you of the good will of the United States by shortening the war and saving American lives. And perhaps it would save Swiss civilians from further accidents as the fighting gets closer."

"You have incredible gall."

Dulles checked his watch with dramatic flourish. "Time is short, General. Please think about it. You would not want to find out that your precious neutrality is a fiction."

Cullen grabbed Tanner's arm. "I think you should come outside with me."

Tanner did as he was told. It was evening and the first thing he noticed was a distinct chill in the air. It was further evidence that the days of warm weather were drawing to a close. The mountaintops were often hidden by mists. They formed a cover that did not always disappear the next day. In only a few more weeks, serious snowfalls would begin, making campaigning in the Alps a virtual impossibility.

Cullen again grabbed Tanner. "Quit gawking at the scenery and come with me."

"Yes, Mother."

They came to the tent that housed Father Shanahan's Catholic chapel. Cullen pushed Tanner inside and closed the flap, leaving him alone. It took a couple of seconds for his eyes to adjust. When they did, he saw Lena standing by the makeshift altar. She was crying and had an envelope in her hand.

He ran to her and held her while Cullen tactfully disappeared. "Is something wrong?" he asked and realized it was a terribly dumb question to ask. Of course something was wrong. She handed him the envelope. "It's a letter that Father Shanahan got. It's from my father. He's alive," she laughed and added, "obviously."

"That's great. How is he?"

"He says he's in good health and has been looking for me. Even more amazing, he's in *New York*."

Tanner laughed. "How on earth did he get there?"

"He says it's a long story and he'll tell me when we're together. He's working in a pharmacy and trying to get his doctor's license back. He says that isn't going to be difficult once his English improves. He wants me to come to New York as well."

"Is that what you want to do?" Of course it is, Tanner thought. There would be nothing for her in Czechoslovakia.

"Yes, but I'm not going anywhere without you. The army will give me a glowing recommendation to expedite my status as an immigrant. But you have to come with me. You *do* love me, don't you?"

"You wouldn't believe how much," he said and they hugged again.

Lena stroked his cheek. "Once upon a time, you told me that you could get a medical discharge because of your problems with trench foot and pneumonia. Why don't you do that, and we can get married and go to America."

Tanner took a deep breath. "That sounds like the greatest idea I've heard in a long, long time. However, I don't think we're going anywhere until this war is over or at least this battle has ended. Not only would the army shoot down any request of mine right now, despite what Hagerman says, but I don't think I could leave without doing my part."

"I understand. However, that means you have to do one more thing for me. You have to promise me that you will do everything in your power to stay alive."

Sure, he thought as he made the promise. Words are easy. But how would it be on a landing craft headed for the coast of Lake Constance and the German capital of Bregenz? Survival had always been his number one priority, and it was even more important now that he'd met Lena.

Rather than thinking dark thoughts, they both thought it was best if they spent these precious few minutes holding each other and wishing they had more than a few minutes.

Another betrayal, thought Josef Goebbels as he contemplated the message he'd just been handed. What remained of his intelligence service said that the Swiss were moving large numbers of troops towards the border. This was coming on the heels of their

surprising announcement that any deserters from the
German army would be welcomed with open arms by
the Swiss government and not returned to Germany
against their will. Obviously the Swiss had succumbed
to pressure from the Americans. Air drops of leaflets
proclaiming this had inundated the German lines.
So far there had not been a mass exodus towards
Switzerland, but he could only wonder when it would
happen. More than ever he needed the strong and
harsh efforts of his loyal SS.

That assumed, of course, that they remained loyal.
How many would emulate Hahn and try to disappear?
How many had false papers and money hidden away,
waiting for just the right moment to disappear? Probably most of them, he thought wryly—after all, he did.

And now the Americans were also littering the
place with pamphlets promising death and destruction
on a level never seen before if the Wehrmacht did
not surrender. The pamphlets hinted broadly at the
expanded use of napalm, of an atomic bomb, and,
perhaps most terribly, poison gas. Even the dumb-
est or most fanatic German soldier could tell that
the Thousand Year Reich was in its death spasms. A
thousand years? Goebbels laughed harshly. It had not
lasted two decades. Hitler was dead and Germany
was in ruins. Any idea Goebbels had of dying as a
noble martyr had long since passed. When the time
came, he would do as Hahn and so many others had
done. He would cross the border and use the chain
of safe houses that had been established for just such
a contingency. He had the necessary false papers and
the money to get away safely. It was a shame that he
was so recognizable. He walked with a limp and his

face and nose were not easily forgotten. Perhaps he could disguise himself as a woman, or have a doctor put a fake cast on his leg?

The sirens went off again. He swore. It was another damn raid by the Americans. What would it be this time, more pamphlets or napalm? He'd just gotten word that the Yanks had taken Lindau, only a few miles up the coast. The Yanks were exerting steady pressure against Vietinghoff's units to the east. No major frontal attacks, just a constant nibbling from positions of power.

Napalm. The woods were burning. Hummel and Pfister could smell the stench of burning woodland as well as cooking flesh, much of it human.

Pfister was near his breaking point and wide-eyed with fear. "Do you think there will be a forest fire?" he asked. The thought of a wave of flames overcoming them and scorching them was terrifying.

"It's too wet," said Schubert and both Hummel and Pfister stared. Their shell-shocked companion had been responding to questions more and more lucidly. Maybe he really was on the road to recovery.

Schubert looked around him and continued. "Where the bomb lands it'll burn, but there's little wind and everything is wet. There will be no firestorm like the Americans want to let loose on us."

"What should we do?" Hummel asked. Despite what Schubert had said, he'd begun shaking with fear.

"Stay here," said Pfister. "But we keep an eye out for signs of a fire coming towards us. If that happens, we run like the devil."

Hummel was about to say something when there

was an intrusion. "What the hell is going on? What are you cowardly shits up to?"

It was an SS captain. They didn't know his name, but they'd seen him before. Their assessment of him was that he was an arrogant prick. He was associated with the SS antiaircraft detachment that had moved in too close to them for comfort.

Pfister snapped to attention while Hummel and Schubert got to their feet. Hummel noticed that Schubert had gotten his hands on a pistol, which was tucked in his belt. Why hadn't he noticed that before and where had Schubert found it?

Pfister answered. "Sir, we are trying to stay out of sight. We believe that your battery of eighty-eights will draw American fire from the lake, or even their planes. Therefore, we will stay hidden until the Americans actually move towards us from the lake. Then we will return to our positions and chop them to pieces."

The captain sniffed and then sneered. "I doubt that you will chop anything to pieces. I think you are a pack of cowards. I think you are planning to skulk here until the Americans come close and then you will surrender. You will be of no use to me unless you move closer to where my guns are dug in and waiting to take on the Americans. Now get up and move back to your real positions."

Hummel's mind was racing. That was the last thing he wanted to do. Pfister, however, seemed reconciled to it. "As you wish, Captain," he said.

The captain walked over to Schubert who now seemed very confused and shaken. "What is your problem, soldier?"

"I don't want to die," Schubert said and began to weep.

The SS captain was shocked. "Fucking coward," he said and smacked Schubert across the face. "I'm going to take you back and see that you are hanged."

"No!" howled Schubert. He pulled the pistol from his tunic pocket and fired point blank at the SS man, emptying the clip into his chest. The SS man fell backwards and immediately began vomiting copious amounts of blood. He tried to get up but couldn't. He looked around at his killers and then lay back down.

Pfister checked his pulse. "Dead," he said with a smile. "Good job, Schubert."

"He *wanted* us to die. I don't want to die. I just want to go home."

"We all do," said Hummel. He held out his hand and Schubert took it. Hummel spoke gently. "I think you should let me take care of that pistol while we get rid of this man's body." Schubert nodded and handed over the weapon. It was a Mauser C96, a weapon that had been issued to the Wehrmacht in the thirties, but was now considered obsolete. Again he wondered just how the devil Schubert had gotten it? Hummel asked and Schubert said he didn't remember. He also didn't have any more ammunition.

"Somebody's likely to miss the swine sooner or later," said Pfister as he jabbed the body with his foot. "Speaking for myself, I do not want to get in a gunfight with our own army. We will find someplace safer."

"May I suggest we leave him here with his pistol in his hand?" Hummel said. "Perhaps someone will think the obnoxious bastard committed suicide?"

"Hummel, that is an absolutely evil solution. I like it. However, how would someone shoot himself eight or nine times? No, we will strip him, hide him in the woods and hope he's an unidentifiable mess by the time he's discovered. Maybe we can find a place where napalm has started a fire that is still burning, and leave him there?"

CHAPTER 20

CAPTAIN CHARLEY WARD FROM THE PROVOST MAR-shal's office was not comfortable. "You know you don't have to do this," he said.

Lena smiled. "But I want to. It's time to set things straight, if only in my own mind."

Gustav and Gudrun Schneider had been swept up by the Americans and been arrested. To her utter astonishment, they'd listed her as someone who could provide them with an alibi and keep them from being tried as war criminals. As the jail where they were being held was only a few miles from where she lived and worked for the 105th, she convinced Tanner to go with her to see them. He wasn't certain such a confrontation with the Schneiders was a good idea, but she said it would help her get over what had happened to her, and he reluctantly agreed. They also had a candid and somewhat uncomfortable conversation regarding what she would say.

Lena and Tanner met the Schneiders in what had been a doctor's waiting room. There were chairs and a table. Ward said he had to be present and Tanner said he wanted to. Lena squeezed his hand and said she wanted him there as well.

Ward cleared his throat. "The last thing we want to do is send innocent people to prison. Miss Bobekova, the Schneiders are claiming that they took you into their house and kept you safe during the war. They say they fed you, clothed you, gave you shelter, and treated you with courtesy and respect. What do you say to that?"

Lena stared at the Schneiders. They looked smaller now, and petty. It was hard for her to believe that they'd once held the power of her life in their hands. "In large part, it is true. I did have a roof over my head and what food they had was shared with me. They got the larger portions, however. Mine barely kept me alive." She pulled a photo out of her purse and handed it to Ward. "As you can see, I was little more than skin and bones."

Gustav protested. "But we gave you what we *could*. No one had food during those last days."

"But *you* always did," Lena said. "I saw the stores of food hidden in your basement. You took food shipments meant for the German people and for me. You stayed fat while others starved."

"But you lived," Gustav continued. "So many Jews like you didn't. We could have sent you east to the camps in Poland. You would have died almost immediately in a place like Auschwitz. And for that we are fighting for our lives, and our children were brutally assaulted."

"I will give you credit for taking me in, but I think it was only because there was doubt about my being a Jew. That and you needed someone to work in your house and I happened to be handy and qualified. That doesn't excuse your keeping me a slave for those years. Nor does it excuse you for raping me."

Even though he knew about it, Tanner froze when she said it so calmly. Lena continued. "You forced yourself on me. And as thanks for being your slave you were going to have me sent to a factory where I would have been worked to death in a short length of time. You two forgot that I had ears and was not part of your furniture. I overheard much of your plans. If I hadn't escaped I'd be dead. Your two children had the misfortune of finding me trying to escape so I had to hurt them in order to get away. Part of me says I am glad they survived, but it would not have bothered me if they had died."

Gustav had begun sweating. "I am truly sorry that I assaulted you. I was drunk."

Lena laughed harshly. "Yes, you were drunk. So drunk, in fact, that you were practically impotent, but that was the first time. There were many other times, or had you forgotten?"

Gudrun gasped and stared at her husband. "You swine, you swore there was only the once."

"Are you that stupid, Gudrun, that you believed Gustav's lies?" Lena said and enjoyed both of them wincing at her use of their first names. It was a clear sign that she was on top and they were below the bottom rung.

"Gudrun, there were many times when your pig of a husband would come to me and take me because he said that having sex with you was like humping a large piece of cold meat."

"You bastard," Gudrun screamed and struck Gustav, splitting his lip.

"It's not true," Gustav protested as blood flowed down his chin, and she hit him again, bloodying his nose.

Lena smiled coldly. "And let's not forget the innocent people you sent to the Gestapo if they couldn't pay the bribe you insisted on. And sometimes, Gudrun, that included sending over their wives and daughters if they didn't have enough money or anything else of significant value."

Gustav began to blubber while Gudrun screamed at him. Ward nodded solemnly. "I think this marriage is in serious trouble. Irreconcilable differences, if you ask me. I think we've all heard enough. This hearing is over."

Lena stood and took Tanner by the arm. Together they walked out and Ward followed. "Miss Bobekova, Lena, I don't think they'll be calling on you to be a character witness anytime soon, and I'm glad. I don't think you should have to relive your experiences and have them put on an official record."

"What will happen to them?" Tanner asked.

Ward shrugged. "It's kind of up to them. We'll offer him five years in prison if he confesses and implicates others and ten if he goes to trial and is found guilty. And he will be found guilty. As to Gudrun, she'll probably get a few months' hard labor. Quite frankly, these two are small fry. We want people like Goebbels. I think Herr Schneider will decide that five years is a bargain, especially if it keeps his wife away."

As they walked to the car, Lena took Tanner's arm and squeezed. "Even though much of what I said was a lie, I'm glad I did it. I saw real fear on the faces of the Schneiders and I'm glad."

Lena had told him that she'd been assaulted only the once by Gustav Schneider. She'd said she was going to exaggerate to frighten him. She hadn't expected Gudrun's violent outburst but it didn't upset her. It was their turn to know fear. Ward had been in on the charade as well. Nobody wanted Gustav Schneider executed. It would have been a waste of a noose or a bullet. She just wanted justice and that included frightening him as he had frightened her. If he went to prison for a number of years, that was enough for her. They were brutal filth, but they had kept her alive, at least until the last moment.

"I think I could walk all the way across the lake without getting my feet wet," said Tanner.

"That would be good," said Cullen. "Doc Hagerman says you're still supposed to keep them dry."

"Go to hell," Tanner said good-naturedly. It was the kind of stupid, nervous banter that men who were about to go forth and try to kill other people would sometimes engage in. It also was an attempt to drown out the thought that they could be killed at almost any time. They were not invincible and they now knew it. Their experiences in the war had proven it.

Tanner used his binoculars to scan the vast array of landing craft and other, more lethal warships. He fervently hoped that the sight of the armada would scare the Nazis into surrendering. Sadly, he didn't think it would happen. Maybe some would give up, but far too many would fight until the end or until they were given orders not to. Maybe they weren't crazy fanatics like the Japs, but the Nazis were bad enough.

"At least we won't be in the first wave," Tanner said. Their orders had them placed in the fifth wave, which was still no picnic. Worse, they would have General Broome in the boat with them. The general was not a glory hound but did feel it was his responsibility to be as close to the action as possible. Tanner and the others admired him for it, but it also meant that they would have to be closer to the action as well.

They had been awakened in the middle of the night and told to be prepared to board the boats. This would be the day. They did not call it D-Day. That was reserved for the landings at Normandy and the term was now considered almost sacred. This had been designated R-Day for Redoubt. Some were happy it hadn't been called G-Day for Gas, which was on all their minds. Of course, G-Day could have stood for Germanica, too.

Only a few moments earlier, the officers had been gathered and told that there would be no poison gas used. Instead, it would be a nonlethal combination of tear gas and white smoke that would hopefully terrify and confuse the Germans. While there was relief that poison gas was not on the agenda, there were mixed emotions. No gas meant that Germans who weren't terrified and confused would be alive, ready, and able to defend against the landing.

The men were still ordered to wear the awkward and sweaty gas masks. First, even a light dose of tear gas could incapacitate a man, and, second, it was hoped that the sight of U.S. soldiers storming ashore wearing the masks would unnerve the Germans who had precious few of them.

"Well, it sure as hell unnerved me," said Cullen. Tanner and the others heartily agreed even though they didn't quite believe the denials from on high. The government and the army did funny things and often at the expense of the troops in their command.

Shortly before dawn, the long caravan of landing craft headed out onto the clear blue waters of Lake Constance. The waves were negligible, which didn't stop one of the sailors from puking, which then got a bunch of soldiers joining him. The sky was bright, clear, and blue, marred only by the odd white contrails made by high-flying planes. At least they're ours, thought Tanner. He hadn't seen a German plane in months, well before they arrived to attack the Redoubt.

The landing craft circled and jockeyed for position. There were to be six waves, each consisting of thirty boats. It was hoped that a full regiment, along with armor and artillery, could be delivered in a very short time against what was hoped to be a shocked and demoralized enemy that was expecting to be slaughtered by poison gas. When unloaded, the craft would circle back and pick up more soldiers, repeating the process until the 105th Infantry Division had landed and joined up with the Tenth Mountain Division.

"What the hell!" yelled Tanner. "I thought we were supposed to be in the fifth wave where it's safer."

General Broome was in the bow of the boat. If he heard, he didn't show it. Broome and his staff, Tanner and Cullen included, had just found themselves in the second wave, where it was far more dangerous.

A lieutenant from Broome's staff grimaced. "He

asked for the change just a little while ago. He said he wanted to be closer to the action so he could support the troops by being seen."

"Shit," said Cullen, "I'd like to inspire them by being invisible."

Artillery fire erupted from the shore. Shells splashed among the small craft, sending up geysers of water and shell fragments. One came close to their boat, dousing them with water and spent metal. No one was hurt.

Another shell hit a landing craft directly, and it erupted in flames. Men jumped overboard and into the cold lake. Only a few managed to get out of their gear. Most of them sank, a couple waving their arms futilely as they disappeared under the water.

"We don't stop," yelled the young ensign in charge. Tanner understood. War consisted of terrible equations and values. They were still about a mile away from shore. More men loosened their gear to the point where it was barely hanging on them. If they were thrown into the water, the hoped they could get out of the gear and not be dragged down to drown.

The line of destroyers began shelling suspected German positions. Insanely, some of the German gunners began shooting at the destroyers and not at the landing craft. But not all. A shell hit the bow of their craft, shaking them violently and destroying one of the machine-gun mounts. Tanner crawled over to see if he could help. The two men working the gun had been pulverized. Someone was screaming. The skipper of the LC had been hit by shrapnel and disemboweled. The only thing Tanner recalled was his name, Kubiak. He'd seemed like a decent guy and now he was going to die. Medics were swarming over him, but they would only ease his passing by heavily dosing him with morphine.

The landing craft was taking on water and in danger of sinking. No, Tanner thought, it was definitely sinking. The water was up to his ankles and rising quickly. They were only a few yards from shore when the LC hit ground and stopped. Someone in the crew ordered the ramp dropped and men poured out into the still frigid waters. This is just like crossing the Rhine, he thought, and realized irrelevantly that the lake *was* part of the Rhine. His feet were getting wet along with the rest of him. He jumped into the lake and waded the last few yards to the shore.

He looked around and saw the general helping people make it to land. "I hope he's happy," Tanner said to a bedraggled Cullen.

Cullen looked skyward and over the coast where a white cloud was advancing. Above the cloud, waves of planes were flying over and out into the center of the lake after dropping their loads. "Oh, God. Now we're gonna find out whether the army was lying to us or not."

Sibre and Schafer hadn't seen so many airplanes in their young lives. Hundreds of fighters were escorting many hundreds more bombers. They would carpet bomb Bregenz and the areas around the German capital.

The two pilots were towards the rear of the extended column. The lead planes had the task of taking on German planes and positions. There would be no enemy planes, so that left them free to attack antiaircraft batteries. By the time they arrived overhead, however, many of these had been silenced by other planes or naval gunfire. This gave them a clear view of what was going to transpire. They had heard the denials of the use of gas and kind of believed them. Better, they were many thousands of feet above ground, and gas couldn't climb to their height. They hoped. They didn't have gas masks. None had been issued to pilots despite their protests that they might be forced to land and might need them.

Bomb bay doors opened in the bellies of hundreds of bombers. At a signal they began dropping thousands of small bombs. From where they were, it looked like a snowfall. A minute later, the bombs began impacting. Clouds of white smoke erupted and, taken by the wind, began swirling towards the lake, blanketing the German lines.

"Dear God," muttered Sibre. "Can you begin to imagine what's going on down there?" Schafer could not. What looked like blankets of death were heading though Bregenz and towards the lake. It was a vision of the Apocalypse. Inside the cloud, he visualized four deadly horsemen riding their skeletal steeds and mowing down victims with their scythes. He shuddered. Sometimes having a vivid imagination was a curse.

He shook off his bleak thoughts. He and Schafer were the victors and to the victors belong the spoils. Tonight a bunch of them would go to Stuttgart and head directly to that whorehouse where the hookers pretended to be nuns and the place a convent. Both he and Schafer had gone to Catholic school, so it was deliciously decadent to screw pretend nuns in a make-believe convent. They had to admit that the madam, Sister Columba, ran a hell of a fine place.

★　★　★

Hummel screamed as the cloud enveloped him. He and the others had tried running, but the gas was inexorable. Like an all-consuming monster, the wind, favorable to the Americans, drove it towards them and the lake, finally overtaking them.

As it approached and in their panic, they had thrown away their weapons, clawed out of their bunkers, and headed away as fast as they could run. Mindlessly, they'd headed in the direction of a once peaceful Lake Constance that was now covered by American landing craft that were moving ever closer. They could see that the Yanks were wearing gas masks and would be safe. They, poor German soldiers, would not be. Once again, their Nazi government had sold them out. Hummel cursed as his eyes watered and he choked. He was going to die and he wanted vengeance and it didn't matter who would be on the receiving end.

An SS officer, his mouth covered with a rag, confronted them. "Get back to your positions, you fools. This is just tear gas. You aren't going to die!"

Hummel had never endured tear gas before, so he had no idea whether the officer was telling the truth.

The officer, his eyes wide and running and streaming tears, waved his Schmiesser machine pistol and pointed it at Schubert. Without thinking, Hummel fired his own pistol, shooting the SS fanatic in the head and dropping him instantly. He looked around to see if he was going to be arrested and realized that nobody cared. It was the same as when Schubert had killed that other SS man. The body had never been discovered and no fuss had been made about one more soldier gone AWOL. It didn't matter if the missing man had been SS or not.

Hummel was in the middle of a swirling mass of

humanity all headed towards the lake. He also realized that he *wasn't* dying. His eyes burned and he
had begun coughing but it was nothing he couldn't
handle. He had never smelled tear gas, but realized
the SS man had been right. Coughing and retching,
he grabbed his comrades. "Get to the lake. We can
wash this shit out of our eyes."

"Then what?" asked Pfister, all pretenses at differences in rank forgotten.

Hummel howled with glee. "Then we throw down
our guns and surrender to those monsters who are
arriving from the sea."

The U.S. boats were close enough that they had
begun disgorging their human cargo, and they indeed
looked like monsters. They were also protected by
masks that the German military couldn't provide.

Up and down the shore, Hummel could see hundreds
of German soldiers throwing away their weapons and
throwing themselves into the lake. They did the same,
and the irritation from the gas was soon controllable.
The three of them raised their hands and hung close
together as Americans disarmed those who still retained
their weapons. There was confusion but no resistance.

A moment later, an American medic, still masked,
looked at Schubert. "What's wrong with him?" he
asked in passable German.

Hummel answered. He was now their leader. "Shell
shock. He got it a couple of months ago."

"You want me to get him to a hospital or you gonna
watch out for him yourselves?"

"We'll take care of him," Hummel said softly. "He
is our comrade."

★   ★   ★

Goebbels had finally found somebody with a radio. After a couple of tries, he made contact with Doctor Esau and ordered him to launch the rocket immediately.

Goebbels heard nothing but silence for a few moments, but finally, "It will be as you wish. We will launch in a couple of minutes."

"Hurry, you fool. We might not have a couple of minutes."

"Yes, Minister."

Goebbels raged at the now silent phone. The next few minutes would determine whether or not he lived as the head of state or died in a town that was being overwhelmed by the enemy. It occurred to him that those in the Fuhrer Bunker in Berlin must have had the same feelings as the savages from the Red Army closed in and were only a few hundred yards away.

He fondled the box with the poison. Soon, he thought. Just not yet. And maybe never.

Overhead, Lieutenants Bud Sibre and George Schafer were breaking off their latest attack when Schafer noticed something on the ground through the thinning cloud of tear gas.

"Would you mind telling me just what the hell that is?"

"Not certain," said Sibre. "But it looks an awful lot like a V1 rocket that's about to be launched."

"Say, buddy, why don't we *do* something about that?"

The pilots dived and lined up to strafe the rocket, which was unmistakably a V1. They were just about to open fire, when the tail of the rocket belched fire and launched it into the sky. They tried to give chase but it was no use. The rocket was too fast.

They watched in fascinated horror as the V1 headed towards the massed landing craft in Lake Constance. They would not be able to stop it.

Sibre's hands began to shake. "Jesus, I hope that isn't what I think it is."

Tanner heard the roar of the rocket's engine through the sound of battle. He looked up and saw the odd-looking craft streak over him. He could clearly see the stove-pipe design. "What the hell?" he wondered as did everyone else who could see the evil thing.

Then the rocket's engine cut out and there was a brief moment of silence. They all knew what that meant from reports of the attacks on London. It was through flying and was about to strike. The rocket's nose tipped forward and it knifed into the water only a couple hundred yards away. Everyone froze and waited for an explosion.

None came.

"I wonder what that was all about," Cullen gasped. They were all breathing heavily.

"If the army wants us to know, I'm sure they'll tell us."

Goebbels screamed in impotent fury as he got the report of the rocket's failure. "Schoerner, find those bastard Jew scientists and kill them immediately. Don't worry about hanging them, just shoot them. They lied to me. They lied to Germany. They are traitors."

Schoerner tried to calm him. "I will send some soldiers to their bunker. That is, if I can find any. Esau and his assistants have doubtless run away and we don't have time to chase them now. We have more important things to worry about. Our survival must be our first goal."

Goebbels shook his head to clear his thoughts. "Of course. We must escape and begin again to build another Reich. We will catch those swine some other time."

"Where the devil is Sergeant Hill?" Tanner yelled.

A very nervous PFC responded. "Sir, Sergeant Hill said to tell you that he's gone snipe hunting and that he'll be back shortly."

"He said that, did he?"

"Yes sir. He also said to remind you that it's easier to ask forgiveness than permission. If it matters, he was heavily armed."

"Private, just where was he headed when you last saw him?"

"Sir, he was headed for Bregenz and, oh yeah, he was carrying a German officer's tunic. I have no idea where he got it."

And it doesn't much matter, Tanner thought. Sergeant Billy Hill had been chafing at being idle. Being attached to division headquarters didn't leave much time for excitement. Hill's skills as a sniper were becoming legendary, and so was his wanting to go hunting for kills. Was that what he was going to do, kill more Germans before the war came to a halt? That seemed plausible. And what difference was there between a snipe and a sniper? He wished the sergeant well. It would be a tragedy for him to get his ass blown away this late in the game. Of course, the same held true for himself.

Tanner dismissed the private, but not before telling

the man to let him know the moment Hill returned. *If* he returned, that is.

Josef Goebbels and Field Marshal Ferdinand Schoerner decided that whatever happened, they would look the part of world leaders. Schoerner dressed in an immaculate field marshal's uniform complete with baton, while Goebbels wore an expensive blue suit made for him an eternity ago by an exclusive tailor in Berlin. They would cross into Switzerland and claim sanctuary, confident that there were enough German sympathizers in the Swiss government to protect them. From Switzerland there was the probability that money would talk and that they could be sent secretly to South America. Argentina would be their ultimate destinations and a new Reich was their goal.

Only the gas masks they were wearing marred the effect. As they approached the door that led outside they could hear the sounds of chaos. Schoerner drew his pistol and suggested that Goebbels do the same.

"Some panic-stricken soldiers could try to take our masks from us in order to save themselves," he said. "And it wouldn't matter if they recognized us or not. Terrified men will not obey orders or be impressed by rank."

Goebbels nodded agreement and pulled his pistol from his shoulder holster. They opened the door and stepped out. They had not actually seen the gas clouds when they blew in, but what was left did not appear too thick. Could these wisps be lethal? Or was the wind causing them to diminish? It occurred to him that the German soldiers he did see were running around aimlessly and not lying dead in the streets. In fact, there were no bodies in the streets.

"Schoerner, either there is no gas or it has dissipated. I think we can remove our masks. We might even be safer that way."

"If it's all the same with you, Reichminister, I'll keep mine on for a while longer. Although," he said thoughtfully, "it does look like you might be correct. Was this a huge charade to cause our army to panic? If it was, it worked marvelously."

"Halt!" A soldier had worked his way behind them. He had a Thompson submachine gun pointed at them. Curiously, he was wearing the tunic of a German officer, a captain. Something was wrong, terribly wrong. This was no German. It was an American who'd gotten this far in the panic.

"*Scheisse!*" howled Schoerner. He pulled out his pistol and fired. He missed. The American ducked and fired his Tommy gun. A dozen bullets struck Schoerner in the head and chest. He collapsed like a bloody wet rag. Something slammed into Goebbels' shoulder and dropped him as well. It was over. He had to get the cyanide capsule into his mouth.

"No you don't," said the American. He pinned Goebbels' good arm and ignored the screams as he tied it to his wounded one. He ripped off Goebbels' gas mask and flung it away. In the back of his mind, Goebbels realized that he could indeed breathe. Calloused hands pushed his mouth open and fingers probed for a capsule disguised as a tooth filling. Through his agony, Goebbels regretted never having had that done. He hated dentists and he'd constantly put off having one inserted.

The American took off the German tunic and threw it away. He searched Goebbels' pockets until he found the jewelry box. He opened it and laughed. Then he continued to search, convinced that where there was one poison cache there might be two.

Satisfied, the American pulled Goebbels to his feet. More American soldiers had arrived and, on seeing that it was Goebbels, began to cheer.

A grinning medic slapped a bandage over Goebbels' wound and pronounced that it wasn't serious. "The fucker'll live long enough to hang. You want me to take him to the hospital or you got plans for him?"

Staff Sergeant Billy Hill grabbed Goebbels by his good elbow and began to propel him towards the shore and through crowds of Americans who were pushing other Germans towards prison pens that were being hastily thrown together.

Hill laughed. Captain Tanner would be pleased rather than pissed by his running off. Damned if he hadn't caught the biggest snipe of all. The publicity he'd get from this would almost guarantee his getting elected to sheriff. Hell, maybe even to Congress.

Damnation, but this was a good war.

General Heinrich von Vietinghoff sat behind his desk and drummed his fingers on the highly polished surface while he listened to the reports. Every one of them said that what was left of the German Army was being destroyed. What fools. He tried to tell them that so many months ago. There was no way what remained of the army could withstand the overwhelming might of the Americans, even without their British and French allies. How many lives had been lost or changed because people like Goebbels wanted to save a thousand-year legacy that would last only a little more than a decade?

He had long since seen the light when he was commander of German forces in Italy. He had initiated contact with the Americans through Allen Dulles and tried to negotiate a surrender of German forces under his command. His plans had fallen apart when the now abortive attempt to create an Alpine Redoubt and call it Germanica had begun.

Vietinghoff sipped some very bad and cold black coffee and looked at the reports chronicling the litany of disasters. The gas attack that had been no gas attack had sown panic and confusion among much of the army. As a result, the Americans were in Bregenz and tens of thousands of German soldiers were now prisoners of war. All he had left were a few under-strength divisions situated east of Bregenz.

The Americans had announced that Schoerner was dead and that Goebbels was a prisoner. Vietinghoff thought that it should have happened sooner. An aide had unctuously informed him that he was now the ranking person in the Third Reich, the new Fuhrer. The aide had the good sense not to suggest that he would likely be the last Fuhrer. What, therefore, were his plans?

Vietinghoff stood and glared at his staff, as if daring them to argue with him. They looked so defeated he didn't think was likely. "Gentlemen, we have a choice. We can choose either life or death. I choose life and I order you to choose it as well. I wish to be connected with General Truscott."

A few moments later and the raspy-voiced Texan

was on the radio. There was an interpreter, but he wasn't needed. The German general's English was up to the very basic task before them.

"General Truscott, I wish to surrender what remains of the German army. I am in the process of ordering all units to cease fire and lay down their arms. I sincerely hope that you will command your units to accept my army's surrender and that it occurs both quickly and without incident. I wish to bring an end to this foolish extension of a war that should never have been fought. We can arrange a formal signing of a surrender document at any time and place of your choosing. In the meantime, I wish to stop the killing."

"My orders are going out as we speak," said Truscott. To Vietinghoff it sounded like the American's voice was heavy with emotion. Well, his was too. Perhaps someday he would be able to go home.

Archie Dixon's Sherman tank plowed through the knee-deep water and onto dry land just outside Bregenz. As instructed, their hatches were closed. Even though the white cloud might not have been deadly, it was, they were told, uncomfortable and could incapacitate Driver and play hell with Gunner's vision. That meant closed hatches, even though that might make them targets for fanatics with Panzerfausts or Molotov cocktails. As it was, a few bullets had pinged off their hull and turret. No harm had been done to men or tank, but it had been unsettling.

Dixon was pleased that Gunner had fired on seeing the flashes and hit the target with the first round. The building hiding the shooter had already been badly damaged and the rest of it flew to pieces when their

76mm shell hit and exploded. Dixon had trained them all well.

At first they'd thought it annoying that they had to wear gas masks. But now, as they drove slowly through throngs of choking, gasping and terrified German soldiers and gaunt, frightened civilians, they changed their minds.

Dixon stopped his tank in the charred mess that had been the town square of Bregenz. He was amazed. He had just seen *Josef Goebbels* being hustled onto the back of a truck. Even better, he and his new crew had survived the war. He climbed out of the tank and his crew followed. They looked at him with apprehension and a little bit of fear. He had been a monstrous and cold taskmaster. But he had won. They had all survived. He could be a human being again.

Dixon slipped off his mask and took a quick breath. The tear gas was almost gone, dissipated and blown away. He took a deeper one and signaled for the crew to do the same. They did and looked around in amazement. Several German soldiers came up, lay down their rifles and stood with their hands up. Some grinned sheepishly like this whole thing had been a silly mistake and could we all go home now?

For the first time in a long while, he grinned and turned to his crew. They had climbed out and stood beside him. "Guys, what say we go find a bar and get a beer or six?"

Lena found Tanner in Doc Hagerman's clinic. He was sitting on a table while a medic swathed his feet in ointment and wrapped them in white bandages. Hagerman looked at her. "I told the foolish little boy not to get his feet wet, so what does he go and do? Why he spends all day playing soldier in cold mud and water. So now he has a flare-up that was caused by his initial trench foot incident. This has to stop."

"So what are you going to do?" she asked timidly.

"Why, after I'm through curing him again, I am going to sign papers that will have his worthless ass thrown out of the army. You two might as well book passage on a ship back to the U.S., unless you'd like to fly. I've got some friends in the air force who can arrange it."

She slid easily into Tanner's arms. Neither cared who saw. "I think flying is a great idea," Tanner said, and Lena nodded. "I've had enough of Europe."

Swiss soldiers had moved several hundred yards inside what had been the German border. It was necessary in order to control the large numbers of people who wanted to leave the remnants of Germany. The Swiss were meticulous. They would ultimately admit everyone, but they wanted to know who each person was. That some of the more odious Nazis would disappear was obvious and none of their business.

Ernie Janek was getting used to life on crutches and enjoying the scene. The curtain on the final act of the Third Reich had fallen. The Twilight of the Gods part of the Wagnerian opera had ended with a ludicrous whimper and not in flames of glory. An entire army had run from a terror weapon that wasn't. The German army might never recover from the embarrassment. Good.

Winnie slipped her hand in his. "I've arranged for us to go and see Vietinghoff formally surrender. It's going to be across the lake in Constance. You'll have to be careful of your leg."

"I was planning on it."

"I've also arranged an elegant suite for us in a hotel overlooking the lake. With all those American warships out there, the view won't be as lovely as it could be, but who plans on looking out a window? I just want to learn how to make love to a man with a broken leg."

"Carefully," Ernie said, "very, very carefully."

In the White House, Werner Heisenberg was well on his way to being drunk. He was being toasted for the failure of Germany's atomic bomb. He'd almost passed out when word that the warhead on the rocket had been a dud. Heisenberg wondered if there had even *been* a warhead on the V1. Esau had likely been working in a secure area and could have filled the warhead with sand.

He'd even been hugged by Harry Truman, who clearly had been crying. He'd been informed that his incarceration would cease immediately. He could go wherever he wanted, but with one exception. General Groves said he would not be able to work with the American scientists in what was called the Manhattan Project. So be it. He'd had enough of nuclear weapons. He would go back to Germany—the American zone, of course—and try to pick up the pieces of his life.

EPILOGUE

THE NEWSPAPER SAID IT WAS THE FOURTH OF JULY, 1960. In the United States they would be celebrating their independence with fireworks, picnics, baseball and beer. Not so Alfonse Hahn, former general in the SS. The war in Europe had been over for almost fifteen years. The world had changed and not for the better. Hahn still could not fathom a world where the Jews had their own nation and had defeated other countries in order to keep it. Who knew that Jews could and would fight? And now they had their own secret police force, the Mossad. Like the worms they were, the Mossad slithered all over the world and part of their job was to seek out and either kill or capture what they referred to as Nazi war criminals.

Just last month, Israelis had located and kidnapped Adolf Eichmann from a suburb of Buenos Aires. This had shaken Hahn. He lived only a dozen miles from Eichmann and had seen him on several occasions, although he had never approached the man. He respected what Eichmann had done in planning the disposal of the Jews, but he personally thought the man was nothing more than a pale, mousy clerk. At least, Hahn thought, he himself had been a Nazi warrior, not a glorified railroad engineer.

But Eichmann's capture meant that the Jews were close by and still looking. He'd read some of the magazines and seen lists of those Nazis the Jews were looking for. He was high on the list. Hitler was first even though most people thought he was dead. Josef Mengele, the "Angel of Death" who decided who would live and who would die on arrival at Auschwitz, was high up as well and nobody knew where the hell he was. It was an honor to be in such company. Still, he had been small potatoes when compared with the Nazi hierarchy. He had personally killed only a few dozen people, mostly Jews, although he had shipped off large numbers to die in the death camps. He had only killed two Americans, yet they were still infuriated by it. A surviving witness named Tanner had written a book about it. It had become a bestseller and that galled Hahn. What a book he could write and what stories he could tell! Sadly, that would not happen.

Hahn's escape from Italy had been fraught with danger. His companion, Diehl, had been killed in a gunfight with Italian partisans only a few days after escaping through Switzerland. Hahn had used the money and identification he'd taken from Bregenz to get on a steamer to Spain and then to Buenos Aires, where he'd lived a quiet and simple life in a small apartment overlooking a quiet street. It was far from the glamor and glory of the days when he'd been an SS general, but it would do until the Reich rose again.

On a positive note, young Hans Gruber had gone

to East Germany where he had joined the East German secret police force, the Stasi. His sources said
he was quickly rising in rank. Good. He had even
survived the scandal when his wife, the former Astrid
Schneider, had been murdered by her brother, a man
driven crazy by the war.

Today Hahn had to be even more careful than
usual. Today was the day he went to the post office
to pick up the envelope that contained his monthly
allowance. It was his only source of income and he
lived in fear that his unknown benefactor would either
die or get caught.

He entered the small grubby post office building
after checking to see if anything was out of the ordinary.
Some familiar people were coming and going along
with the inevitable scattering of strangers. Nothing
looked wrong. He had no idea how Eichmann had
been found but he did know that the man had made
himself a family. Probably someone blabbed or bragged.
It was another good reason to live alone, which he
did. If he needed sex, there were prostitutes in the
neighborhood and he only frequented the regulars.

A truck driver leaned on his horn and began to
curse loudly, attracting everyone's attention. A woman
pushing a baby carriage jumped in front of him. Hahn
was distracted by the woman and barely noticed that
someone had bumped him until he started to lose his
balance. Something was terribly wrong. He tried to
speak but couldn't. He collapsed onto the sidewalk
and heard people calling for help. Someone looked
down at him with real concern. He heard a siren
screaming and growing closer.

The ambulance stopped and medics jumped out.

They put Hahn on a gurney and into the vehicle. As they drove off, Hahn heard people comment that the poor man had been fortunate that the ambulance had been so close.

After a few blocks, the siren was turned off and Hahn, still unable to move, realized that he was living a nightmare. They drove in silence for a few minutes and into another building. He was removed from the ambulance. He could see that they were in a large garage. The men laid him on a table where they cut off all his clothes and replaced them with a hospital gown.

A man leaned over him. His expression was cold. "Hello, General Hahn. Yes, we are Jews, and, yes, we are Mossad. And how we located you doesn't matter. I don't know and wouldn't tell you if I did. Probably someone talked. Money always does that, although sometimes fear works as well, as you well know.

"At any rate, you are now going on a plane ride, a very long one. You will be transported by a private aircraft that has you listed as a severely psychotic mental patient who must be kept tranquilized for his own safety and that of those on the plane. The destination is listed as a sanitarium outside Paris, but, of course, we won't go there. Your final destination will be Tel Aviv."

The Israeli spat into his face and laughed as the spittle ran down Hahn's cheek. "Mazel tov."